The eagerly awaited sequel to SILKEN SAVAGE by Leisure's leading lady of romance . . .

CATHERINE HART

Ever since her first novel, FIRE AND ICE, won a treasured place on every romance lover's bookshelf, Catherine Hart has captured the hearts of readers around the world.

Now she has reached new heights of soaring ecstasy with the enthralling story of Summer Storm and her fiercely passionate Cheyenne warrior.

"Beautiful! Gorgeous! Magnificent!"
—ROMANTIC TIMES

Part II

Book Two

Also by Catherine Hart:

FIRE AND ICE
SILKEN SAVAGE
ASHES AND ECSTASY
SATIN AND STEEL

CATHERINE HART

Summer Storm

LEISURE BOOKS NEW YORK CITY

A LEISURE BOOK

Published by

Dorchester Publishing Co., Inc.
6 East 39th Street
New York, NY 10016

Copyright ©1987 by Diane Tidd

Printed in the United States of America

I
dedicate this book, with great respect,
to the American Indian.
When I see the eagle flying high and free
overhead,
I will see the undaunted heart of your people
flying with him—
free and proud in spirit,
now and always.

Catherine Hart

1

The rain came down in torrents, driven by fiercely gusting winds. Lightning ripped through the darkened summer sky like blinding white swords of vengeance, while thunder reverberated across the land, making it shudder as if thousands of buffalo hoofs were pounding upon it. Above the rain-beaten earth, black clouds boiled in the heavens, turning the afternoon sky nearly as dark as night.

In the face of this ferocious summer storm, all creatures had sought shelter. The Cheyenne had done the same. Huddled in their tepees, they awaited the passing of the fierce tempest. Rain and wind battered the buffalo hides that covered their lodges. Strong gusts tore at the pegs that held down the outer edges and whistled through the skin-draped entrances, sending rain spraying inside and woodsmoke swirling from the fires.

In the center of the village stood the tepee of the warrior chief, A-Panther-Stalks, with distinctive black claw marks etched upon it. Like the others, it was closed tightly against the raging storm, but inside this particular lodge, yet another drama of Nature was taking place.

Lightning lit up the sky with a sudden brilliant display; immediately afterward, thunder shook the earth violently with a tremendous roar. Then, for just a moment, the wind held its breath, and between crashes of lightning and thunder, a new sound was heard. Above the din of the drumming rain came the faint cry of a newborn child, quickly hushed. Once again the storm resumed its furious pounding, in its own way heralding the birth of this newest arrival upon the earth.

Inside the tepee, Tanya Martin Savage, known as Little Wildcat among the Cheyenne, lay back upon her mat, a weary smile etching her lips as she viewed her newborn daughter. Perspiration gleamed upon her forehead and darkened her honey-gold hair. Her unique tawny eyes gleaming with pride and love, she examined the tiny, perfectly created life now wriggling in her arms. "She is beautiful," she murmured softly, tears stinging her eyes.

"How could she not be, with you for her mother?"

At his words, Tanya's gaze sought that of her husband. In his dark eyes she found the love and approval she had recognized in his voice. "Panther, I should be apologizing for presenting you with a girl-child, but I cannot. It would be a lie to tell you I am not pleased to have a daughter this time."

In the faint light, she saw his teeth flash white against his bronze skin as he gave her a knowing smile. "You have earned your right to a daughter after providing me with two strong, fine sons, Wildcat. I, too, am pleased."

Returning his smile, she asked, "Will you not

8

regret the celebration that would have honored another son?''

Each time a son was born to a Cheyenne chief, great revelry broke out, with a celebration that usually went on for days.

"My pride will survive, Wife of My Heart," he assured her.

With long, dark fingers, he reached out to stroke the downy black head nestled contentedly on her breast. "What will you call her?"

Surprise registered on Tanya's face as she realized that she would be the one to name their child this time. When a boy-child was born, one of the men— usually an uncle or grandfather—received that right. Only with daughters were wives given the choice. Before Tanya could answer him, another burst of lightning and thunder split the air. In its echo, Tanya smiled down upon her now sleeping babe. "She will be called Summer Storm."

Tanya sat in the clearing between her tepee and that of Winter Bear, Panther's cousin and fellow chief. Shy Deer, Winter Bear's wife and Tanya's best friend, sat beside her. Together they labored over the precious buffalo robes they were preparing for the coming winter. As they worked, cleaning and softening the skins, they chatted easily.

Anyone watching the two women could not help but see the differences between them; yet there were similarities also. Both were still young, having seen but twenty-three summers. Each wore her hair in long thick braids, held away from her forehead by a decorated headband, and each was beautiful in her own right. Where her doeskin dress did not cover it, Tanya's skin was darkened by the summer sun to a shade barely lighter than Shy Deer's. Yet, while the sun had tanned her flesh, it had also lightened her tawny hair, streaking it with golden highlights until it resembled ripening wheat. Her fair hair contrasted with Shy Deer's midnight braids as their heads bent together over their work.

If an observer were to see only their hands, calloused and working with equal skill over the hides, he would not guess that one of the women was Cheyenne by adoption instead of birth. Neither could he tell by their talk, for both chattered fluently in the guttural Cheyenne tongue. About Tanya's wrists were the engraved copper wristbands that matched Panther's, symbolic of his ownership of her through marriage, a proper wedding gift from a Cheyenne warrior to a great Chief's daughter. Only when Tanya's skirt shifted high on her thigh as she stretched over the buffalo skin, was the brand revealed that proclaimed she had once been the slave of her beloved husband. And while one woman's eyes were like polished onyx, the other's were a gleaming topaz, like those of a cougar caught in a shaft of sunlight.

The sounds of a rider approaching them brought both heads up. Panther, astride his big black stallion, rode slowly toward them. Before him on the horse he carried Summer Storm, now three summers old. Tanya stared in amazement at her mud-drenched daughter.

With an easy grace that never failed to draw Tanya's admiration, Panther slid from Shadow's back and swung his daughter to the ground. "This little mud toad claims she belongs to us, but I am not sure. Will you claim her, Little Wildcat?" he teased, a smile tugging at his lips.

Summer Storm giggled, her once-black hair coated with mud and straggling from long plaits no longer neatly braided. Head to toe, she was plastered a mud-brown, with barely a trace of copper skin showing through. Only her teeth gleaming white in her face, and her golden eyes twinkling out from layers of dirt, declared her identity.

Tanya shook her head ruefully. "Surely this cannot be my daughter, who not long ago wandered off with her friends to play. If this truly is Summer Storm, her mother wants to know how a clean daughter now comes home so filthy."

The stern tone of her mother's voice sobered Summer Storm immediately. "It was Kicking Elk's fault, Mother," she hastened to explain. "I only wanted to play stickball with my brothers and the other boys, but Kicking Elk called me names and pushed me into the mud."

"Did your brothers properly punish Kicking Elk for shoving someone so much younger and weaker than himself?" Tanya asked more gently.

Summer Storm's head bobbed up and down affirmatively. "Hunter hit him in the nose, but only after Sly Fox had hit Kicking Elk first." Sly Fox was Winter Bear and Shy Deer's oldest son, two years older than Summer Storm.

"And what was Mark-of-the-Archer doing while Sly Fox and Hunter-of-the-Forest were defending you?" Tanya questioned, referring to her second son.

"Mark was picking me out of the puddle."

"Were you hurt?"

"Only a little on my bottom," Summer Storm admitted, rubbing her posterior with mud-coated hands. "But I didn't cry, Mother. I was very brave."

Tanya smiled at her. "Then I am proud of you, little one. It was good of Sly Fox to fight for you alongside your brothers."

Again Summer Storm nodded. Then she gazed solemnly up at her father, standing so tall and straight at her side. "Father, Kicking Elk is mean. He called me a white-eyes, and he said Mother is a white-eyes too. He said we are not Cheyenne, and called us bad names."

Tanya and Shy Deer barely stifled horrified gasps, and Tanya raised hurt eyes to her husband.

Bending down to his small daughter's level, Panther spoke calmly to her, his anger evident only in his gleaming black eyes. "Listen to me, little one. Hear me and know that what I tell you is true. Your mother is Cheyenne, and so are you. Even when I took her from her white family, in her heart she was Cheyenne. My uncle, the great Chief Black Kettle knew this when he adopted her as his daughter. Her blood mingled with mine at our wedding. Let no one tell you otherwise." Taking Tanya's hand and holding it next to Summer Storm's and his own, he said, "Look at our hands, Summer Storm. Your hand and mine are darker than your mother's. Her hair is fair while ours is dark. Your eyes and hers are the same, as are your brother Hunter's, while mine and Mark's are black. But in our hearts, where our blood flows with truth and honor, we are all Cheyenne. Do you understand my words?"

"Yes, Father," Summer Storm answered with a slight frown, "but what of my Grandfather Edward and Grandmother Sarah in the place called Pueblo? And what of your mother, my Grandmother Rachel? Are they Cheyenne, too?"

Panther sighed and smiled down at her. "No, daughter, they are not Cheyenne, but that does not make you, or your brothers, or your parents any less Cheyenne. As young as you are now, I know this is hard for you to understand, but you must believe what I tell you. Do not let Kicking Elk or anyone else tell you differently. You are Cheyenne, the daughter of a chief, and you come from a proud line of great

Cheyenne Chiefs. Hold your head high at this knowledge and let no one's teasing words dim your pride in your noble heritage.''

"Yes, Father,'' the little girl agreed. "And next time I will hit Kicking Elk myself,'' she added with determination, her childish chin held at a jutting angle.

Tanya laughed and guided her small daughter toward their tepee. "Go now, little she-warrior, and have Walks-Like-A-Duck wash the mud from you so that you look like my daughter once more. Tell her I will be along soon to help prepare the evening meal.''

As Summer Storm trotted off to do as she was told, Tanya turned to her husband. "Thank you, Panther, for explaining to her what I could not have found the words to do. Our sons are young and strong enough to fight their own battles, but Summer Storm is still so vulnerable to the harsh words of others. Her tender nature is more easily wounded. While the adults know what is true, children are often cruel in their attitudes and hurt without meaning to do so, and speak without thinking first.''

"Still, I shall have a talk with Kicking Elk's parents, and if the child echoes his parents' thoughts, they will know my displeasure.''

"And mine, also,'' Shy Deer agreed, her dark eyes glittering. "No one does more for the welfare of the village than Little Wildcat. No one is more esteemed or worthy of calling herself Cheyenne.'' To Tanya she added, "You are my sister, Little Wildcat, in heart and blood, and I will be the first to proclaim this to all our people. We love and honor you as a chief's daughter and wife, and one of our own.''

"My heart is glad,'' Tanya said, her own eyes shining with gratitude. "And I will thank your son for defending my daughter. Sly Fox is a fine boy, and you can be proud of him. He watches over Summer Storm more protectively than her own brothers.''

''He adores her,'' Shy Deer said, as she picked up her robes and prepared to go into her own lodge. ''He feels it is his right to look after her.''

As Shy Deer ducked into her tepee, Tanya speculated on the satisfied gleam in Panther's eyes. ''What did Shy Deer mean by her words, Panther? Is there something she knows that I do not?''

Panther did not try to evade her question. He met her gaze directly. ''Winter Bear and I recently made a pact, Little Wildcat. It is our wish that Sly Fox take Summer Storm for his wife when she is grown.''

By now Tanya was too steeped in the Cheyenne ways even to consider arguing with her husband over matters which by tradition fell into his domain. Squelching her initial tendency toward anger, she allowed only surprise to show on her face. ''And Sly Fox, at the tender age of five summers, knows of this and accepts it?'' she asked.

''He not only accepts it, but he embraces the idea with great delight. Chief Winter Bear's son will make a fine husband for our daughter.''

''I do not doubt that, husband, but will Summer Storm feel the same when she learns of your plans?'' Tanya wondered aloud.

''She will abide by our wishes, as any good daughter is expected to do,'' Panther stated, ''but I see no reason why she should object. Sly Fox will be a strong, handsome warrior when he is grown, and she should be proud to be his wife.''

''I hope this is so, but as your daughter, she has inherited your stubbornness, Panther,'' Tanya pointed out. ''If she sets her mind against this, I can see problems ahead.''

"Put your face into the water, Summer Storm," Sly Fox instructed. "If you wish to learn to swim, you must keep your body in a straight line, not curved like a bow."

"My body is straight enough. I do not like water in my eyes."

Sly Fox sighed. "Now I see why your brothers refused to teach you. You are a stubborn little squirrel and too smart for your own good, but everyone knows that the fox has more cunning than the squirrel. Now, do as I tell you, and put your head down—or are you afraid?" he taunted.

Summer Storm's lower lip came out as her small chin jutted upward. "I am not afraid." Her golden eyes glared up at him.

"Then let me see you do it right this time," he challenged, meeting her look with a superior smile.

From the bank of the river, Tanya watched her daughter and Sly Fox. The breeze carried their words to her, and she smiled to herself at Sly Fox's patience and cunning. The boy was only five summers, just two years more than Summer Storm, yet he seemed older. Perhaps it was the hard life the Cheyenne led these days, but Tanya knew he was much more mature than a white boy his age would be.

Tanya barely heard Panther's silent footsteps as he joined her. Seating himself beside her on the grass, he reached out to lay his hand possessively over her protruding stomach. Dark eyes held those of gold in a long, smoldering look. "How is the mother of my children?" he asked quietly.

"I am getting more round and awkward with every sun," she replied with a wry smile. "This is the price I pay for your show of virility. While you strut through the village like a proud cock pheasant, I lumber about like a fat buffalo."

Panther laughed. "Is it my fault that my seed falls on such fertile ground?"

"But, Panther, to have four children within six and a half summers! I am the only woman in the village to do so, and I feel as if I am an oddity among our people. No doubt everyone has begun placing wagers as to how large our family will eventually become."

"Should I take another wife to help ease your burden?" he offered.

His words startled her until she caught the teasing gleam in his black eyes. "I will live with the embarrassment of your great and famous virility, husband. And I will make do with help from Walks-Like-A-Duck. You need not go to such bother just for my sake."

"It would be no trouble," he was swift to assure her, stifling a ready laugh.

"It would be more trouble than you could deal with," she promised, her eyes narrowing dangerously.

His deep chuckle shook his broad chest. "Would you be jealous, my Little Wildcat?"

"Only until I murdered her in her sleep."

He rewarded her with a tender smile and a stolen kiss. "As long as you satisfy my desires so well, I have no need of any other woman."

His gaze strayed to Summer Storm, still floundering in the water. "How is our littlest fish? Is Sly Fox able to teach her anything?"

"In time, I suppose. Sly Fox is very good with her, and she adores him for all his attention. He has promised her a ride on his pony when she has learned to swim."

"If she is anything like her mother, she will learn quickly. Soon she will want a pony of her own."

"Between you and Sly Fox, she will soon be thoroughly spoiled. Perhaps it is good that she will no

16

longer be the baby of our family.''

Panther's thoughts became more serious. "Once the child is born, we should try to find time to visit your parents. It has been a while since they have seen their grandchildren.''

"Those visits are hard, Panther,'' Tanya confessed on a troubled sigh. "Each time, they want us to stay. I can scarcely bear the tears in my mother's eyes when we leave. Even your mother has trouble hiding her heartbreak when we must leave the ranch and return to our lives here.''

"My mother knows where my heart lies,'' Panther said. "She resigned herself to it years ago, when I chose to live with my father's people.''

"Still, she waits for the day when you will return for good, to take over running the ranch. She will not be truly content until then.''

"That day will come soon enough, Wildcat.'' Panther's fine features drew into grim lines. "Before our children are much older, we will be forced to choose. Most of the tribes are already settled on reservations. It is only a few of us who still wander the plains. The buffalo are scarce; the game scattered. The bluecoats nip at our heels like hungry dogs. With no hides and little food to see us through the winters, we too will soon be forced to surrender our way of life.''

Tanya swallowed the lump in her throat. "It is sad to see it happening and be so helpless to stop it. If only the whites would be satisfied with the lands they have already taken! If only the government would uphold the treaties and not be so greedy! If only the soldiers were less glory-hungry and would leave us in peace!'' she exclaimed.

"That is not possible, Wildcat. We both know you are reaching for rainbows that do not exist.'' Panther's dark eyes were filled with sorrow for the future. "No, one day we will be forced out of this life forever. Then I will take you and our children, and we will go to Pueblo. There I will once again become Adam Savage, white rancher. Our children will trade their moccasins for hard leather shoes and their deerskin for clothes of cloth. They will go to school and abandon their Cheyenne ways. My mother's Spanish heritage and dark coloring will explain their appearance, as they once did mine. No one will suspect their Cheyenne blood. In time, they will think of the old ways and their life here as if it were all just a far-off dream. Already they speak English as well as they do Cheyenne.''

Tanya's hand curled about his arm, and her tear-filled eyes sought his. "I will do my best not to let our children forget this life, Panther, or their proud heritage as children of the Cheyenne. Always I will seek to keep the traditions alive in their hearts, as they will be in ours. This I promise you, my dearest love.''

His deep voice whispered through her tawny hair as he drew her close to him. "How is it, Wildcat, that I often feel you are more Cheyenne than I? What spirits have I pleased to deserve a love as fine and true as yours?''

All through the long, hot summer the Cheyenne tribe followed the buffalo, sometimes joining with other bands they met. Too often they came across the carcasses of vast herds slaughtered by white buffalo hunters and left to rot on the prairies. Though the United States government did not sanction such destruction, neither did it move to stop it. Officials and military alike merely closed their eyes and ears to the facts, for this was one sure way to defeat the remaining renegade tribes. Without warm robes, and tepee covers, and food for the winter to come, the

Indians would weaken, and many would die.

The buffalo were scarce; other game scattered. Hounded by the soldiers, the tribes often had to leave their best hunting areas hurriedly to avoid capture. Confrontations with the military were avoided when possible, not so much out of fear, but in order to secure needed stores of food and skins for their people. Scouts were sent ahead and posted in strategic positions to alert the tribe of approaching danger, while more experienced hunters stalked the elusive game.

Undaunted, Panther and his cousin Winter Bear led their people across the plains. Though harassed by the bluecoats and frustrated by the scarcity of buffalo, they persisted. By summer's end, they had enough meat and hides to sustain them through the worst months of winter. Unless they met with unexpected disaster, they would survive.

While the men hunted, the women cured the hides and dried the meats. They dried summer berries and dug for roots, using virtually everything nature provided. They collected nuts, honey, wild plants and gourds. Smaller game was snared near the camps. Evenings found the women straining their eyes in the firelight to sew winter garments for their families. Great joy sounded throughout the village when the men found time for a few raids and came home with sacks of stolen corn from settlers' fields. Now there would be cornmeal to add to their meager diets. Once Panther took a small raiding party for a night foray into a small settlement, returning with such treasures as coffee, flour, and sugar. Slowly but surely, the tribe readied itself to withstand a long, harsh winter hidden away in a mountain valley far from the reach of the soldiers who would pursue them even then.

When the hunting was done, and the deep snows

had not yet fallen to hamper horses, Chiefs Panther and Winter Bear took their warriors on raids against the smaller troops of soldiers who dared to wander farther from the forts than was wise. Often, it was merely a case of luring soldiers who were already following the tribe into a well-set trap. The Cheyenne now harassed the settlers and military in turn, tearing up train tracks and cutting telegraph wires where they would. Farms and outlying settlements were ransacked and burned. Poorly guarded wagon and supply trains were attacked with a vengeance, leaving hardly enough in the burning rubble to attract a vulture.

Had Tanya not been expecting her fourth child, she, too, would have gone along on these raids. Years before she had learned the skills of a Cheyenne warrior. Panther had instructed her well, and she was much revered by the tribal warriors. Though still barred from tribal councils and traditionally male ceremonies, she was readily accepted on war raids, her skills and bravery admired and lauded.

It was late in the Moon of the Dying Grass, the month the white men call September, when Panther returned from one of his numerous vengeful raids. As word went out, the entire tribe came together to greet the returning warriors. The head chiefs, Panther and Winter Bear, led the procession through the village to its center.

It was here, outside their tepee, that Tanya awaited her husband. Her eager eyes scanned his bronze body for signs of battle, glad to find no new wounds. Panther rode tall and proud upon his great black stallion, his long dark braids lying across his muscled shoulders, the eagle feathers that announced his many coups ruffled by the breeze. His onyx eyes gleamed with victory in his handsomely sculpted face. With his high cheekbones, firm lips and bold straight nose, he was the ideal picture of a noble warrior.

Tanya's gaze swung from her husband's face to the man stumbling along behind Panther's horse. The captive's hands were bound behind his back, a rope lashed about his throat. His clothes were torn and caked with dirt and blood, but still recognizable as a cavalry uniform. What angered Tanya was the fact that the man was obviously an Indian, his skin and braids proclaiming him so even as his uniform declared him a scout—a traitor to his own people. Two more Indians in cavalry uniforms were led behind other Cheyenne warriors. All three were Utes, and as such, long-standing enemies of the Cheyenne, but even more hated now for their cooperation with the U.S. military. Their fate at the hands of these enraged Cheyenne warriors was sealed. They would betray no more of their Indian brothers.

That night, beneath clear star-studded skies, the Cheyenne drums beat loudly in celebration of the warriors' victories. Campfires blazed brightly as the tribe gathered in the center of the village to sing and dance and to thank the benevolent spirits that protected them.

Tanya sat near her husband, her own collection of scalps adorning the belt about her greatly enlarged waistline. Throughout the evening of revelry, she was unusually quiet. According to her station as a chief's wife, she saw that food and drink were offered to the warriors, but she ate very little herself. Her position decreed that she oversee the celebration, seeing to the comfort of the braves and the arrangements for the captives. Before the sun rose to greet the next morning, the Ute captives would be slowly tortured to death. It was a ceremony Tanya had observed and participated in many times, and though she could not truthfully say she approved, it was a part of the

Cheyenne way of life, and she had learned to accept it.

This night, however, her mind was elsewhere. The preparations for the feast had exhausted her, and her condition was making itself felt. As soon as possible, she seated herself, propping several robes behind her to support her aching back. Listening to the warriors' accounts of their victory, she unconsciously rubbed her hands over her protruding stomach in soothing circles. The hours wore on, and with them her discomfort increased, the ache in her back extending itself to her stomach. When the others began preparing to torture the Ute captives, Tanya rose. Finding Shy Deer, she explained her predicament and politely excused herself from the proceedings.

As she walked toward her tepee, where Walks-Like-A-Duck was watching over Tanya's three sleeping children, Panther stopped her. "Now is not the proper time to leave the celebration, Wildcat." His words, though quietly spoken, told her of his displeasure at the timing of her exit. He had long been aware of her dislike of these tortures and knew she endured them only because she must.

Tanya touched his arm and smiled serenely. "Now is the only time, husband. It cannot be helped." A sharp pain lanced through her belly, nearly doubling her over with its force.

Panther's strong arms supported her until the pain had passed. A look of understanding cleared his brow. "Your time has come," he said softly.

Tanya nodded, and when she found the breath to speak, she said, "Go back to the festivities, Panther. Shy Deer has gone to find Root Woman to attend to the birthing, and Walks-Like-A-Duck will be with me. We will send word when your child is born."

Compared to her others, this birth was long and

hard, lasting throughout the long dark hours of the night. The night's revelry had finally ceased, the last drumbeat faded away, the final shouts dying on the morning breeze. Dawn was just testing the new day with lovely colors of pink and gold when Tanya's second daughter made her entrance into the world. Filled with the peace of the quiet, beautiful morning, Tanya named her daughter Dawn Sky. At last she slept, her daughter in her arms.

When she awoke, Panther was at her side, his dark eyes caressing her face. "Good morning, Wildcat."

She smiled and reached out to touch his cheek gently. "Good morning, Panther. Am I forgiven for presenting you with yet another daughter?"

"There is nothing to forgive," he assured her. "She is a beautiful girl-child. This time I finally have a child with your honey-gold hair, though I think her eyes will be dark like mine."

"Perhaps the next will be another son for you."

Her softly spoken words made him frown. "No, Wildcat," he said, shaking his head. "Root Woman has told me how difficult this birth was for you. She has warned against endangering your life with further childbearing. You must take her advice and guard against this. She will give you a mixture of herbs to prevent future fruitfulness."

Tears misted Tanya's vision as her gaze slid away from his. "Perhaps you should seek out a second wife after all, Panther. She could give you more children to fill your tepee."

His long fingers caught Tanya's chin, bringing her eyes back to meet his. Panther's gaze was tender as he smiled down at her. "My tepee is filled to bursting now, Wildcat. I have no need of another wife and no wish to personally populate our tribe. Four children are plenty for any man to boast. I am well pleased with you and our fine sons and daughters.''

"I love you, Panther. You are the sun that lights my days so brightly.''

With restrained passion, Panther met her uplifted lips with his own in a sweet, sweet kiss, "And you are my very life, Wildcat.''

2

Summer Storm's eyes were as big and bright as those of the two cougars her parents kept as pets. Kit and Kat, as the female and male mountain lions were named, would have loved all the brightly packaged gifts surrounding the créche in Grandmother Rachel's parlor. The two big cats would have had the packages torn open within minutes, had they not been left behind in the Cheyenne village. Summer knew exactly how they would have felt, for she longed to do precisely this herself. Only her father and mother's stern admonitions kept her from doing so.

Today was something everyone kept calling Christmas Eve. It was some sort of celebration of a great chief's birthday, as near as Summer could figure. All the family was coming together at Grandmother Rachel's ranch. Grandmother Sarah and Grandfather Edward were coming, with Great Aunt Elizabeth, Uncle George and cousin Jeremy. Aunt Julie and Uncle Roberto were already here, with Summer's cousin Linda; and Mother's good friend Melissa Kerr and her husband Justin, and Judge and Mrs. Kerr, were bringing someone called baby Steven. Even Sheriff Middleton was invited.

Everything was strange here at Grandmother Rachel's house. There were many rooms altogether in one lodge, and the fires were lit inside the walls rather than in the center of the rooms. Father was dressed in cloth leggings and shirts, though he still wore his moccasins and headband. Mother wore a beautiful cloth dress the color of the sky, and her hair was arranged in waves upon her head instead of in her usual long braids. Here, everyone spoke in English, or sometimes Spanish, and called Father "Adam" instead of Panther. Mother, they called "Tanya," which Summer thought a very pretty name. Even her own name sounded different when spoken in English, and Summer found it confusing at times to know who was addressing whom.

Summer liked her cousin Linda, whose name meant "pretty" in Spanish. Linda was Summer's age and had curly brown hair and bright blue eyes. She was nice to play with, which was good since all the adults were so busy talking or fussing over Dawn Sky and Melissa's baby, Steven. Besides, Linda had the most beautiful dolls, and she didn't mind sharing them.

Summer felt quite grown up in the pretty new dress Grandmother Sarah had made for her. It was a color called "pink" and had white lace along the collar and sleeves, and it felt so light and soft to touch. Mother had washed Summer's hair and left it in loose curls flowing down her back.

There was a bit of confusion at mealtime. Here, it seemed, everyone ate at once, rather than having the men served first and the women and children eating afterward. Then there was the strange feeling of sitting so high off the floor on this thing called a chair. At first Summer had difficulty managing the odd utensils until her mother showed her how to handle the fork. The square cloth called a napkin kept falling from her lap onto the floor, instead of staying to keep her new dress clean. Still, Summer managed to get her fill of the delicious foods heaped on her plate.

"It is so good to see everyone again," Tanya was saying. "I am glad we made it back in time for Christmas."

"Yes, the holidays are such special family times," Rachel agreed.

"Tanya, do you remember those Christmases we spent together with the Cheyenne?" Melissa asked softly. "I'll never forget how you went out of your way to make them special for me. You talked Adam into shooting a turkey just to make a traditional holiday dinner."

Tanya laughed in remembrance. "Everyone thought we were crazy to make decorations and hang them on the pine trees, even though Adam would never allow us to cut one down and bring it into the tepee."

"Do you still do that?" Edward asked curiously.

"No, not since Melissa left. There is no need. I never miss it when I am there."

"But, surely, for the children's sake . . ." Sarah said.

"No, Mother, Cheyenne children do not understand or celebrate Christmas. They have their own traditions and festivities."

"Still, your own children should be taught the Christian holidays. One day they will live here and—"

"Sarah, there will be time enough for them to

learn all they need to know later, when they are older and not so easily confused,'' Elizabeth put in.

Tanya flashed her aunt a thankful smile. ''Aunt Elizabeth is right, Mother.''

''Have you any idea when you might come home to stay, Adam?'' Tom Middleton asked.

Adam frowned as he answered, ''The way things are going, it will be sooner than we want; a few years at most.''

''What a perfectly horrid thing to say, Adam!'' exclaimed Tanya's sister, Julie. ''I, for one, will be happy to see Tanya home where she belongs, as well as these poor children who are growing up so fast! Mother and Dad would love to get to see their grandchildren on a regular basis. Goodness! We didn't even know Tanya was expecting another child, and in you walk carrying Dawn!''

''We barely recognized the older three, they have grown so!'' Roberto said in support of his wife's statement.

''We get back as often as we can,'' Adam stated quietly.

''And we try to understand,'' Rachel told him, ''but we want you home, son.''

''Our home is with my father's people. As their chief I am needed there.''

''Your mother needs you here, too, Adam,'' Judge Kerr pointed out.

''Not as badly as the Cheyenne.''

''If things are so bad now, shouldn't Tanya and all the children stay here, where they will be safe?'' Edward asked hopefully.

Adam met his father-in-law's look squarely. ''No, my wife and children will go where I go and live where I live.''

''Tanya, surely you can see the sense of this,''

Sarah pleaded.

Tanya shook her head and gazed lovingly into Adam's dark eyes. "No, Mother. I follow my husband, our children with us," she stated firmly. "Our lives are intertwined. Whatever else the future holds for us, I will never again be separated from him. The pain would be too great to bear."

They stayed for ten days, sharing the holidays with one another. For Summer it was bliss. Among her Christmas presents she found two more lovely dresses. There were dozens of colorful hair ribbons and a wooden box in which to store them that played a magical tune when the lid was lifted. But the gift she treasured most was a beautiful doll all her own; a doll with dark hair and sparkling blue eyes painted on her shiny hard face, and her own tiny pink and white checkered dress with a frilly white pinafore made to fit.

The spring that preceded Summer Storm's fourth birthday brought many changes to their lives. Now that Dawn Sky was old enough to be left with someone else for a while, Tanya was once again going on a few raids with the warriors. In late spring Panther and Winter Bear led their people south, where they had been invited to participate in a Comanche Sun Dance ceremony hosted by the Comanche Chief Quanah Parker. Several tribes converged at Elk Creek for the sacred ceremony and to exchange news.

The news was not good. With winter past, the cavalry was preparing for renewed campaigns against the tribes. Now, just as the Indians were about to begin their spring hunts, the white buffalo hunters were once again slaughtering and scattering the few remaining herds.

The Indians were angry and desperate. Winter food stores were depleted, and they needed the buffalo now more than ever. Time and again they would come across the decaying remains of hundreds of buffalo scattered over miles of prairie.

In retaliation for all the heedless carnage, several bands of Comanche, Kiowa, Cheyenne and Arapaho joined in attacks against the buffalo hunters. The hapless men who were caught were tortured and killed, but there were many more white hunters who escaped the Indians' wrath, and too much damage and waste had already been done. Twice, though, the tribes managed to come upon the buffalo hunters immediately after a kill. Not only did they have vengeance against their enemy then, but the Indian women were able to salvage much meat and many precious hides.

Tanya was with the Cheyenne raiding party early one summer morning when they tracked several white buffalo hunters to a ramshackle cabin. So swift and sure was their attack, the white men had no time to defend themselves. Not a single gun shot was fired. Within minutes two buffalo hunters lay dead in the dirt before the cabin. Three others stood awaiting similar fates.

The Cheyenne warriors ransacked the cabin, scavenging for knives and guns. Cast iron kettles and cookware would be carried home to their wives, fine gifts from a successful raid.

Just as they were preparing to set fire to the shack, one of the warriors came from the cabin pulling a woman behind him. He threw her to the ground at his feet. The woman never moved to block the blows he aimed at her with his fists and feet. Nor did she look up or cry out, other than to groan softly when the brave's foot connected heavily with her ribs.

She was painfully thin, with lank dark hair so filthy it was impossible to tell its true color. Her skin was dark from the sun, her hands rough, her dress little more than a drab brown rag to cover her.

Tanya had witnessed such scenes time and again. Redwing would either kill his captive or take her back to camp as his slave. Tanya paid little attention as she wrapped the iron skillet, her prize from the day's raid, in her pony blanket. Her hands stilled as, suddenly, something about the woman touched a familiar chord in her memory. Tanya's gaze slid curiously to the woman, studying her with a new intensity. All at once, as Redwing grabbed the tomahawk from his side, recognition came to her.

Just as the warrior aimed the weapon at the woman's skull, Tanya called out to him, "Redwing, wait! If you do not want the woman, I will trade my iron skillet for her."

He eyed her skeptically. "You want this worthless piece of dogmeat?"

"Yes." Tanya nodded.

Panther, who had now walked to her side, said quietly, "Wildcat, if it is a slave you want, I can find you one who is younger and stronger. This one has a witless look about her."

With a secretive smile, Tanya disagreed. "I would have this one, husband."

Only later, in the privacy of their tepee, did Panther come to know his wife's true reason. Under all the filth and bruises, Tanya had recognized Rosemary Walters, one of the four other women who had been captured along with Tanya by the Cheyenne years before. Rosemary had long ago been traded to another tribe, and Tanya had not seen her since.

Of course, this was not the same Rosemary that Tanya had once known. The years of captivity had taken their toll on the older woman. For a while, Tanya feared Panther was right—the woman was a silent, broken shell. While she obeyed commands and diligently carried out all her duties, Rosemary shuffled about with a vacant stare and hunched shoulders. She had become a beast of burden, with absolutely no will of her own.

Bit by bit, with patience, Tanya pieced together the story of Rosemary's life since they'd last met. Rosemary's Cheyenne master had sold her to a half-breed trader. For a few months she followed him as his squaw woman. Rescue came at Ft. Larned, where a group of well-meaning Christian women helped her gain her freedom at last. A few weeks later, Rosemary finally had word of her husband and family. The news was devastating, for with it went the last of her hopes and dreams, rendering her newfound freedom mean-ingless. Harry Walters had only recently given up hope of Rosemary's survival. He had remarried, finally providing his daughter and four sons with a step-mother. Betty, his new wife, was soon to bear him another child.

For a while, Rosemary had stayed on at Ft. Larned, but her life with the Indians had tainted her. Her husband had refused to come to the fort to identify her, for to do so would make him a bigamist. Harry staunchly claimed that his first wife was dead. Rejected by her beloved husband, forsaken by white society, Rosemary was distraught and heartbroken. Nearly out of her mind with grief over losing her family a second time, she made her way to Wichita. She tried to find work as a laundress or waitress, but her past seemed to haunt her even there. No decent family would take her in, no reputable establishment give her work. Even the church refused her refuge. Inevitably, in order to survive, she ended up selling her body to anyone with the price of a meal and a bottle of cheap whiskey in which to drown her sorrows. Lower and lower she sank into her private pit of oblivion, until one day she simply ceased to care about anything at all. She drifted from place to place, from man to man, uncared for and uncaring, existing in body but not in spirit. This was her situation when the band of buffalo hunters had taken her with them to serve their joint needs, and it was thus that Tanya had found her.

As she had once done for Melissa, Tanya now made it her mission to restore Rosemary's spirit and body. With patience, kindness, clean clothes and decent food, Tanya set about her self-appointed task. Here Rosemary would be safe and cared for at last. In Tanya's lodge the woman would once more know a family of sorts. As long as Rosemary accepted the Cheyenne ways and served her new mistress well, she would be treated decently. Her work would be hard, but she would be rewarded for it instead of beaten. Under Tanya's protection, she would never again be forced to accept the unwanted attentions of any man. While it was not the best life a woman could ask for, neither was it the worst; and under Tanya's benevolent friendship, Rosemary slowly began to heal.

"There, but for the grace of God, go I," Tanya said softly as she watched Rosemary head for the river to fill the leather pouches with water.

"What did you say, Wildcat?" Panther sat nearby repairing a bow.

"That could have been me, Panther, if not for your tender love and care."

Panther followed her gaze to Rosemary's bent, shuffling figure. "No, Wildcat. I doubt your spirit could ever have been broken as Rosemary's has. Your pride and your heart are too great."

"I don't know. If another warrior had chosen me as his slave, my life would be very different today. To be constantly beaten and used and degraded by an unfeeling vile beast of a man would break any woman. To be handed from man to man and treated worse than a camp dog—it is a wonder Rosemary's mind did not snap altogether."

"I was not sure it hadn't. At first I wondered at the wisdom of letting her care for our children. I was sure she would poison us or try to kill us all in our sleep one night."

Tanya laughed and poked fun at his words. "I thought the Indians revered a person who was crazy, Panther."

"Perhaps 'awe' is a better word, or maybe 'fear'," Panther explained. "We avoid them when possible, and we never deliberately harm a crazy one for fear of the powerful spirits that have taken over his mind. It is very bad medicine to kill such a person, for then the evil spirits must seek a new body to invade."

"Well, we needn't worry, for Rosemary has not lost her mind. She is recovering steadily."

"It would be good if you could convince Walks-Like-A-Duck that this is so," Panther said, laughing softly. "She will not come near our tepee when Rosemary is inside, not even to see the children. Once I saw her turn pale when she realized she was standing in Rosemary's shadow. It is the first time I ever recall seeing Walks-Like-A-Duck come close to fainting."

"I will talk with Walks-Like-A-Duck," Tanya promised.

"It is good, what you are doing for Rosemary, Wildcat. You have a loving heart."

Tanya smiled, and then sighed. "I suppose many of our people will say I am doing this because she is white, but that alone does not win my sympathy. She

34

has lost so much, Panther—her family, her husband and children, her pride. I look at her and I feel so fortunate in my own life, so blessed by your love.''

That summer was long and hot and dry. It brought the worst drought in memory. Shimmering waves of heat danced over the prairies, while the sun baked the grass and plants into clumps of shriveled brush. Creeks and riverbeds dried up as if they'd never been more than dusty gulches. The few that still ran were little more than rivulets of mud. The land came to resemble a desert, and with the hot winds came choking dust storms. Wildlife left in search of food and water, and the plains became a barren wasteland that season.

The tribes convened in a secluded canyon known to the Indians as The Place of the Chinaberry Trees. Few whites knew of this place; those who did called it Palo Duro Canyon. Quanah Parker was there with his Kiowa, Panther and Winter Bear with their Cheyenne, and several other tribes.

Here the land was still green. The waters ran clear and game was plentiful. Here the tribes found the elusive buffalo. For many weeks the tribes camped in peace and plenty, hunting and curing their hides as in the old days, with no white man in sight, no soldiers or buffalo hunters to disrupt their lives. It was a beautiful time of peace and renewal, a reprieve from the trials that constantly plagued them.

It was during this peaceful interlude that Shy Deer presented Winter Bear with their second child, a daughter as lovely as Shy Deer herself. They called the girl-child Sweet Lark, for her little trilling voice was as clear and sweet as that of the lark's song.

Tanya adored Sweet Lark, but she was not quite as charmed with another sort of baby that came her way that summer. Kit and Kat, the cougar pets she'd raised from cubs, had gone off on their own that spring. Kat, the huge sleek male, had returned within a few weeks. Now, finally, Kit had returned from her mountain foray, bringing with her a new little cougar cub.

The spotted cub was darling, as are all kittens, but Tanya knew how rambunctious they could be. She and Panther had worked hard to train Kit and Kat and keep them out of constant trouble. While she loved them, she was not looking forward to training yet another curious cub.

Summer, however, was delighted with her precious new pet. Dawn Sky was not yet old enough to be a real playmate, but Meow, as Summer dubbed her, was lots of fun. Surprisingly, Kit trusted the entire family with her kitten, knowing instinctively that no one would harm her newest baby. This was the first of her cubs she had brought home, and Tanya could only wonder why she had done so now. At any rate, everything chewable was now hung high out of reach, for nothing was safe from Meow's bright golden gaze and sharp teeth.

For many weeks the tribes enjoyed the contentment of Palo Duro. The braves hunted with renewed spirit, and the women went about with a new feeling of security. Even the children felt the added sense of freedom, laughing and playing without a worry in the world.

Then, somehow, the sense of peace drifted away like smoke on the wind. While some ignored the change, Tanya could not.

"Something is about to happen, Panther. I know it. I feel it. It is time to leave this place, as much as I love it here."

Panther, too, felt change in the air. "There is trouble on the wind. Some of the people want to go on hunting yet, but the Cheyenne will travel with the sun's first light.''

''We will be ready, Panther.''

Once more they were a tribe on the move from place to place, always with a sharp eye watching for the cavalry. A month after their tribe left Palo Duro, news came that the pony soldiers had attacked those still camped in the canyon. At the surprise attack, many had tried to flee, leaving behind all their possessions. The Indians had been rounded up and driven like cattle to Ft. Sill, where the warriors and chiefs had been jailed.

Further north, gold hunters had invaded the *Pala Sapa*, the sacred Black Hills country of the Sioux, Cheyenne and Arapaho. The hated General Custer had made an army reconnaissance in the Black Hills that summer and reported gold to be found just by pulling up the grass and shaking it loose from the roots. Chief Sitting Bull of the Sioux was angered that the whites dared to invade what was, by treaty, Indian territory. When the U.S. Army did nothing to stop the gold-hungry hordes, the tribes took matters into their own hands and Indians and whites alike were on the warpath with a vengeance again.

Summer Storm sat watching her mother apply the red and yellow streaks of war paint to her face. ''Mother, when I grow up, can I become a warrior woman like you? I don't want just to cure hides and sew and cook and make babies.'' Summer's bow-shaped lips pursed in distaste at this idea.

Tanya hastily stifled her ready laughter. ''To be a warrior woman you must first pass all the tests, Summer Storm. This is not easy to do, or anyone could become a great warrior. There is nothing shameful in being a wife and mother. The women of the tribe render great service in their own way. Without them there would be no order in our village.''

"But I want to ride and fight with the men."

"Sly Fox might have something to say about that, my daughter. Perhaps he will not want his wife to be a warrior."

"Then I will not marry him," Summer Storm said with a frown.

"I thought you *wanted* to marry Sly Fox when you are grown. You seem to like one another a great deal."

"Sometimes I think I will marry him, and sometimes I do not know what I want."

"Well, little one, there are many years before you must decide," Tanya counseled.

"There is so much I do not know, Mother, so much I am curious about."

"What things do you wish to know?"

Summer dipped her fingers into the colorful paints. "Why is the grass green?"

"That is easy. Mother Earth likes the color green for her growing things."

"Why does the frog hop and the bird fly?" Summer persisted. "How does Sun get to the East from the West when he sleeps? Does Moon push him so that Sun wakes again in the eastern sky?"

Tanya shook her head in mock dismay. "For such a pretty child, you certainly have an active mind. Your thoughts scurry through your head like a chipmunk!"

"Have you no answers for me, Mother?" Summer Storm asked.

"No one can answer all your questions, daughter. Many you must discover on your own as you grow and learn about the world around you."

Summer Storm thought about this a moment. "Yes, but each year I find more questions in my mind," she complained.

"Then you must decide which are most important to you," Tanya told her wisely, "and concentrate on finding the answers to those first."

There were times in the next months when Tanya wondered whether her children would grow old enough to find their answers. Times were very hard, and the tribe constantly on the move to avoid capture or massacre at the hands of the military. Even the deep snows and cold of winter did not deter the government troops. For the Indians it was a struggle just to provide food and shelter for their families, let alone defend them from the ever-present threat of cavalry attack. Panther and Tanya often discussed these problems and the uncertain future of the tribe and their own small family.

"I wonder what will come of this special Medicine Lodge Ceremony that Sitting Bull has called." Tanya spoke softly as she banked the fire for the night. On the far side of the tepee her four children and Rosemary already slept.

"We cannot see into the future, Wildcat, unless the spirits send us dream visions. The tribes are gathering to pray for strong medicine against the invasion of the whites into yet more of our lands. All we can do is pray and prepare to defend what is ours."

Panther's breech cloth fell to the ground next to his empty moccasins. With supple grace he lowered himself to sit cross-legged and naked on the sleeping mat he shared with his lovely wife. "Let us forget tomorrow and enjoy what is left of the night." His jet eyes gleamed with anticipation as he watched her come to him.

At the edge of the mat, Tanya shed her dress, glorying in the love and possessiveness etched on Panther's face as his dark eyes played across her nude form. She stood proudly before him, knowing her body pleased him now as much as it always had. He had yet to move, but Tanya felt his desire reach out to her as his avid gaze slid over her soft curves. A trembling began in her limbs, a fire in her belly. She felt her breasts tighten and her nipples pucker as her body responded to his silent commands.

"Come, woman, unbind my braids." His words took her thoughts back to that first night he had made her truly his—the night he had stolen her soul and made it his own. That night, too, he had made her perform this service for him. This night her hands shook only slightly less as she loosened the leather thongs and unwound the thick black plaits. With her fingers she separated the long heavy strands, letting them whisper across her palms in a midnight caress.

In his turn, Panther unbraided her hair, letting it spill in tawny waves across her shoulders, a sheer silken curtain over her taut breasts. His broad hands slid beneath the golden strands to find her breasts, cupping them, teasing the pert nipples with his long fingers. His blazing dark eyes held hers in a burning look. Then he brushed the hair aside, and his mouth enclosed the rosy nub of one aching breast, his lips pulling at it.

Ripples of liquid flame raced through Tanya's body, pooling low in her belly. A soft sound of desire hissed from between her parted lips as she pulled his head closer to her. With fevered flesh, her body melted toward his, willing the touch of his naked flesh against hers. Her hands found the muscled breadth of his broad shoulders, then slid in a loving caress to his warm smooth chest. His heart thundered beneath her palm.

Together they sank onto the mat, limbs tangling, hands caressing. Panther's touch was fire, igniting her passions with expert ease. With lips and tongue he traced a hot, wet path from her shoulder to her jawline, laughing softly as she shivered beneath him and arched even more closely into him.

With a twist of her head, Tanya found his firm, sensuous lips with hers. Their lips clung, parted, and met again in pliant desire. His tongue pushed past her parted lips to twine with hers, to probe the dark sweetness of her mouth.

Then Panther was leading her in the ancient mating dance as his leg parted hers and he came into her, full and powerful in his male supremacy. Her soft gasp became the whisper of his name from her lips. They moved together, his hands on her hips lifting and guiding her as she writhed beneath him. Tanya's hands stroked his back and clutched at his shoulders, her nails furrowing his flesh in her rising need. Passions built to an unbearable level—that point where agony and ecstasy meet—and the explosion sent them hurtling skyward through clusters of brilliantly shining stars.

Afterward, Tanya nestled in the curve of his shoulder. She felt the soft caress of his lips upon her damp forehead and sighed contentedly. No matter what else happened in their future, as long as she and Panther had each other, she would be happy. With his strong heartbeat pounding reassuringly against her ear, she slept.

3

The year was 1876, and while the rest of the nation was preparing to celebrate the centennial, the Indian tribes were struggling for their mere survival. This past December, during the Moon when the Wolves Run Together, Edward Smith, the U.S. Commissioner of Indian Affairs, had ordered all Sioux and Cheyenne Indians living off the reservations to report to their agencies by the end of January. If they did not comply willingly, military forces would be sent out to compel them.

When the deadline had passed by a week, the Great Father in Washington, President Grant, authorized General Sheridan to commence action against all hostile Indians. In turn, Sheridan ordered Generals Crook and Terry to begin preparations for military operations in the direction of the headwaters of the Powder, Tongue, Rosebud, and Bighorn Rivers.

That it was entirely unfair and unreasonable to expect the tribes to be able to travel such long distances through bitter winter weather in such a short time, with their families and belongings in tow, the government did not care. Snug in their civilized homes in the cities, they gave no thought to the brutal winters of the plains, where snows came up to the bellies of the horses or beyond, and the howling winds brought the temperatures plummeting well below the freezing mark.

Government and military officials alike wanted only one thing—to free the Black Hills for gold hunters and settlers, and to see every Indian safely confined within a reservation. It mattered not that they were breaking yet another in a long line of broken treaties. It mattered not what hardships the Indians might endure, or that the reservation lands were poor in water or wildlife. Who cared if the Indians were cheated, as long as the whites got what they wanted—and right now they wanted the gold and land in the Black Hills.

Fierce blizzards and winter storms prevented many tribes from hearing of Edward Smith's order, let alone responding to it. Those who did learn of it could not possibly travel to their agencies by the deadline date, even if they had wanted to. The snows were too deep, the weather too bitterly cold. There were women and children and old people to think of, and they would never survive such a trek over many miles of frozen and snow-drifted land.

In mid-March, during the Bud Moon, Panther and his people were camped in the Black Hills with Two Moons' tribe of Cheyenne and several bands of Sioux. They were camped peacefully, anxiously awaiting the coming spring, for food supplies were treacherously low.

Near dawn, just as the women were rising to stoke the morning fires and the men beginning their prayer chants to the rising sun, the surprise attack came. The peace of the early morning was suddenly shattered as gunfire ripped the air. In those first crazy moments bullets were flying everywhere, cries of alarm and pain mingling with those of the charging cavalry. To Tanya, it seemed like the Washita Massacre all over again.

But there was no time for fearful reminiscence. Panther was barking orders as he gathered his weapons and raced to join his warriors. "Grab only what you can carry, and take the women and children up the mountain. To run along the riverbank would be suicide."

"What of our horses?"

"Leave them. They'll never make it up the steep slope. Hurry!" With that he was gone, Kat at his side.

The children were wide-eyed with fright, Dawn Sky howling as Tanya stuffed her into her cradleboard and swung it onto her back. The two older boys hurriedly dressed and began to gather the weapons as their mother instructed them.

"Robes—gather robes and what food you can fit into these." Tanya tossed the two parfleche bags at Rosemary.

Summer clutched at her mother's leg, frightened nearly to death at the noise and confusion around her. Looking down, Tanya saw the naked fear in Summer's golden eyes and could find no words to console her child. Grabbing the first dress her hands touched, Tanya tugged it over the girl's head and stuffed her bare feet into a pair of moccasins.

"Come," Tanya commanded. "We must flee now. Keep as low to the ground as you can, and run like the wind. Hunter, you must find Shy Deer and bring her to us," she told her eldest son. Tanya followed Kit and her cougar cub from the tepee.

It was Kit who showed them the safest route up

the steep mountain slope. As they clambered over the jagged, icy rocks, Tanya could hear the sounds of fierce fighting behind them. The warriors were giving their families precious time to escape, at great risk to themselves. Finally the warriors gave up their defense and joined their tribes in retreat.

Then began the long journey through the snow-bound Black Hills, with little clothing, no shelter, and almost nothing to eat. Behind them, General Crook's troops had captured all their ponies and burned everything else to the ground. The smoke of their burning possessions could be seen for miles. Ahead of them lay the long walk to Crazy Horse's camp, their nearest refuge.

That night several of the warriors returned to the village, and beneath the very noses of the sleeping soldiers, stole back their captured ponies. Now the Indians once more had mounts, but they could do nothing to ease the cold, howling wind and the sub-zero temperatures that threatened the lives of their people. Many had fled without robes or moccasins, and there was a red trail of bloody footprints in the fresh snow. A few of the old ones could not keep pace. Falling behind, they sat and waited for death to claim them, refusing to endanger the others by slowing them.

Walks-Like-A-Duck was one who chose death in this way. Though Tanya tried to urge her on, the old woman would not budge. "If it is my time to die, let me choose the manner in which I will join my ancestors," she declared stubbornly.

"Please, Grandmother," Summer Storm begged, using the familiar term for this woman who had helped to raise her from the very day of her birth. "Please do not give up. I will help you. You can have my robe to keep you warm. I do not want you to die and leave us." Tears froze on her wind-chapped cheeks as she pleaded with her friend and teacher.

Walks-Like-A-Duck gathered the shivering girl close to her for one last embrace. "Little one with the golden eyes, I have loved you like my own granddaughter, and it is not my wish to make your heart heavy with sorrow. You are learning now that life can be hard, and there are things that we must accept because we have not the power to change them.

"I am old. My eyes have seen much in my lifetime. I have seen great joy and great sorrow. Now I am weary. The voices of my ancestors cry out to me to join them, and I must heed their call. In the spirit world I will be warm and young and beautiful again, as I was in my youth. I will be with my husband and son, whom I have not seen in many years. I will sit and laugh with my mother and sisters once again. I will be happy.

"Do not hold me back from this with your tears, Summer Storm. Your sorrow will bind my spirit in this world, where I no longer wish to be. Release me gladly, Granddaughter. Walk away and do not look back. Do not call again for me to join you when my heart yearns for what awaits me on the other side of death."

Summer Storm choked back her tears and nodded. "I will miss you, Grandmother," she whispered quaveringly.

"I will think of you, and I will be watching you grow into the lovely young woman I know you will be one day," Walks-Like-A-Duck promised.

With a final farewell, Tanya led her small daughter away. Neither looked back, though Summer Storm's thin shoulders shook with the effort to stem her sobs, and two pair of golden eyes glistened with tears.

For three long, cold days the tribe marched onward. Quill Woman lost her unborn babe, and four of the younger children froze to death on the way. Their bodies were buried in deep snowdrifts and left behind. Two other small children were saved when their father killed his horse and placed their tiny bodies within the warm cavity of the animal's belly. One of the wounded warriors succumbed to his untended injury.

At the end of the third day, they limped into Crazy Horse's camp, starving and homeless. The Sioux welcomed them with open arms, weeping with them over their losses, and sharing with them their own shelters and meager supplies. Cheyenne and Sioux, they were brothers in this war against the greedy, malicious white men—and their hearts grew hard with anger and hatred and thoughts of revenge.

Spring came late that year to the Black Hills. Though the Sioux shared what they could spare with their Cheyenne brothers, it was never enough. Every time one of the children cried out in hunger, Tanya thought her heart would break. Four and five families crowded together in each tepee, and though rarely a complaint was heard, they were constantly bumping into and stumbling over one another. There were not enough robes to go around. Three and four people would huddle together under one robe at night, hoping their combined body heat would combat the chill of the cold nights and damp ground that the fires never seemed to quite dispel. Hunger and cold combined to weaken the smaller children and old folks. Many sickened and died before the weather finally broke and the sun sent warm winds upon the land once more.

"It was not supposed to be this way," Panther

told Tanya as he held her thin, shivering body next to his. His words were spoken softly so as not to disturb the others sharing their lodge. The night was crisp and bright, and sleep was long in coming as he worried over his family and his tribe.

In the glow of the dampered fire his dark, saddened eyes lingered on her features. His fingers reached out to touch the sharp bones of her cheek and chin, then wandered down to trace the line of her protruding collarbone. "You are so thin, my love. By touch alone I can count each of your ribs. I have seen you give your share of the food to the children, and always after you serve me the larger portion. You cannot keep on doing this, Little Wildcat, or you will soon become weak and ill.

"You are a warrior, Panther, and our chief. You need more food to maintain your strength to hunt and fight for us. As for the children, how am I to swallow my food when their big, hollow eyes follow each bite from my bowl to my mouth? When their silent faces beg me for enough food to ease the constant ache in their bellies? Sometimes I forget what it felt like to be full and warm, and I wonder if we ever will be again."

"Yet never once have I heard you complain. Always you are helping others and trying to ease our discomforts," he said. "You shame me, Wildcat, even as I shame myself."

Tanya frowned at him. "Why should you feel shame over something you cannot control, my husband?"

With a sigh, he tried to explain. "When I first stole you away from the wagon train, I knew I was bringing you to a life far different from anything you had ever known. Yet you adjusted and thrived. It made me proud to see how well you learned our ways, and how quickly you adapted. You were strong and willing and determined, and you soon stole my heart for your own.

"Everything was different then. As a young warrior I was so eager and so sure of myself. Never did I doubt my ability to provide all of our needs and to protect my people. The buffalo were plentiful; the deer roamed the plains at will, as did the tribes. The white men were still too few in number to be considered any real threat. Our world was as it had been for countless lifetimes.

"Now, in just a few years, all this has changed. No longer can I provide the food and skins my beautiful wife needs to feed and clothe our family properly. We live in a tepee given to us by others. Even the clothes on our backs were worn by another first—not caught and skinned and sewn by our own hands. Daily I watch my wife and children grow thin with hunger, and my heart grows heavy with sorrow and shame that I can no longer provide and protect as a husband and warrior should, as a Cheyenne chief is honor-bound to do."

Taking his face between her palms, Tanya caught back a sob. "Panther. Oh, my love, do not berate yourself so. None of this is your fault. Always you have given your best. Place the blame where it truly belongs—on the soldiers who raid and plunder and burn our villages, never giving us respite or peace; on the ever-growing greed of the white men for land and gold that is not theirs to claim. *They* have slain our friends and families. *They* have killed off the buffalo and scattered the game. *They* have stolen our lands and our very way of life.

"There is nothing you or any of the other chiefs could have done to prevent it. There are too many whites and too few Indians, and with each moon that passes more settlers arrive from the east and more soldiers come to protect them. Every sunrise they pry a little more of our land from between our fingers. As much as we wish to, we cannot change this. My heart, too, aches to see it, but what more can we do that we have not already tried? No, Panther, the blame does not lie on your shoulders. You are a good husband and a great chief, and always you will have my love and my deepest respect."

"Even though I probably deserve neither," he murmured into her soft hair. "Truly I do not deserve a wife as lovely and tolerant as you, my Wildcat. Even now, when you need your rest, you listen to my problems and try to ease my troubled mind. My head tells me your words are true, but when I see my children shivering in the cold and growing thin with hunger, my heart cannot contain its sorrow. My soul yearns for days gone by, for a way of life fast vanishing. And from the depth of my despair arises an anger and resentment such as I never before imagined. It is an immense hatred that lives and grows daily like a raging fire fed by a fierce wind—and it will not be appeased until I have extracted my revenge against those who have harmed my people."

Panther's revenge against at least one of his most hated enemies would come sooner than he expected, but first would come the matter of survival and recouping some of their vast losses. With the help of the Sioux braves, they hunted the sacred Black Hills and brought back a good number of antelope and deer, as well as buffalo from the plains. While their successes helped greatly, they did not come near to what was needed to make up their losses.

Help came suddenly to the Cheyenne from an unexpected source. A week into May, two wagons came rolling into the encampment, closely guarded by several mounted Sioux and Cheyenne warriors. Summoned by the commotion, Tanya came forth from her lodge and warily approached the crowd gathered about the wagons. From where she stood, she could see that the drivers, both slim youths, were white.

"For God's sake, Tanya! Call off these renegades before they scalp us both! Tell them we come in peace."

Stunned, Tanya stared at the first driver. It was Jeremy Martin Field—her dear little cousin Jeremy! Only he was not so little anymore. She had forgotten he was a young man now; that he was twenty years old and nearly full-grown.

"Jeremy!" she exclaimed, her surprise turning to delight and lighting up her face. As she started forward to welcome him, the driver of the second wagon removed his hat. A wealth of dark curling hair tumbled down about "his" shoulders, and Tanya cried out in renewed surprise as she recognized Panther's mother, Rachel.

"Rachel! Jeremy! What in the world are you doing here? How did you find us? What is going on?" Her questions tumbled out as her mind scrambled to make sense of their sudden appearance.

"Would you believe we came for a nice little visit?" Jeremy asked with a wide, beguiling grin. His straight white teeth flashed in his tanned face, and he reached up slim fingers to brush an errant lock of sun-bleached blond hair from his forehead. His forest green eyes twinkled in merriment.

Tanya laughed up at him. "Next you'll be telling me those two wagons carry your luggage."

Rachel hopped down from her seat, dusting off the rear of her breeches. "Don't believe a word of it, Tanya. You know how I detest life with the Cheyenne. I wouldn't be here now if it weren't necessary."

SUMMER STORM

"I still don't understand," Tanya said, watching Jeremy alight from his wagon. When had he grown from a lad to a man so tall and straight and handsome? Not long ago he'd been a mere boy, and now she had to crane her neck to meet his eyes.

"Well, we started off with one wagon," Rachel began. "When we heard of the trouble you were having, we had to do something to help."

"How did you hear? How could you know of our problems?"

Jeremy's face darkened. "Word gets around fast when big-mouth soldiers brag of routing Indian villages. The family was frantic when we heard tell Panther's tribe was burned out. For a while we had no idea if any of you were still alive."

"It was bad, very bad," Tanya admitted grimly. "We lost several from our tribe trying to reach safety with Crazy Horse's people."

"It was a relief to hear that Panther and most of his band had escaped. Still, we knew you would be desperate for food." Rachel gestured toward one of the wagons. "We raided your Uncle George's mercantile for all the food and blankets he could spare. There are kettles, cloth, utensils, even some hatchets and knives—anything we felt you would need."

Tanya's golden eyes swam with tears at their compassion. "And you risked your lives to come all this way to aid us."

"You don't know the half of it!" Jeremy claimed. "We started out with one wagon-load of goods. The second wagon was a bonus of sorts."

"Only if you discount the fact that for the last week we've been looking back over our shoulders, not to mention the putrid smells radiating from that horrid contraption!" Rachel declared, turning her nose skyward.

Jeremy laughed at Rachel's antics and Tanya's puzzlement. "Yeah, Rachel, but can you think of anything these people need more right now than a wagonload of buffalo hides? Of course, some of them might be too ripe to be of much use, but the majority should be okay. They were the freshest load we could steel from the railroad yard. Cripes! They hadn't even been unloaded yet!" He winked rakishly at Tanya.

Tanya was flabbergasted. "You stole hides for us?" she squeaked. "A whole wagon full of buffalo skin?"

"Sure did, wagon and all. Slick as a whistle! Heck fire, Tanya, they were just settin' there practically begging to be taken, and not a soul around to notice at the time."

"You could have been shot or worse!" Tanya exclaimed, her eyes travelling between Jeremy and Rachel in stunned disbelief. "If you'd been caught . . ." Her words hung in the air.

"Luckily for us, we weren't!" Rachel put in. "I still don't know how Jeremy had the nerve to pull such a fool stunt, but there was no talking him out of it. Truth be told, I'm glad now that he did it, though it sure set my nerves on end at the time and for quite a while afterward just wondering if we had an enraged bunch of buffalo hunters hot on our trail."

"Oh, you wonderful, beautiful scoundrels!" Tanya hugged each of them in turn. "We will never be able to express our gratitude for such an act of courage and generosity."

Jeremy actually blushed as she kissed his cheek. "I figured those buffalo hunters had stolen what was rightfully yours. All I did was get a bit back for you. If I'd known we'd run into such luck, I'd have brought help along and carted more up here for you."

"I still don't know how you managed to find our

camp, or how you got through Indian territory with all your hair.''

"The credit goes entirely to Jeremy,'' Rachel volunteered with a slight shudder. 'I would have had us eternally lost, and any Cheyenne I once had learned has long since left my mind.''

Jeremy grinned. "Tanya, you didn't think I'd forget all those valuable lessons you once taught me, did you? Why, I can track and read signs better than anyone around Pueblo, soldiers included, thanks to you. And you'll never know how glad I was to remember just a few words of Cheyenne. It saved our hides more than a few arrow holes, I'll admit.''

Rachel and Jeremy stayed with them for three days, during which time Jeremy spent hours hunting with Panther and the other warriors and learning tribal ways. He was having a fine time and enjoying himself immensely.

Quite the opposite was true of Rachel. "*Por Dios!* I had forgotten how dark and dingy these hovels can be!'' she complained. Her nose wrinkled distastefully as she watched Tanya and the other women salvaging the precious buffalo hides. "How I managed to live with White Antelope as long as I did surprises me. The dirt, the smells, the bugs, the cramped quarters—the absolutely primitive conditions! Tanya, dear, how you can prefer this to life at the ranch is beyond my understanding.''

Tanya smiled gently. "I love your son, Rachel, and where Panther desires to be, so shall I stay.''

"I loved White Antelope, too, but I simply could not abide life in the Cheyenne village. I was miserable every moment, yet you seem so content.'' Rachel shook her head in bewilderment.

"Truly, I am happy here. If only the soldiers and buffalo hunters would stop harassing us, life would be so good, as it was just a few short years ago. To live in peace, free to roam our lands at will in search of food and shelter is all we ask. I want to raise my children to value this simple life—to hunt, to be at one with nature and her splendor, to work and play and appreciate their proud heritage. There is such a basic and uncomplicated beauty here, such as I never knew in the white world."

"Beauty?" Rachel echoed, looking slowly about her with a frown. "Therein lies the difference between us then, Tanya. Where you see beauty, I see only dust and dirt. Where you found contentment, I found only heartache. You labor lovingly over smelly skins and I see only backbreaking work beneath a relentless sun. You readily don buckskin, while my heart cried out daily for satin and lace and ribbons to adorn my hair. I would never trade my world for this."

"Nor I this life for yours," Tanya replied softly, "yet I know in my heart that one day Panther and I must do just that. When that day comes, I will follow him willingly back to Pueblo and the ranch, but a part of me will always yearn for this life and I will miss it terribly."

Though Summer Storm had always liked Jeremy the few times she had met him previously, she came to truly adore him during his short stay in her village. To her he was the most magnificent of men. Surrounded by people with dark eyes and hair, she was dazzled by his blond good looks and unusual green eyes.

Not only was he handsome to behold, he was also kind and fun to be around. Along with the many necessities, he had also brought sweet sticks of flavored candies for the children of the tribe. Unlike many Cheyenne men who rarely found time now to give a child much attention, especially a girl-child, Jeremy took time to devote himself to the younger ones. He never excluded the girls from these hours of fishing and games, even little Dawn Sky, who was but three summers of age, and he seemed to favor Summer Storm most of all.

"How is my beautiful little Cheyenne princess?" he would say, making her cheeks glow hot with pleasure. He teased her about how pretty she was and what a heartbreakingly beautiful woman she would be one day. "I am tempted to wait for you to grow up, and if you are half as lovely as I suspect you will be, I just may marry you myself, Golden Eyes," he jested.

Though she knew he was only joking with her, Summer Storm was pleased. Nonetheless, she thought it only fair to inform him. "I am already promised to wed with Sly Fox."

Jeremy seemed shocked at this. "What! At your age, how can you possibly be promised? Who told you such a wild tale?"

Summer Storm returned his gaze with utter solemnity. "It is true. You may ask my father and mother."

Jeremy did exactly that. He confronted Tanya with the matter. When she confirmed Summer Storm's words, he was stunned. "Lord, I thought such things went out with knights and dragons and damsels in distress! Summer is just a child. How can she know at six years old who she may want to marry when she's grown? What if she doesn't love the fellow? Has she no say in her own life? This is unbelievable!"

"Do not fret, Jeremy. Summer Storm accepts this already. She adores Sly Fox, and he her."

"That is all well and good, but it seems so—so cold and unfeeling to decide a child's fate for her."

"Arranged marriages are nothing new," Tanya

argued in defense. "Throughout the ages they have succeeded admirably, and many couples learn to love one another dearly. Summer Storm and Sly Fox know and like one another. I foresee no problems between them."

"Well, what if they didn't agree? What if they hated one another? What then? Would you condemn your own child to a life of misery?" he persisted.

Tanya threw up her hands in exasperation. "What if . . . What if! If a snake had wings, he would fly! Really, Jeremy, you are worrying over nothing, but if it will ease your mind any I will tell you that neither Panther nor I would see our daughter married to a man she found repulsive or who would mistreat her. Now, will you please let the matter rest?"

"For now," he conceded reluctantly. "But don't think you've heard the last of this from me."

Promised to Sly Fox or not, by the end of his visit, Summer Storm nearly worshipped Jeremy. Her eyes followed him everywhere and she delighted in the special attention he showered upon her. She had literally lost her young heart to this tall, golden sun god, and when he left she was desolate for days afterward. Her only consolation was Jeremy's promise to return one day soon and bring her another doll to replace the one lost in the raid.

4

With the help from Rachel and Jeremy and much hard hunting and work, the tribe gradually recovered from the winter raid. At long last, the warriors were free to avenge their losses with warring forays and raids of their own. They concentrated their efforts on the gold-hungry men invading their sacred Black Hills in search of shining wealth. These foolish fellows, with dreams of vast and instant riches, often wandered through the land ill-prepared to meet any challenge but that of digging into the gold-laden earth. Many came alone or in pairs, wrongly believing the cavalry would protect them and hold the Indians at bay while they peacefully raped sacred land. Many a poor dreamer's scalp found its way to an Indian belt that spring and summer.

After all she and those she loved had endured, Tanya found not a morsel of sympathy for these stupid gold-crazed robbers. Rather, she joined Panther and his warriors in their efforts. She rode straight and proud beside her husband, her battle cry echoing with his. The legend of her bravery and prowess grew as she boldly threw herself into battle. Never hesitating, her aim as true as any other warrior's, her weapons ran red with white men's blood. This golden-haired, tawny-eyed Mate of the Panther inspired many an awesome tale retold over night campfires of Indians and whites alike. Small as she was, it was said her warbelt could not hold all the scalps she had earned. Only those who knew her well knew what an exaggeration this was. While she spilled her share of enemy blood, her aversion to scalps was such that she often left her victims' scalps attached. Her status in the tribe was great enough to allow her this option now, and she readily took advantage of it.

That is not to say the raids always went smoothly, or in their favor. Each time they rode out of the encampment, they faced death and danger. It was a matter of confronting one's enemy bravely and with daring—and hoping everyone came back alive to fight yet another day.

This day they had come upon the camp of eight rough mountain-wise men. The prospectors had holed themselves up behind a tumble of boulders, and were not about to give up their claim without a fight. Bullets and arrows pelted the air furiously as the two sides challenged one another.

Finally, when the barrage of bullets had nearly ceased, Panther motioned for his warriors to move forward cautiously. ''They must be nearly out of ammunition, for now they are more careful in their aim.''

Within a few minutes, there came a lull in the gunfire. Of one accord, the warriors kneed their horses and bounded toward the rocks. This was what the white men had been awaiting and fearing, but they had saved a few rounds of ammunition in a last-ditch

60

effort to rout their attackers. As the fearsome battle cries split the air, a final burst of gunfire spent itself.

The first indication Tanya had that something was wrong was an oddly painless feeling of impact hard against the side of her head. A thud that knocked her slightly sideways on her horse. Then a strange stinging began, and a buzz started in her ears. A tingling sensation raced through her limbs, and she could feel the strength leaving her fingers, then her arms and legs, all in a matter of mere seconds. As her vision began to blur, she raised her hand to her head in a slow, disoriented move so unlike her usual quick reflexes. Her fingers came away covered with her own blood. The world about her began to waver and darken alarmingly in coordination with the numbing that was taking over her entire body.

Tanya shook her head trying to dispel the dizziness fast overcoming her. "Heaven forbid!" she spoke hazily to herself. "I think I'm about to faint!" Her last conscious act was purely instinctive, a move drilled into her by Panther when he had trained her to be a warrior. With her last ounce of flagging consciousness, she leaned forward and locked her arms about her horse's neck, tangling the reins about her hands, her legs wrapped as tightly about his middle as possible. This was the last thing she remembered before the dark clouds of unconsciousness wrapped about her, blotting out everything around her.

Colors of pain swirled about her, invading her peace and chasing away the blessed oblivion that held the hurt at bay. Though Tanya's eyes remained closed, she sensed the mist of unconsciousness lifting from her. As a wave of pain crashed through her head, she groaned with the agony of it.

Even as the sound left her lips, she felt warm arms

tighten about her in a gesture of comfort. "Hush, my heart. All will be well. I will let no more harm touch you."

Panther's voice, so warm and deep, cut through Tanya's pain to soothe her. Gentle as rain, she felt his touch as he bathed her temple with a wet cloth.

Slowly, and with much effort, her eyelids fluttered open. Tanya gazed straight up into eyes as dark as a moonless night, so black she could not tell where his irises left off and his pupils began. It was like gazing into a bottomless lake. Her thoughts flew back to the very first time she had seen this magnificent man who was to become her husband. She had lost consciousness in her fight to escape him, and his fathomless black gaze had been the first thing she'd seen upon opening her eyes. Then, as now, their eyes had caught and locked, gold to black. She'd been mesmerized for countless moments, nearly hypnotized by twin onyx mirrors that threw back her own reflection from their shining depths.

Now those eyes were blessedly familiar, concern haunting them as he gazed down into her face. "Wildcat, can you see me, my little one? Can you speak?"

Tanya made the mistake of trying to nod, and the pain in her head set the world to spinning again on a brightly colored pinwheel. Her breath hissed loudly between clenched teeth as she inhaled sharply. Her fingers dug into Panther's bare arms as she clung tightly, fighting the pain and dizziness. "Panther." The word was less than a whisper, yet he heard.

"I am here."

"My head . . ."

"Just a graze," he assured her gently. "A deep one, but not too serious, I think. Is your vision blurred?"

"A little, but I can see."

"You were fortunate. Your headband deflected the bullet enough to save you serious injury." His arms tightened about her once more. "When I think how close you came to death . . ." His voice was gruff with the agony of nearly losing her.

"Do not think of it, my beloved. Just hold me and let me feel your strength surround me." Once more her eyelids fell closed, but this time she drifted into a healing sleep.

When she awoke again, her head was cradled gently on Panther's broad chest. Beneath her, she could feel his even breathing and his steady heartbeat, and she felt warm and safe in his embrace. The sky was just becoming the pearl-gray of pre-dawn, and Tanya knew she had slept the night away.

She raised a hand to gingerly touch the side of her aching head, and her slight movement immediately awakened Panther. "How are you feeling?" he asked.

"Better. The pain has eased some." Now, instead of hot lances, she had drums pounding inside her skull.

He brushed her hand from the bandage encircling her brow. "You will leave the bandage on until we reach the village. Then Root Woman can see to your wound."

"Panther?" Her voice was low and hesitant, betraying her fear. Carefully easing her head from his chest, she sought his eyes. "Will I have a hideous scar?"

"No," he hastened to assure her, and she read the honesty in his gentle look. Then his dark eyes took on a twinkle and his lips twitched with the urge to smile. "Your only scar will not be on your face, but beyond your hairline. You now have a second part in your hair, that is all."

Relief flooded through her, though she did not appreciate his humor overmuch. "You are a beast to tease me, Panther."

"And you are vain, my love."

Vain or not, Panther thanked the benevolent spirits that had spared her life, for he did not think he could bear to be parted from her. If he ever lost her, he would himself be lost. All the way back to the village he held her before him on his horse, lest she become dizzy and fall; he held her close to his heart and cherished her.

In May, Chief Sitting Bull sent out invitations to the other free tribes for a Sun Dance to be held the following moon. Thousands of Indians from various tribes were expected to gather together on the banks of the Rosebud River. Crazy Horse was eager to go, and Panther and Winter Bear agreed that their Cheyenne should also attend. The Sun Dance always brought out the best in the warriors, giving them the opportunity to renew their faith and courage. It brought strength, and good medicine and unity to the tribe as the warriors sought closer contact and guidance from the spirit world.

For Tanya and the children it was a chance to renew friendships with others they had not seen in many moons. While the children played, the women exchanged ideas and gossip. In the midst of troubled times, it was a brief reprieve—a time of laughter and pleasantry so rare these days.

While much of the ceremony was strictly for the men, some of the celebration was publicly enjoyed by all. Tanya particularly liked the dancing, with the men attired in their finest garments, their bronze bodies gleaming in the firelight. Faces and bodies were painted in vibrant colors with creative artistry. Feathers and beads, shells and bone adorned the warriors from head to ankle in intricate and bold design. Never had these proud warriors looked more fierce, more handsome, or more defiant. Their courage and confidence radiated from them like rays from a hot summer sun.

June was half spent when word came to the camp of advancing military troops. Crazy Horse led a successful rout against General Crook's cavalrymen, badly defeating the soldiers. Crook retreated, and the Indians celebrated this victory with high revelry.

After the confrontation with Crook's troops at the Rosebud, the Indian chiefs decided to move west to the valley of the Little Bighorn to camp and hunt. In all, about ten thousand Indians relocated to the Little Bighorn, nearly four thousand seasoned warriors among them.

Exactly one week after the skirmish with Crook, a few hours after sunrise, the southern end of the enormous camp was hit with a sudden, surprise attack. For several minutes Tanya and the others were unaware of any hostile activity, since the Cheyenne were camped near the northern end of the village, away from the attack. Literally hundreds of tepees separated them from the military action. Not until Panther rode up some time later, did they learn of it. It seemed a Major Reno had launched an unsuccessful attack, was backed into a nearby woods, and was now pinned down on a bluff by a ridiculously small number of braves.

Panther shook his head in curious disbelief. "What was the man thinking of, to attack such a large encampment with so few troops?" he wondered. "Does the man have a death wish?"

Tanya could not understand the major's strange strategy either. Surely it was baffling—unless— "Unless he was expecting reinforcements, or to combine his attack with additional forces to hit from yet another direction,'' Tanya thought aloud.

Hearing her, Panther frowned. "Do you suppose?''

The words were barely out of his mouth when a cry went up from the nearby northern end of the village. Two Cheyenne women, out collecting firewood, had spotted advancing military troops to the far north. A rider had already been sent to determine its direction and strength.

Word had spread, and the warriors were gathering their weapons when the scout pulled his lathered mount to a halt before Winter Bear's tepee. "It is Long Hair,'' the brave shouted. "The general with the long yellow hair comes this way, from the north.''

"How big is his army?'' one chief asked.

"Around two hundred and fifty men, all mounted.''

Compared with the number of warriors now encamped in the valley of the Little Bighorn, Custer's troops were pitifully small. It was laughable to think that Custer would pit his forces against a strength so much greater than his. So ridiculous was it that many of the warriors snickered outright, even while hoping that this most hated enemy would indeed attempt just this. Immediately the tribes began plans to set their trap and spring it upon the arrogant general and his hapless men.

After a quick council of all the tribal leaders, it was decided that Custer should be allowed to cross the river approaching the camp. Well before Custer reached this point, several bands of warriors would ride into the river and up a hidden ravine to lie in wait there. Other bands would retreat from the river to the blind side of a natural rise of land between the river and the Indian encampment.

"Surely, Custer does not realize our size or force, or he would not approach so openly," Crazy Horse commented. "That, or the man's mind has deserted his head."

"His arrogance leaves no room for reason," Sitting Bull predicted. "His head is filled only with thoughts of his own importance. Today, it will bring his defeat. By concealing ourselves, we will lure Custer across the river and over the hill, where he cannot retreat fast enough to avoid us. Before he realizes his mistake, we will have surrounded his entire troop. Then we will have him at our mercy."

Another chief spoke up. "And shall we show mercy, Chief Sitting Bull? After the atrocities the man has shown our people, I say no."

"No mercy."

"Let not one soldier live to tell of the battle."

"Let their dead bodies proclaim our victory."

"All must die."

"Let the ground run red with their blood."

One by one the tribal leaders voted unanimously for death to "Long Hair" and all his soldiers. This day, there would be no survivors, no prisoners, no pity shown. Victory would be theirs, and they would savor the sweet taste of revenge against this murderer, this brutal ravager who called himself a great general.

"I want you to stay here, Wildcat. You will protect our families from any other attacks the soldiers might have planned."

"No, Panther."

Panther stared hard at Tanya. His usually obedient wife had stunned him with her refusal. "Would you defy me, woman?"

Tanya's small chin jutted out stubbornly. "In this,

I would, Panther. I, too, am a warrior, and though you are my chief and my husband, I ask you not to deny me my own revenge against Custer. This man led the Washita Massacre, where my beloved adoptive parents were brutally murdered, their bodies trampled to bits in the icy river by his rampaging soldiers. He caused the deaths and mutilations of so many of our friends and relatives. He destroyed our village. He is responsible for so much misery for so many of our people. Because of his attack, you were critically wounded that day, almost dying. I was forced to return to my parents in Pueblo, dragged there and held for months against my will. Custer caused our painful separation.''

"Lieutenant Young had something to do with that, too, as I recall,'' Panther reminded her.

"Yes, my fiancé was at fault, but so was that strutting peacock of a general who admires only himself and lauds his own victories as if he were some supreme god. Panther, I want to see his blood spill from his vile body onto the ground. I need to see his death with my own eyes; to witness his lifeless corpse, to participate in his final defeat. Surely you can understand this. You, too, must need this revenge as badly as I.''

She was reminding him of all the pain and misery this one man had brought to both of them. Chief Black Kettle had been Panther's uncle, his father's brother. Yes, he wanted revenge against Custer very badly, indeed. How, then, could he deny Wildcat the same release?

With a curt nod, he gave his permission, his dark eyes already eager for the thrill of battle. "You shall have your moment of vengeance, Little Wildcat. Come. Let us speed the general to his death.''

"And may his black soul rot eternally in Hell,'' she

added to herself, as moments later she hastily applied her warpaint.

Summer Storm watched her mother ready herself for battle. She listened as Tanya recited the chant that would call up her protective spirits to defend her in battle. Part of Summer was just a little frightened at Tanya's swift transformation from gentle mother to fierce warrior, yet another part of her heart was swelling with pride. Each time her mother rode out at her father's side, Summer feared for her safety. When Tanya had returned with the head wound, Summer's heart had nearly stopped. After being convinced that her mother would soon recover, she had crept away and secretly cried great tears of agony and relief. Summer could not stop her fears, for she loved her mother dearly; yet neither could she stem her pride and admiration for this brave, beautiful woman who had given her life. She watched anxiously as Tanya rode off once more.

As Tanya watched with Panther, General Custer led his men across the river with the easy assurance of a man accustomed to victory. The Indians kept their silent vigil until the last soldier had crested the hill. Suddenly, with the lightning speed of an eagle swooping down upon its unsuspecting prey, the warriors attacked. The air rang with their fierce war whoops as they swiftly encircled the outnumbered cavalry. Completely cut off from any avenue of retreat, with no shelter of defense available, the soldiers panicked. For some unknown reason, the order came to dismount, which put them at a further disadvantage to the mounted warriors. The somewhat baffled Indians witnessed the predictable result—the frightened cavalry mounts immediately bolted, adding to the confusion of the moment as they sought to escape the barrage of arrows and gunfire being exchanged. A few of the men met their death not by arrow or lance, but trampled beneath the flailing hoofs of their excited horses.

The cavalrymen had no chance to rally in their own defense. Though most had wits enough to try to return fire, they were no match for the sea of warriors that melted over them like a giant, engulfing wave. Many had not time enough for a single shot before the tip of an arrow found its lethal mark. Not one soldier lived long enough to fully empty his revolver. At close range, with the Indians soon among them, their firearms were virtually useless anyway. Most quickly resorted to swords and knives, in fierce hand-to-hand combat with the savage enemy.

By some strange unvoiced agreement, the warriors whittled away at the men surrounding Custer, fast diminishing their number but leaving Custer with only superficial wounds. More and more of the cavalrymen fell, until only a handful stood helplessly with their stunned leader. With wild yells of victory and an unholy gleam in their dark eyes, the warriors relished this long-awaited moment. Slowly and with great ceremony, they circled the few remaining bluecoats. One by one they picked off the survivors, until at last only General George Armstrong Custer stood alone. In the midst of his slaughtered troops, his uniform coated with dust and flecked with blood, his long yellow hair straggling with sweat beneath his cap, he faced the very people he had harmed most. Not one face of the hundreds surrounding him held an ounce of pity, any hope of reprieve.

Tanya was savoring the moment every bit as much as the other warriors. All the hatred and vengeance of the years was reflected in her gleaming golden eyes as she halted her horse next to Panther's.

A sneer distorted her beautiful features as she watched Custer's face turn a ghastly gray and beads of sweat pop out along his forehead.

Calmly, silently, the warriors let Custer's fear build. They smelled his fear, felt his nearly unbearable panic, and thoroughly enjoyed watching the involuntary movements of his body. Jerkily, he twisted about, viewing the unbroken ring of warriors around him. Now the Indians did not bother to cover their hate-filled glee as they watched him squirm.

The waiting soon became intolerable, as the warriors knew it would. "Shoot me, if you're going to, you damn red bastards!" Custer screamed. "You're going to kill me, so do it!"

Not one warrior twitched a muscle at his raving taunt, but sat staunchly and silently, watching and waiting with the eternal patience of their forefathers.

"What are you waiting for?" he yelled again. His voice cracked. "What the hell are you waiting for?"

At last he cracked completely and began to plead —for life—for death—for anything but this continued agony of wondering. Sweat and tears mixed and ran down his cheeks, his shoulders slumping in defeat. Still the warriors waited.

Finally Custer could bear no more. His panicked gaze traversed the circle in indecision. Then he took one step forward; and then another.

This was the signal the Indians awaited. Of one accord, several raised their weapons and took careful aim. Then as if by prearranged plan, each in turn let fly his missile. One by one, with incredible accuracy and deadly vengeance, they shot.

Hate glittered in Panther's black eyes as his arrow found its mark; and as Tanya's joined his, the smile on her twisted face was savage in its silent fury.

As each individual missile embedded itself into

his body, Custer lurched and cried out. Unable to stand, he fell to his knees and finally sprawled lifeless onto the blood-soaked earth.

It was as if a giant weight had been lifted from Tanya's heart when Custer breathed his last. Closing her eyes, she released a shuddering sigh of such immense relief that it amazed her. Her next breath seemed to bring a cleansing to her entire spirit. She opened her eyes and smiled up at Panther. "It is done. The debt is now paid—at last."

"My heart, too, is glad," he said, matching her smile with his own.

Then came the part that Tanya liked least. With great revelry, the warriors proceeded to collect scalps and souvenirs of their victory. Since several had contributed to General Custer's death and none could claim sole victory over this enemy, all declined his scalp, though a couple cut off locks of his long yellow hair. Panther chose as his reward the gold braid from Custer's military cap, but Tanya declined all but one gold button from his jacket. Even this she took with reluctance, wanting nothing that had belonged to this evil man. Still, she took it as a reminder of his humiliating end at the hands of the people he had tormented for so long.

Just as the Indians were preparing to return to the village, two braves rode up with a horse in tow.

"It is Custer's horse," one said. Others nodded in agreement, recognizing the general's well-bred mount. "All the others have either run off or been killed in the fight. What shall we do with this animal?"

Quickly the other brave spoke. "Perhaps we should shoot him and leave him beside his master. Certainly, it is of no use as an Indian pony."

Several warriors readily agreed.

"Wait." All eyes turned toward Tanya expectantly, respectfully awaiting her opinion. "I say we let the horse live. Leave him here to mark Custer's defeat."

"What is your reasoning for this?" Sitting Bull asked.

Tanya favored the Sioux Chief with a cat-like smile. "Custer calls this horse 'Comanche', Chief Sitting Bull. Would it not be appropriate for the only survivor of this battle to be named after one of our own tribes? Years from now, when the events of this battle are retold, would it not be a special coup—an extra bit of victory for us? Something to laugh and gloat over?"

The older chief laughed openly. Looking at Panther, he said, "Chief A-Panther-Stalks, your warrior wife is not only beautiful and brave in battle, she has a sharp mind and a sly wit. You are a fortunate man to possess such a woman."

To Tanya, he said, "It will be as you suggest, Golden Mate of the Panther." Still chuckling, he gave the order and led the victorious march back to the village, while buzzards gathered to feast on the bodies of the dead cavalrymen. Very few of their own warriors had been killed in the brief fray. These they took back to camp with them for proper burial.

During the next ten moons, Summer Storm became accustomed to seeing her mother return from raids and battles with blood on her weapons and clothes. It was a harried and horrible time for all the tribes. Those already confined to reservations often suffered the worst. Since the American government could not locate the Indians responsible for what they termed the Little Bighorn Massacre, they took spiteful action against peaceful reservation tribes instead. First, General Sherman received authority to assume military control of all reservations in Sioux territory, and to treat the Indians there as prisoners-of-war, even though they'd had nothing to do with the battle at the Little Bighorn.

Directly following this, Congress made a new law requiring the Indians to give up all rights to their Powder River territory and the Black Hills. Also, they thought it wise to relocate the Indians to a new reservation on the Missouri River. The American government threatened to cut off all rations to reservation Indians unless this new treaty was signed.

A few weeks later, eight companies of U.S. Cavalry, under the command of MacKenzie, who had led the Palo Duro attack, marched out of Fort Robinson into agency camps. There they confiscated all Indian ponies and guns, searched and dismantled tepees, and placed all male Indians under arrest. The tribes were marched back to Fort Robinson, to live there directly under the watchful guns of the soldiers.

That fall, to avoid further confrontation with the military, Chief Sitting Bull took his people north along the Yellowstone River. There they settled and hunted buffalo for the coming winter. Panther's tribe joined them, and compared to some of the less fortunate tribes, spent a relatively uneventful, if frozen, winter.

Meanwhile, while searching for Crazy Horse, General Crook came across Dull Knife's Northern Cheyenne village in late November. Most of this tribe had slipped away from the Red Cloud agency after the U.S. government stopped the rationing. They were a peaceful group, wishing only to hunt and provide for their families away from the reservation. General Crook sent MacKenzie to attack the village, which they did one cold, snowy dawn. As before, the warriors held off the soldiers as the women and children escaped. Then they walked three days, barefoot and hungry in sub-zero temperatures and drifting snow, to reach Crazy Horse's camp on Box Elder Creek. Crazy Horse again provided refuge, and soon thereafter moved the entire camp in order to avoid the soldiers.

The spring of 1877 brought no relief to the weary tribes. Most were faring worse than ever before, and the future looked bleak indeed. Crazy Horse, tired of constantly being hounded by the military, finally agreed in April to bring his tribe to Fort Robinson. He was lured by the promise of a treaty giving him reservation land along the Powder River. With Crazy Horse went Dull Knife, Little Wolf, and another smaller Northern Cheyenne tribe. Crazy Horse's Sioux remained at Fort Robinson, but the Northern Cheyenne who surrendered were sent south into Indian Territory to the reservation of their Southern Cheyenne and Arapaho brothers at Fort Reno.

Upon hearing of the surrender of several major tribes, and after a conflict with soldiers building roads and a fort along the Yellowstone River, Sitting Bull decided he had endured enough. Rather than surrender and accept life on a reservation, he decided to take his people and flee across the border to Canada. There he hoped at last to find peace and freedom for his tribe.

After conferring with the others of their tribe, Panther and Winter Bear declined Sitting Bull's offer to accompany him to Canada. Their people did not want to go that far from their homelands. In a council of warriors, a final heartrending decision was finally reached. With Sitting Bull leaving, and most of the other large tribes already confined to reservations, they could not hope to stand alone much longer. Their time of freedom was done. It was agreed that Winter Bear would lead the Cheyenne tribe to the reservation at Fort Reno, where they would surrender voluntarily. Panther would take his small family back to Pueblo, Colorado, there to resume ranching under his white identity as Adam Savage. Heartbreaking though it was, it was the only path left open to them, and they could no longer avoid or deny it. All had to reconcile themselves to this wretched fact, accept it and learn to adapt. Bleak though it may be, it was the only road to survival.

Parting from his people, who held such a special place in his heart, was the most difficult thing Panther had ever done. He would rather have cut off his right arm than desert them now, in their darkest hours. These were his father's people, and long ago Panther had made the choice between this and the white world to which his mother belonged. Through hard times and good, he had never regretted that decision. Now he listened with heavy heart to his cousin Winter Bear's solemn words.

"We are beaten," he told Panther, defeat in his eyes and voice. "The end is in sight, and there is no reason for both of us to lead our people to their final humiliation. Take Wildcat and your children and go back to your life in the white world. There teach your sons and daughters both ways of life, white and Cheyenne. Teach them to be proud of their Cheyenne cousins and their illustrious ancestry, but teach them also how to excel in the white man's world. Perhaps in some way you can better aid our cause from outside the reservation, and someday perhaps your children can help bridge the gap between the two worlds— white and Indian."

Panther agreed reluctantly, but as he had always known he must. In parting, he had these words for Winter Bear. "Our hearts and blood are forever bound in brotherhood, and our thoughts will often travel the same paths, but the time for parting has come. We shall meet yet again from time to time, in this life,'' Panther promised solemnly, "but we will ride and hunt together eternally in the next. If you have need of me, send word and I will come. If the need arises, send your children to me, and I will raise them as my own. I give you my solemn oath, on my life's blood, that I will never deny you anything which is in my power to grant. Though I walk away now, I shall never turn my back on the people of my heart.''

Tanya, too, was heartbroken at leaving her Cheyenne family and friends. She and Shy Deer shared a sad and poignant farewell. Hunter and Mark, at ten and eight respectively, well understood the importance of what was happening. Regret darkened their eyes as they said goodbye to those they knew and loved, knowing how much they would miss their Cheyenne brothers. Neither would reach manhood within the tribe, with all its colorful ceremonies and solemn rituals. Neither would dance the glorious Sun Dance, or earn the status of warrior or chief in the traditional manner. Their feet would now walk a different path.

At seven, Summer Storm knew only that her life was about to change drastically. They were going away to live at the ranch from now on. Remembering previous visits, Summer was excited about going. She loved Grandmother Rachel and the different life there. Still, she was saddened at having to leave her friends behind, especially Sly Fox.

"Do not cry, Summer Storm," he implored, drying her wet cheeks with his fingers. "We will see one another again. This your father has sworn.''

"But we will be so far away," she sniffed. "Now you will not marry me.''

"You are promised to me," he reminded her.

"When you are grown, we will marry. You have my word on this."

"You will wait?"

He nodded. "I will wait."

Panther and Tanya had released Kit and Kat into the wild, but Summer Storm gave her cougar cub to Sly Fox as a parting gift, and as a measure of her infinite trust in him.

When the final parting came, Panther and his family rode slowly away, not looking back once they had left the village. Deep sorrow was etched on all their faces and tears ran unashamedly down the proud bronze cheeks of Chief A-Panther-Stalks.

5

"Mother! Dawn has borrowed my best white blouse again, and there is a horrid berry stain on the collar!" Summer's agitated complaint preceded her into the kitchen, where Tanya was paring vegetables for lunch. The young woman entered the room in a huff, her long wavy black hair falling in charming disarray about her shoulders. Her golden eyes flashed their irritation. Her normal copper complexion was flushed with more color than usual, emphasizing the high cheekbones and arrow-straight nose that hinted strongly of her Cheyenne heritage. At seventeen, Summer Storm was already an arresting beauty. Tall and long of limb, her vital young body already flaunted the delightfully alluring curves of a woman— a siren's call to every young swain within miles of Pueblo.

"Will you please make her stop?" Summer continued. "It's not as if she doesn't have plenty of clothes of her own. Besides, she has no bosom yet, and my outfits hang on her. Could you talk some sense into her?''

Tanya smiled. Summer did have a point. Dawn was a petite thirteen, just now beginning to develop a hint of a figure. "Yes, Summer. I will talk to her. Now, bring me the blouse, and I will see about removing the stain.''

"Now? I'm trying to get ready to go to town with Mark.''

Tanya leveled a telling look at her oldest daughter. "You found time to complain about your sister. You can find a minute to bring your blouse to me. I am not unbusy myself, Summer.''

Summer wrinkled her nose in the spoiled, arrogant manner that was fast becoming a habit with her. "Mother, why are you bothering yourself with all this when we have kitchen help? Rosemary or Nora should be preparing the meal. Then you could be free to do something else—something you want to do.''

"You know your father prefers my venison stew,'' Tanya answered, shaking her head.

"So, once again Father commands, and you obey, like a trained dog!'' A sigh of impatience came from Summer's throat. "You would think you were the only woman who knew how to patch a tear or sew on a button. Sometimes I think you are nothing more to him than the perfect slave.''

"Summer! That is quite enough!'' Tanya's own temper was fast rising. "I am your mother, and as such you will show me proper respect.''

"Why? No one else around here does? Certainly not Father! And Hunter and Mark are becoming just as bossy. Honestly, Mother! I don't know how you can stand them! When I marry, my husband will not treat me as if I were a menial.''

"Oh? And how can you be so certain, my dear?" While still irritated, Tanya was also somewhat amused at her daughter's statement.

"We will have that understood before the wedding," Summer answered her. "The man I marry will love me and respect me. He will cherish me above everything else, and provide for my every need."

"My, my! And does this paragon of men exist beyond your dreams?"

"Oh, I'm sure he does. He just doesn't know it yet himself. When he finds himself in love with me, he will be eager to meet all my requirements."

Unable to hold back any longer, Tanya burst out laughing. "You have such a lot to learn yet, daughter."

"One thing I know already. I will marry no man who thinks I was put upon the earth solely to serve his needs. He will love me enough to respect my feelings and needs, too."

"Does this mean that you believe your father does not love and respect me, Summer? Because if this is what you think, you are so incredibly mistaken. No one, anywhere, could love me more than he does, and I return that love fully."

"I know that, but he certainly has a strange way of showing it sometimes, the way he orders you about. It sickens me sometimes to see you leap to do his smallest bidding."

"That is none of your business, sister, nor mine. Now apologize to our mother for your sharp tongue." Both women spun about to see Hunter standing in the hallway door.

"I do not take orders from you, brother dear," Summer said scathingly.

"You will either apologize immediately, or I will personally drag you out behind the barn and tan your spoiled behind with a willow switch,'' Hunter warned. Though he never raised his voice, it was plain that he meant every word.

"I'm sorry, Mother," Summer said, though it galled her to back down before her oldest brother's threat. To Hunter, she added spitefully, "Now are you satisfied?"

"Only if I never hear you speak that way to our mother again. You are so spoiled and pampered that it scares me sometimes, Summer. Have a thought for someone's feelings other than your own once in a while. And you can thank your lucky stars that it was I who overheard your smart remarks and not Father," he added as he walked through to the back door. "He would have taken the skin off of you with his belt for some of your hateful comments."

"And just how long were you standing there eavesdropping?" she called after him.

"Too long," came the dry reply.

If others shared Hunter's opinion that Summer was spoiled, perhaps her willfulness was made most noticeable in comparison with Dawn Sky's sweet and gentle nature. Dawn was a quiet little person, very pretty but also fairly shy. Only with her family and very good friends did her humor and playfulness really show through. Unlike Summer, whose temper could flare at the slightest cause, Dawn hardly ever became truly angry, and then she forgave the offense quickly. To her credit, Summer rarely held a grudge either, her temper cooling nearly as fast as it appeared.

Of the four Savage children, Hunter and Summer were definitely the most stubborn, though Mark, too, was prone to fight if he was sure he was right. Hunter was so much like his father that Tanya was stunned each time she saw Adam and Hunter together. They behaved similarly and looked alike, with the exception of Hunter's golden eyes. At twenty, fully grown now, Hunter was content to follow in Adam's footsteps and become a cattle rancher. He loved the ranch and the daily challenge it offered.

Mark, now nearly nineteen, was home from Harvard University on summer break. Studying to be a doctor, he would begin his second year in the fall.

In the ten years since leaving their Cheyenne village, Tanya and Adam had done their best to keep the Cheyenne values and beliefs alive in the hearts and minds of their children. It seemed they were only partially successful in their efforts. The two boys had been old enough to remember much of their lives with the tribe. Even while they adapted quickly to their new lives and all the changes, they clung to the memory of the ways they'd left behind. At school, they practiced their reading, writing, history and arithmetic in English. In the privacy of their home, they often fell back into the familiar Cheyenne tongue, or sometimes Spanish. They traded their breechcloths and moccasins for trousers and boots, but they continued to join their father in his morning prayer chant at sunrise. Each spring they counted the days until school would be out, then eagerly awaited their annual visit to the Cheyenne reservation where they would once again see all their childhood friends.

The girls, too, were trilingual, but with much grumbling and less enthusiasm. Though Summer recalled a great deal of her first seven years as the daughter of a Cheyenne chief, she much preferred the life she led now.

Dawn had been too young when they had left to recall much of it. Her memories were all to do with growing up on the ranch and frequent visits to town to shop and see her grandparents. Both girls reluctantly practiced the Cheyenne tongue, endured their yearly visits to the reservation, and did their level best to sneak out of Tanya's lectures on Cheyenne customs and traditions.

Summer particularly balked. She enjoyed being the daughter of a prominent rancher. Though she did not care overmuch for school, she adored living in a warm, comfortable house, being clean and well-fed. With each passing year, she pushed more of her Cheyenne teachings behind her. Not in her wildest dreams could she envision trading in all her lovely frilly dresses, perky bonnets, and lace gloves for garments of buckskin. Never again did she want to live in hunger and want. A bed with fresh linens was preferable any day to a hard mat on a dirt floor. Why would she care to sit cross-legged on the ground when she could eat at a finely set table from china plates and crystal goblets? No, give her a closet full of pretty gowns and plenty of ribbons and lace, and Summer was very content just as she was, thank you.

Of course, she did have other interests. The Savage ranch prospered primarily from cattle, but they did raise a few horses, and they were what interested Summer most. Not only did she love to ride, she had an unnatural interest in breeding and an uncanny talent for treating a sick or wounded horse. They seemed to respond to her as if she communicated with them on some deeper level which they instinctively trusted. This rapport extended to other animals, too. No one could fully explain it, but Summer definitely had a way with creatures.

Because of her fascination with animals, she had urged Jeremy to teach her all he could about veterinary medicine. Six years before, Jeremy had returned to Pueblo with a degree from the Iowa State College. He was Pueblo's first bona fide veterinarian, and Summer's idol. If she had lost her heart to him at age six, now she practically worshipped him. From the time she was eleven she trailed about behind him, watching him work, observing and learning. When she was with Jeremy, whether it was helping him heal a sick animal or delivering twin calves, Summer was at her happiest.

Summer truly adored Jeremy. In fact, she was more than a little in love with him. With his blond hair and marvelous green eyes, she was sure he was the most handsome man on earth. It pleased her that they shared this common interest in animals. There was a problem, however. Jeremy had known her since she was a child. Infinitely patient while explaining how to treat an injury or set a broken bone, he still viewed her as a child. She had grown up before his very eyes, and even as Summer did everything she could think of to please him and make him take notice of her as a woman, he seemed blind to the fact. Too many years had gone by in braids and pinafores, too many skinned elbows and dirty knees and toothless smiles. The man was impossibly dense—kind, sweet, thoughtful, incredibly handsome—but dense!

Of course, there were plenty of other fellows ready to notice what Jeremy would not. Most of them were nearer to her own age, but next to Jeremy they were terribly immature in Summer's eyes, which was only natural since Jeremy was thirty and long past boyhood. There were several that Summer liked, one or two who had even kissed her, but none that measured up to Jeremy.

This increasing attraction to Jeremy, and Summer's marked preference for what she termed a "civilized existence" did not please Sly Fox at all. As far as he was concerned, Summer was promised to him and they would one day marry. To his mind this was an inalterable fact. Summer would just have to put away her childish dreams when that time came. That she might not want to or be able to readjust to Cheyenne ways simply did not occur to Sly Fox. She would do so because she must.

In addition to the visits the Savage family made to the reservation each summer, Sly Fox had also come to Pueblo. He had appeared on their doorstep one fall morning two years after Panther's departure from the tribe. Panther-Adam had discovered him when he came out for his morning prayer.

"Sly Fox. What brings you here?"

"My father has sent me to you for the white man's learning. He says I must go to school." Sly Fox was not all that impressed with the idea himself, but he would not disobey his father.

Sly Fox had tried going to school for a while, but it was soon evident that this was not going to work out. Through Tanya's teachings he could already speak English well, but he could neither read nor write in the language. Nor did he have any concept of their number system. Because of this, he was placed with Dawn Sky's group of first grade beginners. Not only was he obviously not white, but because of the age difference he towered over his fellow classmates. He was an oddity and it was very uncomfortable for him. Still, he was determined to learn and please his father.

Adam and Tanya tried to help Sly Fox in this difficult situation. They bought him shirts and trousers and boots like those the other children wore to school. This helped some, but because Sly Fox did not wish to cut his long braids, he still stood out from the others. His only friends were the four Savage children.

Hunter and Mark took him under their wing as best they could, as did Summer Storm. They were the only ones to play with at recess and lunch. The others his age ridiculed him for his differences. Because he was behind them in their learning, they called him "stupid" or "dumb." Those were only some of the nicer names. They ridiculed him at every turn and teased him unmercifully. When the name-calling turned to fist fighting, Sly Fox finally retaliated. If it was blood they were after, he would spill some of theirs. Fair was only fair, except that he was vastly outnumbered, even with Mark and Hunter on his side. Still, he was the son of a Cheyenne chief, and he would bear no more humiliation at the hands of these hateful white children.

The day all three boys returned home battered and bruised was the last time Sly Fox ever set foot in the schoolroom. Even Summer returned with her dress torn and dirty and scratches on her face and arms, but she had fared the best. Hunter's right hand was swollen, the skin scraped and bleeding across his knuckles. His face was bruised and his nose had been bleeding but luckily was not broken. Mark was not so fortunate. The younger boy's left arm was hanging at an odd angle, indeed broken, and he sported a bruised cheek and torn breeches as well. Sly Fox had a blackening eye as the day's souvenir. It was a dandy shiner! In addition to varied other bruises and lumps, his lip was split so badly that he could barely talk or eat.

Tanya was appalled that the other schoolboys would gang up on Sly Fox in such a despicable manner, and she was proud that her children had rushed to his defense. Adam took one look and asked wryly, "What does the opposition look like?"

That question was answered Sunday afternoon when the Savages went to dinner at Tanya's parents' home. "You should have been there, Adam," Edward gloated. "I've never seen so many black eyes and broken noses in my life! Into the church they filed with their parents, limping and dragging along so bruised and battered that they looked as if they'd been through the war!"

Adam laughed appreciatively. "Then our boys didn't do so badly after all."

"Looks like they gave as good or better than they got," Edward agreed.

Be that as it may, Sly Fox refused to have anything more to do with school. He would not set himself up for ridicule so readily again; never again would he be the butt of someone's joke, someone to be laughed at or humiliated. For the rest of that school term and the next, he stayed with the Savages, but Tanya tutored him now. Summer Storm and her brothers helped Sly Fox with his lessons.

His mind was quick and his progress was remarkable. In no time at all, he was reading and writing fluently and had a good grasp on arithmetic. As long as he could study on his own, Sly Fox did not mind learning. In fact, he enjoyed learning and was proud of his accomplishments. At the end of the second term, however, he decided that anything else he learned would be at home with his own family. On their future visits to the reservation the Savage family always brought books for Sly Fox, which he gratefully accepted but said little about afterward.

Each year, Sly Fox looked forward to seeing Hunter and Mark again, but he waited especially to see

Summer Storm, hoping her attitude to reservation life would have softened over the months. Always he was disappointed. The older she got, the more beautiful she became, and he was proud to know that one day she would be his wife. If she had been stubborn and willful as a child, she was more so with each passing year. As a young child her prettiness and perky energy had overshadowed her stubbornness, making it less noticeable, but as she grew it became more and more obvious that Summer Storm would have her own way or wonder why. Though Sly Fox admired a certain amount of assertiveness in the woman of his choice, he realized early that he would have to find a way to temper this dubious attribute in Summer Storm. Otherwise she would be the very devil to live with. He could not have his wife thinking she could dominate their tepee.

On their visits, Sly Fox and Summer Storm always became reacquainted and had a wonderful time together as long as he refrained from mentioning marriage. Then she would cloud up and pout or suggest as gently as she could that perhaps they were now too different from one another to marry.

"Perhaps we should forget the idea altogether and just remain friends," she had said the last time they'd met. That was two years ago, when he had been seventeen summers and she fifteen.

"Do you find me repulsive to be near or to look upon?" he had asked, hurt by her continued rejection.

"Oh, no, Sly Fox!" she hastened to assure him. "You know that I do not. I care for you a great deal. I always have."

"Then why is it you cannot even remember to call me Windrider instead of Sly Fox when we meet? It has been two years since my vision quest—two years since I became a man and took the name Windrider. If you care for me as you claim, I would be in your thoughts often enough for you to at least recall my name,'' he rebuked.

Her face red with embarrassment, she said, ''I am truly sorry, Windrider. Forgive me. It is just that I knew you for so long as Sly Fox that I still think of you that way.''

''That is the problem, Summer Storm. You still think of me as a boy instead of a man, while I have been thinking of you as the woman you are becoming.'' His dark eyes boldly raked her blossoming figure, making her blush wildly.

''Please do not press me on this, Windrider. I am too young to think of marriage yet.''

''Many Cheyenne women marry at your age or younger,'' he reminded her.

''I am not Cheyenne!'' she blurted in confusion, shaking her head in agitation. ''I am not Cheyenne. I am not white or Mexican. I am nothing!'' With an exclamation of distress and tears glittering in her golden eyes, she ran from him.

For the remainder of that visit, she had been subdued, and he had respected the distance she had placed between them. She had not come last summer with her family, and soon it would be two long years since Windrider had set eyes on his promised bride.

''Grandmother Rachel, may I stay with you and Tom again this summer while the rest of the family visit the reservation?'' Summer asked. A few years before, her grandmother had surprised everyone by accepting Sheriff Middleton's marriage proposal. Rachel had promptly turned the ranch over to Adam's care and moved into Pueblo. She and Tom had bought

you are starting to show more interest in Jeremy than the animals he tends."

"Oh!" Summer was at a loss for words, not knowing how to comment on her grandmother's observations.

Rachel's smile was sympathetic. "It's quite all right, Summer. It is not at all unusual or wicked for a young girl to be infatuated with a handsome man—and he is quite undeniably good-looking."

"I'm not infatuated with him, Grandmother," Summer hesitantly admitted. "I'm in love with him. I have loved Jeremy for more than two years now, and I think I always shall. If only it were he instead of Windrider who was asking me to marry."

After a moment, when Rachel had failed to comment, Summer asked, "Do you think he is too old for me?"

"Hardly," Rachel answered with a light laugh. "How old is he—thirty?" At Summer's nod, she said, "And you are seventeen. That is thirteen years difference. Not so awfully many years, really. Why do you ask? Does the age difference matter to you?"

"Oh, no! Not at all! I just thought that some people might think so."

"You can't go around all your life worrying about what other people think of you," Rachel advised.

"Then why did you pretend that my father was not Cheyenne and pass him off as Spanish and English when you first came to Pueblo?"

Rachel blanched at Summer's direct question, but she answered truthfully. "Because I was young and ashamed and easily influenced by my father's wishes. He knew that if Adam's Cheyenne blood were known, both my baby and I would be scorned. He did not want to see that happen, for none of what had been done to me had been my fault or Adam's. My father was wise enough to realize that most people would not view it that way. By concealing Adam's Indian blood, we were spared much embarrassment and ridicule. It was, perhaps, cowardly of me, but I was not strong enough to stand alone against a town full of strangers who might despise me or my child.

"Your mother was the strong one, Summer. She thumbed her nose at the entire town and dared them to comment on her two Cheyenne sons. She openly declared her love for the Cheyenne chief who had married her and given her two sons."

"But, I don't understand, Grandmother," Summer interrupted with a frown. "Since Father was both Panther and Adam Savage, why do they tell everyone that Dawn Sky and I are darker-skinned because of our Spanish heritage? Why hide the fact that we, too, are Cheyenne, as Mark and Hunter are? It makes no sense to me. Not that I mind at all, but it is so confusing sometimes."

"I know, honey. Let me try to explain it to you. It is because of my original deception. Very few of the townspeople here in Pueblo know of your father's dual identity. They know him only as Adam Savage."

"But Father was publicly accused of being A-Panther-Stalks. Mother has told me how Lieutenant Young had him arrested."

"No," Rachel corrected. "Tom arrested Adam in order to save him from Jeffrey Young's military courts. Then your mother devised his escape. To answer your question, no one believed Young's rash accusations. The man was crazy in love with your mother and would have done anything to have her back again. No one believed his outlandish tale about Adam being Panther. How could this young man they had known all his life as Adam Savage be a famed and feared Cheyenne chief? It was too preposterous!''

"So no one knew except Tom and you and my mother's family?'' Summer concluded.

"And Melissa, who had been captured with your mother and lived with the Cheyenne. Also, Justin Kerr was told, and Judge and Mrs. Kerr. It was Judge Kerr who married your mother and father and drew up adoption papers for Hunter and Mark so that Adam could legally claim them as his sons.''

"Which they already were,'' Summer added.

"Yes, but hardly anyone knew that then or now. You and your sister were born after Adam and Tanya were married here in Pueblo. When they went off again, no one guessed they went back to the Cheyenne camp. Unless we were to now admit that Adam is indeed a Cheyenne chief, you and Dawn cannot be Cheyenne in the eyes of the town. You are his and your mother's daughters only; Spanish–Mexican, English, and a little Dutch, but Cheyenne to no one but your family.''

"Why haven't Father and Mother admitted that he is Cheyenne; that he is Panther? Neither one of them is ashamed of it, I know.''

Rachel smiled a little sadly. "It is mostly for my benefit that they are silent, Summer. They will not expose my lies after all these years and shame me before the town and all my friends.''

"But your friends would understand,'' Summer insisted, "and Tom already knows.''

"There are other reasons, dear. The Indian wars are still too fresh in mind, and many people here have lost friends or relatives to Indian raids in past years.

Feelings still run high against the tribes. More for you children's sakes and mine than their own, they keep silent. Also, Indians cannot now inherit or own land off the reservations, so I have asked Adam to keep his silence on the matter of his Cheyenne ancestry, or the ranch my father and I built cannot be handed down to my own son or his children. It would break my heart to see that happen.''

"You may rest assured that I shall never tell anyone,'' Summer was quick to reassure her grandmother. "It would suit me nicely if no one were ever to know that I am Cheyenne.''

Rachel frowned. "Are you ashamed of your Indian blood, Summer?'' she asked softly.

"No—yes—oh, Grandmother, I don't really know! I am so confused sometimes! When I was small and we lived with the Cheyenne, it was easy to be proud of my Indian heritage. Then we came here and I was warned to say nothing of our previous life in the camp. Later, I saw how hatefully the other children treated Sly Fox, merely because he was not white like themselves. I was angry and confused, but I was also grateful that no one knew that I too was Cheyenne. Even while I berated myself for my cowardice, I was thankful no one knew and fearful they would guess. I knew my friends would turn away from me, and I didn't want that to happen. I was both ashamed of my reactions and ashamed of my Indian bloodlines at the same time. Truthfully, I still am even now. Once, long ago, my father told me always to be proud of my Cheyenne heritage. Now I am too embarrassed to even admit to it. What am I to do? How am I to think? Which way do I choose? What traditions do I cherish?

SUMMER STORM

Grandmother, on the very brink of my womanhood, I do not know myself! My heart aches, and I am torn with wondering *Who am I?* Will I ever really and truly know? Will I ever resolve this conflict within myself?''

6

"Jeremy, have you ever thought of raising thorough-breds? Breeding them, I mean?"

"Mmn." That was the sum total of his answer to Summer's all important question. Not that he meant to ignore her, he just had his hands full at the moment—full of one warm, squirming, about-to-be-born foal. The birth had been a long and difficult breech birth, and the mare's work was nearly done, thanks to Jeremy's expert manipulations. One last mighty heave and the foal was finally free, warm and wet and all legs.

"Gosh, he's a beauty!" No matter how many times Summer witnessed the miracle of birth, she was always awed by it.

"Another colt for your father's fine stable. You're right. After he grows into those legs and ears, he'll be a real beauty, all right."

"I want to raise horses, Jeremy." Summer went back to her original train of thought.

"You've got a good start already," he answered

absently, watching as the mare turned to cleaning her newborn.

"No, I mean on my own ranch. Father raises mostly cattle. I want to breed horses, the most beautiful horses Colorado has ever seen."

"No reason why you can't, I suppose."

"Jeremy, you're only half listening to me," she complained. "Pay attention. This is important."

Jeremy threw her an indulgently amused look, his leaf-green eyes laughing at her. "I'm listening, princess. You want to raise horses."

"Don't you think it's a grand idea, Jeremy? Haven't you ever considered it for yourself? With your knowledge of breeding, you could have the finest breeding farm ever!"

He shrugged and a lock of golden hair drooped low over his damp forehead. Summer's fingers itched to touch it, to brush it back into place. "If you are talking about thoroughbreds, I don't think you could make a go of it as a business. Not in these parts. Here the ranchers need good cow ponies, quarter horses born and bred for ranch work."

"But thoroughbreds are so much more beautiful," she argued.

"They are also flighty and high-strung," he pointed out. "Quarter horses have more staying power for this terrain and for working cattle. They are patient and hardworking, they train well for riding and roping . . ."

"They're dull!" Summer concluded snappishly.

"They're reliable, and their legs are better suited than the long spindly legs of a thoroughbred," Jeremy corrected.

Summer answered with an exasperated huff. "What have you got against long legs?"

"Not a thing, except that I want the mount I'm

riding to have four good legs beneath him so I don't end up walking home through miles of mountains, or getting thrown into a milling herd of cattle because my horse snaps a foreleg.''

The foal had found his feet at last, his wobbly legs precariously balanced beneath him as he searched his mother's belly for his first meal. Jeremy and Summer let themselves out of the stall and stood watching from behind the closed gate. Outside, it was raining, the steady downpour making a rhythmic din against the stable roof. The warm smell of horseflesh mingled with the sweet scent of fresh straw bedding to create a cozy atmosphere inside the stable.

''Why do you always find fault with my ideas?'' Summer pouted.

''That's unfair, princess. I don't always find fault; only when you don't stop to think an idea out first. Then I correct you, but I don't 'find fault'. Not the way you mean, at any rate.''

Summer conceded the point. ''All right, you correct my erroneous thinking. Thank you *so—o* much, Dr. Field.'' She wrinkled her nose at him and he laughed.

''You are quite welcome, princess.''

''It's raining harder,'' Summer said, looking toward the door. ''Shall we make a run for the house or wait it out here?''

''I want to keep an eye on the mare for a while yet. You can go up to the house if you want.''

''And drown by myself? No, thanks. I'll wait with you.''

''Afraid you'll melt?'' he teased. ''What are you, a cinnamon-sugar princess?''

''Are you making fun of my heritage, Doctor?'' she countered with fake hauteur.

''Would I do such an ungentlemanly thing?'' His

eyes were laughing at her again, making her heart do strange things in her chest.

"I do believe you would." She could barely get the words past her constricting throat. "After all, everyone knows that women are naturally nicer than men. It is a scientific fact. You can't help being nasty, I suppose."

"And just how do you deduce such a fact? I demand proof if you are going to defame my character to such a degree." He was stalking her now, and she was slowly but steadily backing away, a wonderfully wicked grin on her face. Summer delighted in baiting him every bit as much as he enjoyed teasing her. It was a game they had played and perfected over the years. She had grown up trying to match his quick wit with hers, striving to outwit him with her sharp young mind and agile tongue. More often than not, she lost their verbal battles, but it delighted her immensely when she managed to win a round here and there.

Now her topaz eyes sparkled with deviltry as she playfully taunted him. "Why, learned doctor, don't tell me your education has been so sadly lacking that you have never acquired such basic and elementary knowledge. Everyone knows that girls are made of sugar and spice and all things nice." Her husky laughter bounced off the stable walls as she broke into a giggle. As his hands reached out for her ticklish ribcage, she shrieked and tried to back away, only to find herself cornered against a nearby stable. "And boys . . ."

"Yes?" Jeremy looked down at her, a daring smile on his face as his fingers edged even nearer.

"Boys are made of sticks and stones and puppy dog bones, so they are nasty little creatures!" she finished in a rush. Summer tried to duck beneath his arm and dash for safety, but Jeremy was too quick for her. Catching her arm, he caught her off balance. As Summer fell, she took him with her down onto a mound of fresh, soft hay.

"You outrageous little imp!" Laughing, Jeremy started to lever himself up off of her, but instead of clasping her arm, he misjudged his position. Instead, his hand encountered the firm, round contours of her full breast. His unintended touch surprised them both, and the breath seemed to freeze in both their lungs. The smile melted slowly from his face as his startled eyes flew to meet hers. For a long moment, neither moved as they stared at one another.

Summer's tongue snaked out to moisten lips gone suddenly dry. Deep green eyes followed the movement and lingered on her full, inviting mouth. A groan sounded from deep within Jeremy's chest as he fought a losing battle with himself. His awakened senses overrode his better judgment, and he found his mouth lowering to meet her shining lips. "Oh, princess! How you do tempt a man!"

Any answer she might have given was cut off by his warm lips against hers. Truthfully, her mind was spinning so by now that thought and speech were impossible anyway. Her heart was thundering against her ribs, and she was sure he could feel it pounding against her breast still cupped gently in his hand.

His lips were warm and firm against hers, moving and tasting and sending magic tingles of sensation through her. Then his slick tongue was tracing the sensitive outline of her lips, nudging them apart to seek entry into her pliant mouth. His tongue slid across hers, learning the shape and taste of her mouth and leaving Summer weak with a melting desire more wonderful than anything she'd ever imagined.

A new, sharper shaft of longing seared through her as his fingers sought her aroused nipple through the thin material of her blouse. With a strangled moan, she moved closer to his touch, her arms coming up to entwine about his neck, her slim fingers delving into the golden hair at his nape and holding his mouth firmly to her own.

By the time his lips left hers to wander across her cheek, Summer's breath was coming in short, painful gasps. Jeremy was in similar straits, as his labored breathing near her ear proved. Novice though she was, Summer had been around nature and the animal world long enough to realize what was happening when she felt his swollen manhood hard against her thigh. It thrilled her to know that she could elicit such a response from him. Surely Jeremy could no longer regard her as a child after this. With a shaky, happy sigh, she twisted her head about to seek his lips again.

His kisses became more demanding as she freely gave herself up to his guidance. How much further things might have gone, Summer was never to know, for the mare chose this point to demand their attention with a loud neigh.

Abruptly, Jeremy broke off the kiss and stared at her flushed face. The look of wonderment faded from his face, to be replaced by a dark look of self-censure. "Damn! I'm sorry, Summer. At my age I should have better control over my senses."

Summer stared up at him in hurt confusion. "You're sorry?" she echoed weakly. "Why?"

"I should know better than to behave this way," he said, pushing away from her to sit upright. He brushed the hay from his clothes refusing to meet her look. "I really don't have any excuse for what I did."

Summer rose, straightening her blouse. The tips of her still-aroused breasts stood out boldly beneath the fabric. "And what did you do that was so awful, Jeremy?" she asked in rising agitation. "You kissed me! And I enjoyed it! So, I think, did you! What is so terrible in that?''

He glared up at her, his anger directed more at himself than her. ''My God, Summer! I'm twice your age! A man of my years has no excuse for taking advantage of an innocent girl like you! Your father would be well within his rights to pound me senseless.''

Summer was angry now too, tears glistening in her huge eyes. ''Look at me, Jeremy. I am seventeen, a woman fully grown.''

''So I have recently noticed,'' he admitted wryly. ''Still, that doesn't change the fact that I nearly tumbled you in the hay a few moments ago. You trusted me, and I nearly destroyed that trust in a moment of pure stupidity on my part. I accept the blame entirely. You are young and innocent and in no way responsible for my incredible lapse of control. All I can say is that it won't happen again. You have my solemn word on it.''

''How magnanimous of you, dear Dr. Field,'' she retorted sharply. ''Don't I have anything to say about this? Doesn't it occur to you that I might have enjoyed your kisses? That I might want more than kisses from you?''

''Experiment with someone else, Summer,'' Jeremy stated flatly, rising to look down at her sternly. ''I'm too old to be satisfied with a few kisses and a bit of heavy breathing. You may have talked me into teaching you some veterinary medicine, but I'll be damned if I teach you anything else. This is where I draw the line, princess. I'm a man, not a eunuch.''

''And I am a woman, not some untouchable princess!'' she countered, nearly screaming at him. ''I hate it when you call me that! It makes me seem so cold and unapproachable, but I'm not! I'm as warm and feeling as anyone else. I've loved you for a long time now, Jeremy, but you have refused to see that I am no longer a child.''

"Oh, I've noticed. Believe me, I have noticed," he sneered, thoroughly annoyed at both of them. "God knows I've also tried my damndest not to."

"Why not?" she demanded. "What's wrong with it, Jeremy? What's wrong with me?"

Jeremy shouted back. "There's not a blasted thing wrong with you, except for the fact that you are entirely too young to be interested in a man nearly old enough to be your father!"

"That's stretching the truth a bit, don't you think, since you are only thirteen years older than me? I love you, Jeremy! Doesn't that matter at all to you?"

Jeremy closed his eyes and sighed heavily. "Summer, you are infatuated with me. That is all. It happens to girls your age all the time. I'm trying to understand that and deal with it, but you aren't making it any easier for me at this point. If I didn't respect you and care for you as much as I do, I could easily take advantage of your feelings. Any other man might have by now."

"Oh, but not the fine and noble Dr. Field," she cried out on a broken sob. "Oh, no! Perish the thought!" She took a deep breath to steady her trembling voice. "If you truly cared for me, you would believe me when I say I love you."

In a calmer, kinder tone, he said, "I believe you *think* you love me, Summer. Can't you let that be enough and give yourself time to discover that what I have told you is the truth?"

"No! It is not nearly enough! Not when I want you to love me in return!"

"I'm truly sorry, princess, but you ask too much of me. What nearly happened here today was a mistake. I regret it more than I can tell you. Nothing can come of it.''

"But, Jeremy . . ."

"No!" His tone was implacable. "In view of what has happened and the things that have been said, I think it is best if we stay apart for a time. You will not accompany me on any more of my veterinary calls for a while. Until you come to your senses and realize that there can be no romantic relationship between us, I will not risk another episode such as this. The embarrassment from today alone will put a strain on our friendship. We will both need time to recover from it.'' He turned from the hurt on her face, unable to bear the sight of her tears. Instead, he focused his attention on the mare and her foal.

Her light touch on his arm made him flinch. "Jeremy," she said softly, hesitantly, her voice trembling. "Will you not reconsider?"

Without looking at her, lest she see his own pain, he shook his head. "No."

After she had left the stable, Jeremy rode home in the rain, lost in his thoughts of her. He had long been in love with Summer, though he knew he was too old for her. He had watched her grow from child to nearwoman and lost his heart to her more each day. He knew that his was a hopeless love, and he had valiantly reconciled himself to the fact. To have to deal with this infatuation of hers was a cruel trick of fate.

Jeremy could have kicked himself for nearly losing control with her the way he had done, but it had been such a shock to feel her soft feminine curves suddenly beneath him that he had lost his head temporarily. The temptation of her moist lips had been more than he could resist. It was like a stolen moment out of one of his relentless dreams of her. The reality of her kiss had been even better than his dreams, and for a few brief moments he had let his heart and his senses overrule his better judgment. In one way he was glad, for he would cherish the memory of that brief embrace forever. In another way, he regretted it deeply, for having tasted of her sweetness, he would forever hunger for more of her forbidden fruit.

Summer was devastated by Jeremy's blunt rejection of her. She had innocently and honestly declared her love for him and he had refused to listen or believe. Oh, she felt like such a fool! While she had not consciously provoked the scene in the stable, she had been glad it had happened, that Jeremy at long last had seen her as a woman. His kisses and caresses had thrilled her, and she was not sorry he had touched her.

Still, that was the only positive result of the entire episode. Now he refused to see her at all. How was she to convince him that her love was true if he would not see her? How would he ever return her love if he were not around, if she could not be with him? It wasn't fair! It just wasn't fair! Her only hope was that Jeremy would reconsider once a few days had passed and he'd had time to reflect on what had occurred.

Several days later, Summer was coming to the realization that time was not helping matters. Jeremy had kept his distance, and the one time she had tried to approach him, he had immediately and uncaringly sent her away. Something had to be done. This separation was not aiding her campaign to win his love.

Meanwhile, several of Pueblo's unattached boys had continued to call on her. Only a few were dissuaded by her lack of interest. The others persisted. One fellow in particular was especially insistent. Roger Watkins, the son of a well-to-do nearby rancher, would not be persuaded to give up his courting. Day after day he came to the ranch, plying her with flowers and candy and sweet praise. His constant pleas for her company were a balm to her bruised ego, and soon Summer found it easier to accept his offers than to suffer his wounded looks if she refused. They went riding, or took pleasant walks together.

Though Summer did not want to encourage him, she hated to reject him continually. Twice she invited him to Sunday dinner.

The more Summer saw of Roger, the more she became aware of his faults. He held a very high opinion of himself, which Summer found irritating at times. Roger, it seemed, was a snob. His father's prominence in the community made Roger feel vastly superior to most of his friends and neighbors, and he never failed to point out his better qualities to Summer.

He was also extremely opinionated, which only accentuated his lack of knowledge to others, but Roger, in his exalted ignorance, failed to realize this. He looked down his nose at persons less fortunate than himself. "They could make something of themselves if they wanted," he would say.

He also gossiped incorrigibly about friends and foes alike, and Summer could only guess what he said about her beyond her hearing. "Old Addie McFarland tripped over her cat and broke her hip last night," he informed her. "If she wasn't such a persnickety old bat, she'd have found a husband years ago and wouldn't have needed the silly cat for company." "Dennis Long's wife had her baby Sunday. Nearly didn't make it home, so I hear. This is their fifth in seven years. No wonder they can't get ahead. All they ever do is make more mouths to feed." "I ran into Fred Hill at the feed store yesterday. Amos refused him any more credit. Can't say I blame him, though. Fred owes everyone in town. He hasn't got the business sense his father had. Of course, he's not alone. The bank is about to foreclose on Frank LaRue's farm. He's so far behind on his mortgage that he could live to be a hundred and never catch up. Anyone could have told him it was stupid to try and plant all that acreage in wheat last year.''

What Roger or his family bought was always the best, according to Roger's estimation. What he didn't know wasn't worth knowing. What he hadn't seen or done was below his consideration. Other people's opinions were inferior, if Roger hadn't thought of it first. For a mere boy of nineteen, he was cruelly critical of others, and fully expected everyone to praise his ideas and agree with him. When they didn't, he became angry and sulked for hours.

Summer soon became so sick of Roger she could barely tolerate him. However, he was the most handsome of her suitors, and suited her new plan very well. Since it was obvious that Jeremy was intent on ignoring her, Summer was now resorting to more devious means. She set out to make Jeremy jealous, if that were possible. Failing that, she hoped he would believe that she was over her so-called infatuation with him and allow her near him once more. Only then could she hope to gradually lead him around to her way of thinking.

Hence, Summer continued to see Roger, much to her family's dismay. As time went on, they disliked the rude, spoiled young man more and more. They put up with him only because Summer seemed so taken with him, though they failed to see why. When any of them dared to question her choice, Summer would politely, and sometimes not so politely, tell them to mind their own business and leave her to tend hers. She and

Hunter got into several heated rows over Roger and what Hunter considered his sister's faulty judgment of character.

Tanya had also tried to talk with Summer about the matter. "Just how serious are you about this young man, Summer?" she had asked, trying to hide her growing dismay.

"Why do you ask? I've only been seeing him for a short time," Summer hedged.

"Has he asked you to marry him, or haven't things progressed that far yet?"

"Would you object?"

Tanya debated how to answer. "I'm not sure he's right for you, dear. Roger is so—so opinionated and critical sometimes."

Summer laughed. "Be honest, Mother. I'd have to be blind and deaf not to know that Roger is narrow-minded and rude much of the time." Tanya's sigh of relief was nearly audible. At least Summer was aware of the boy's faults.

"He does adore me, though," Summer pointed out. "He certainly is handsome and well-bred, and he's not at all stingy with his gifts. He'll provide very well for his wife, I'm sure."

Going back to a previous question, Tanya asked again. "Has he proposed, Summer?"

"Just this evening, as a matter of fact," Summer said with a satisfied nod.

"Oh, dear! You didn't accept him outright did you? Your father would have a fit!"

"Don't worry, Mother. I merely told him I would consider his offer." Summer hid a private shudder of revulsion at the very thought of living as Roger's wife.

"I doubt your father will ever approve such an idea," Tanya warned, detesting the thought herself.

Knowing her father, Summer was positive he

wouldn't. Adam was still holding out hope that Summer would eventually marry Windrider, as he had planned years before. She said as much to her mother. "I'm surprised that Father has not resorted to singing Windrider's praises, since his hopes still lie in that direction."

"Windrider is a fine young man," Tanya said, her eyes glittering defensively. "There is nothing at all wrong with him."

"Nothing at all," Summer agreed, "except that if I married him I would have to live in a dingy tepee on that horrid reservation."

"I still say you would do well to marry him. He is a good and honest man. Material possessions do not always insure happiness, daughter. Windrider loves you. He would treat you well and provide for you as best he could. He will give you strong, lovely children and be a faithful loving husband."

"But I don't love Windrider in that way, Mother."

"Perhaps you would grow to love him, Summer."

"And perhaps not. Would you see me tied to a man I do not want?"

"Rather that than bound to the one you seem to want now," Tanya stated flatly.

Matters came to a head a few days later. Jeremy still had not shown any interest in Summer's supposedly growing attraction for Roger, and Summer was forced to continue seeing him. She had again invited him for Sunday dinner with the family. This day, both sets of grandparents were coming out, which meant they too would be forced to endure Roger's obnoxious behavior. It was when Roger's comments took on a distinctly prejudiced flavor that things began to heat up.

"I admire the way this house is built," Roger said,

tendering a rare compliment. If he had stopped there, everything would have been fine, but he had not. "It has definite Spanish lines, but I still like it. There's not much those lazy Mexicans do well, but their architecture is lovely."

Summer's eyes widened in despair as she looked quickly about the table, assessing her family's reactions. A deadly silence had immediately followed Roger's insulting comments. "Oh, Lord!" she thought. "Here it comes!"

Rachel was the first to speak, which was appropriate since it was her family that was of Spanish-Mexican descent. "My father and I built this house," she said coolly, directing a penetrating dark look at Roger.

Dense as he was at times, Roger still had not realized his error. "Then you must admire their architecture, too," he concluded, smug in his own opinion of himself.

"I ought to," Rachel told him with royal hauteur. "My entire family comes from Mexico originally, and before that from Spain." Her smoldering eyes pinned him to his chair.

Roger at least had the grace to blush guiltily as his thoughtless words came back to him. "I—uh—I beg your pardon, ma'am. Now that you mention it, I do recall hearing that somewhere."

Treading on thin ice, Roger immediately tried to get back on firmer ground, only to make matters even worse. "I meant no offense. There are a lot of fine Mexican folks just like yourself, I'm sure. Unlike those savage redskins. If there's anything my father hates, it's a damned Injun!" Unmindful of his second consecutive offense, Roger continued blithely voicing his shallow opinions. "I have to agree with Dad. Why, when I was still in school a few years back, we had this

Indian boy attending school. He had these long, greasy braids and a real sneaky look to his beady black eyes, and he was so dumb it was laughable. We finally got rid of the little weasel. A group of us boys beat him up real good, and he never came back to school after that.'' A proud, conceited smile etched Roger's mouth as he awaited their praise.

An unbroken circle of hostile glares bored into him, Summer's included. As the tense silence continued, even Roger could not remain unaware of the intense hatred directed his way.

Hunter at last broke the silence. ''Windrider is my Cheyenne brother, you insolent bastard,'' he sneered. ''I helped to defend him that day against a group of bully cowards that outnumbered him ten to one. We beat you fairly, if you recall correctly. We did not run from your puny fists.''

Mark took up the defense. ''I also fought you that day. You did not defeat Windrider or cause him to run from you. We were the victors. Even Summer cannot deny this. She was there fighting alongside the three of us, even though she was just a young girl.''

Roger looked to Summer, only to meet her scornful golden gaze. ''My brothers are right, Roger. I was there defending Windrider. I would do so again if I had to.''

''Well spoken, daughter,'' Tanya said. ''It does my heart good to hear you guard your fiancé's honor.''

Roger finally found his tongue. ''Fiancé!'' he squealed. ''What do they mean, Summer? What kind of joke is this? I asked you to marry me, and you never said a word about this!''

From the head of the table, Adam spoke up, his deep voice ringing with unchallenged authority. ''My daughter is not required to tell you of her intentions toward another man, but since you doubt my wife's words, let me reinforce them. Summer is indeed promised in marriage to Windrider. She has been for many years.''

''Summer, is this true? Are you really going to marry that filthy Indian?'' Roger was aghast, and beyond even thinking about tempering his words.

It was Summer's anger that forced her into the answer her father had long awaited. At the time, she was too furious to guard her tongue or mind the wording of her reply. She simply blurted out the first thing to come to mind, wanting only to set Roger back on his heels. She did not realize the trap she was stepping into until it sprang closed upon her.

''Windrider is not a filthy Indian!'' she declared heatedly, her face flushed with defiance, her head held proudly upright as she glared golden daggers at Roger. ''He is a brave and noble man, the son of a Cheyenne chief. He is strong and handsome and a hundred times the man you are or can ever hope to become. Yes, he is my promised husband, the man I am pledged to marry, and I would be proud to be his wife. I would gladly bear his name and children, even as I would never consent to marry a conceited ass such as you!''

The moment the words were out of her mouth, Summer knew she had made an irrevocable mistake. She sat in shocked silence over her own stupidity. Even while she wished she could recall her hasty remarks, she knew she could not. She had just committed herself publicly to wed Windrider, and her honor would hold her to that unwisely spoken vow. A Cheyenne's word was a solemn pledge, never to be broken or taken lightly. Summer had lived under the influence of this strict rule all her life. Though she had rejected many of the Cheyenne teachings in her white life on the ranch, this was one of the ironclad rules she adhered to, one that Adam and Tanya adamantly insisted upon.

Summer recalled many times when she had unthinkingly promised one thing or another, later to regret her rash words. Always, her mother and father had made her uphold her promises. Once, when she had been fourteen, she had invited a girlfriend to stay the weekend at the ranch, only to find herself invited to a party in town which she desperately wanted to attend. Summer wanted to arrange to have her friend stay another weekend, so that she would be free to go to the party. Tanya had quickly dismissed that plan.

"You promised Lenore she could come this weekend, and you will stand by your word, Summer. A Cheyenne does not break her pledge."

"But, Mother," she had argued. "Everyone will be at Betsy's party, and I did not know about it when I invited Lenore to stay with me."

"Is Lenore invited to Betsy's party?" Tanya had asked.

"No," Summer admitted sheepishly.

"Then it would be wrong to change your plans and hurt Lenore by going to Betsy's party. If Lenore were included, you could go together and spend the rest of the weekend here, but since that is not the case, you will spend the weekend here with Lenore and forget going to the party. You know the rules, daughter."

"Cheyenne rules!" Summer had stormed. "I am not Cheyenne any longer!"

Tanya's golden gaze had flashed a warning. "You *are* Cheyenne, now and for all your life, like it or not, and you are also a member of this family. A Savage does not tarnish his or her honor with broken promises. The matter is settled. No more will be said about it. You will have Lenore here next weekend, as arranged, and you will behave in a polite and proper manner, or pay dearly if you do not.''

Another time, when Summer was just ten, she had begged her father to allow her to have a puppy all her own. A neighbor's dog had just whelped a litter, and Summer was enthralled with the tiny, furry creatures.

"If I let you have a pup, you must promise to assume all responsibility for it,'' Adam had said. ''You must feed it and care for it yourself. I will not hear of your neglecting the dog or pushing its care off on someone else, or I will take the animal from you and give it away.''

Summer had eagerly agreed to the terms. For a while, she had done well, but after a few weeks the novelty of her new pet had worn thin, and her interest in the pup began to wane as her attention turned to other things. It became a chore to look after the dog. All too soon, several days passed with Summer barely giving the pup a thought. Its food dish would stand empty until someone else thought to throw it a bone or some scraps. Its fur became tangled and matted with burs.

One day Summer came home from school and noticed that the pup was not there to greet her. Nor was he in his favorite spot beneath the porch, or anywhere to be found. Guilt rose up in her as she spied his empty food bowl. With a sinking feeling in the pit of her stomach, Summer confronted her father.

Adam's stern look had held disapproval and disappointment as he gazed down at her. ''The dog has been gone for two days, daughter, and you are just now asking about him? I warned you what would happen if you neglected him. You promised to care for him, yet you did not. Therefore, I gave him back to his previous owner. He will no longer suffer from your lack of attention.''

Tears had filled her golden eyes. With trembling

chin, she had begged, "Can I have him back, Father? Please? I will take proper care of him this time."

"No, Summer. You must learn to honor your pledges from the first moment you speak them. You must not give a vow lightly, only to disregard it as it suits you. I must know that when my daughter offers a promise she speaks truly, and will uphold her pledge. You must learn that, in this house, your word is binding, and I shall hold you to it. Think carefully before voicing your pledges, for they are your solemn word of honor; and once spoken, they cannot be recalled."

Her father's solemn admonishment came back to her now, haunting and mocking her hastily spoken words. Summer had just pledged herself to Windrider. Stunned as she was, Summer did not hear Roger's exclamations of disbelief. Nor did she see her brothers gleefully escort the offensive guest out of the house and on his way. Her mother's tearfully gratified look did not register with her. The only thing that held her attention was the victorious look on her father's face and the satisfied gleam in his deep dark eyes.

"We will leave for the reservation in a week. I will send word ahead to Winter Bear and Windrider so that they may begin preparations for our arrival."

The feeling of doom deepened around her with every word her father spoke. Each felt like a nail driven into the coffin that would seal her into a life of misery. Yet by her own mouth she had condemned herself. She could blame no one else.

What hurt most was the realization that she had ruined any possibility of a life with Jeremy. Already her heart cried out for her lost love, a love that had never stood a chance from the start. Now she would never be able to convince Jeremy of her love for him, or to win his heart for her own. By her own hand she had strangled that delicately budding love, and now it would never grow to see full blossom, never spread its petals to the sun, nor reveal its wondrous beauty to the world.

Jeremy was stunned to the depth of his being on hearing of Summer's impending marriage to Windrider. Of course he had known of the agreement between Adam and Winter Bear for several years, but he had also known of Summer's intense dislike of the reservation. He had never expected Summer to relent to Adam's wishes once she had come to prefer life in Pueblo. Also, he was sure that Adam and Tanya would never force Summer into accepting Windrider, no matter how badly they wanted her to do so.

Something drastic must have happened to make Summer change her mind so suddenly, and Jeremy badly wanted to know what it was. He had been fighting a battle with himself since that day in the stable. Though he tried to tell himself that not seeing Summer was best for both of them, he was as miserable as he'd ever been in his life. How badly he wanted to believe that she truly loved him, as he did her, but how could he be sure that it wasn't merely a schoolgirl's infatuation that she would soon outgrow? If he leaped in too quickly, they would both pay for his impetuosity later.

Now it seemed he had waited too long. When Summer had begun seeing Roger Watkins so regularly, Jeremy had been eaten alive with jealousy. Still, he had forced himself to hold back and be patient. If Summer truly cared, she would soon send Watkins on his way. Perhaps this was merely her way of repaying him for rejecting her and hurting her pride.

The more she saw of Watkins, however, the more it frightened Jeremy. He began to wish he had taken

Summer more seriously, and had begun to reconsider his ideas. Maybe Summer really did love him as she claimed. Was it possible for the two of them to build a life together? He began to consider that possibility and had nearly come to the conclusion that it was worth taking a chance.

Then, out of the blue, he learned that she was to marry Windrider after all! Why? Had Watkins done something that had triggered Summer's sudden about-face? Or was he, Jeremy, primarily responsible because he had rejected her so cruelly and seemingly thoroughly? Heartbroken and riddled with guilt, Jeremy knew he must see Summer before she left. He must talk with her and find out why she had made such a hasty and irrevocable decision.

"Hello, Jeremy." Summer forced herself to smile as she walked into the parlor. "Have you come to wish me well?"

They were alone in the room, so Jeremy could talk freely. "I have come to ask you why you have suddenly decided to marry Windrider after being so opposed to the idea these past years."

"I have been promised to him since I was three," she said, schooling her face into serene lines.

"That is not an answer, Summer. Why are you doing this now? Just a few short weeks ago you claimed to love me. Are you truly as fickle as you seem, or was I right all along in thinking you were too young to know your own heart?"

At his cruel words, her composure cracked. Along with sudden tears came a burst of anger and frustration. "Damn you, Jeremy! I did love you—I do! How can you be so unfeeling to come here now and throw my words in my face? Don't you think I regret the foolish, impulsive promise that led me into this situation? I was angry when I said I would marry Windrider, but once I had agreed I could not retract my words! Now I must marry him whether I want it or not!'' Hot tears raced down her cheeks faster than her shaking hands could brush them away.

Her tears tore at his heart. Moving to her side, Jeremy drew her tenderly into his arms, cradling her face against his chest. ''Oh, princess! What a mess I have made of everything! Tell me, was it me you were angry with when you agreed to marry Windrider?''

She shook her head. ''No. Roger had been degrading all Indians, and Windrider in particular. I'm afraid I became overzealous in my defense of Windrider, and before I knew what was happening, I had announced that I was marrying him. Naturally, I did so before my entire family, and now I am trapped by my own rash actions. There is no way I can change my mind now that I have committed myself. Father has already sent word to Windrider. I must follow through on my promise.''

Regret washed through him. Oh, to come so close, and still to lose her! ''I'm sorry, princess. I'm so sorry.''

Mistaking his heartbreak for pity, she drew back from him. ''What have you to be sorry for, Jeremy? You certainly did not want me. You made that perfectly clear the last time we parted.''

Her sharp words cut into him like a knifeblade. ''That is not entirely true, Summer, but it is too late to help either of us now. We must each go our way and learn to live with our choices.''

''Jeremy, are you saying that you *do* love me after all?'' she asked, her golden eyes searching his face for the answer she sought.

A look of utter, weary sorrow etched his handsome face. ''I am saying it is best for both of us not to dwell on what might have been. Fate has decreed that we be no more than friends, and we must accept that and go on. I want you to be happy in your new life with Windrider. I wish for you all the best that life has to offer.''

"I don't want just to be your friend, but if that is all I can have of you, then I accept. Jeremy, will I ever see you again?"

"Be sure of it, princess," he promised. With one last, lingering embrace, they parted; both harboring heartaches and regrets and wondering what the future held in store for each of them.

7

The downcast look on Summer's face as they rode onto the reservation was far from the joyful anticipation of the usual bride. Her normally full lips were drawn into a thin, straight line, her face tight, and her lively golden eyes gone dull with misery. At least there were no more tears. She had long since exhausted those.

Tanya, seated next to her daughter in the wagon, cast Summer a sympathetic look. ''It would be better if you could try to look a little happy, Summer, if only for Windrider's sake. He has looked forward to this time for many years.''

Summer nodded. Her mother was right. None of this was Windrider's fault, and it was not fair to appear before him sullen and sorrowful. She cared for him too much to shame him before his friends like that. Yet she knew, too, that she could not pretend a joy she did not feel. The most she could hope to project was a serene acceptance. With determination, she schooled her features into more placid lines and tried to muster a small smile to her stiff lips. This she did for Windrider, her childhood friend. After all, it was not Windrider she dreaded so much as the drab, hard reservation life ahead of her.

The wedding would not take place right away. Realizing her daughter's lack of skills, Tanya had requested a few weeks in which to tutor Summer in the ways of her new life. For the remainder of the summer, she and Shy Deer would attempt to teach Summer all she needed to know in order to be a proper and helpful mate to Windrider, and Summer would work hardest of all in that short time. Sadly lacking in her knowledge, she had much to learn before her wedding.

The added time, while spent in the Cheyenne camp, would also allow Summer and Windrider to become better acquainted. For this Summer was thankful. It would be hard enough wedding a man who had always seemed more like a brother than a fiancé, let alone someone she had not seen in two years. They would almost be strangers to one another, and Summer needed to get to know the man who would be her husband. She had liked the boy, now she wanted the reassurance that she would also like the man. She would be sharing his life, his mat—bearing his children. The thought of such intimacy with Windrider was strange and somewhat frightening to her. She needed to know what kind of man Windrider had become and she prayed she could come to care for and respect him, if not actually love him.

As the wagon rolled slowly through the village, friends and relations came forward to greet Panther and Wildcat and their family. To Summer's eyes, nothing had changed much in two years. The many tepees still stood in their circular pattern, their tops blackened by smoke from the interior fires. Crude drying racks with strips of meat stood outside most of the structures, as well as hides of all sizes and shapes stretched or staked alongside. The grass surrounding the lodges had long since disappeared, replaced by dust in dry weather and muddy quagmires in the rainy seasons. With hollow dismay, Summer acknowledged that this drab, dismal place would be her home from now on. The poverty surrounding her did nothing to raise her sagging spirits.

Only the sight of Windrider awaiting her outside his family's tepee made her feel glad that she had come, but even then she was consumed by guilt. Here stood the proud, honorable brave who would soon claim her as his bride, a man who had wanted her and waited for her since childhood, and if not for her one rash moment of anger, he would be waiting still. Summer wished she could return the love he offered her. He did not deserve a reluctant wife who could not give him her whole heart, and Summer did not have that to give.

Summer was surprised at the changes in Windrider since she'd last seen him. Gone was the boy she had known. In his place stood a tall, broad-shouldered bronze brave. His body had filled out and his face matured. He was a handsome young man with glowing black eyes set over the high, proud cheekbones and the arrow-straight nose of his ancestors. His teeth gleamed straight and white as he flashed her a quick smile. Only the long thick braids, the smile, and those incredibly dark eyes were familiar to her as reminders of the boy she had known as Sly Fox.

Windrider was experiencing similar surprises of his own, though with more delight. Summer Storm had become even more beautiful than he had anticipated. Her long curling hair was brushed back from her face, fully revealing her features to his avid gaze.

Her face was perfection, with smooth, flawless skin and full red lips that looked slightly sullen in a sultry sort of way that made a man ache to feel them beneath his own. Her figure was more developed now, with the enticing curves of a young woman. It was her eyes that caught and held his attention, however. Framed against the blue–black mantle of her hair, they were like huge golden coins, like gleaming topaz jewels stolen from some magnificent crown. If sadness lingered in their shadowed depths, Windrider tried not to notice. He would soon dispel the sorrow from them.

"Welcome home, Summer Storm," he said solemnly, coming forward to greet her.

The strength of his arms amazed her as he lifted her effortlessly from the wagon and set her on her feet before him. Unsure of how to respond to this new Windrider, Summer laughed nervously. "Heavens, Windrider! What have you been doing these past years —lifting tree trunks? You're so strong!"

Windrider returned her smile, a bit derisively. "Hardly," he said, his eyes travelling over the barren landscape outside the camp. There was barely a tree in sight, only a few short scraggly ones near the river.

As he watched the color rush to her face at her blunder, he took pity on her. "I work wild horses, Summer Storm. I break and train them for profit."

"I see."

An awkward silence followed their short exchange, until Hunter stepped forward. "You look well, brother. Soon you will truly be my brother, when you marry Summer. I pity you her sharp tongue. Are you sure you want such a shrew for a wife?"

Used to her oldest brother's teasing, Summer merely threw him a disgusted look. Windrider laughed. "I think I can handle it, Hunter. I look

126

forward with great anticipation to having Summer Storm in my lodge."

Bright color again stained her cheeks, and Summer could not think of one word to say. Thankfully, Shy Deer took over. "You will be pleased to know that you and Windrider will have your own lodge, Summer Storm. You must come and see all the fine things our friends are preparing for your new home."

When Tanya erected Panther's tepee soon thereafter, Summer received her first lesson as a Cheyenne woman. First the poles were tied together for what would be the top of the frame. Once upright in a cone-shape, the skins were laid over the framework until it was completely covered. The bottom edge was lashed by thongs to pegs driven firmly into the ground.

Tanya and Shy Deer worked quickly and efficiently, instructing Summer as they went along. They made it look so easy! Then, to Summer's surprise, they began to dismantle the tepee, showing Summer step-by-step how this was done.

"But, Mother! Why are you taking the tepee down again?" Summer asked in confusion.

Shy Deer hid a smile as Tanya explained. "Because you need to learn how it comes down as well as how it is erected. Also, you are going to set it up again by yourself while Shy Deer and I supervise."

Summer's jaw fell open in dismay. "You expect me to put that entire huge structure up by myself? Mother! Those poles weigh a ton!"

"Not quite, but they are not light either. You'll soon get used to handling them. Just be thankful the tribe does not move around constantly, as it did when your father and I were with them. Then the women had to repeat this chore very often, indeed."

Summer's first attempt to erect the tepee by

herself was very awkward. It did not help that several of the other Cheyenne women had now gathered to watch. Some of the more helpful of them offered suggestions or encouragement. Others watched in amusement, often giggling uncontrollably at Summer's inept attempts to place the poles correctly. The longer she struggled under their curious eyes, the more frustrated and angry Summer became. If it hadn't been more humiliating to admit defeat, Summer would have given up and walked off in a huff. Instead, she worked on under the hot July sun, her hair straggling in damp strands across her face and perspiration dripping down her arms and back in itchy rivulets.

At long last, after several disastrous attempts, she had the framework up properly. Then she had to drag the heavy skin coverings onto it and lash them into place. Finished with this part at last, Summer stood back to survey her accomplishment. Somewhat lopsided, the covering hanging a bit crookedly, it was not as neat as her mother's work, but it was up.

"For your first time, it is not too bad, Summer," her mother told her. Then, almost hesitantly, she added, "I really hate to tell you this, but you have the entrance in the wrong place. It must always face East."

Summer wanted desperately to cry. Her arms and legs ached, her head was pounding from the heat of the sun, and huge blisters had risen on her palms. Had it not been for her audience of onlookers, she would have sat down and burst into tears then and there. "What difference does it make what direction the darn thing faces?" she wailed.

"It makes all the difference. It must be redone correctly."

For a moment it looked as if Summer would

refuse. Her face was clouded in rebellion. Then, with a resigned sigh, she said, "Alright! Does the whole blasted tepee have to come down?"

"No, dear. Just the covering. Then you must tie down the edges and you will be done."

"Thank heaven for small favors," Summer muttered as she began to disassemble the skins.

"Oh, and Summer? You must remember to speak Cheyenne. It is extremely rude to speak a tongue the others cannot understand."

"Is it, now?" Summer retorted indignantly. "Well, I think it was rude of them to laugh at me, so I guess that makes us about even."

Mealtime was another revelation for Summer. She had forgotten that the men always ate first, and the women and children afterward. Because they had been so long in putting the tepee together, Shy Deer had provided the evening meal, and they all gathered in Winter Bear's lodge to eat. While the men sat talking, the women served them their dinner.

As Summer served Hunter his bowl of stew, her brother grinned up at her in devilish delight. "You know, Windrider, I really ought to move back here myself," he said. "I rather like some of the customs. Don't you, Summer?" he taunted.

"Eat your meal before I throw it on you and break the bowl over your hard head," Summer responded sharply.

Hunter's smile widened. "What did I tell you Windrider? She has the tongue of a riled rattlesnake."

"Stop teasing her, Hunter, or I won't get my dinner at all," Mark said. "I can't count the times you and Summer have gotten into a fight and I've ended up paying for it in some way. Let's just have a peaceful meal for a change."

Over the next few days Summer relearned many small but important points of etiquette which she had forgotten, such as never walking between another person and the fire. Women also walked behind their husbands or fathers for the most part. If a woman was having her monthly flow of blood, she could not prepare a man's meal or touch his weapons or share his mat. Here in the camp, Summer never saw her father embrace or kiss her mother outside the privacy of their own tepee. Public displays of such emotion were not proper here, though she had often seen him do so at home on their ranch.

"Summer Storm. Summer Storm!"

Summer turned to find Windrider approaching her, a frown creasing his brow.

"Are you in the habit of ignoring your friends now?" he asked, giving her a measured look.

"I'm sorry, Windrider. I didn't realize you were calling for me. I am not accustomed to hearing my name pronounced in Cheyenne. Besides, hardly anyone calls me Summer Storm anymore."

"Then what are you called?"

"Summer," she answered. "Just Summer."

Windrider shook his head negatively. "No. You are Summer Storm. It is what your mother named you at your birth and the name you will carry through all your life. It is the name I carry in my heart for you. You are Summer Storm."

"Why is it you can change your name, yet I cannot? That does not seem fair to me."

"That is the way of things," Windrider said with an indifferent shrug. "When a boy enters manhood, he goes on his vision quest. According to what the spirits reveal to him, he chooses his adult name."

Curious, Summer asked, "What did your vision show you, that your name is now Windrider?"

"I cannot reveal that to you, Summer Storm. It is forbidden. Do not ask again."

Windrider's thoughts turned inward, to the time of his vision quest. He had seen many things in his vision, some that he understood and others that would only come clear with the passage of time. He had first envisioned himself as an eagle, riding the air waves on wide, outspread wings. Then he had glimpsed bits and pieces of his future, and Summer Storm had been there, cradling his child to her breast. This was the reason he did not doubt that they would marry, but he could not tell her this. A brave's vision was a sacred and private thing, a privilege granted by the spirits.

A frown marred Windrider's brow as he reviewed the secrets revealed to him and tried to solve the puzzling mysteries. In his vision, he had seen himself in a large city, Summer Storm by his side. His mind could not fathom what this meant, for Windrider had hated Pueblo, and would certainly avoid such places if he could. It was much easier to accept the vision of himself leading a band of warriors. This, at least, was reasonable.

More puzzling yet were scenes portraying himself, Summer Storm, and Jeremy Field together. There seemed to be much warmth and friendship between the three of them. Windrider could only wonder at this. What part Jeremy Field would play in his future, he knew not. Again, only time would bring the answer.

His vision had exuded a feeling of love and contentment for the most part, yet threaded throughout was a strong sense of danger, a lurking menace in the dark course of his dream. It brought with it a shrouded sense of his own mortality, almost a warning of his own death, though Windrider could not clearly determine what the gloomy shadows truly foretold. With it came a fierce feeling of protecting someone. Later, perhaps, he would understand these things, too. He knew only that when he had seen this clouded part of his vision, he had felt great pain—had sensed his life ebbing away. Then, miraculously, the pain was gone, and he was once more transformed into a mighty eagle, proud and noble and free, effortlessly soaring the cloudless blue skies.

Windrider had often pondered the various aspects of his personal vision and, doubtless, he would do so many times more in his efforts to unravel the riddle of his future. His destiny was interwoven in the fabric of the spirit-dream. Of this he was certain, yet so much remained unclear to him. That, too, would serve a purpose, he supposed, for no man should know his full fate. Windrider wisely accepted this fact, as he accepted the custom of keeping the revelations of his vision a secret, even from the woman who was destined to be his mate—perhaps especially from the one who would most closely share his life and future. As he traveled the winding paths of his life, he would cling to his vision and to Summer Storm, gradually discovering the deeply-hidden mysteries of both.

Windrider's mind snapped back to the present as Summer gave a disgusted huff. "I fail to see what the great secret is, or why it is forbidden to reveal your vision. It seems many things are forbidden the women here, but the men are free to do much. Why don't women go on vision quests?"

"They just do not. It is not our way. Vision quests are for braves and warriors."

"My mother is a warrior. Why didn't she get to

choose a new name?''

"Your mother is a special woman and a fine warrior. She trained very hard to pass the many tests to become a warrior, but she never went on a vision quest. That is for men of the tribe alone.''

"Naturally,'' Summer grumbled. Suddenly she asked, "Could I become a warrior, too, Windrider?''

He laughed ruefully. "I think not. It is hard enough for the men of our tribe to become warriors these days, restricted as we are to these reservation lands. We train for battles that never come, coup that are never earned. How can we prove our cunning and bravery penned as we are like dumb cattle?'' His voice was ripe with hatred, his black eyes glittering with it.

Summer looked at him in surprise. "*You* don't like this place, either,'' she realized suddenly.

His blazing look warned her not to press him on this. "No. We all wish we were free to roam our lands once more, lands the white man now claims as his. Instead, we are put aside on land unfit for white men and told to grow corn like women!'' His bitterness was alive and real.

"Yet you readily condemn me to the same fate,'' she accused softly.

"*I* am your fate, Summer Storm.'' His ebony eyes blazed into hers, his anger and bitterness still strong upon him. "It is time you realize and accept this. I am your fate and your destiny, for what is a summer storm without the Wind to carry it? It is but mere rain. It is the Wind that drives the rain hard upon the earth, that gathers the clouds in the skies to bring mighty Thunder and Lightning. For a true Storm you must have a strong Wind. I am the Rider of the Wind, born to guide the Wind to the heart of the Storm, to give life to the Storm. I am your life, Summer Storm—your true mate.''

Hidden as they were by the slight rise of the riverbank, no one saw as he pulled her into his strong arms. Surprise held her speechless as he tipped her face to his. "Look at me, Summer Storm, and know me for the one who will bring you to life, the Windrider who will build your strong passions and satisfy them as none other."

"No!" This single word was all the response she was allowed, as Windrider's lips lowered to lay claim to hers. Even as she pushed at his hard chest, he drew her nearer. Caught in the iron web of his arms, she could only wait until Windrider was ready to release her.

If only it were that easy! If only she could endure and ignore his mouth pressed so intimately to hers, but his lips were warm and tasted of salt and sunshine. They moved with such tempting skill over hers, heating and molding her own as if they were his to command.

Confusion tore at her. When she had allowed herself to think of kissing Windrider, she had imagined it would be like kissing her brother. It wasn't supposed to feel like this—so warm and good! She loved Jeremy! How could Windrider's lips tempt her so when her heart belonged to another? And yet . . .

Windrider's tongue slid past her parted lips and into her hot, moist mouth and lightning bolted through her. If candles could feel, this must be what they felt when lit by the match, this feeling of heat and light and glorious melting! As his mouth plied hers with its magic, Summer's trembling fingers ceased to push at his chest. Now they lay soft and shaking against the smooth naked skin. Beneath her palm, she felt his heartbeat, strong and rapid.

Unconsciously, Summer's lips softened beneath his, fitting themselves more willingly to his. Her hand brushed against the dark braid that lay across his shoulder, and without thought she caught at it, stroking its smooth coils in sensual agitation. Still unaware of her own participation, her other hand rhythmically stroked his broad bronze chest; her lips now clinging to his, savoring the taste and feel of him.

Lost in his kiss, Summer could not think. She could only react to what Windrider was doing to her. His hands were roaming her sides and back, claiming and possessing her as he held her close. His lips were ravaging hers with heat and desire. He was wind and fire, and he was fast consuming her.

When at last he set her away from him, Summer was in a daze of confused feelings. "You see, Summer Storm, how perfectly matched we are for one another?" she heard him say. "Together, you and I will ride the skies, Windrider and his Summer Storm."

His midnight eyes bore into hers with such fiery intensity that Summer could not hold his gaze. Embarrassed and confused, she turned from him, seeking to calm the racing turmoil that threatened to overwhelm her.

Windrider caught her arm, swiveling her about to face him once again, but she refused to meet his curious gaze. "Why do you turn away from me?" he asked. "Surely you cannot now deny that we are meant to be together. I felt you tremble in my arms and your soft touch upon my body. Your lips answered mine."

"I didn't mean for them to." Her mind was whirling with the mystery. How could she have responded to Windrider like that when she knew she still loved Jeremy? How could her traitorous body have overwhelmed her mind to such an embarrassing extent? Was she a wanton, that any man could touch her and bend her body to his will?

"What is wrong, Summer Storm? You are much more upset than one embrace warrants." Windrider had watched the emotions revealed on her lovely face —embarrassment, confusion, and something closely resembling guilt, but why? Surely Summer Storm was not so shy that a mere kiss would bury her in guilt. The girl he had known had certainly never been shy! She had been a little hoyden!

Anger and confusion sent red flags of color to her stinging cheeks. "Perhaps I'm not used to being kissed by near-naked men!" she said sharply. "Back home, all the boys and men wear shirts and trousers."

"Pueblo is no longer your home," he reminded her. "This is your home, here with me."

"So everyone keeps reminding me, as if I were too dull-witted to realize the grief I have brought upon myself!" Summer picked up her water bags and trudged back to her family's tepee, leaving Windrider to consider her last comment with a frown.

Summer set her mind to learning all the hard and strange new tasks, not because she wanted to please Windrider or her family, but because she had to. She used her work and her lessons to avoid Windrider as much as possible. Since the day he had kissed her, she had ceased to see him in a brotherly fashion. Thinking of him in that way was virtually impossible now.

She was still bothered by her physical response to him. How she wished she had Grandmother Rachel here to talk with about it. Rachel was the only one to whom she had confided her love for Jeremy. Also, Rachel understood Summer's dislike of the Cheyenne village and sympathized with her granddaughter's plight. To Summer it seemed she was the only one who did, who truly understood her feelings. It was Rachel Summer wanted now, not her warrior mother who had taken as readily to the Cheyenne life as a duck to water. Then, too, Summer found it easier to discuss matters of the heart with her grandmother.

Without Rachel, Summer had to try to resolve her conflicting emotions on her own. There was no one else in whom she wanted to confide her present troubles. First of all, she knew she still loved Jeremy. One simply did not fall out of love in a few days. Besides, she missed him terribly. He was never far from her thoughts, and memories of him readily brought tears to her eyes.

In all honesty, Summer had to admit, to herself if no one else, that she had more than enjoyed Windrider's kiss. Herein lay the problem. What kind of woman was she to love one man and enjoy another's touch? Was she some sort of wanton—an immoral woman? Would she respond to any and every man in such a ready manner? The very thought was revolting and ever so sobering!

Trying to reason this out by herself was very difficult, but Summer did come to some logical conclusions. Once she really thought about it, she realized that Roger had not had such an effect on her. Quite the opposite in fact. She had been repulsed by his touch and had literally had to force herself to accept his kisses when necessary. While not as extreme, she recalled being disappointed when other suitors had failed to excite her. No, it seemed just to be Jeremy and Windrider to whom she responded so intensely, though why was still a mystery.

Perhaps, she thought, there was something similar about the two men. But what, pray tell? Both were tall and handsome, but there the likeness stopped. Jeremy was fair-haired, green-eyed, an educated and dedicated veterinarian several years older than Windrider. Windrider had dark hair and eyes. The old tribal ways were ingrained into his personality as well as his bronze skin. He was utterly and totally Cheyenne, every proud, tall inch of him! Try as she might, Summer could find nothing about Windrider that reminded her strongly of Jeremy or would draw her to him out of loneliness for Jeremy.

So her dilemma remained. Now she could no longer even argue that she cared for Windrider as a brother. That was certainly not a brotherly kiss he had bestowed upon her, and no sisterly response either! Summer knew she did not love Windrider in a romantic way, but his touch had set her head to spinning. Of course, if he were soon to be her husband, it was nice to know that she could enjoy his advances. It was a definite advantage she had never expected to discover. It would make her marriage much more comfortable than having to endure a man whose touch she found abhorrent.

Strangely, it was Summer's brother, Mark, who helped her sort things out. "You know, Summer, in one way you are doing much better here than I'd hoped, and in another you seem more miserable than I'd expected. You are learning so fast; but you are so unhappy, so befuddled all the time."

"I never wanted to come. You know that."

"It's more than that. It has something to do with Windrider himself. Are you afraid of him, Summer?"

"Afraid of Windrider?" Summer was astounded that Mark could even think such a thing! "What a preposterous idea! I've known him for years! He's been like another brother to me!"

"Oh, so that's it!" Mark nodded his head wisely.

"What is it? What are you talking about now?" With every word, Summer understood Mark less.

"Simple. You are wondering how you can marry a man for whom you feel more sisterly than wifely devotion.''

Knowing she should be angry at his interference, Summer was, instead, amused more than anything else. ''Well, I'm certainly glad you have it all figured out, Dr. Savage.'' After enough pause to allow him to feel pleased with himself, she added, ''However, you are wrong. There is nothing sisterly in the way I feel about Windrider now. In fact, that is part of the problem, Mark. How can I find myself desiring him, when I know I do not love him as a woman should love her husband? It is all wrong!''

''There is nothing wrong about it,'' he surprised her by saying. ''Good grief, Summer, is that what has been bothering you?''

She nodded. ''I am not in love with him, yet his touch excites me. I thought only bad women felt that way. A good woman should love the man before she wants him, shouldn't she?''

Mark stared at her in numb disbelief. ''Where do women get these distorted ideas?'' he muttered half to himself. ''Are they passed down from generation to generation like favored recipes?

''Summer, the man is not some disfigured troll. Windrider is a young, handsome, virile man. Of course you would desire him. I would think there was something wrong with you if you didn't!''

''But Roger was handsome too, yet he didn't excite me in this way,'' she argued.

''Thank God! Still, that has nothing to do with Windrider. Feeling desire for Windrider does not make you bad, Summer, even if you do not love him yet. For some reason, you are drawn to him. This being so, you will naturally respond to him. That doesn't mean you would respond to anyone else in the same way, you understand.''

''No, I do not understand. Tell me, Mark. What if I

were in love with someone else? Would it still be possible to feel this way about Windrider then? Would that make it wrong?''

''Why do you ask?'' he questioned suspiciously. ''Are you in love with Roger after all?''

''No, I just want to know. Would it make me bad to love another man and still find myself attracted to Windrider?''

''It wouldn't be advisable, but it certainly wouldn't be unusual either. Neither would it make you bad. My professors at school call it biological. It is a physical response, and quite normal. As long as you are not married to one man and betraying him with another, it is not immoral either.

''This is simply a natural reaction between you and Windrider, two young and attractive people, and quite fortunate since you are to be his wife soon. Many women would envy you for it. Odd as it seems, many women who truly love their husbands cannot bear their physical touch for some reason. That would really make marriage a trial for both partners, I suspect.''

''You certainly seem to be learning more than medicine in that fancy eastern college, brother dear,'' Summer teased, relieved to find out there was nothing so very bad about her behavior after all.

''There is more to medicine than most people think,'' he responded. ''Summer, who is this man you love?''

Summer stared at him in surprise. Mark was more perceptive than she'd given him credit for. ''I'd rather not say. Besides, it is best forgotten now. As you said, Windrider and I will soon be married.''

Mark did not miss the hastily hidden tears or the sorrow in her voice. He wondered who had stolen his sister's love. He could only hope that Summer could still find room in her heart for Windrider, for they deserved to be happy together.

"Perhaps you can love Windrider, too," he suggested gently, "if you give yourself the chance. Do not reject the idea, Summer. Anything is possible if you try hard enough."

She smiled sadly. "Yes, Mark, I suppose anything is possible. Perhaps in time I'll even come to like this awful place. Do you think?"

8

Day after miserable day, Summer prepared herself for life as a Cheyenne wife. Each morning she arose before the sun. After preparing the morning meal and getting the day's kindling and water, she joined the other women in the dusty fields. Crops had been planted in the unlikely soil, tenderly nurtured to life by the backbreaking work of the women who hoed and pulled weeds, and hauled bag after bag of water from the river to the thirsty fields.

When the sun became too hot to bear, the women retired to their tepees. There they sewed or cooked or cleaned. If there were clothes to wash, a trip to the river was a welcome relief from the heat of the day. Summer much preferred beating buckskin against a wet rock to preparing stinking hides. Of all the endless and detestable chores, that was the worst.

Though game was scarce on the poor reservation land, the men still hunted. Often the hunters strayed beyond the legal limits in search of food, but as long as they were not caught none were the wiser.

Usually Tanya would have prepared the meat Panther brought home, and cured the skins. Now she supervised Summer's work and helped where she was needed. First the meat had to be removed from the hide. This was either cooked immediately for the next meal or cut into strips, and salted, and dried on a rack outside. Then the remaining organs, bones, sinew, and brains were cleaned and set to their particular uses.

Summer soon learned that nothing went to waste. Everything was put to use in some way. Glands were used in medicines, or for their fat content. Stomachs and intestines became waterproof bags, and linings. Sinew took the place of thread, and bones were made into everything from needles to cooking utensils. Brains and fat were combined to form a special mixture to be used in curing the hides. This was laboriously rubbed into the hide to soften it. Special tools were used to remove the hair from hides, but the process was still long and tedious. Again and again the skins were stretched and rubbed and scraped and dried, then wet again. The process went on and on, until the hide was at last ready to be sewn into a garment.

Summer hated working the fresh hides. It was a nasty, smelly business at best. With the hot sun beating down on her, and flies buzzing incessantly about the fresh kill, the hours dragged by like a jail sentence. By the time she was finished, her hands and knees were raw and bleeding and her back nearly broken from bending and stretching so long over the skins. Then, just as the work was finished, a fresh kill would need the same grueling attention. It seemed a never-ending process, and the most unsavory of chores.

Sewing the garments was much less distasteful, but still a tedious process. The deerhide, no matter how finely worked, was still thick and cumbersome to cut and sew, especially with bone needles and sinew. Summer missed working with more manageable cloth, fine thread and sharp silver needles. Still, she had always enjoyed sewing and found she still did, no matter what the material. She especially enjoyed decorating the garments once they were sewn. With dyed quills and colored beads, she painstakingly fashioned intricate designs on the finished clothes.

Much to her dismay, Summer soon found herself garbed in deerskin like the other Cheyenne women. As soon as her first dress was sewn, her mother had confiscated Summer's cotton gowns, and the girl had not seen them since. While finely sewn and decorated, and wonderfully soft to the touch, it was much more hot in the summer heat than the airy cotton to which she was accustomed.

"I'm melting beneath this thing!" she complained miserably. "No wonder Cheyenne men go about dressed only in a breechcloth and moccasins. I am tempted to do the same myself!"

Tanya laughed. "You are not the first woman with that wish, but so far none have yet dared. You'll soon get used to it."

"That is what you said about curing those stinking hides!" Summer said with an accusing glare. "Forgive me, Mother, if I don't quite believe you."

"It would help if you braided your hair instead of having it lay so thick and heavy over your shoulders. Besides, it is so much neater and stays out of your face that way."

Summer made a face. "I outgrew braids several years ago, and I am not ready to go back to them now. I will agree to wearing a headband, though, since it keeps my hair from falling into my eyes while I am working." Once she had become accustomed to them,

145

Summer had also found moccasins much more comfortable than shoes, though she admitted this to no one but herself.

Watching as Summer fringed the yoke of an overblouse, Tanya said, "Have you thought what you would like to give to Windrider as a wedding gift? With your talent, you could make him a beautiful shirt and leggings."

"No." Summer shook her head. "I would rather not make him clothing."

"What, then?"

"I don't know yet. I will think of something. When I have the right idea, I will know it."

Summer and Tanya were sitting in the shade of the overhang outside their tepee entrance. Here they could enjoy the breeze that blew in off the river as they busied themselves with their sewing. Dawn Sky, Shy Deer, and Sweet Lark had joined them there. Concentrating fully on the complicated quill design she was applying, Summer was not aware of Windrider's approach until a brace of dead quail landed at her feet.

"What the devil?" she exclaimed, surprise making her revert to speaking in English. She looked up to find Windrider grinning down at her, proud and arrogant, and handsome as ever. Without a word, he turned to leave.

Instant fury charged through Summer. How dare this man just walk up, throw two stiff quail at her, and leave? With deadly accuracy, and no hesitation whatever, Summer retrieved the birds and heaved them at Windrider's retreating back. They hit him square between the shoulder blades.

Shock was a mild description for the expression on Windrider's stunned face and he spun about to confront Summer. His confused gaze traveled from her angry features to the birds lying in the dust at his feet, and back again. Before he had a chance to question her strange actions, Summer was railing at him, oblivious to the others who were avidly watching.

"What do you mean by throwing those creatures at me? Haven't I enough to do without you coming around to add to my work?" Summer shook a threatening finger at him. "If you think I'm going to cook for you before we are even married, think again, Windrider! Cook your stupid birds yourself if you can't find someone else to do it. I certainly won't! By heavens, next you will expect me to launder your clothes and mend them! Enough is really enough!"

Before Summer was halfway through her indignant speech, Tanya was convulsed in laughter. Holding her aching sides, tears racing down her face, Tanya rocked back and forth while peals of glee echoed through the air. Drawn from nearby, Panther came immediately, curious to discover what had set his wife into such hysterical laughter. Looking up to find him patiently watching her strange behavior, Tanya tried to compose herself, but it was impossible at this point. Panther's all-suffering expression only seemed to set her off again, and it was several minutes before she could regain her breath enough to speak. "The quail," she squeaked.

"What about them?" His dark eyes took note of the birds still lying at Windrider's feet and the tension between the young brave and Summer.

Wiping at her wet face, Tanya explained, "Windrider brought them as a gift to Summer."

As she stopped to collect her breath, Windrider inserted huffily, "I fail to see humor in your daughter rejecting my offering, Little Wildcat."

Now Panther *was* confused. "She did that?"

"Most emphatically!" Windrider assured him.

"She—she threw the birds back at him!" Tanya managed, then broke into fresh gales of laughter. "You should have seen it! She was so magnificently angry!"

Panther turned a stern look on his daughter, who was by now more than confused herself. "Summer Storm, why would you do such a thing? It is expected for a young man to present his intended bride with such a gift. In doing so, he is showing that he will provide well for you when you are wed. By accepting it, a woman is also symbolically accepting the man's attentions. It is all part of the courting ritual. As you have already consented to the marriage, you were supposed to accept the gift graciously, not throw it back in his face!"

Embarrassed by her lack of knowledge of proper courting customs, Summer's anger diminished quickly, but not entirely. "I am sorry, Father, but I was not aware of all this. I had no idea what was behind Windrider's pompous actions. Had he offered them to me politely instead of tossing them at me with that highhanded male attitude of his, I might have been inclined to accept. How is it I am expected to know everything when no one has bothered to explain beforehand? It really is unreasonable and extremely aggravating as well!"

Now Tanya spoke up in defense of her daughter. "Summer is right, Panther. It slipped my mind, and I forgot to mention it to her. Naturally, she thought it odd that Windrider would bring her two quail. She thought he was . . ."

"I thought he was being an overbearing ass expecting me to cook for him already, when we are not yet married," Summer interjected by way of explanation.

"But you *are* supposed to cook the quail, Summer Storm," Shy Deer said quietly. "Just as Windrider's part of the ritual expresses his desire to provide for you, by cooking the quail and presenting part of it to him, you are demonstrating your skills and willingness to please him in the ways a wife should."

"Oh!" Summer glanced hesitantly at Windrider's indignant expression. He was waiting for a well-deserved apology. She had more than dented his pride this day. "Forgive me, Windrider. I am not yet familiar with all the customs. I am sorry if I offended you, but you could have been more polite in presenting your offering."

"Are you a woman or a goddess, that you expect such tribute to yourself?" he countered stiffly, his dark eyes glowing in suppressed anger.

Summer's jaw stiffened in renewed irritation. "I am used to much more courteous and gentlemanly behavior from my suitors, Windrider. Something that seems singularly lacking in this society where men reign supreme in all things and women are but lowly subservient beings. You must be patient with me if it takes me a while to adjust to your ways. There will be times, I am sure, when I will forget my place!" Her words and tone conveyed the sarcasm and disdain she felt so strongly.

With inbred pride, she walked directly up to him, meeting him scowl for scowl without flinching. Then she bent to retrieve the birds at his feet. "I'll go prepare your quail now, but I must warn you that I am not the best cook. Don't be surprised if you choke on a few feathers, dear intended husband!"

As Summer stalked away, Tanya's smile would not be held back.

"What *is* so funny, woman?" Panther asked with a stern glower.

149

"Our daughter is so much like I was when I first came to this camp, Panther. Yet, she has a lot of your conceit and pride too. There were many times when I, too, felt like throwing something at you or shouting back when you issued an order in that all-important manner of yours, yet I never had the nerve to actually do so. Seeing Summer dare to lose her temper today, after working so hard to learn a way of life so foreign and restrictive to her, did my heart good. And the expressions on both their faces was priceless! Our daughter's spirit will not be broken, my love, and I am glad for that. Coming here and giving up all that she knew before has been hard for her, but Summer will survive the change. She may not ever grow to like it, but she will weather it well."

Turning to Windrider, Tanya tendered her own apologies. "What happened here today was mostly my fault, Windrider. Summer Storm could not be expected to understand what I had failed to explain to her. I am sorry if it has angered you or caused you grief."

"My promised bride is very willful," he answered thoughtfully.

"And hardheaded and opinionated, and stubborn to a fault," Panther agreed, shaking his head ruefully. "She is filled with pride." A smile much like Tanya's creased his face as he considered his daughter's righteous anger. "I must ask you to be patient with her, Windrider. We have spoiled her dreadfully."

"I should have remembered this. Summer Storm was also very willful as a child." Windrider shared a smile with his future in-laws. "Do not despair. Even as I teach her to obey, I will not break her proud spirit. If she were meek and mild, she would no longer be the Summer Storm I have always loved. I will earn her respect, and then she will willingly follow my lead."

"She may not be easily won," Panther warned.

A self-assured grin was Windrider's only answer —that and a speculative glance toward the tepee where Summer Storm even now was preparing the quail.

The ritual of accepting the food and preparing it for Windrider had officially declared Summer Storm off-limits to any other interested Cheyenne man. She now belonged to Windrider in nearly every way, with the exception of the actual ceremony which would soon give him the right to her body as well. This restriction of other suitors bothered Summer not at all, for she had no desire to be courted by other Cheyenne braves. If, by some stroke of luck, Windrider was to decide he did not want her after all, she would not stay around seeking other proposals. No, she would hightail it back to Pueblo and Jeremy so fast her feet would never touch the ground!

If Windrider had been just an ordinary brave and she a run-of-the-mill Cheyenne maiden, there would be no formal wedding ceremony. He would simply negotiate terms with her father. Then he would lead her into his tepee, and having crossed the threshold together, they would be wed. It was not to be so simple for them. Their fathers were both respected chiefs, held in high esteem by the tribe. Therefore, a more elaborate joining was due.

The bride price of twenty horses was an immense sum in these days, but that is what Windrider had offered for her, and Panther would not injure Windrider's pride by suggesting lower terms. In response, Panther sent him twenty head of prime cattle as Summer's dowry, as well as twenty extra to be distributed among his tribe. This would help see them through the long winter ahead and give them hides as well as meat to offset the loss of buffalo now long gone from the plains. It was Panther's contribution to his beloved tribe; his way of aiding them in staving off starvation in this barren place, since the United States government rarely upheld the terms of the treaty by providing adequate food and supplies to the Indians.

Windrider and Summer Storm's new tepee was now completed and nearly furnished for their needs. Preparations were well underway for their wedding some weeks away, and still Summer had not decided what to give Windrider as a wedding gift. Tanya was constantly urging her to make up her mind soon, as Summer would need sufficient time to adequately prepare a gift befitting the son of a chief. Time was running out.

This was uppermost in her mind as Summer walked along the riverbank. She, Dawn Sky, and Windrider's younger sister, Sweet Lark, were scavenging for firewood along the banks. They had wandered far from the camp in their search this day, and they were about to turn back when Summer heard a strange screeching sound.

"Hush!" she commanded the other girls, putting a finger to her lips. "Be quiet and listen."

Just as she began to think she had imagined the sound, she heard it again.

"What is it?" Dawn Sky whispered.

"I'm not sure. It sounds like a wounded animal." Summer was already starting in the direction of the noise.

"Wait, Summer Storm." Sweet Lark placed a detaining hand on Summer's arm. "Perhaps we should not look for whatever it is. I have heard that wounded animals can be very dangerous. We should get one of the men to investigate for us."

At thirteen summers, Sweet Lark was a dear child,

and Summer had grown to like her future sister-in-law. The girl was right. In pain, even a normally docile animal could turn dangerous, but Summer had faith in her own abilities. Many times she had been able to calm a frightened creature that even Jeremy had been leery of approaching.

"It is all right, Sweet Lark. I will be very careful. You and Dawn Sky may wait here for me if you wish."

The other two girls followed cautiously at a distance as Summer threaded her way through the tangle of weeds and brush near the river's edge. Every few feet she would stop and listen for the distress call.

At last she found what she sought. There, not three feet in front of her, was the most magnificent eagle she had ever thought to see. Its wing span alone was over seven feet wide, the regal white-tipped feathers the envy of any war bonnet. Frightened though it must have been, the bird drew itself up, ready to defend itself. Valiant as the effort was, its right wing continued to drag at an awkward angle.

"Oh, you poor thing!" Summer crooned, warily approaching as close as she dared. "You've broken your wing."

The huge bird squawked at her, flapping its good wing and nearly toppling over with the effort to lunge at her with its sharp talons. Summer thought she'd never seen anything so beautiful as this proud, injured creature. The eagle's majestic head cocked at an angle, its curved beak open and ready to strike, its golden eyes daring her to come closer.

"All right, have a good look," Summer said calmly, seating herself just out of reach. For countless minutes golden eyes stared into golden eyes, as the two assessed one another. Finally the eagle relaxed its defensive pose.

Still Summer sat where she was. In a quiet,

soothing tone, she began talking to the creature, letting it become used to the sound of her voice. At the same time, she warned the other two girls not to talk or make any unnecessary movements. After an interminable time, she edged closer, talking all the while and never taking her eyes from the bird for even an instant.

"Let me help you, proud fellow, I can, you know. I can fix the wing as good as new, and before you know it you'll be soaring the skies again. Don't let your pride and fear stand in the way of recovery, my friend. You'll die if you reject my help."

Cautiously she slid her hand beneath the bird, catching hold of both his legs above the razor-sharp claws. Then just as the eagle began to panic, she brought her free hand about his neck just below his head, gently but firmly holding him.

"No, no. You don't want to bite me, pretty bird." Her sing-song voice served to calm him somewhat, though he held himself alert to her next move. It took all the strength in her arms to steady the enormous creature, lifting him to her chest while still maintaining her hold on his neck and legs. Cradling the eagle against her body and trying to support the broken wing was a feat in itself, let alone tottering awkwardly to her feet with him in her arms.

"Trust me, my beauty. I only want to help you." In the same gentle tone, she called to Dawn Sky. "I need something to use as a hood over his head. He will be easier to manage if he cannot see."

Summer nearly laughed aloud as her sister gingerly wrapped her own underdrawers about the eagle's head. "Oh, Dawn," she said softly, "what a solution!" It was the only material small enough and manageable enough to suffice, and Dawn had been quick to think of it. "Thank you, sweetie."

"If you ever tell anyone about this, I'll never speak to you again," Dawn warned on a whisper.

All the way back to camp Summer held the eagle to her as gently as possible, though her arms felt as if they would break beneath his considerable weight. She nearly cried with relief as she came within sight of the village.

Word quickly spread of the unusual sight approaching the encampment. Curious onlookers gathered to watch in amazement as Summer walked slowly to her father's tepee.

"Mother, please help me," she called softly to Tanya. "The eagle has broken his wing. I need a safe place to tether him so that I might set the bones."

Quickly Tanya secured a thong from the central pole of the tepee to the eagle's feet, tying it tightly but gently. In the same efficient manner, she wound a thin strip of leather about its beak, leaving the hood in place over the big bird's eyes.

Finally, in the safety of the tepee, away from the distraction of the gathering crowd, Summer gently released her lame captive. Flexing her numb arms, she turned to Tanya. "Thank you, Mother. I doubt I could have held him much longer."

"Can you mend his wing, Summer? Will he fly free again?" Tanya asked.

"Yes." There was no doubt in Summer's mind that she could do as she claimed. For years she had learned at Jeremy's side, and now she would prove her own healing skills. "It will take time for the bones to knit properly and I shall have to keep him near to watch over him."

Tanya shrugged philosophically. "We have had unusual pets before and survived it. We can do so again. At least this one won't chew up our clothes and drink all my coffee."

Summer set the break with astonishing ease, then tied the wing securely to the eagle's body to prevent further injury to it. Only then did she remove the covering from the bird's head. For the time being she left his beak and legs bound. "There you are, fine fellow. Time and nature will tend to the rest of the cure."

As she watched the eagle survey its new surroundings, a plan began to form in Summer's mind. If she could gain this great bird's trust, perhaps she could train it as her parents had the cougar cubs. What a spectacular gift it would make to present Windrider at their wedding—one windrider to another, true brothers in spirit!

Though everyone in the village knew of the eagle within moments of its arrival, Summer swore her family to secrecy about her plans to try and train it. Hunter thought she was crazy. "It can't be done, Summer. This is a fully grown eagle, wild and used to its freedom. Perhaps if it were a younger bird."

"I do not intend to curtail its freedom once it can fly again. It will be as free as ever, but I would like to train it to trust me, perhaps to come when called or to protect my family."

"To attack your enemies and warn you of danger?" Mark teased.

"Yes." Summer leveled a serious look at him. "Is that such an impossible goal?"

Her brothers thought so. After watching Summer first approach the eagle, Dawn Sky reserved judgment. She had already seen her sister do the impossible in merely catching the creature and setting its wing. Having seen many strange and inexplicable things in their lives, Panther and Tanya calmly waited to see the result of their daughter's scheme. Stranger things had happened.

Windrider was amazed and delighted by Summer's unique talent, even while he had no idea of her future plans for the wounded eagle. To be able to approach a wild, wounded creature and calm it as she had done was truly remarkable. "Where did you learn such a thing?" he asked.

"I didn't. Animals have always trusted me for some reason I really don't understand," she explained. "That is why I was so interested in learning more about them, and I talked Jeremy into letting me learn from him how to treat their ills. He is a fine animal doctor. Without his teaching I would not have known how to set the eagle's wing."

It did not pass Windrider's notice how Summer Storm's voice and face softened as she spoke of Jeremy. His dark eyes narrowed thoughtfully as he studied his future bride. "You speak of your mother's cousin, the man with the yellow hair and eyes like new grass?"

"Yes. I'd forgotten that you have met him."

Not only had Windrider met him, but Jeremy was one of the few white people Windrider had liked. Now he was not so sure. "Were you with him often to learn from him?" He was careful to keep the suspicion from his voice as he questioned her.

A tender smile touched Summer's lips as she recalled those happy times at Jeremy's side. "I followed him everywhere like a puppy. He was always so gentle with the animals, and so patient with me no matter how ignorant I seemed or how many questions I asked." Her voice trailed off to a broken whisper. "I adored him."

Lost in her memories, Summer had forgotten it was Windrider to whom she was speaking. She came to herself with a start as Windrider stated harshly,

"You loved him."

As much as Summer wanted to deny his claim, she could not. She would not deliberately hurt Windrider, but neither would she lie to him. Summer said nothing; she merely turned away and stood staring off into the distance.

"You still love him. That is why you delayed coming here for so long. Is that not so, Summer Storm?"

"That is not the only reason, Windrider. You know I've always detested this reservation."

"Then why did you come?" His eyes were darker than usual with hurt and anger. "Why have you agreed to become my wife when it is another man you want?"

Summer whirled on him, tears making her eyes glisten like golden suns. "Because I had committed myself, and I hold to my pledges. If you still want me, I will marry you. If not, just say the words that will free me, and I'll go back to Pueblo." Her small chin jutted out stubbornly as she tried valiantly to hold back her tears.

"And does Jeremy return your love?" Now that he knew part of it, Windrider was compelled to know the rest.

"Not at first."

"But he does now?" At her answering nod, he asked, "Then why did he let you come to me, Summer Storm? I would never let you go to another man, not while I had breath in my body."

"Because he is an honorable man," she sobbed. "He knew I was promised to you. He knew there was no way I could break my promise to marry you. We both knew it. My honor and his were at stake. In the end, we agreed to remain only friends."

Every line of his face was drawn taut as he stared

intently down at her, his eyes blazing into hers. "Is that all you were? Were you never lovers, Summer Storm?"

"No!" She was shocked that he would think it. "Have you so little respect for me that you think I could come to you and have you take me as your wife after having been with another man? Windrider, I could never do such a thing to you. I would never seek to deceive you that way."

"Yet you would come to me with no love in your heart, offering only your body," he pointed out coldly.

She closed her eyes against his accusing glare. "I did not deliberately fall in love with him, Windrider. I did not choose for it to happen this way. And no matter what you think of me now, I do care for you. I always have."

"As a brother?" he sneered.

"No, not any longer," she answered, letting him read the honesty of her reply on her face. "You confuse me, Windrider. I truly do not know how to define what I feel for you now."

"How do I confuse you, Summer Storm?"

Though it embarrassed her to admit it, she answered truthfully. "With your touch," she said softly. "With what I felt when you kissed me."

"So!" His knowing arrogant look mocked her. "Even while you claim to love another, you respond to my touch. Your body already knows its master. In time, your mind will also concede the contest. Then you will be mine completely, for your heart will soon follow. I will have all of you, Summer Storm, body and soul, and you will surrender gladly in the end."

"You speak as though you will own me," she said hesitantly, not at all sure of herself at the moment.

"I will, my Golden Eyes. Don't you know that? You will be my most treasured possession."

Summer's palm itched to slap that insolent smirk from his face. "Never!" she claimed staunchly. "No one will ever control me that completely. I belong to myself."

Windrider simply smiled that self-satisfied smile that was fast becoming irritating. "It might prove very interesting and enjoyable teaching you differently. How quickly do you learn, little one?"

In the next instant, he had her trapped in his arms, his lips burning down upon hers. For just a moment, surprise held her motionless. Then she was fighting him, twisting and struggling to break free of his hold on her. His arms were like steel bands about her, making it hard to draw sufficient air into her lungs as his mouth covered hers so completely. Her struggles only increased the problem, and she was soon weak and breathless, unable to withstand his greater strength.

The advantage was his, and Windrider grabbed it greedily. With his lean fingers he urged her stiff jaws apart, leaving her mouth ready prey to his invading tongue. His lips ravished hers; his tongue a hot spear dueling with hers.

Summer was awash in strange emotions, afloat on a sea of delirious desire. The strength seemed to seep from her bones, replaced by a churning heat that seared through her. All she could do was cling to the strong male body that held her ever closer and hope that Windrider would keep her safe from drowning in this spinning whirlpool.

So subtly that neither really noticed, the kiss changed. Lips that had demanded now persuaded. Tongues that had dueled now stroked. Summer's passion-swollen lips softened to accept tribute from his, accepting and returning his kiss with her own. On and on it went, this giddy, soul-destroying mating of mouths; giving sweetness and taking it, tasting, testing, caressing.

He did no more than kiss her, yet she felt conquered. When he pulled his mouth from hers and released her, he stood and assessed the result of his power over her. Her mouth was soft and swollen and moist from his, her golden eyes large and glazed with passion. "You are mine," he said simply. Even as he left her, she felt strangely possessed.

9

As the time for Summer's wedding drew nearer, Tanya pressed her harder. There was much to learn yet; religion, ritual, customs, history. There were robes and winter clothes to make and stores of winter food to be dried and laid up. From before sunrise to long after each sunset, Summer was busier than she'd ever been in her life. When her weary body finally found her sleeping mat each night, she was too tired to miss her big feather bed back home.

Youth was in her favor, for her healthy young body was not long in adjusting. No longer did the muscles of her arms and legs rebel so terribly. Her friends back in Pueblo would have been revolted by the calluses on her palms, but Summer was thankful that the days of seeping blisters and bleeding cracked hands were past.

Bit by bit she was earning her place in the tribe and the respect of the other Cheyenne, particularly the women who had seen her try so hard and learn so much that had been strange to her before. War Bonnet, as Summer had named the eagle, had gone a long way toward helping her gain the esteem of the tribe. Nearly everyone was astonished by her instant rapport with the bird, and they greatly admired her skill at healing.

War Bonnet was healing rapidly, and Summer was making great strides with him. Once accustomed to his new surroundings, he adjusted faster than anyone would have thought. While still wary of the others, he readily attached himself to Summer, as if he knew she was special in some way. To Summer's delight, the bird seemed to favor Windrider as well, being much less feisty and nervous around his two chosen humans. It was as if, out of everyone else, he had decided to adopt Windrider and Summer Storm as his new family. Summer was thrilled.

With buckskin padding over her shoulder and arm, Summer carried the eagle about with her, a short tether attached to one of his legs. After the first few days it was no longer necessary to bind his feet and great curved beak. Though he sometimes tried when others came too close, he never again attempted to claw or bite Summer. The bird instinctively seemed to trust her, and slowly and unobtrusively Summer taught him to extend that same trust to Windrider. Later, after the wedding, she would teach Windrider to call the eagle, and also prompt War Bonnet to respond to Windrider's call as well as her own.

This was what she now taught War Bonnet—to come on command, though she would not truly see the result of her work until the bird could fly again. If all went well, War Bonnet would be fully recovered by her wedding. It was not necessary to teach the valiant creature to protect her. This he did instinctively. He also set up a raucous alarm whenever someone approached them suddenly. By nature a predator, and therefore used to hunting and killing his own food,

War Bonnet had to learn to accept the fresh kills Summer provided for him. This was a new experience for both bird and girl, for to do so Summer had had to learn to set snares and traps for smaller animals. It was just one more thing out of many she had never thought she would do.

Little by little in the course of the passing days, Summer began to make friends with other young women her age, and as she did so her loneliness and feelings of isolation began to disappear. Luckily, her little-used Cheyenne returned readily to her tongue, for her new friends spoke no English. Before long she and two of the other girls, Singing Waters and Snow Blossom, were as close as sisters. Together they gathered wood and washed their clothes and pulled weeds. The three friends became inseparable. It was rare not to find them together, talking and giggling and sharing girlish secrets.

Singing Waters and Snow Blossom taught Summer many things her mother did not think to. From them she relearned songs from her childhood, and beautiful poems handed down from her ancestors. She learned stories and folklore handed down through countless generations, the kind of tales that made all Cheyenne children feel close to nature and an integral part of the world about them. Through her friends she now recalled old fables and many treasured memories long forgotten. Their friendship was invaluable in so many ways, and Summer cherished their open acceptance and the closeness that grew up between the three of them.

Windrider was especially glad to see Summer Storm and Singing Waters come to like one another so well. His own best friend, Two Arrows, had just approached Singing Waters' father with an offer of marriage. They were now negotiating the young woman's bride price and dowry. It would be nice to know that his friend's wife and his own got along well together. Having grown up together, Windrider and Two Arrows were like brothers. They spent a lot of time together, and it would have been very uncomfortable if their wives could not tolerate one another. Fortunately, this would not be the case with Singing Waters and Summer Storm.

Of all the Cheyenne women, there was only one who truly seemed to dislike Summer. More and more, Summer noticed the girl's malevolent glares. At first she paid it no heed, but soon it began to bother her. "Who is that woman staring so hatefully at me?" she asked Singing Waters one day.

"Oh. That is Morning Moon. Pay no attention to her. She always looks as if she has eaten sour apples," Singing Waters told her.

"If looks alone could kill, I would have been dead a thousand times over. Perhaps I am mistaken, but she seems to have taken a particular dislike to me. I cannot recall having ever offended her in any way."

A quick look passed between Snow Blossom and Singing Waters, but Summer noticed. "What is it? What do you know that I do not?"

"We should tell her," Snow Blossom said to Singing Waters. "She has a right to know why Morning Moon acts as she does."

"It will pass. There is no need to trouble Summer Storm with this," Singing Waters insisted.

"I disagree. You know how vicious Morning Moon can be when she wants. What if she plans some harm to Summer Storm? Our friend should be alerted so that she can guard against this."

"What are you two talking about? Would you please tell me what is going on?" Summer Storm was more than suspicious by now.

Singing Waters relented with a resigned sigh. "Morning Moon dislikes you because you are going to marry Windrider."

"Dislike is a mild term for the hatred I see in her eyes," Summer informed her friend. "Why should she be angry that I am marrying Windrider? Is it because I am new to the reservation? Doesn't she think I am good enough for him?"

"That has nothing to do with it," Snow Blossom said. "Morning Moon wanted Windrider for herself. She would hate any woman who claimed him."

"I see," Summer said quietly. "And did she have reason to believe that Windrider returned her affections? Was he paying court to her before I arrived so suddenly?"

As serious as their conversation had been, the other two girls burst out laughing at Summer's words. "No, Summer Storm," Singing Waters assured her with a giggle. "There are not enough magic charms in the universe to attract Windrider to her. Morning Moon has the disposition of a bear with his paw in a trap, and all the young men keep their distance from her. She will be fortunate to ever find herself a husband."

"But she is so pretty, or could be if she would only smile," Summer argued.

"Cheyenne men are wise enough to know that beauty is not enough in choosing a wife," Snow Blossom said. "They also need peace in their lives and someone who will soothe them, not present them with more problems than they have already. With Morning Moon, their troubles would never cease."

"Besides," Singing Waters added, "can you imagine having to wake up each morning to that sullen face? A man's whole day would be dreary with a beginning such as that!"

All three girls broke into laughter at the image Singing Waters' words projected.

"Then Windrider did nothing to encourage Morning Moon's affections? He was not attracted to her at all?" Summer asked again.

"Not in the slightest. Any attraction between them was all in Morning Moon's mind, though she did not hide her feelings for him. She has made a fool of herself before the entire village by her constant attempts to get Windrider to notice her."

"Why did she choose Windrider?" Summer mused. "Why not any of the other braves?"

"Who can guess the workings of her mind?" Singing Waters shrugged. "She has always been a strange one. Perhaps it is because he is a chief's son, and will one day take his father's place in our tribe, or maybe she was smitten by his fine looks. He is quite handsome, you must agree."

Summer Storm blushed as her friends laughed at her. "I have noticed," she acknowledged.

"If I were Morning Moon, I would set my sights much lower," Snow Blossom said. "In truth, if I wore her moccasins, I'd accept the first offer I received and count myself fortunate."

Singing Waters chuckled devilishly. "Perhaps there is yet hope for her. Old Crooked Toes is in need of a wife, and he is deaf as a stone. Maybe he will offer for her. At least he would not have to listen to her constant carping all the time."

The day War Bonnet flew again for the first time, Summer fully experienced her own self-worth. She had succeeded at a practically impossible task. She was so deliriously happy that she could hardly bear to keep her victory a secret. Only by telling herself how surprised Windrider would be later, was she able to keep quiet now.

That the bird returned when she whistled for him was an added thrill. Then, when he killed a rabbit and brought it to her, dropping his prize at her feet, Summer was ecstatic. Her pride in herself and the magnificent eagle burst its bounds.

Her confidence and buoyant spirits bubbled over. It was evident in the lightness of her step and her joyous smile. She even found herself humming a tune as she scraped the flesh from an odorous hide—a job she ordinarily detested. Her high spirits were obvious to one and all.

It came to Windrider's attention that Summer Storm was extraordinarily merry this day. He had never seen her so content, so completely happy. As he greeted her, she smiled up at him, her eyes shining and her face aglow.

It was several minutes before he realized yet another difference in her appearance; and when he did, he was astounded at how deeply it affected him. Today was the first time he had seen her with her hair in braids.

Almost reverently he reached out to stroke the shining black plait lying across her shoulder. "You have finally braided your hair," he said softly.

"It was time." She spoke without raising her eyes from her work.

"Why now?"

"Because today I finally feel a part of the tribe, like I belong here and am accepted."

It was what Windrider had long hoped for, a day he had feared might never arrive. Relief flooded through him. "Your words please me, Summer Storm."

"Then I am glad I spoke them." Summer looked up at him. "I will not always plait my hair, Windri-

169

der," she told him. "I prefer my hair loose at times. I like the weight of it on my back and the feel of the wind blowing through it. There is a freedom about it that pleases me."

It was his turn to smile. "Then leave your hair loose when you choose, for it is beautiful any way you wear it."

"Sometimes I will braid it, if you prefer," she offered, returning his tender look.

"And sometimes I will unplait it for you," he said with a teasing grin, "so that I may have the pleasure of running the shimmering strands through my fingers as I make love to you."

In all the time she had been on the reservation, over two months, Summer had never seen Windrider work his horses. Mostly she had avoided him and kept herself busy with her own chores. Many times Singing Waters and Snow Blossom had urged her to go with them to watch him gentle the wild horses, but she had always found some excuse until now.

Standing at the railing of the corral, she and her friends watched as Windrider slipped a rope halter over the head of a dainty gray mare. To the halter he attached a long lead line. Standing in the center of the corral, Windrider proceeded to lead the horse in wide circles around the area.

"He's really wonderful," Snow Blossom remarked admiringly.

"She," Summer corrected. "The horse is a mare."

Snow Blossom giggled, and Singing Waters joined in. "I was speaking of Windrider, Summer Storm. He is very good at training the horses."

Summer took their good-natured teasing in stride. "You do that to me all the time. One or the other of you is always deliberately teasing me."

"We do it because we like to see you blush,"
Singing Waters gaily confessed. "You embarrass so
easily."

As they watched, Summer was willing to concede
that Windrider *was* talented in his chosen endeavor.
With the mare he was gentle, yet firm, leading her
easily through her paces. Talking to the horse in soft,
even tones, he laid a short horseblanket over her back.
When he added the padded saddle, the mare barely
shied at all.

"Why is he doing that?" Summer was curious to
know. "I thought most Cheyenne rode bareback."

Singing Waters answered. "The men do, but most
of the women prefer a saddle on their mounts. Since
we ride less than the men and usually have bundles
and babies to carry with us, the saddle is very handy.
The pommel is convenient from which to hang a
cradleboard. Blankets and food and a few clothes can
be tied to the back where they are easily reached. A
saddle is steadier, safer, and more comfortable for us
most of the time. For short rides we will go without it,
but on longer trips, a saddle is much better."

"I see." Singing Waters' explanation made sense
to her. "Is Windrider training the mare for a woman?"

"Not necessarily. It is better to have a horse who
is trained to the saddle. Then, whether ridden by a
man or woman, the horse accepts this, and either
person can ride."

Summer continued to watch and admire both
man and horse. The mare was a beautiful little
creature. Her legs were long but daintily formed, with
four black stockings to match her long mane and tail.
The rest of her trim, sleek body was a soft gray, with
the exception of a jet-black blaze down her slim nose
and broad, intelligent forehead. Summer had never
seen a horse with such beautiful markings and such

deceptively delicate conformation. The mare would be fast, definitely a runner with those long lovely legs. Yet she would also be strong enough to endure the longer run and the rough terrain. Yes, her dainty looks were indeed deceiving to the untrained eye, but Summer could see the mare's hidden attributes.

Summer wondered wistfully if the mare were Windrider's or if he trained her for someone else. How fortunate one would be to own such a marvelous creature as this! Just watching the sweet little mare made Summer desire to have her as her own, but by now Summer was learning not to yearn for unnecessary things, no matter how tempting or pretty. What would she need a horse of her own for here on the reservation? She never left the village! Even if the tribe moved to a different section of the reservation, Windrider would most likely give her the loan of one of his horses.

Moreover, each time she wished desperately for something, it never came to pass anyway. She had wanted Jeremy, but she could not have him. She desired to live in Pueblo, but she had ended up here instead. She yearned for pretty dresses in lovely colors, with decorations of satin and lace, but she now had to content herself with deerskin. No, it did not do for her to want anything too much.

There was to be a feast, the first big celebration Summer had seen since her arrival. The festivities were in honor of the young men who had recently returned from their vision quests, to celebrate their new maturity.

Actually it was a dual celebration, for the first of the sweet new corn had been harvested. There would be dancing and singing and much revelry. Mounds of food were being prepared; corn, summer squash, an assortment of meats, nuts and berries.

After all her work and hard-earned accomplishments, Summer was looking forward to the celebration. It would be nice to relax and have fun for a change. In honor of the occasion, she took special pains with her appearance. When she found herself seated between her mother and Windrider, Summer was glad she had.

On this night, both the men and the women took part in the songs and dances, and there were several times when they danced together as partners.

Since the festivities went on for many hours, this was also one of those rare occasions when everyone ate when they wanted, the women and children along with the men.

Though many of the ritual songs and dances were still strange to her, Summer was enjoying herself immensely. She gamely joined in the fun, hardly finding time to touch her food between activities. She only managed a few bites here and there, but she didn't really mind. She gladly set her meal aside each time Windrider invited her to dance with him, both of them laughing at her attempts to follow the intricate steps and his attempts to teach her.

At ease and smiling, Windrider was this evening more like the boy she had known as a child, and Summer found herself enjoying his company. They talked easily, and even when he teased her openly and often, Summer took no offense. It was an evening of pleasure and harmony between them, a night to relax and celebrate being young and alive.

They made a remarkably striking couple, this tall young brave and this beautiful woman with the glowing golden eyes. To Summer, Windrider seemed extraordinarily handsome this evening, and anyone with eyes could see that he was well and truly smitten with her. Many a smile passed between them, many a happy gaze was exchanged.

"Whew!" Summer sighed breathlessly as she seated herself once more. "Those dances take a lot of concentration and stamina! I really need to rest for a few minutes."

Windrider laughed. "Perhaps I *should* let you eat something. The evening is young yet and you will need your strength."

Summer had just begun to eat when one of the children dashed by, knocking her bowl from her hands. Food spilled into her lap, quickly staining the skirt of her dress.

It had been an accident, and Summer was in too good a mood to bother about reprimanding the little girl. She recalled how thoughtless and active she had been as a youngster. Still, she could not wear the dress like this.

"I must go and change my clothes," Summer said.

"You will come back and dance again?" Windrider wanted to know.

"Oh, yes!" she assured him, her eyes sparkling and bright. "I will not be long at all."

Summer had all good intentions of changing her dress and returning to the festivities as soon as possible. However, by the time she reached the tepee, she was beginning to feel quite peculiar. Her vision was starting to blur and she suddenly felt very dizzy. She managed to stagger into the tepee and brace herself against one of the lodge poles. By now she was perspiring profusely, and there did not seem to be enough air in the large lodge.

"Oh, God!" she thought fuzzily. "What is happening to me?" Just a few moments before she had been fine, but now she knew that something was drastically wrong. Shaking her head to try and clear it,

Summer reached for a fresh dress hanging nearby. She never touched it, for suddenly she was hit with the most severe stomach cramps she had ever experienced. As she sank to her knees, her arms hugged tightly about her, she began to cry. She knew she must have help, but she could hardly move for the pain in her stomach and chest. The last thing she remembered, through a haze of pain, was trying to crawl to the entrance of the tepee to call for help.

"Summer Storm has been gone a long time," Windrider commented to Tanya with a frown.

"Perhaps she has gone to sleep. She arose very early this morning and has worked all day helping to prepare food for this evening's feast."

Windrider shook his head. "No, Little Wildcat. She promised to return after changing her dress. If nothing else, Summer Storm always keeps her word. If she were tired or had changed her mind, she would have come and told me."

Now Tanya was becoming concerned. Windrider was right. She did seem to be enjoying herself this evening. "It is odd that she would stay away and miss all this gaiety when she was so excited earlier. Perhaps I should go and check on her."

Moments later Tanya was staring down at her daughter's prone body. Summer lay just inside the tepee entrance where she had collapsed. Her arm was still outstretched, as if in her final conscious plea for help.

"Summer! Oh, Summer!" Tanya dropped to her knees beside her daughter. Summer's labored breathing frightened her. The girl moaned in agony as Tanya gently turned her over onto her back. Though her eyelids fluttered slightly, she did not awaken or respond to her mother's desperate calls. Her face was deathly pale, with rivulets of perspiration wetting her face and hairline. Even as Tanya watched, Summer's body began to convulse violently, her arms and legs jumping and twitching as if pulled upon a puppeteer's commands.

Tanya feared leaving Summer even for a moment, but she knew she must get help immediately. Though she had studied herbs and cures under Root Woman's wise hand, this was beyond her own knowledge. Tanya could only hope the old herb woman's expert curing powers would be enough.

Tanya's frantic call for help, quite unlike her usual calm demeanor, immediately brought everyone running. Panther and Shy Deer helped her carry Summer to her mat and settle her there, while Windrider ran to find Root Woman. Outside the tepee, Winter Bear, Summer's brothers and sister, and their friends anxiously wondered what had happened to strike Summer Storm so suddenly ill. No one seemed to notice Morning Moon standing to one side, a sly smile on her face as she, too, watched the flurry of activity and waited for word of Summer's illness.

Root Woman took one look at Summer Storm's ashen face and shallow, labored breathing and knew it would take all her expertise to save this young woman's life. She immediately ordered Panther out of her way, keeping only Tanya and Shy Deer to aid her. The first thing she did was to get Summer Storm out of her clothes, calling for plenty of fresh cool water to bathe the girl's convulsing body. With quick expert touches, she quickly determined that Summer's stomach muscles were cramping severely. In examining the state of her eyes, limbs, and tongue, she noted a peculiar odor about Summer's breath. It was several long seconds before her mind sifted through all its stored knowledge to give her the answer to the puzzle. The peculiar odor, in combination with the other symptoms Summer exhibited, indicated only one thing, and it was not a favorable diagnosis at all.

"Poison," she said at last.

"What!" Tanya could not have been more shocked. "How?"

"How, we can determine later," Root Woman stated authoritatively. "How long ago and how much of it she took into her body is what we need to know now. Beaver poison works very fast and is usually fatal."

"Beaver poison?" Tanya echoed.

"Cowbane, Mother," Mark said as he brought more water into the tepee for the women. "More commonly known in other parts of the world as water hemlock."

"Hemlock? My God, when Root Woman taught me about plants and herbs, I never realized that beaver poison was actually hemlock! Mark, that's almost always lethal!" Tanya's voice quivered as her panic rose. Looking down tearfully at her oldest daughter, she stared in wide-eyed shock. "Is there no cure at all?"

"None. Mother, I am sorry. There is little we can do for her." Mark's face twisted in his own agony at his sister's fate.

Root Woman snorted impatiently. "What do *you* know, Mark-of-the-Archer? You think you learn so much in that fancy school! Even with beaver poison there is hope, if caught soon enough. Let us pray that we are in time."

No one objected when Mark stayed to watch and assist. One day he would be a doctor, and there was much he could learn from Root Woman now that even his finely educated professors did not know. Besides, he was very concerned about his sister and wanted to help in any way possible.

It was Shy Deer, when folding Summer Storm's dress, who noticed the spill on it. "What is this on Summer Storm's dress?" she asked. "Did she lose her stomach on it?"

"It is just where her food bowl was tipped over onto it," Tanya answered distractedly.

"Let me see that." Root Woman did not let the seemingly unimportant fact slip her sharp notice. Carefully she examined the stain. A serious, worried frown pulled at her lined old face. "The hemlock was in her food," she announced soberly. "Perhaps in the turnips. The root of the water hemlock looks very similar."

"She ate very little of her food this evening before the bowl was overturned," Tanya recalled hopefully. Then another thought struck her. "The spirits only know how many others ate that same tainted food this night."

Shy Deer and Mark left at once to find out if anyone else was feeling ill. To their relief and amazement, all of the others were well. When they checked what was left of the food, Mark determined that the food in the large bowls was not poisoned. Only Summer's portion had contained the water hemlock, it seemed. Still, just to be safe, all of the remaining food was thrown out.

When they related this information to the others, Panther stated the obvious. "If the common bowls were not tampered with, and only Summer Storm's meal poisoned, then this despicable act was planned and deliberate! Someone among us has tried to kill my daughter!"

"We will not let this go unpunished, Panther," Winter Bear promised. "We will discover who is responsible."

"And I shall kill him, as he has tried to do—may still succeed in doing—to her," Panther vowed, his face an angry stormcloud.

"With poison, slowly and painfully," Windrider added with a low growl. "Let the guilty one know the same suffering he has brought to my bride. I will hold him while you force it down his evil throat!"

"Have any of you thought that the culprit might just as well be a woman of the tribe?"

For a moment following Singing Waters' surprising statement, everyone stared in mute shock. "Either way, the guilty one will pay," Hunter said at last, an ugly look of vengeance distorting his features. "Man or woman, they will not get away with poisoning my sister."

Snow Blossom happened to look around in time to see Morning Moon slip quietly away from the gathering. Her brow puckered in wary consideration. As soon as she knew whether Summer Storm would live or die, she would discuss her suspicions with Singing Waters. It seemed incredible to even think that the girl's jealousy would lead her to deliberately poison Summer Storm, but then it seemed unthinkable that any one of the tribe would have. But, obviously, someone *had* done the terrible deed. Those gathered outside Panther's tepee could only pray that the attempt would not be successful.

Root Woman and the others tending to Summer Storm had their task cut out for them. Once the source of the illness had been determined, time was precious. Working together, they did as Root Woman directed.

First the old woman concocted a noxious mixture to induce vomiting. Mark and Tanya supported Summer's unconscious body as her stomach reacted to the brew. Next they held her head and massaged her throat as cup after cup of water was poured into her. Then Summer was made to swallow another of Root Woman's strange remedies, this one to soothe her and hopefully further reduce the effects of the poison. More water followed, as well as continuous bathing with a cool wet cloth. When the girl's convulsions returned from time to time, they strained to hold her down, for Root Woman was adamant that Summer be kept as still as possible.

By noon the next day, it was fairly certain that Summer Storm was going to live. Still, Root Woman warned that her recovery might not be total. "Much depends on how much of the poison spread through her body. Her mind could be affected, or her muscles."

"Meaning she could be lame?" Tanya asked worriedly.

"Or completely paralyzed," Mark interpreted soberly. The outlook was still dreary. "Or her lungs could be seriously damaged. Hemlock often affects the respiratory system."

On the second day, with continued care, Summer at last regained consciousness, but she was too ill to move at all or to recognize anyone. The others had to feed her broth and water, for she could not swallow on her own.

All this time, Windrider stood guard outside the tepee, praying for Summer Storm's recovery. To think how close he had come to losing the woman he loved made him tremble with fright and rage. The would-be murderer still had not been caught. There was no evidence of hemlock anywhere in the village, for Panther had ordered an immediate and thorough search. Whoever had done the deed had been very careful to cover his or her tracks.

Four full days after the attack, Summer spoke for

the first time. And when, a few days later, she was able
to move about a bit and sit up on her own, her friends
and family were elated. Not until then did Root
Woman finally pronounce her patient cured and
predict a full recovery with no lasting ill-effects from
the poison.

Fortune had smiled on Summer Storm at last.
When told all that had happened, Summer realized
how very lucky she was to be alive at all, let alone to
expect a full recovery. She had much to be thankful
for.

Everyone was amazed, but most of all Mark, who
swore it was nothing short of a miracle. Root Woman
had put his medical professors to shame, and she had
his undying admiration.

The only thing that marred Summer's recovery
was the undeniable fact that someone hated her
enough to try to kill her. She determined to be on her
guard until that person was discovered. While it did
not slow her recovery, just knowing the culprit might
try again served to dim the joy she should have felt at
getting well once more. There was a shadow on her
life, and until she could shake free of it she would
tread very warily, indeed.

10

Autumn was upon them, and suddenly so was Summer Storm's wedding. Summer had just regained her full health after the poisoning, only to realize that her wedding was less than a week away. Suddenly the magnitude of this important step in her life struck her full force. It was frightening to consider. Never again would she fall under her father's protection. Windrider would take over that responsibility. Where her parents had led and guided her, she would now have to rely on what they had taught her, and her own judgment. No more would her mother and father provide for her needs. Windrider would provide food and the new materials for clothing. It would be Summer's responsibility to prepare the meals and garments, and to make their tepee a comfortable home for the two of them.

In a few days, her childhood would be past. Vows would be made that would bind her to Windrider for all time. She would be a wife, with all the joys and worries of a married woman.

"Mother, I'm scared," Summer admitted in a nervous panic.

"Of Windrider?" Tanya asked curiously. She had already told Summer what to expect on her wedding night. The girl seemed to understand and accept the explanation.

"No," Summer said, shaking her head. "It is the whole idea of marriage that frightens me. I don't know if I am prepared for it—all the decisions and responsibilities it entails."

"Bridal nerves," Tanya said with a gentle smile of understanding. "You will do fine, Summer. You have learned most of what you must know to be an excellent wife to Windrider. Every woman worries whether she will be able to please her husband. Most discover they worried for nothing."

Suddenly a look of absolute dismay crossed Summer's features. "Mother!" she shrieked. "My dress! We forgot to make my wedding dress!"

Tanya only laughed. "I wondered when you would think of it, daughter."

"How can you sit there so calmly?" Summer jumped up and began to pace the tepee in agitation. "How could I have forgotten something as important as my own wedding dress?"

"You were busy learning all the Cheyenne ways again. Then you were so ill. I suspected you might forget a few small details."

"A few small details!" Summer wailed. "Mother, what are we to do?"

Tanya was already rummaging through a traveling trunk she'd brought from the ranch. "We are going to do as I'd planned all along. You shall wear my wedding dress, Summer—the one I wore when I married your father in the Cheyenne ceremony years ago." With that, she unfolded the beautiful doeskin dress before

Summer's astonished gaze.

"It is so lovely, Mother!" Summer exclaimed in awe over the feather-soft, cream-colored dress. Intricate beadwork decorated the bodice and elaborate fringe hung heavily from the fancy yoke, the arms and the skirt.

"Woman-To-Be-Hereafter made it for me," Tanya said wistfully, remembering with fondness the woman who had been her adoptive mother. "It was sewn with love and hope in every stitch."

It was a wonder Tanya still had the dress. It had survived the Washita Massacre when Tanya had been forced to pack but a few of her possessions and travel to Pueblo with the very cavalry that had attacked the village and murdered so many of her friends and family. Chief Black Kettle and Woman-To-Be-Hereafter had been killed in that attack.

When Tanya and Panther had escaped back to the Cheyenne camp, Tanya had had to leave the dress behind, packed in a trunk in Rachel's attic. Now, after all these years, her daughter would be married in it, in another Cheyenne wedding to another handsome young Cheyenne brave. It was like watching history repeat itself. Tanya could only hope that Summer and Windrider would find the lasting love and joy that she and Panther had.

The morning of the wedding, Summer awoke to find herself without a moment to herself. It seemed every woman in the tribe had gathered about their lodge.

"What is happening, Mother?" Summer rubbed her eyes and peered about. "Why are all these women here?"

"They have come to prepare you for your wedding."

"Now? The ceremony is not until this evening."

Tanya merely smiled and nodded.

Never, in all her years, had Summer experienced anything like the next few hours. Dignity flew right out the door, swiftly followed by any objections of self-consciousness! These ladies took their project seriously, and the order of the day was to wash and groom Summer Storm.

This they did with a thoroughness that was mortifying to the uninitiated. Summer nearly died of embarrassment when over a dozen laughing women stripped her of her clothing and took charge of her bathing. Down to the river they went, where with handfuls of sand they scrubbed her skin until it glowed and tingled. Another group worked on her long dark hair, washing it until it squeaked, then brushing it dry until it shone like polished onyx. A few drops of scented oil made it smell like a field of wildflowers, and magically tamed her natural curl into shining waves that cascaded down her back and over her shoulders.

Gloriously clean, Summer thought the ordeal done. In truth, her giggling tormentors had barely begun. Pumice was vigorously applied to her knees, elbows, feet and hands, to soften the rough skin. Next, her nails were neatly trimmed and buffed. It would not do to go to the marriage bed feeling like a prickly cactus! Then her body hair was removed with a deft precision that left Summer feeling like a cleanly plucked chicken. It was all she could do not to beg for mercy.

All the while, her entourage chatted and laughed and gossiped. Their high spirits were contagious, even to the highly embarrassed bride, who blushed prettily under their ministering hands and endless teasing. An invigorating massage, with much pounding, prodding and pummeling, was followed by a final wash in the cool river. Then more of the deliciously scented oil was applied to every inch of her glowing body. At last Summer was deemed ready to don the beautiful dress and do it justice.

Never before had Summer felt so shining and beautiful. Her reflection in the still water told her she had never looked this lovely. Her skin had bronzed under the hot summer sun, clearly pronouncing her proud Cheyenne ancestry. The copper glow enhanced her unusual golden eyes, making them seem larger and more luminous behind their shelter of thick lush lashes. Her black brows arched delicately beneath the intricate headband Shy Deer had presented to her. She had no need of lip or cheek rouge, even had she had it available, for excitement had naturally heightened her coloring.

Her hair had been left unbraided, bound only by her headband, and three dangling silver discs had been clasped into its gleaming length. The butter-soft doeskin dress hung gracefully on her lithe form, flowing nearly to her moccasined feet.

The beaded moccasins had been loaned to her by her mother for this special occasion. "It is my wish for you that, by walking in the very moccasins I wore to my own wedding, your heart will follow the paths of joy and peace that mine have found," Tanya had said, tears glistening in her own amber eyes so like her eldest daughter's.

A silver disc pendant hung about Summer's neck. Matching scrolled armbands were fitted about her upper arms. These were gifts to her from her parents, symbols of the daughter of a Cheyenne chief. Replicas of those given to Tanya by Chief Black Kettle on her adoption, these were Summer's to keep. They marked her as a great chief's daughter, and by her supreme efforts these past weeks, she had earned the right to wear them now.

From her pierced ears hung silver and turquoise earrings designed in the shape of the revered thunderbird, whose flashing eyes and great wings created the lightning and thunder. Windrider had sent this special gift to his bride, to be worn on their wedding. The sight of them vividly recalled his words to her mind—the words in which he claimed that destiny had already decreed her as his, for what was the storm without the wind to guide it? Perhaps he was right all along. Who could fight Fate, after all?

In return, Summer had sent to Windrider a braided chain made of long strands of her own hair. He would wear it about his neck this evening. This personal gift represented the act of willingly handing over her care into his capable hands. It was a pronouncement of faith much appreciated by Windrider.

As he stood now, watching his bride approach, Windrider's heart swelled with pride. Surely she was the most beautiful woman in the world! Her ebony hair streamed in waves across the creamy doeskin dress. Though he could sense how nervous she was, she held herself proud and erect. Huge golden eyes sought and held his as she walked slowly toward him, the heavy fringe of her dress whispering in echo with her steps.

For just a moment, Summer was tempted to turn and flee. Then she saw Windrider waiting for her. He looked so proud, and though he did not smile, she could sense his happiness at this moment. She could not hurt him now. She could not dishonor him, herself and both their families. She had promised to marry him, and now she must see that vow through.

With renewed determination she turned her gaze

to Windrider. He was so handsome in his wedding finery. This night, for this special ceremony, he wore a heavily fringed buckskin shirt and breeches. His shirt was elaborately decorated with fancy bead and quillwork, and his breechcloth was painted with an intricate design. In his unbound hair hung silver discs much like her own, as well as two eagle feathers from his ceremonial headband. Riding high on his upper arms were two gleaming silver armbands, also denoting his status as a Cheyenne chief's son. About his wrists were his personalized copper wristbands, specially engraved with eagles and scurrying clouds. His onyx eyes gleamed in his handsome face as he stood proudly awaiting her.

Before she could gather her thoughts, the tribal shaman was inquiring as to the bride price and dowry. Satisfied that both had been acceptable, he waited as Summer Storm and Windrider knelt before him, facing one another. The shaman began the traditional chant for long life and fruitfulness, waving a bowl of smoking embers above their heads to ward off evil spirits that might mar this union.

In a stunned state, Summer heard her own voice agreeing to honor and obey her husband, to follow where he would lead, to raise their children and see to Windrider's comforts and needs. Windrider's solemn pledge followed hers; to honor her place in his life, to protect and provide for her and their children. In the final act of the ceremony, Windrider placed about Summer's wrists two copper bands to match his own, symbolic of his ownership over her in this marriage.

It was done. Summer Storm was his from this day forward. Before the feasting began, their friends and family would present gifts to them. First, however, their gifts to one another would be exchanged.

Windrider signaled, and a path was immediately

cleared. Two Arrows came forward, leading close behind him the beautiful gray mare Summer had so admired. Windrider's generous gesture brought tears shimmering to Summer's eyes. "Oh, Windrider! How can I thank you for such a wonderful gift?"

"I am happy that you like her. I trained her especially for you." His glowing eyes told her he would soon find ways she could properly thank him for the gift.

"I hope you like your gift as well," Summer said, gesturing to Dawn Sky. Her sister carefully stepped forward, balancing War Bonnet on her arm.

Windrider was speechless. At first Summer was afraid she had made a mistake in her choice of gifts, but Windrider's wonder-filled eyes assured her differently.

While Windrider was still struggling to find words, Summer told him, "I have trained the eagle to come on command. He is called War Bonnet. My only request is that you allow him to remain free, to soar among the clouds as he was born to do."

"You have my solemn pledge on it, Summer Storm," Windrider promised in an awed voice. "I cannot believe you have given me such a magnificent gift as this. I have no words with which to thank you."

Her amber eyes sparkled up at him, laughing at his sudden loss of words. "I am sure you will think of a way to show your appreciation, husband."

Hours later, a cluster of laughing women again gathered about her, this time to escort and prepare Summer Storm for her wedding night. They led her to the new tepee she would now share with Windrider. Inside, everything was ready for the newly married pair. Even the latest gifts had already been brought to the lodge and put away.

As they had earlier, the women once again

undressed Summer. The dress was carefully folded and put aside, as was the rest of her wedding finery. Even the silver discs were removed from her hair. Only her earrings and wristbands, both bestowed upon her by her new husband, remained. Laying Summer upon her mat, and arranging her hair about her to provide a modicum of cover, they left her to await Windrider's arrival.

Nervous beyond belief, Summer found it impossible to lie there. Expected or not, she simply could not remain still. Arising, she began to anxiously pace the confines of the tepee.

This is how Windrider discovered her when he quietly entered their lodge. So soundless was his arrival that Summer was at first not aware of his presence.

He stood for a moment just watching her. In the light of the fire, her body was golden perfection, one movement flowing into the other with a natural grace that drew Windrider's appreciation. The long midnight hair was a fluttering veil that shifted as she walked to reveal tantalizing glimpses of firm breasts and buttocks. Her legs were long and lovely to behold.

He must have made some sound, however small, for she suddenly turned to face him. Her eyes were huge and wary, like those of a trapped fawn, but golden like a cat's. Her hands were clasped together, one gripping the other in an agitated manner; but now they flew to her chest as if to keep her heart from flying away, or perhaps to cover her breasts from his view.

For a long moment they stood staring at one another in silence. Then softly, as if afraid he would startle her, he said, "Come to me, Summer Storm."

Slowly, cautiously, she approached him. When at last she stood before him, she stopped, unsure of what to do next. His hand came up to cup her chin, and inadvertently she jerked. "Do not be nervous, Summer Storm. I will not harm you."

Her eyes now refused to meet his. "I know. I can't help it," she whispered.

His hand lifted her chin, making their eyes meet. "I will be gentle with you, Golden Eyes. I will tenderly initiate you in the ways of love." His palm caressed her burning cheek, brushing the hair back from her face. Lacing his fingers into her hair, he slowly lowered his face to hers, catching her trembling lips with his.

The kiss he bestowed upon her was tender and seeking, in no way urgent. It gentled rather than demanded, and when his arm came about her, she willingly stepped into his embrace. The kiss deepened, drawing on her raw emotions, pulling the last of her resistance and fear from her. Her lips were no longer still beneath his, but moving in rhythm with his, pliant and soft. When his tongue sought access, she parted her lips to let it enter. Sweetly, so sweetly did his tongue mate with hers, her lips cling to his.

His hands were caressing her bare curves and stroking her thick mane of hair. Softly he touched her, like the wings of a butterfly brushing her skin, yet every place he touched came instantly alive beneath his hands. Lightly he caressed just the tip of her breast, the lock of hair half covering it shifting sensuously between his fingers and her nipple. The nipple sprang to life, sending ripples of sensation through her. Her knees gave way, and he held her firmly against him, supporting and caressing her as she quivered beneath his touch.

Her low moan told him that she was finding pleasure in his touch, but it also served to remind him that while his bride was naked, he was still fully clothed. Gradually he brought his lips from hers, nipping and nibbling and finally breaking contact. Her quivering body rested against his. "You tremble in my arms like a small bird," he said softly.

Gently he led her to the mat and laid her down upon it. Her eyes were wide with wonder, and she watched as he stood to remove his clothes. When she realized what he was doing, she blushed and immediately turned her head.

Windrider chuckled. "Do not be shy with me, Summer Storm. Are you not curious about your new husband, as I am about you?"

Her color deepened but she turned back again to see him standing nude before her. His words were true. She was, indeed, curious, even after all the animal husbandry she'd learned from working with Jeremy. When she was younger, she had seen her brothers swimming naked in the creek, so she was not ignorant of a man's body. Yet this was different. Husband or not, this was the first time a man had touched her naked body. Soon her body would know the feel of his upon it.

Slowly her eyes travelled over his unclothed form, the long legs, the muscled calves and thighs. His waist was trim, his hips compact, and between them his manhood was aroused and fully erect. Summer's eyes flew past his flat, hard stomach and smooth broad chest to his face, where they clashed immediately with his. Black as jet, she could see the desire in their shining depths, but she also detected a glint of humor.

"Do you approve, little bride, or have I failed your inspection?" he asked laughingly.

Angry flags of embarrassment stained her cheeks. "Would it make any difference what I say?" she retorted smartly. "You know you have the body of a god. You don't need me to tell you how handsome and well-formed you are.''

"But it is nice to know that my wife thinks this is so, since I also find her so beautiful and tempting.''

Windrider dropped to his knees beside her, running his hands along the sides of her breasts to her waist, and on to cradle her hips. "You are truly captivating, my lovely one. You are like a fine colt, all legs and eyes, with a long flowing mane as soft as the silk of new corn.''

His hands were reviving the strange fluttering sensation he had awakened earlier. "If you tell me how great my withers are, I'll choke you, Windrider,'' she said softly but defensively.

He laughed gently, his dark eyes shimmering into hers. "No, but your hips are nicely rounded, and your waist is so small that I could span it with my hands.'' His long lean fingers proceeded to do just that, sending shivers through her as his thumbs then strayed to stroke her quivering stomach.

Her small gasp drew his attention to her parted lips, so lush and tempting. "I love you, Summer Storm,'' he whispered as his lips sought hers. "I always have and I always will.''

At his soft, heartfelt words, and the warmth of his lips against hers, Summer was lost. Her senses came alive under his knowing touch. Her head spun with delight, driving all reason out of her pleasure-fogged mind. All of her thought and feeling were centered on Windrider alone as he played his fingers along her sensitized skin. His tongue slid along hers, learning the feel and taste of her, and soon she was caught up in the enticing whirl of sensation herself. Without thought, her hands sought his shoulders, unconsciously measuring the breadth of them. Her seeking fingertips savored the satin-hard feel of his muscled chest. She, herself, deepened their kiss; sucking his tongue into her warm mouth, plunging hers into his to taste his sweetness.

When his palm cradled her breast, she unwittingly responded by nestling closer to his touch. A moan escaped her lips as his fingers circled the erect tip and finally caught it in a light grasp. Shafts of lightning darted through her veins to gather at the center of her being.

His lips left hers to trace a path across her damp face, lightly feathering across her cheeks, her eyes, her nose. Then his moist breath was tickling her ear, sending shivers tingling across her skin and up her spine. Of its own volition, her body arched upward, seeking his touch.

Sensing this, Windrider obliged her. As his lips wandered down her neck to find the throbbing pulse at the base of her throat, his hands traced the gentle curves of her body from shoulder to knee and back again. His warm, wonderful mouth moved lower to seek a waiting breast. With teasing licks he tasted of the swollen globes, tracing their rounded contours and the valley between. After countless moments that had her gasping for breath and arching helplessly into him, his mouth closed upon one pert nipple. Desire shot through her with the force of a whip, lashing at her again and again as he suckled and laved the captive bud with his hot sweet tongue.

Summer's head thrashed back and forth on the mat, her breath coming in sharp spurts, her hands clutching at his shoulders, her fingers tangling in his unbound hair as it trailed silkily across his shoulders to caress her bare skin. Her heart raced giddily in her chest.

Beneath her palm, Windrider's heart was pounding heavily, thudding against his ribs as he strove to control his passion. While his head was warning him to go slowly with his inexperienced bride, his body was urging him to hurry. Her eager hands were caressing his chest and back, tantalizing him with her touch, teasing and pleasing him as he had always dreamed she would. It took all his willpower to hold back, to check his reeling emotions as he continued to build her desire to meet his.

A sigh of pure delight escaped her lips as his mouth sought her other breast, giving it the same loving consideration as its twin. His hand now caressed her quivering stomach and slid lower to trace the inner curve of her hipbone. Then his long fingers sought the sweetness hidden in the dark tangle of curls between her trembling thighs.

Her startled gasp brought his lips back to cover hers, as his fingers tenderly stroked the bud of her womanhood. Sensation raced from her head to her toes like a runaway horse, sending her completely out of control. As she twisted beneath his wondrous touch, small strangled whimpers of desire caught in her throat. His fingers found entry to her secret cove, gently testing and preparing her for him. "Windrider, please!" she whispered urgently, her body aching for his. "Please."

Unable to withstand her impassioned pleas, he brought his body down to hers. With infinite care he entered her, feeling her maidenhood give way beneath his insistent pressure. With his mouth over hers, he caught her startled shriek of pain. Everything within him strained toward completion, yet he held back, giving her time for the pain and discomfort to ease. When at last he felt her tense muscles relax around him, he began to move in smooth, easy strokes. He kissed her tenderly, his mouth moving from hers to touch her forehead, her temple. Soft words of love fell from his lips to her ear, soothing her even as his body was exciting hers once more.

Wondrous waves of passion were washing her in hot, multi-colored glory. Her body melted beneath his, opening to him like a flower welcoming the sun, welcoming him to the deepest reaches of her being. His long thrusts, while still gentle, were becoming more and more urgent. Her long legs were wrapped lightly about his waist and his hands cradled her hips, steadying and guiding her. Each delicious thrust brought him to a greater yearning, building their desire, taking them to higher and higher plateaus of passion. Gently, but insistently, he took her with him on his stormy ride through the night sky. Flames danced through her like a roaring forest fire, engulfing her in their heat and light. Then, suddenly, her world exploded into fiery fragments, sending her reeling into the heavens on a collision course with the stars. Windrider's hoarse cry echoed her own, and his arms tightened about her, as together they created their own wild lovestorm, one that even Nature could not rival.

11

Summer awakened to the feather-soft caress of Windrider's hands lightly stroking her body, his dark eyes blazing down into hers. Even in sleep her body had responded to his touch, for already she ached for him, her nipples erect and her skin tingling.

By the light creeping in around the edges of the tepee, Summer knew that it was near dawn. Twice during the night they had awakened and made love, each time more glorious than the last. Then Windrider would pull her close to him, her head cradled on his shoulder, and she would sleep again wrapped in his arms.

Now, in the light of day, she blushed to think of their heated lovemaking and her own abandoned behavior. "It is morning," she whispered, stupidly stating the obvious.

Windrider laughed, his fingers teasing along the soft sensitive skin of her inner thigh. "And my shy bride has returned with the light. Summer Storm, couples *do* make love during the day, too. After last night, it is too late for maidenly protests, my dove.''

Her eyes glowed bright and golden into his, a soft sweet smile curving her lips. ''I was not protesting, Windrider. Not in the least.'' Reaching out, she brought his hand to her breast. ''Kiss me,'' she said softly, offering her lips up to his. ''Make love with me.''

It was the teasing looks of their friends and the knowing faces of the other villagers that had Summer's shyness returning later that morning. This soon faded, however, for there was much work to be done. The entire camp would soon be moving to its winter grounds several miles west along the river. There they would stay in the shelter of the low hills, where the winter winds would not blast them full force, as on the open flatlands they now occupied.

Windrider and Summer Storm would depart ahead of the others, he had informed her. It would give them a little time alone together, time most newly married couples needed and appreciated, but rarely received. For several days Windrider, with help from Hunter and Mark, was busy transferring his horses to the new location. Once this was accomplished, Summer Storm's brothers stayed in the hills to guard the small herd from thieves, while Windrider returned for Summer Storm.

Summer's family was returning to Pueblo. Mark had to go back to college soon, and Panther and Hunter had work of their own to do on the ranch before winter set in. Dawn Sky had another year of school to attend, and classes had already begun back home. They had stayed as long as they could.

Summer hated to see her family go. They were

her last link to her former life. Once they were gone, she would truly be on her own. Oh, she would have Windrider and her new friends and family, but that final tie would be broken. Her old life would truly be behind her then.

Thoughts of Pueblo also brought memories of Jeremy—sad, poignant remembrances that tore at Summer's heart. For a time she had forced him from her mind. She had kept busy and tried to adjust to her new life, for her own sake and for Windrider's. Now, just days after her wedding, she found herself pining for him; for the sight of him, for just the sound of his dear voice.

Her morose mood was obvious, but most of all to Windrider. At first he told himself that she was sad over her family's imminent departure, but in his heart he feared it was more than this.

Panther and Tanya rode with them as far as the location of the new camp. There, Hunter and Mark would join their parents to travel together toward Pueblo. Each mile that took them closer to parting made Summer's heart ache a little more. Even the thrill of riding Mist, as she had named her new mare, did not brighten her spirits. Nor did the welcome sight of green trees and rolling hills, which she had so longed for. The new camp site was a vast improvement, but Summer was too depressed to really appreciate it as she might have.

As she and her mother worked to erect the two tepees, tears kept stinging Summer's eyes. This one last night, and then it would be nearly a year before she saw her family again. How she wished she was going home with them!

"Do not be so sad, Summer." Tanya gave her daughter a loving hug. "Time will pass quickly and soon we will see you again."

A sob caught in Summer's throat, nearly choking her. "I will miss you so, Mother!" she cried. "I will miss all of you so awfully!"

"I know. We shall miss you, too, but there comes a time for each of us when we must begin our own lives. Windrider will be here for you, and his family. You will not be alone." Tanya smiled. "You will soon begin your own family, you and Windrider, with children of your own to love and to fill your lives. Then you will not have time to miss us so badly."

Early the next morning, her family departed with the dawn. Summer watched forlornly as they rode away, standing and looking after them long after they had passed from sight around the bend of a hill. With every part of her, she yearned after them, wishing she was leaving with them and returning to the comfort and convenience of the ranch. Tears ran down her face unchecked as she stood helplessly crying for everything she had lost and could never have again, not the least of which was Jeremy.

Guilt washed over her as she thought of how passionately she had responded to Windrider's love-making. She could not help feeling she had betrayed her love for Jeremy each time she had succumbed to Windrider's persuasive touch. Yet was she not betraying her husband now by dwelling on her feelings for Jeremy? Was she doubly guilty then? Did she not betray both men, and herself, by her confused emotions?

Thankfully, Windrider gave her time to herself that day. He busied himself tending to his horses and beginning work on a small corral. Summer had her own chores to see to. Though separated by only a few yards, they practically ignored one another.

SUMMER STORM

Summer was grateful that Windrider was so busy, for she found it difficult to hide her tears from him. When she had prepared his meal at midday, she left him to eat it alone as she walked by herself along the riverbank. Not wanting to add laziness to her growing list of faults, she gathered firewood as she went. Then she sat for a long time staring into the water and trying to calm herself.

As busy as he was, Windrider watched Summer Storm as he worked. From time to time she would look up to find his quizzical gaze on her, but he did not approach her or attempt to get her to talk. He left her to sort through her turmoil on her own. Later, if need be, he would take matters in hand himself.

Two days went by this way, with little spoken between them. Summer had ceased her weeping, but she was still downcast and quiet. She went about her daily chores like a heartbroken ghost, and at night, while she did not refuse him her body, neither was she the joyously enthusiastic wife of their first times together.

The evening of the third day, Windrider had had enough. As they prepared for bed, he told her this. "When you come to our mat this night," he warned in stern tones, "you will bring yourself as well as your body. I will no longer abide a wife who acts as if it is a pronouncement of death just to enter my arms."

Her head came up sharply at his terse words. In his dark eyes she could see pain as well as anger. "I am sorry, Windrider. I have not been myself these last days."

He accepted her apology with a short nod of his head. "You have had time now to recover sufficiently from parting with your family, Summer Storm. I am your husband, and I can make you very happy if you let me.''

Lying back on their mat, Windrider watched as Summer removed her clothing. When she joined him on their bed, she came into his arms more willingly. ''I will try to please you, Windrider,'' she said quietly. ''I will try to be a good wife to you.''

She accepted his touch and his ardent kisses, and her body readily responded in appreciation and anticipation. Her breasts swelled to fill his large palms, their tips aroused and sensitive. Her lips moved, wet and pliant beneath his, quickly following his lead. Her hands reached out to tentatively return the sweet caresses he was giving, her body arching into his touch as if to better receive it. Yet her mind was not thoroughly involved. While her reactions were not faked, there was no joy in her, no sweet murmurs of delight from her lips.

Windrider had moved over her and was about to join their bodies, when suddenly he stopped. Still kneeling above her, he gripped huge handfuls of her flowing hair, his fingers tightening hurtfully until her eyes flew open in surprised pain. Sparks of rage rained down at her from his midnight eyes, and when she would have turned her head he held it firmly, the taut hair wound even more tightly in his strong fingers. When she cried out in hurt and confusion and would have asked why he was so angry, he shook his head.

''Do not speak, Summer Storm. I shall speak now, and you would be wise to listen and heed my words well.''

He paused to gain her full attention, and when he spoke once more, Summer was astounded by his words. ''My mat is not large enough for three persons, wife, and I will no longer make love to you while your thoughts dwell on another man.''

"I am not . . ."

"Do not speak falsely to me, Summer Storm!" he hissed furiously, the quieter tone more ominous than if he had shouted at her. "The ghost of his memory lies between us in our bed. I can see this in your face; I feel it in your touch."

Her guilty gaze slid away from his, but he tugged hard on her hair. "Look at me," he ordered gruffly. "Look at me and know me. I am your husband, the man who owns your body, the only man on your sleeping mat, now and always. It is my body that makes yours sing sweetly with ecstasy; and it will be I alone who rule your thoughts when you are in my arms. Do you understand?"

Another sharp tug at her hair brought a swift reply. "Yes," she gritted through clenched teeth, tears sparkling in her wide eyes. "Yes, Windrider."

"I will gain your heart as well as your thoughts and your beautiful body, if it is the last thing I do on this earth," he vowed fervently. "I will gain your very soul as my own."

With his determined promise still echoing in her ears, he plunged into her, arching her body up to his in urgent demand. He took her roughly but not hurtfully, insistently yet with gentle command, considerate of the need to build her passions as well as his own. His powerful body moved over and within hers, mastering her very will, compelling her into an eager submission she could not deny him. Never had she felt so dominated, so entirely out of control of her own body and mind. Emotion ruled her completely as Windrider pushed her onward, ever higher, taking her with him to rapture's realm.

Tiny whimpers and delighted moans were their music, as their bodies blended in glorious harmony. So tightly did she cling to him as her world spun crazily about her! Inside her, the tumultuous tempest rose, until finally, when she had thought she could bear the torment no more, it burst its bounds at last. As the heavens split about her and the earth disappeared from beneath, she clung to him wildly. Her nails scored his back and her teeth bit sharply into the flesh of his shoulder as rapture engulfed her. His name was the frantic cry that was torn from her throat. Her fierce fulfillment triggered his, and together she and Windrider rode out the storm.

Neither of them doubted that at least part of Windrider's threat had been made good this night. There had been no room in her mind for thoughts of Jeremy as Windrider had mastered her body with his own. Summer had conceded the victory to him with barely any resistance. This thought was extremely humiliating. Tears rose into her eyes. What a humbling surrender! Disgusted with herself and with him, Summer turned her back to him, intent on ignoring her triumphant mate. Then, much to her surprise and his, she turned back to him flinging her arms tightly about his neck and burying her wet face in his throat.

"Damn you, Windrider!" she sobbed. "Damn you! How dare you degrade me so!"

His arms tightened about her quaking body, his big hand tenderly stroking her hair. "I have not dishonored you, Sweet One. I hold you in great esteem; in the highest reaches of my heart."

"Always hold me there, Windrider. Hold me tightly and never let me go."

The next few days, unlike the last two, were spent in pleasurable pursuits. Once again they were two young people enjoying the fresh new days of their marriage. And in their playfulness, they discovered a new unity between them, a bond of mutual honor.

Summer made a private pledge to herself to try not to think of Jeremy, to attempt to put her love for him behind her and go on with her life; to make Windrider her future and to be content with her chosen path. If thoughts of Jeremy crept in, as they inevitably would from time to time, she determined never again to let them come between her husband and herself.

Windrider was as pleased with War Bonnet as Summer was with Mist. He was amazed that the eagle's wing had healed sufficiently to allow the bird to fly once more. "It is miraculous!" he declared. "And you are amazing."

He was equally astonished when Summer taught him to whistle for the bird and War Bonnet instantly obeyed the special signal. "The eagle is a magnificent creature," Windrider said wondrously, watching the bird soar high above him. "We are blessed to have him bestow his trust upon us."

"Who better to trust than his brother and namesake, the Windrider?" she suggested with a loving smile. "Still, I know how you admire War Bonnet's plumage, and I must tell you that if I ever find so much as one of his feathers adorning your attire, I will personally skin you alive."

Windrider returned her smile with a wry one of his own. "As you did with your fingernails the other night, when you tore the skin from my back in your mad passion?" he teased.

"Exactly!" she agreed, willing the sudden rush of tell-tale color from her face. Then she eyed him shyly and said, "I am sorry, Windrider. I never meant to do that. I guess I became overenthusiastic.''

Her apology met with raised eyebrows and a devilish look. ''You have my permission to become overenthusiastic under those circumstances any time you wish. The rewards far outweigh the pain, my Sensuous Summer Storm.''

A beguiling light turned her eyes as golden as ripe wheat. ''Then come, Mighty Eagle, and test your seductive skills on me once more. Let us see if you can again bring me to such incredible heights that I forget myself in your arms.''

They laughed and loved and cavorted for hours. They rode and swam and chased each other like children. It was a glorious time together for them.

''I am glad to see you remember how to swim. It seemed weeks before you finally learned.''

''That is right,'' she recalled with delight. ''I had forgotten that you taught me when Hunter and Mark would not.''

''When you learned at last, I think you became part fish. You were forever in the water. You would emerge resembling a chubby little brown grape, all shriveled and wrinkled.''

Summer stood in the chilly waist-deep water and faced him. ''Do I still look like a fat, shriveled grape?'' she taunted.

Windrider's dark eyes were like black velvet as they caressed her glistening wet body just inches away. ''Only here,'' he said huskily, his hand coming up to touch one pert, rosy nipple. ''And here,'' as he caught the other uptilted tip with teasing fingers. It was a long while before they came out of the cool river, but neither noticed how cold the water had become.

"Come. Today we are going for a longer ride, and I will show you the magic Father Frost has brought to the hills." Windrider held the mare's reins out to Summer.

"Shall I pack a lunch for us?" she asked.

Windrider laughed. "Still a city girl despite all our efforts! No, Summer Storm. There is no need to carry food with us. Mother Earth will provide our meal, as Sun will give light and warmth to our travels, and Nature will display all her beauty before our eyes."

Indeed, the day was beautiful. A clear blue sky covered the heavens and set the perfect background for the panorama of color. The frost had turned the leaves to red and gold and orange, and the air was crisp and clean with the smell of autumn. Here and there in the vivid, rolling landscape, a pine tree still lent its green to soothe the eye.

Compared with the dry, flat area surrounding the present Cheyenne village, this land was lush. "Why did our people set up camp there instead of here in the hills?" Summer questioned. "It is so much nicer here. There are more trees to provide firewood and the river is still close."

"Yes," Windrider agreed, "but the wildlife here would not sustain the number of our tribe all year long. In summer we must move down to the prairie, where the land is more suited to growing crops. If we are fortunate, we can still find a few buffalo there, or a small herd of antelope. Also, thanks to George Bent and your father, we now have cattle to provide us meat and hides, since the buffalo are so scarce. In summer they grow fat on the grasslands. In winter, after we have slaughtered those we require, the rest are brought here where they can find shelter and forage among the small valleys and hills, to perhaps survive the killing snows and freezing winds."

Summer shook her head in bafflement. "That is just the opposite of what my father and Hunter do each year. In summer, the cattle are allowed their summer ranges in the mountains, and in winter they are herded down to their valley pastures where the men more easily can provide feed for them if necessary."

"But we have no feed for *our* cattle, Summer Storm," Windrider pointed out in bitter irony. "Left on the open prairies they would most certainly freeze and starve. These small hills are not like the rugged, towering mountains around your father's ranch. Here the cattle are not trapped so much as protected from the elements of winter. Here they find small areas where the snows do not collect and cover the ground completely, since the dumb creatures would stand and starve before they would paw away the snow to uncover the grass as a horse would do. They take cover in the lee of the hillsides and among the trees, and if they find enough food for themselves, they survive. Still, each year we lose many to the harsh weather."

"Survival of the fittest, and prone to the fickle whims of Nature," Summer mused thoughtfully. She could not help wondering if that same axiom now applied to herself as well.

As if he had read her thoughts, Windrider spoke assuredly. "We are strong, Summer Storm. Together we will withstand all that we must. Not only will we survive, but we will grow stronger through all of it, good and bad." Taking her into his arms, he held her tightly to him. "With you by my side, who could defeat me?"

"And with you to defend me, who can ever do me harm?" she answered softly, her eyes shining up into his.

A few days later Summer awoke to find, not Windrider's black eyes gazing down into hers, but two huge golden eyes much like her own. These, however, were set in the sleek furry face of a mountain lion. Gulping back an instinctive scream, Summer dared not move. The huge creature stood directly over her, his face mere inches from her own. She could feel his warm breath on her cheeks, and the light tickle of his long whiskers on the tip of her nose. His mouth opened to show sharp, gleaming white teeth, and Summer closed her eyes in complete and absolute terror as his great head moved even closer.

"Oh, God!" she prayed. "Please make him go away! Please don't let him eat me!"

Instead of teeth, she felt the sloppy slap of a wet tongue across her face. Despite all her best warnings to herself, she let out a small strangled shriek. "Windrider!"

From across the tepee she heard his amused laughter. "Come, Pouncer," he called, still chuckling heartily. "I do not believe my wife enjoys your morning kisses as well as mine."

Incredulous at her husband's words, Summer's eyes popped open. The huge cat gave her a baleful look and backed off. With a disdainful grace, it wandered over to where Windrider sat and unceremoniously plunked its head into his lap.

Nearly speechless with shock, but no longer frozen with fear, Summer sat up and stuttered, "I—uh —you—uh—" As words failed her, she reverted to English, which Windrider understood perfectly, to express her stunned disbelief. "Hell's bells and little fishes! Would you mind explaining what the devil that cougar is doing in here?"

Her words brought tears to Windrider's eyes as he laughed even harder. "Summer Storm, meet Pouncer. He is the grandson of your old pet. You do remember Meow, the mountain lion you gave into my care when you left to live on the ranch?"

Summer's mouth dropped open in surprise. As fond as that particular memory had always been for her, she wondered how she could have forgotten it now. "Oh, for goodness sake!" she exclaimed. A slow smile spread across her face as a warm delight engulfed her. "Of course I remember Meow, but I thought she must have died by now. I never expected that any of her young would still be coming around."

"Meow died a few seasons past," Windrider told her solemnly. "Pouncer is the only one of her offspring to acknowledge me, and I suspect he only does it in order to enjoy the comforts of a warm lodge in winter. Each summer he departs again, and goes off on his own somewhere."

"Is he tame?"

Windrider shrugged. "As tame as any wild creature can be. He will not attack anyone unless severely provoked, or if he thinks I am in danger. And he never relieves himself inside the tepee or chews things up now that he is no longer a cub. In that respect, you could say he is trained. And we have an understanding that he will hunt on his own and leave the cattle alone."

"What about me? Will he accept me as a friend, too?" Summer cast a wary but covetous look at the cat.

Windrider's smile reeked of deviltry. "That might

depend on how nicely you treat me, my little coward.''

"Hmph!'' she snorted indignantly. "We'll see about that! After all, I do have a certain affinity with creatures myself.''

Now he was laughing at her offended pose. "Go ahead and laugh, you big brute! I am willing to wager that you would not have come within twelve paces upon first meeting the pet I once had on the ranch!''

"And what manner of pet was this?'' he asked in that irritating superior tone of his.

Summer smiled wickedly. "A skunk!'' she declared triumphantly. "I had a pet skunk named Stinker, and believe me, he certainly earned his name many times over!''

Pouncer readily extended his friendship to Summer once she had shown him that she did truly like him. As with Windrider, the cougar also designated himself as her protector, though he had to share that honor with War Bonnet. The eagle and the mountain lion struck an uneasy truce, barely tolerating one another at first. As time went on, they gradually became accustomed to one another. They certainly were a strange pair when first seen together, often causing the unprepared observer to stop and stare in mute disbelief, shaking his head as if to clear from his sight what he knew he could not actually be seeing.

Windrider and Summer had been on their own for half a moon, when one evening they received unexpected but welcome company. Toward sunset, Two Arrows and Singing Waters rode into their solitary camp. After the initial greetings, Two Arrows announced proudly, "Singing Waters is now my wife." Since they had arrived alone, the other two had already deduced this fact, for Singing Waters would never had been permitted to travel alone with Two Arrows otherwise. Still, the news was exclaimed over, and hearty congratulations extended.

"I am sorry we missed your wedding, Singing Waters," Summer Storm told her friend.

Singing Waters smiled joyously, her dark doe eyes shining with love and happiness. "Our union was not as elaborate as yours," she confided, "but it was still wonderful."

"We hope you do not mind our joining you in your seclusion," Two Arrows said, half explaining and half apologizing. "We, too, wanted to be away from the entire tribe for a short time."

"You are our friends. Wherever we erect our tepee, you are always welcome," Windrider assured him. Summer echoed his sentiment wholeheartedly.

For two more weeks, the two couples had the area all to themselves. It was a time of love and laughter and shared friendship, and the four of them founded a lasting relationship that all cherished greatly. They talked and ate and swam and rode together, and each evening they parted to their individual tepees. They were together a great deal and grew incredibly close; yet even during the day, if one pair desired privacy, the other two newlyweds seemed to sense this and quietly wandered off without comment.

"Seeing you again, I suddenly miss Snow Blossom," Summer confided to Singing Waters one day.

Singing Waters sighed happily. "I hope that someday soon Snow Blossom can find the love we have found, Summer Storm. Gray Rock has finally begun to court her seriously, and she is hoping he will offer for her before long. She loves him nearly as much as I love Two Arrows and you love Windrider.''

Summer made no comment to her friend's statement, but she sat quietly contemplating her words. While she had been very happy this past month, she had not considered herself in love with Windrider. Now Singing Waters' words suddenly pulled her up short and made her take a long look at herself and her situation. With some surprise, she realized that her friend was right. Somehow, someway, she *had* fallen in love with Windrider these past weeks, without ever realizing it. It had taken Singing Waters' innocent declaration to clear the fog from her mind, to make her see clearly what had been before her all the time.

A glorious sweetness filled Summer's heart, making it sing with happiness. Suddenly she could not wait to share her discovery with Windrider. How surprised and pleased he would be to learn of her new feelings for him—or perhaps not surprised, for he had vowed all along that he would capture her heart one day, but even he would be amazed that he had succeeded so soon and so easily. Yes, he had done as he had warned. He had won her completely: body, heart, and soul.

12

One full moon after Windrider and Summer had come to the hills, the entire tribe relocated to its winter quarters. Shortly afterward, November brought the first snows and winter settled in around them.

If Summer hated summers on the reservation, she detested winter. The cold winds howled around the tepee, and the bitter cold crept in around the edges no matter how carefully the bottom was tied down. Freezing temperatures and drifting snow made even short excursions impossible. Having heard tales of "cabin fever", Summer was positive that before spring came she would have "tepee fever" instead.

Outdoor fires were not practical now. All cooking had to be done inside, and everytime the entrance flap was opened, the sudden rush of air caused smoke to billow about the tepee instead of up and out the top draw hole. Even if she could cook elsewhere, the central fire was the only source of heat. Actually, if one discounted the inconvenience of stinging eyes and everything becoming smoke-blackened, the constantly fed fire kept the tepee comfortably warm as long as you stayed away from the drafty edges.

Other than feeding them, there was little Windrider could do with the horses now in the way of training. He spent a good deal of his time either in their own tepee, or the lodges of his friends. Often the men would all gather in the larger council lodge for days at a time. What they did there or talked about so long, Summer did not know. She suspected they gossiped every bit as much as the women did when they gathered together to sew.

While Windrider repaired saddles and halters and his weapons, Summer cooked and sewed. Together they spent many companionable hours, and between their chores came many wonderful hours of lovemaking. Once having admitted to him that she loved him, Summer could not seem to tell him often enough, and Windrider never tired of hearing her say it.

Windrider put his arrows and bridles aside long enough to fashion a pair of snowshoes for each of them. Summer was delighted! She detested being confined to the tepee so much of the time.

"You remind me of a plump brown duck!" Windrider chuckled as he watched her struggle along on her snowshoes for the first time. Bundled into a fur cape and leggings, she waddled blissfully ahead of him.

Summer threw him a dark look over her shoulder and nearly lost her precarious balance. "You are not the most graceful of persons on these things either. You look like a huge goose who is trying to learn not to walk pigeon-toed!"

"Pigeon-toed?" he asked laughingly.

"Yes," she said, and proceeded to try and demonstrate. "Like this." Awkward anyway on the novel devices, Summer had barely pointed her toes toward one another when her next step tripped her. Down she went headfirst into the powdery snow, a tangle of arms and legs and giant webbed feet.

Sputtering and spitting, she lifted her face to find Windrider doubled over with laughter, not the least bit concerned with whether or not she had been hurt. "You howling coyote!" she exclaimed. "I'll teach you to laugh at me!" Reaching out, she grabbed him by one ankle and pulled. Windrider teetered for a moment, trying to recover his balance, then toppled in a heap next to her.

For the next few minutes they rolled and wrestled in the snow, until Summer breathlessly surrendered. "You win!" she puffed, pinned beneath his superior weight. For good measure, she gave him one more jab in the ribs with her elbow.

"Oof! Woman, is this any way to treat your beloved husband?" His dark eyes laughed at hers even as they caressed her rosy wet face.

"Husband," she crooned, a smile teasing at her cool lips, "is this any way to treat your loving wife, who even now carries your first child?"

Every feature of Windrider's face froze as he stared at her in stunned silence. "Truly?" he whispered at last. "You are sure? You would not joke with me about something so important?"

Summer nodded. "I am positive. Have you not noticed how swollen my breasts have become, and they are so sensitive now." Her hands came up to touch his cold cheeks, her face suddenly very serious. "You have not said if you are pleased, my love."

"Oh, my little Earth Mother! I am pleased beyond words!" he assured her. Tenderly he brushed the snow from her face. "I love you," he murmured as his lips touched hers.

Long minutes later, her lips warm and tingling

from his ardent kiss, she answered softly, "I love you, too, Windrider. With all my heart, I love you."

According to Summer's calculations, their child would be born in mid-June, during the Summer Moon. With luck, her mother would be able to come from Pueblo in time for the birth. Summer hoped so, for she really wanted Tanya near when the baby arrived. She adored Windrider's mother, Shy Deer, but it was just not the same as having your own mother there when you needed her.

If Windrider was protective of her before, he was doubly so now. No longer would he allow her near the horses. He forbade her to shuffle about on her snowshoes unless he was there to accompany her. He even went so far as to suggest that his sister move into their tepee to help Summer with the heavier chores and to fetch water and firewood for her.

This was where Summer finally put her foot down. "Windrider, will you please stop coddling me so much? I am not ill; I am merely with child."

"With *my* child," he pointed out determinedly. "I do not wish for you to harm yourself or the babe. You should not be carrying heavy loads of kindling or hauling water from the river. What if you should trip, or slip on a patch of ice?"

"Fine, then Sweet Lark can do these chores for me during the day, if you insist, but I prefer that she spend her nights elsewhere."

"Why?"

"Why!" Summer gave her husband an incredulous look. With her hands on her hips, she faced him squarely, shaking her head in disbelief at how dense he could be at times. "Windrider, there are many weeks yet before we will have to cease our lovemaking. If Sweet Lark moves into our tepee, our time together will be shortened by far. Is this your wish? Do you no longer desire me now that I am to grow fat?''

"Summer Storm," he said, with exaggerated patience, "where does Sweet Lark sleep now?"

"In your father's lodge."

"Yes, and do you suppose my parents no longer make love?"

Summer frowned. "I suppose they still do. I don't really know. Why?"

"Believe me, Summer Storm, they do. And so would we, for I will always desire you, even when you are large with our child.''

"No, Windrider. If Sweet Lark comes into our tepee, we will no longer make love. I refuse to do so with my young sister-in-law just paces away from where we lie.'' Summer was prepared to defy him on this point. "I will not perform before an audience, like some trained bear!" she hissed.

Windrider was torn between anger and laughter. His young wife could be incredibly obstinate when she set her mind to it. "I cannot believe how modest you are in these matters!" he told her. "Or are you merely being stubborn now? It is not unusual for several families to share one lodge, or for servants or slaves to live with their masters. Even your mother accepted this, yet you were still conceived.''

"I am not my mother!" she shouted back. "I value my privacy, and I will not be swayed on this! If you insist on having Sweet Lark live with us, you will have to prowl elsewhere to satisfy your lusts! Perhaps you could spend your nights in the whores' lodge!''

Windrider was shocked that Summer even knew of the existence of this tent, let alone its purpose. Furthermore, any other Cheyenne wife would rather have cut out her own tongue than admit this knowledge to her husband.

Though some of the captives had been forcibly surrendered upon entering the reservation, most had not. As usual, the Army soldiers were too ignorant of the various tribes to distinguish one Indian from another. Therefore, nearly all slaves who were not obviously white had been overlooked. Even now, years later, the inhabitants of this tepee were the female children of their immoral mothers, following in their footsteps, though not always by choice. They were social outcasts, never to be accepted by the tribe except in this manner.

Of course, there were some Cheyenne women among them, those who had not prized their chastity or protected their virginity. By dishonoring themselves, they had cast their lot with the other women of loose morals. Now they gave their favors and services to the men of the tribe who frequented this tainted lodge in search of relief for their lusts. In return they received food or clothing as payment. It was their sole means of survival.

In his youth, Windrider had visited this lodge, for where else was he to gain carnal knowledge of a woman's body? How else was he to learn what pleased a woman or himself, and to test his male prowess? Good Cheyenne maidens were carefully protected, and it was forbidden to be together with one of them before marriage. Besides, like most Cheyenne men, Windrider would not have taken to wife a woman who valued herself so little.

"What need would I have to avail myself of their soiled services?" Windrider said now in response to Summer Storm's heated suggestion. "It would be much easier to merely take a second wife. She could help you with the women's work and be of service to me where you refuse."

His haughty tone grated on her, but his suggestion

was too much to bear. "You would not! You could not!" she exclaimed in shock and dismay, fearful that she had pushed him too far, and that he would seriously consider doing as he threatened.

"I could, and I would, if I wished. It would be wise if you would remember that we are not bound by rules of white society here, but by the Cheyenne code. Here a man may take as many wives as he can provide for, and his wives have no say in the matter. If I wanted a second wife, or a third, your objections would not stop me."

"Windrider, please do not do this!" Summer turned pleading eyes to him, tears swimming in their liquid gold depths. "I have tried to accept all the differences of the Cheyenne ways. Truly, I have, and it has not been easy for me. I am not accustomed to such a lack of concern for privacy. In time perhaps I will become used to this, too, but it is unacceptable to me now. Please do not ask Sweet Lark to share our lodge at night. Please do not take a second wife. This would break my heart, and I fear what it would do to my love for you."

"I need no wife but you, Golden Eyes," he confessed, pulling her near to his heart. "I want no other woman in my life. I spoke in anger."

"And Sweet Lark?"

"Sweet Lark need not sleep in our lodge," he relented. "She can help you during the day, but do not let me find you doing all the heavy chores yourself, or in she will come to stay, regardless of your shyness."

Of all the holidays, Christmas had always meant the most to Summer, not so much for its religious significance since her parents had tried to include all their inherited cultures into their children's lives, but for the gathering of the family members and the shared love. This first Christmas among the Cheyenne, who did not celebrate the Christmas holiday at all, was a lonely time for Summer. Never having been away from her family before, she was terribly homesick, and spending Christmas without them only saddened her more. Though she said nothing about it to Windrider, she was sure he noticed her forlorn attitude.

Christmas morning, Summer awoke with none of the usual expectancy of past years. Here it was just another winter day, nothing special at all. As she prepared breakfast for herself and Windrider, Summer wondered what her family was doing right now. Were they all gathered in the *sala* exchanging gifts? Were they sitting down at the big oak dining table to eat their own breakfast? Had Mark made it home from college for the holidays? Was her mother dashing back and forth from the kitchen, with a succulent turkey already roasting in the big oven? Had Dawn, the most religious of the family, gone to church with her grandparents?

Windrider had finished his morning prayer chant. A blast of cold air followed him into the tepee, making the fire blaze brightly for a moment. As his eyes adjusted to the dim light inside the tepee, his sharp gaze caught the sheen of tears in Summer's eyes. Having lived with her family for two winters, Windrider had experienced Christmas as Summer knew it. He knew that this was the day for the great Christian celebration, and he also knew how sad his wife was to be away from her family at this time.

With a secretive smile, he held out his hand to her. "Come, Summer Storm. There is something I wish you to see." Before they left the warmth of the tepee, he wrapped her fur cape snugly about her. Then he led her to the edge of the village, where the trees began.

Shy Deer and Sweet Lark were waiting for them, shivering and smiling in the crisp cold morning air. "What is all this?" Summer asked through chattering teeth.

Shy Deer and Sweet Lark stepped quickly aside, revealing the small pine tree directly behind them. Summer gasped aloud in her surprise, as the other three stood watching her in delight. Before her stood the tiny pine, gaily dressed in all manner of colorful Christmas decorations! Leather stars, and angels, little wooden drums and deer, dangled from its branches.

"Oh, how beautiful!" she exclaimed, bright tears flashing like miniature stars on her reddened cheeks. "How absolutely wonderful!"

"We wanted to make you less sad on this special day," Windrider explained tenderly. "I remembered your Christmas celebration from my times at your ranch."

"I also recalled some of your customs when Windrider told us of your loneliness. When your mother's friend, Melissa, felt as you do, Little Wildcat decorated a tree such as this for her," Shy Deer added gently. "Sweet Lark helped to make the pretty things to hang on the tree. We all want you to be happy here with us."

This was not to be the only surprise this day. Sweet Lark and Shy Deer had prepared a special feast for Summer Storm's Christmas dinner. Windrider admitted that it had taken him nours of hunting to finally find a wild turkey for the meal. The bird had been roasted to perfection, and along with it there was squash and sweet potatoes and a pumpkin pudding that passed for pie. It was the closest they could come to a traditional Christmas feast, and Summer was deeply touched by their thoughtfulness.

After all they had done to cheer her, Summer never expected more. When the meal was done, Singing Waters and Snow Blossom joined them. To Summer's surprise, they presented her with gifts they had made for her for this occasion. From Singing Waters there was a pair of rabbit-fur mittens, and from Snow Blossom a pair of matching leggings for winter. Then Shy Deer and Sweet Lark presented her with a soft new dress, gaily decorated with beads and quillwork.

"We made it bigger, for when you can no longer wear your other dresses," Shy Deer explained gently. Summer had known she would have to fashion herself some new clothes soon, to accommodate her burgeoning figure as the baby grew. She was grateful that the women had thought of it.

With pride, Winter Bear presented his daughter-in-law with a small wooden flute he had carved with his own hand. "One must always have music to brighten one's day," he told her with a smile.

Last of all, Windrider came forward with his offering. It was a hand-fashioned bridle that he had made for her and decorated with enormous care. Intricate patterns were designed along the wide straps and reins. Colorful quills alternated with decorous eagle feathers and ornate fringe. It was truly a work of art, and Summer was delighted with it. It would look absolutely beautiful on her horse, a symbol of her husband's love and pride for all to see.

"I did not pluck out any of War Bonnet's feathers to make this gift," Windrider was swift to tell her. "These are only what he lost naturally, and he gave them freely."

"I was wondering about that," she confessed with a guilty blush. The joyous smile she bestowed upon him should have melted the deep snow for miles around. "Thank you, Windrider. Thank you for making this a wonderful and most miraculous day."

Later, in the privacy of their tepee, she showed him the full measure of her gratitude and love.

Summer soon had reason to express her friendship in return. The following month, in the Moon When the Snow Drifts Into The Tepee, Snow Blossom and Gray Rock were wed. The families of the new couple had prepared the new tepee, and all of their friends had made gifts for their lodge. Summer took it upon herself to plan a special feast in their honor, something not always done unless the maiden or warrior was from a family of high rank in the tribe. With Singing Waters' help, and aid from Shy Deer and Sweet Lark, she arranged the celebration.

The morning of Snow Blossom's wedding day, the preparations were finished. Fresh pine needles had been spread on the floor of the ceremonial lodge, and all the food had been prepared. Everything was ready for the evening's festivities.

Later that morning, with their work done, the four women returned to their lodges to tend to their individual chores. As Summer had no need of her just then, Sweet Lark went with Shy Deer to their own tepee. No one took special notice of Morning Moon's malevolent gaze following their movements, or saw the evil smile that marred her features as she saw Summer Storm enter her tepee alone.

It was Singing Waters who first alerted them to the problem awaiting them. She came dashing to their lodges, calling excitedly to them. When Windrider and the women came out to find out what was wrong, Singing Waters exclaimed, "Someone has destroyed all our fine work! The ceremonial lodge is total confusion!"

As they soon saw for themselves, Singing Waters had not exaggerated. The place was a shambles! The big bowls of food had been overturned onto the ground, the central fire had been doused with water, and the fresh kindling wet down and scattered. Then the culprit had turned several camp dogs loose inside the lodge to create further destruction.

"Oh, no!" Summer wailed. "Look at this mess!"

"Yes, just look at it!" a voice behind them sneered. They turned to find Morning Moon glaring spitefully at them, the full force of her evil look directed toward Summer Storm. Entering the lodge with her were several of the council's high-ranking warriors and some very important women of the tribe. Winter Bear was with them, a deep frown of concern and confusion etching his brow.

Pointing an accusing finger at Summer Storm, Morning Moon announced loudly, "Here is your culprit! What will be a just punishment for such a wasteful and vile deed as this?"

A collective gasp rang among those gathered there. Singing Waters was the first to recover her tongue. "Are you mad, Morning Moon? Summer Storm is the one who planned and arranged this feast. She has worked very hard to see it done properly. Why would she destroy her own labors?"

"How should I know how her evil mind works?" Morning Moon retorted hatefully. "I only know what I have seen."

"And what is that?" someone asked.

"Just after all of you left this lodge this morning, I saw Summer Storm return alone, carrying two large buckets of water. With my own eyes, I saw her enter this tepee, and she was a long while inside. Much noise came to my ears as I stood outside. When she finally came out and walked away, I looked inside, for my curiosity was great. The lodge was as you see it now—in ruins. Just as I was about to run to tell someone of this, I saw Summer Storm coming back again. I hid around the side, and I saw her lead the dogs into the lodge. All this I witnessed with my own eyes!''

"This is a lie, Morning Moon! I never did any of what you claim!'' Summer was appalled at the other woman's hatefulness.

"Does anyone else know anything of this?'' Chief Winter Bear asked, his eyes narrowed thoughtfully at Morning Moon.

"Father, what Morning Moon has said cannot be true.'' Windrider, too, leveled a dark look at his wife's accuser. "Summer Storm returned to our tepee this morning at the same time as Mother and Sweet Lark. I heard them bid her good-bye as she entered, and they went on to your own lodge. From that time until now, Summer Storm has been with me.''

"You speak falsely to protect your wife, Windrider!'' Morning Moon declared. "You were with your father and Gray Rock at that time, in Gray Rock's new lodge. This I know for truth!''

Windrider's smile was ominous, a warning before his words cleared his mouth. "How is it that my comings and goings are of such importance to you, Morning Moon? If you had stayed but a moment longer, you would have seen me leave my father's side and return to my own lodge. I was there before Summer Storm arrived, and I was with her every moment since.''

Panic began to flow through Morning Moon at his words, and the color fled her face.

"My son's words are true. At the time you say this happened, he was no longer with Gray Rock and me.''

"That does not prove he returned to his lodge immediately,'' the woman was quick to point out.

Her nervousness increased tenfold as Shy Deer announced calmly, "He was there when I sent Sweet Lark to borrow a bone needle mere minutes after our return."

Sweet Lark added her testimony to her mother's. "Both he and Summer Storm were there, and Windrider was upset with me for interrupting just then."

Windrider favored his sister with a wry grin. "It was embarrassing to Summer Storm to be caught in such intimate circumstances, sister. You must remember to announce yourself before entering our tepee."

"Summer Storm could not possibly have done this!" Singing Waters declared vehemently.

"Agreed, but who did then, and why would she want to accuse Summer Storm of the deed?" At Winter Bear's statement, all eyes turned toward Morning Moon.

"And how did you know of this before anyone else?" Towering Pine spoke. "It was you who brought us all here."

"I told you! I saw her leave, and I was curious."

"You lie! Since the very day Summer Storm came to our camp, you have hated her merely because Windrider desired her, and not you!" Singing Waters' words rang clear to all who listened. "I have seen the spiteful looks you send her way, and now you dare to accuse her of your own vile deed! I would not be surprised to learn that it was you who tried to poison her before her wedding!"

"No! It is not true!" Morning Moon was frantic now, caught in her own deceitful web.

Winter Bear held up his hand for silence. "Morning Moon," he declared solemnly, "by your deceitful lies you have sought to dishonor another member of our tribe. This act was deliberate and malicious, done solely for personal benefit, and to harm your Cheyenne sister for no just cause. It is my judgment, as chief, that your untruthful tongue be immediately removed from your head. You have broken our code of honor, but never again will you malign another with your evil words.''

As Summer and the others watched, Towering Pine had already stepped forward and taken firm hold of Morning Moon's arms, forcing her to her knees before Summer Storm.

"No! No!'' the girl screamed, twisting and squirming frantically.

With calm deliberation, Windrider removed his hunting knife and placed it in Summer's hand, curling her fingers tightly about the handle.

Her shocked gaze flew to his. "Windrider, I cannot do this!'' she said weakly.

"You must. It was you she maligned with her evil tongue, and it is your duty now to carry out the punishment. At least her life has been spared, which is more than she would have done for you.'' His tone, while soft, told her more than his words. She had no choice in the matter. The Cheyenne laws were strict and unbending. If she were to keep the respect of the others, she must find the strength and the stomach to see her through this. There was no honorable way to refuse.

With trembling hand, Summer held forth the razor-sharp knife. The very thought of what she was about to do made her ill. While Windrider and Towering Pine held the screaming, struggling woman, Summer gulped back the bile that rose in her throat and set the knife. She tried to block out the sound of Morning Moon's strangled shriek of pain, and the agony on Morning Moon's face before the woman's eyes rolled back in their sockets and she fainted on the floor at Summer's feet. The awful deed was done!

In shock, Summer let herself be led to her tepee. Within its confines, she at last allowed herself to be ill. With no one but Windrider to see, she vomited violently until her retching stomach was empty. Still she could not stop shaking. She felt chilled from the inside out, as if she would never again be warm.

Vaguely she registered Windrider's concern as he removed her dress and blood-spattered moccasins and bathed her quivering body with fresh, clean water. "You must calm yourself, Summer Storm, or you could lose our child."

Wearily she nodded and closed her eyes, tears streaming down her cheeks and into her hair. "Burn the moccasins, Windrider," she whispered, knowing he would understand her reasons for never wanting to wear them again. On a trembling sob, she slept, at last successfully blocking out all that she had seen and done this day.

13

The remainder of the winter crept by. As the baby grew within her, Summer's body burgeoned until she felt like a huge overripe pumpkin. By the first of May, her stomach was so far out in front of her, that she hadn't seen her own feet in ages. She could balance her bowl on top of it to eat, if the child within did not decide to kick overhard. This the baby did with vigor, stretching the taut skin of Summer's belly until she was sure he would pop through with his sharp little elbows. The outline of a tiny foot or knee could often be recognized beneath the surface.

Winter finally released it tenacious grip, but slowly and reluctantly. This spring was wet and chilly, with only a few bright days and a barely perceptible warming. Summer thought spring would never come, as she had begun to wonder if her baby would ever arrive. She felt as if she had carried the child inside her forever. Her back ached, and she could no longer sit without something to lean back upon, and once she was seated, it took tremendous effort to rise again.

Ungainly and awkward, she indeed waddled like a duck now, even without snowshoes.

Summer spent the long hours sewing tiny garments for her expected child. With her flair for design, the miniature garments were darling. All her friends exclaimed over them. Singing Waters, who now carried her first child, begged Summer to help her with her own infant's clothing. The gaily decorated little dresses and moccasins, shirts and blankets, served to cheer the women as each awaited the birth of her firstborn.

Windrider also awaited his child's arrival with great anticipation. Like most men, he wanted a son; but because the child was of his and Summer's love, he would not complain if she presented him with a daughter. As he and Summer spent long winter evenings in their tepee, he fashioned an ornate cradleboard for the babe. With love and patience he carved an intricate pattern into it and decorated the straps with bright designs.

In late May, during the Moon When the Leaves Are Dark Green, the tribe decided that it was time to move again. The women needed to plant their summer crops, and the men to find fresh areas in which to hunt. With the child so near to being born, it was not a good time for Summer to move about. It was more than a day's ride to the new location the tribal leaders had chosen.

After deliberation, Windrider decided that the two of them would stay where they were until the child's birth. Then they would rejoin the tribe. Sweet Lark elected to stay with Windrider and Summer since Summer's great girth now so hindered her work.

Before the tribe left, Root Woman explained the birthing procedure in detail to each of them, offering advice and instruction for every possible problem.

SUMMER STORM

Having grown up with Nature's ways, Windrider was already familiar with most of this. So was Summer after so many years tending to animal births with Jeremy. Still, this was her first child, and it was a bit frightening to know that they would be far from help if anything should go wrong.

"Do not worry," Root Woman said before departing. "I tell you these things only so you can be prepared. Summer Storm's mother, Little Wildcat, will be arriving soon. She will tend to everything."

"What if she does not come in time?" Summer asked nervously.

Root Woman smiled secretively. "She will come," she repeated.

"How do you know this?"

"I know," Root Woman said simply.

When she had gone, Summer turned to Windrider. "How can Root Woman know that my mother will be here when our child is born?"

Windrider shook his head. "She is a strange one, and she has many times predicted what later came to pass. If she feels that Little Wildcat will be here, then most likely she shall be."

Four days later, Tanya and Panther rode into camp. Hunter and Dawn Sky had stayed behind at the ranch, but Mark would be coming as soon as college let out for the summer. Summer was ecstatic at seeing her parents again after so many months, and Tanya was overjoyed to learn that Summer was soon to present them with their first grandchild.

"You carry the child high and forward," she commented with a sure eye. "It will be a son."

"How can you be sure, Mother?"

"I know."

After Root Woman's prediction had come true,

Summer was not about to question her mother further.

It was a fortnight before Tanya's prophecy could be proven. The night was bright and clear, with a full moon and a million stars twinkling brightly against a backdrop of deep blue velvet. Summer knew none of this. Her pains had begun early in the evening. Now it was near midnight, the pains hard and fast, as she labored to bring their child into the world.

"Don't fight the pains, Summer," her mother counseled. "Flow with them as a leaf does in a river current."

"Now I know why they call it labor," Summer grunted through clenched teeth, trying to pant dog-like as her mother had advised.

"Scream if you want. There is no one here to condemn you. Your father and Windrider will not think less of you for it, though it might make poor Windrider even more nervous than he is already."

A small laugh coincided with the next pain, coming out as a strangled screech despite Summer's efforts to curtail it. When the pain had receded, Summer glanced weakly at her mother. "Please do not make me laugh again, Mother. It hurts too much."

Tanya smiled and tenderly mopped the perspiration from Summer's forehead. Her daughter was being so brave through this! Tanya's heart swelled with pride. Summer had come so far from the pampered, spoiled child she had been such a short time ago.

Another pain, sharper than the last, came and went. Summer's writhing body relaxed, gathering strength for the next wave. "Thirsty!" she whispered.

Tanya held a damp cloth to Summer's lips, letting her suck the moisture from it. It came away spotted with blood where Summer's teeth had cut into her lips. "Try not to bite your lips, sweet. Grind your teeth and pull at the leather straps, but don't bite your lips or tongue, or the insides of your cheeks.''

She adjusted the thongs she had arranged for Summer to pull on. ''It won't be long now, precious,'' she crooned. As Tanya adjusted the pile of supporting robes behind Summer's back, she wished that Sweet Lark could help; but being an unmarried maiden, it was inappropriate for the young girl to be in attendance.

''Oh!'' The surprised look on Summer's face alerted Tanya that something different was happening now. ''Mother!''

Tanya positioned herself at Summer's knees as the young woman came nearly upright with the pain. She aided Summer in drawing her knees upward. She could just see the baby's head.

''I need to push!'' Summer panted, her breathing hard and quick.

''Easy, Summer. On the next pain, take a deep breath and push hard and evenly.''

Summer did as she was told, though the pain felt as though it was tearing her in half. Once, twice more, she heaved forward, straining at the thongs and pushing with all her strength. On her pile of robes, with her arms wrapped tightly about her upraised knees, she gave a final, mighty shove. Summer felt the child slip from her body into her mother's waiting hands as she watched her baby's entrance into the world.

Drained of strength, she collapsed back onto the mat, her ears straining for her child's first cry as Tanya tended to the newborn infant. ''It's a boy,'' Tanya announced. ''A fine big son.'' Seconds later, a lusty wail filled the tepee, the sound carrying to those waiting outside.

Outside the tepee, Windrider and Panther awaited news of the birth. At the exact moment of the babe's first cry, a shadow moved slowly across the bright moon. Not another cloud was visible in the sky but this one lone shadow. Looking upward, Panther and Windrider beheld the shape of a brave walking across the surface of the full, round moon. According to Panther's calculations, it was now midnight; that breathless pause between one day and the next.

"This child shall walk between day and night; between a world of darkness and light, in the shadow of its blending," Panther predicted, interpreting what he had seen.

As his words drifted off on the night breeze, Tanya stepped from the tepee. "You have a son," she said to Windrider's anxious look. "A strong, healthy son."

"And Summer Storm?" he asked, his eyes turning toward the tepee.

"She is fine. Even now the child suckles at her breast." Tanya smiled gently. "Go to her, Windrider. Go feast your hungry eyes upon your new son and his mother."

When Windrider had ducked inside the tepee, Tanya leaned tiredly against her husband's side. "Our first grandchild, Panther," she sighed happily. "He is a beautiful babe."

Panther held her close to him, sharing her joy at this momentous occasion. "He shall be called Shadow Walker," he told her, "the one who walks softly between two worlds, in the shadow of life's way."

When Summer had recovered sufficiently to travel, the small family group joined the tribe in their new camp. While the men hunted, the women tended their crops and tanned the hides. They picked spring berries and early summer apples, drying them and storing them away for the next winter, when fresh fruit such as this would be but a fond memory. This new camp was a little better than the one of the previous summer, with more grass and trees, and Summer was thankful for this, at least. Day ran into day, and life for the Cheyenne went on as usual.

Then there came a slight but disturbing change. Word had come to the tribe about new action being contemplated by the United States government. Though they did not thoroughly understand what was being considered, they did know that it concerned all the tribes in the Indian Territory, known also as Oklahoma Territory, and their reservation lands. The main concern was that the government meant to steal yet more of their precious if poor lands.

Before long, the government sent a delegation to explain the proposed Dawes Act, or General Allotment Act, to the tribal leaders. Panther and Windrider, both educated in English and able to better understand the confusing document, attended the meetings. They came away with disturbed frowns on their faces.

"This Dawes Act has already been passed in Congress for over half a year," Panther explained as the men sat talking with their wives. "We had no say in the matter at all, as usual." The bitterness he felt was expressed in his voice.

"What does it mean for us?" Summer asked.

It was Windrider who answered. "It means exactly what we feared, though the white men have tried to make it seem just the opposite. They think if they say the words differently and sugarcoat the facts, we will be deluded into believing they are actually doing us a huge favor, when in truth they will be taking more of our lands."

"They come to us now seeking our smiling approval of that which they have already decided," Winter Bear added with rancor, "as though we are but

239

dumb cattle to be led about at their whim. Treaties mean nothing to them but what they can gain by them. Their word is as worthless as spit!" To emphasize his words, Winter Bear spat upon the ground, as if to rid his mouth of some rotten taste.

"How have they taken advantage of us this time?" Tanya asked dispiritedly. It seemed the Indian could never get the better deal these days, and yet the government still shook its head in wonder that the Indian was not more thankful for the privilege of being cheated. With each new treaty and broken promise Tanya was more sickened at the government's stupidity and greed.

"Under this new act, they wish to allot one hundred sixty acres of land to each adult Indian, and eighty acres to each child. In this way, so they say," Panther sneered, "the Indian will own his own plot of land and feel pride for it. The reservations will be divided up into individual farms, rather than a wholly-owned unit."

Shy Deer was obviously confused. "Why is this so terrible? We all know, as the white man fails to see, that whether owned by the tribe or by each person, the tribe will still stand as a whole. If their scheme is to disband the tribe, it will fail, for we are a closely-woven people."

"True, but what my mother fails to see is that, by doing so, we will be losing much of our land. Our numbers are not that great these days, and the allotment of land per person too little, to account for the total acreage we now hold." Windrider growled in disgust. "Yet again we are being cheated, while told with a smile how grateful we should be that the Great Father in Washington is looking after his Indian children!"

Panther nodded. "Added to that, the government

would hold actual deed to the land for twenty-five years. Only then would the titles be given into our hands, and we all know what disastrous changes can come about in a few short years, let alone twenty-five. It is just one more step backward for us if we accept this."

"To add insult to injury, they kindly advise us to work hard at becoming good farmers! Ach!" Winter Bear shouted, waving his arm at the poor land surrounding them. "As if this land could produce more than weeds and rock!"

His dark eyes flamed with broken pride and heartache. "I am a warrior," he exclaimed, "not a woman! Let the women harvest what serves our needs, for it is little and does no harm to the land. I will not scar the flesh of Mother Earth for miles with an iron plowblade and bleed her dry of her life. I will take only what she freely offers of her fruits, and hunt for my meat like a man!"

"If this act is already in effect, needing only our approval, what are we do to about it?" Tanya asked. "What if we do not sign this? Will they take our lands regardless?"

Panther smiled derisively. "Most likely, Little Wildcat. Most likely. For now we must stand our ground and refuse. If they go ahead without our approval, we can do little to stop them, though they break yet another in a long line of broken treaties. Our best defense against this is to ask the government to send someone of high rank to negotiate with us here. Then we must try to persuade them to our thinking."

"Will you do this, Father?" Summer questioned. "Officially, you are not registered as a resident of the reservation. For years now you have been known to others as Adam Savage, a Colorado rancher. How can you now represent the Cheyenne people without

241

forfeiting the ranch and all the influence you presently hold in the white world? You do too much good for our people from the outside to risk discovery now.''

Winter Bear nodded. ''Your daughter is wise to point this out, Panther. You cannot become involved in this except as Adam Savage. Perhaps you can wield some power through those local officials who know and respect you, but someone else among us must represent the tribe.''

''You are the obvious choice,'' Panther pointed out. ''You and I hold equal rank as chiefs. If I cannot do it, then you must.''

''Yes,'' Winter Bear agreed, ''If they come here I will talk with them. But if they want to meet elsewhere, it will not be I who goes, but Windrider. This is why I sent him to you for his schooling in the ways of the white people. Though I can mostly understand the words of the whites, Windrider is fluent in their language. He can read their written word, while I cannot. He knows their ways and will not be fooled so easily by their devious trickery.''

''It is a fine plan,'' Panther said. ''Do you agree, Windrider?''

The younger man nodded his agreement, ''I will go if need be. I will travel to the camp of our most hated enemy and count coup on him in the only way left to me as a Cheyenne warrior.''

''May I suggest something?'' Tanya asked politely, though she held the status of warrior herself and by virtue of that honor could speak among them freely anyway.

''Speak.''

''When Windrider goes to meet the white delegates, Summer Storm should travel with him.'' Tanya went on to explain her reasoning. ''Even educated as Windrider is, there are many white customs that will be strange to him. The white men seem to love to humiliate the Indian publicly, especially if the Indian is unaware of this humiliation. It sickens me to see them convince a great chief that he should dress as the white men do. Nothing looks more a fool than a warrior in a topcoat and stovepipe hat! Have they not done enough to degrade us without displaying us as ignorant buffoons?

"Summer Storm can prevent something of this sort from happening to Windrider. She was raised with whites and knows their manners and customs. She can make certain that they do not succeed in making a laughing stock of a fine Cheyenne warrior. With Summer Storm on guard for their wiles, they will have nothing to snicker about behind our backs while they smile at us with their other faces."

"Little Wildcat's words have value," Panther said. "These government fellows all have two faces and forked tongues."

"If Windrider agrees, his wife will accompany him," Winter Bear decided. "Perhaps she can see past their words to their hearts, while Windrider convinces them of our needs."

"While I do not consider myself ignorant of the white man's ways, I value my wife's opinion. It is true that she better knows their customs and rites, having lived among them for many summers. She will go with me if we must meet outside the reservation."

Summer was elated at their high esteem of her. Her smile was wide and proud. "'Does this mean that I, too, can count coup and become a warrior?" she asked jokingly.

Everyone laughed at this, herself included. Then, surprisingly, Winter Bear said, "If you can learn to ride and track and hunt and fight as well as our warriors, as your mother did, then you can count coup on our enemies at this meeting. Since our warriors can no longer war with other tribes or count coup in battle, this manner will be sufficient. Do this, and your father and I will gladly bestow upon you the title of a warrior.''

Summer's mouth flew open in astonishment. ''Truly?''

Both chiefs nodded, chuckling at her surprise, while Windrider stood torn between pride and amusement at his stunned wife. ''You have our word as chiefs,'' Panther told her.

Her smile, wide before, now nearly split her face, lighting it with joy and making her big golden eyes glow with delight. ''I will do it!'' she exclaimed. ''If Windrider will teach me, I will learn all I need to know.'' Her questioning gaze sought her husband's.

''Yes, Wife of My Heart,'' he answered with a loving look. ''I shall gladly teach you all that I know. But I will warn you now that I will not be lenient. I shall be a hard master, and you must learn your lessons well or forget your fine ambitions altogether.''

Summer could hardly believe that this was happening. ''I will work hard, Windrider,'' she promised. ''I will make you proud of me.''

''I am already proud of you,'' he assured her.

''Then I will make you even more proud, my husband.''

Summer began her lessons immediately, determined to be prepared when, and if, they had to meet with officials from Washington. Meanwhile, the tribal council rejected the Dawes Act, and the government delegation had sent word to Washington, awaiting a reply on what to do next.

Day after day, in addition to her usual chores and tending to Shadow Walker, Summer applied herself to learning the skills of a warrior. True to his word, Windrider was a tough instructor, and when he did not have time to teach her, Tanya took over. After all the years on the ranch, Tanya felt that by helping her daughter she was also honing her own dulled skills. Tanya was, perhaps, tougher on Summer than Windrider.

Summer already knew how to ride. Now she learned how to ride Cheyenne style. She began to think she spent more time along the sides of her horse than she did upon the mare's back. When she had learned to ride without benefit of saddle or reins, guiding the mare with her knees and leaving her hands free for her weapons, she then learned to lay herself flat along her horse's back and sides, using the animal's body as a shield. Mastering that, she was taught to leap upon the back of her horse from either side at a dead run, to mount a moving horse, to drop from above onto the horse's back, and to kneel or stand on the galloping mare's back. Then she did the exact opposite; learning to dismount a moving horse, to leap at an enemy from her mare's back, and to transfer herself from one running animal to another without injury to herself.

This took weeks and weeks of diligent practice. It definitely was much harder than she'd thought, and Summer had muscles aching in places they'd never ached before. In fact, her entire body felt as if it had been beaten with rocks, and she could barely move without groaning aloud in pain.

"Why did I ever decide to attempt this?" she groaned miserably.

"Are you admitting defeat?" Windrider goaded. "If it is too difficult, we need not continue. You can give up this idea any time you wish."

"Never! I shall become a warrior if it kills me!"

Summer added quietly to herself with a silent goan, "And it just might!"

The easiest of her lessons was learning how to shoot both bow and arrow and rifle. Her father had insisted that all of his children learn how to use firearms for defense around the ranch. Her naturally inherited skill and accurate aim helped her here, and she actually enjoyed these practices. However, when she had to combine these skills with riding, and hit her target from the back of a racing horse, it was a true test of her abilities. Then there were lessons with knife, lance, and tomahawk. The degree of difficulty increased, but Summer still liked these lessons best.

The first time Windrider took her hunting, Summer nearly burst with excitement. Her quick mind soon learned the art of distinguishing one animal's tracks from another. Here her veterinary knowledge of various animals aided her speed in learning. Her keen eyesight and sense of smell held her in good stead as well.

The truly difficult thing was learning to sit absolutely still for hours at a time. This was compounded by the fact that Summer was still nursing her newborn son. When they could, they took Shadow Walker with them, hanging his cradleboard from the pommel of Summer's saddle. When the child had to be left behind, Tanya cared for him, and he was nursed by one of the other women. This did not help Summer's predicament at all, since her breasts would soon fill with milk and begin to ache—and sitting still was ten times more miserable then.

Not only did Windrider teach her to track and hunt, he taught her how to avoid being tracked. To move quietly and easily, without disturbing the elements about her, and without leaving telltale signs or footprints, was most difficult for her. While not ungraceful, neither had she ever paid particular attention to walking as softly or carefully as this skill required. This was, perhaps, the most difficult of her required teachings.

When, weeks later and at long last, she could evade both her mother and Windrider, she had passed the test. Then, to try her skills further, Summer was required to track and find her own father, whose skills were revered throughout the Cheyenne tribe. She did manage to track him, up to a point. Then, when she was certain she had lost him and was about to give up, she caught just a glimpse of the blue of his headband among the thick brush.

"You have learned well, daughter," he commended her.

"It was more luck than anything else, Father. I spotted your headband, or I would never have known you were there."

"Then it was my own carelessness that disclosed my position," he decided. "I must be getting lax, indeed, to have forgotten such a thing. Still, it was your own skill that led you to me."

Another required skill, which Tanya and Panther took charge of teaching her, was the art of hand-to-hand combat. This particularly intrigued Summer, who had always naturally assumed that a woman was incapable of matching a man's superior strength. She soon learned differently. It was a matter of balance, of properly distributing one's weight, and leverage.

"Always keep your eyes on your opponent's," Panther instructed. "This is the first and most important rule to remember. By his eyes, you can read his intentions, anticipate his every move. Contrarily, you must learn to conceal your own emotions from your face. If you can foretell your combatant's moves, yet surprise him with your own, victory will soon be yours. This will only be so, however, if you can also learn the proper moves and counterattacks.''

Hours—and days—of practice ensued. Over and over again, Summer met defeat at her parents' hands. Ever so slowly, aching bones, sore muscles, bruises and all, she improved. Then, one day, she surprised all three of them by throwing and pinning Tanya to the ground.

''Mother! Are you hurt?'' Summer exclaimed, thinking surely that was the only reason she could have defeated her mother.

''Would you ask your enemy such a ridiculous question?'' Tanya grumbled as she picked herself up and dusted herself off.

Summer blushed. ''No, but I was concerned. Why did you not anticipate my move, as you usually do?''

Tanya grimaced as she rubbed her bruised hip. ''Because you have finally learned to hide your emotions from me. I did not suspect what you intended. It came as a complete surprise.'' This was high praise, indeed, from her demanding mother/instructor.

Summer's final triumph was defeating Windrider in a private match viewed only by their parents. As he had not been involved in this aspect of her training, he made the initial mistake of underestimating her skills. That error landed him flat on his back in the dust as she effortlessly flipped him over her hip. He recovered quickly, however, and from then on the conflict was more evenly matched. Warily they circled one another, ever watchful of an opening. Both scored points at various times, but neither could gain the edge or pin his opponent for long.

Then Windrider managed to trip her and fall full-length upon her as she lay upon her back. His hard body covered the full length of hers, his large hands clamped tightly over her shoulders. A victorious grin began to spread itself across his handsome face.

It was then that Summer realized something very significant. She could still move her feet far enough to maneuver her ankles about his. This she did, at the same time grasping his own shoulders tightly. Then, before he had time to realize what she meant to do, she rocked quickly twice; and with the deceptive strength of a ballerina, rolled him forward over her head and onto his back, following him over as he went. She was now on top of him, but unlike his pose, she had made sure that she unlocked their legs at the precise moment. This allowed her to fall upon him, her knee coming down hard upon his chest and knocking the air from his lungs. Windrider was senseless just long enough for her to win the contest.

Later, in their tepee, Windrider rubbed his sore stomach, where her bony knee had practically speared him. "It is a good thing your aim was not lower, Summer Storm," he complained, "or our son would be our only child."

"My knee came down exactly where I intended it to," she told him. "Besides, as someone once said, 'All is fair in love and war'."

"Which was this?" he grumbled.

Summer gave him a beauteous smile. "I could never really make war against you, Windrider, so it must be love."

Her smile was having its intended effect. Windrider reached for her, pulling her down next to him on their sleeping mat. His fingers threaded through her unbound silken tresses as he brought her face to his for his kiss. "Try not to love me so vigorously in future, my lovely young wife, or I may not survive your intense affections."

Then all thought of conflict was forgotten as he

molded his lips to hers. In this encounter, she let him take the lead, gladly following him move for move. Their tongues danced and mated, even as their bodies writhed and twined. Loving hands tenderly stroked and discovered countless points of sensuality. Lingering caresses were heightened by sensuous kisses that had both of them unashamedly quivering with desire.

Windrider's big hands shook with tempered need as they tenderly cupped her cheeks, watching her face as he slowly joined his body to hers. Summer's eyes widened with passion, and then her eyelids fluttered closed in ecstatic pleasure as he moved fully, and with infinite slowness, into her. He did not rush their pace, but employed deliberately languid strokes designed to enhance their desire, measured to tantalize them both to the brink of insanity, where pleasure was so intense it was nearly unbearable. Their rapture rose to unbelievable heights before it eventually burst upon them, swathing them in a glowing ecstasy that shook their very souls. Muted cries echoed in the night as the two lovers claimed mutual victory in a battle neither could lose.

14

It had taken Summer over two long months to complete her training satisfactorily. During that time, the tribal leaders awaited word from Washington concerning the Dawes Act. Meanwhile, much was happening.

For one thing, Mark had arrived, reporting that all was well at the ranch. Hunter and Dawn had everything under control there. Mark had offered to bring Dawn with him for a visit, but she had declined, sending her love via Mark instead.

"Does she have a beau?" Summer asked. "Is that why she prefers to stay at home?"

Mark shook his head. "No, I don't think so, though Steven Kerr comes around quite a bit. You know, Summer, I think our baby Dawn may be leaning toward a religious vocation."

Summer blinked twice. Surely she hadn't heard her brother correctly! "What did you say?"

"You heard me perfectly. It really shouldn't come

as such a surprise to any of us. After all, she has always been the most religiously inclined of our immediate family.''

''Wait, Mark. Just exactly what are you saying? How serious is this? Does Dawn want to be a missionary, or a minister's wife, or just sing hymns and play the organ? What?''

Mark pursed his lips and shuffled nervously from one foot to the other. Summer couldn't recall ever having seen him this unsure about anything. Calm, steady Mark was really upset. ''She thinks she wants to be a Sister of Mercy—a nun.''

''Holy Moses!'' Summer exploded, completely stunned. ''Do Mother and Father know about this?''

Mark shook his head. ''She intends to discuss it with them when they come home.''

''Oh, Mark! Father will have raving fits! And Mother . . . well, I can't begin to guess what she will think!''

''Maybe it won't be as bad as we think,'' Mark suggested. ''If this is what Dawn really wants, who can say it won't work out? She certainly has the sweet, gentle disposition required for the work. She would probably make a very good Sister and be very happy at it.''

''Perhaps. Who can say? I will tell you this for certain. I can see Grandmother Rachel's fine hand in this! She is probably singing in the streets at this very moment!''

This brought a reluctant grin to Mark's face. ''You are probably right, Summer.''

''Well, I hate to see Dawn do this,'' Summer said on a sigh, ''but if she has her heart set on it, I wish her all the luck in the world, particularly when it comes to convincing Mother and Father. With you away at school and me here, Hunter and Dawn are the only ones they get to see regularly. They aren't going to want Dawn leaving, too.''

"At least they'll be in a happy mood when they leave here, having gotten to see their first grandchild born,'' Mark said, a smile creasing his face. "I've never seen a more beautiful baby, Summer.''

"As an uncle, you are prejudiced,'' Summer chuckled.

"And as a doctor, I say Shadow Walker is perfect.''

Summer eyed her brother skeptically, holding back the urge to laugh. "If your new nephew is so perfect, then why is he always springing a leak and wetting through his clothes and everyone else's?'' she teased.

"Aw, Summer you know you are so proud of him you could dance on air.''

"You're right,'' she admitted. "He is a most marvelous baby.''

"And Windrider?'' Mark asked hesitantly.

"He is a most marvelous husband.'' The loving glow on Summer's face as she spoke of Windrider told Mark all he needed to know. Summer was more than content; she was truly in love.

Mark was in love, too, though he tried to be less obvious about it. The primary reason for his visit this year was not to see his sister or his friends. He had come to see Sweet Lark. Since last summer he had been taken with her, and all year he had not been able to shake her from his mind.

Sweet Lark was young yet, just fourteen, but in another year she would be of marriageable age. Then, as lovely as she was, all the eligible braves would be wanting to court her. Every time Mark thought of this, he wanted to scream with jealousy. He had three more tough years of schooling ahead of him yet. By the time he was finished, Sweet Lark would most likely be married to someone else and have a child already. In reality, she could be wed by the time he returned to the camp next year.

Mark knew he had to do something. Though he could not marry her now, or for the next three years if he wanted to be practical, he could not bear to think of losing her to someone else. He loved her too much.

His one hope was that his father could arrange something with Winter Bear, as they had done before for Summer and Windrider. If Sweet Lark and he were promised to one another, then perhaps he could return to school in the fall and not worry so.

Of course, a lot depended on Sweet Lark. At this point, Mark could not be certain how the girl felt about him, but no matter how much he loved her, he would not marry her if she did not care for him at all. He would never force himself into her life if it would make her unhappy. However, if Sweet Lark were to agree, Mark knew it would make him the happiest man alive.

Even with her work and her training to become a warrior, Summer made time for her young son. She adored him, from the top of his downy black head to the tips of his tiny toes. To her he was perfect—a wonderful miracle created from the love she and Windrider shared. She never tired of looking at him.

"His skin is as soft as velvet, especially deep down in his neck," she said, wrinkling her nose into that very spot and making Shadow Walker gurgle. "And his hair is like black goose down."

Tanya agreed with an indulgent laugh. "When he is grown, he will resemble his father. Already you can see that he has Windrider's forehead and chin."

"And his noble nose and straight, serious lips," Summer added.

"Let us hope he inherits Windrider's even temperament," Panther jibed, sending Summer a teasing smile.

Windrider laughed at Summer's less-than-amused look. "My son may have most of my features, but he wears his mother's golden eyes. Already they glow with such intensity and intelligence that it amazes me."

"He *is* a smart little squirrel, and so active already," Shy Deer put in. "Already he notices bright objects and follows them with his eyes. This morning he smiled at me and waved his arms for his grandmother to pick him up."

"Indigestion," Mark corrected gently. "At six weeks, he isn't smiling, he has air bubbles in his tummy."

Sweet Lark shook her head. "No, Mark. Regardless of what they teach you in that doctor's school, Shadow Walker smiles. He also laughs, and he plays with his hands."

"When he was left on the mat earlier, he lifted his head clear of the robes and held it upright for several moments." Summer defended her son's achievements. "Just yesterday he rolled from his back onto his side."

"He is a remarkable child, so bright and alert for his tender age." Shy Deer smiled down on her young grandson. Then her eyes met Winter Bear's in shared joy. "I can only hope the child I now carry will be so blessed."

Following Shy Deer's quiet announcement it seemed everyone in the lodge was suddenly and simultaneously struck dumb. Tanya was the first to recover. "Shy Deer, that is wonderful news!" Her topaz eyes shone with happiness for her friend. Shy Deer had long hoped for another child, and now, when she was almost too old to bear one, she was to have her heart's wish.

"I shall make you a dress, as you did for me," Summer promised with a surprised smile. "And I shall see that you do not overwork yourself. Sweet Lark and I shall take very good care of you and this most wondrous child."

Sweet Lark readily agreed. "It will seem strange, though, that my nephew will be older than my brother. Why, my own children will be only slightly younger." Her shy, doe-like gaze slid modestly in Mark's direction, then slipped hastily away as he met her look with burning curiosity. Over their heads, Winter Bear and Panther shared a secret, satisfied look.

Windrider gave his mother a tender smile. "Your news surprises and delights me, Mother. When can I expect to welcome my new brother or sister into the world?"

"In the spring, around the time of the Bud Moon —in the same season as you were born to us, my son."

"It is a good time for sons to be born," Winter Bear concluded confidently. "You shall have the brother you always longed for, Windrider, even though he will not be much of a playmate for you, with so many years between you."

"No, but I will love him nonetheless, and my own son shall be his playmate."

Among the women, babies seemed to be the main topic of conversation for the next several days. Shy Deer's extraordinary news was exclaimed over time and again. Then Singing Waters delivered a strapping son who promised to tower over his father, if his long legs were any indication. Two Arrows immediately named him Long Feather.

It was during this hot, dry early part of August, when the only breeze seemed to sizzle across the land in shimmering waves of heat, that another curious occurrence came about. Ignored for the most part by the white men and soldiers who had relegated them to the reservation, the tribe was now suddenly of great interest, it seemed.

First the delegation in favor of the Dawes Act returned to try yet again to persuade the tribal leaders to accept the terms of the document. Failing this, they returned to Fort Reno, but often visited the tribe, wanting to maintain friendly relations with the Cheyenne. Each time they came, a small troop of soldiers would accompany them out from the fort.

Then came the government agent to inspect conditions on the reservation. In all the time the tribe had been here, they had seen an agent perhaps a total of six times. Why the government was so concerned with the Cheyenne now was anyone's guess.

"Perhaps, with a new treaty being presented to us, they wish to show good intention by at last upholding the terms of our old agreement," Winter Bear suggested warily.

"They are many seasons too late, if that is their thinking," Windrider said. "Where were all the blankets and cattle and seed and supplies when we needed them? Do they think they can soothe our anger now by pretending interest where none was shown before? They put on a false face and expect us to believe, as foolish children would.''

Along with the agent came others. There were advisors to teach them how to properly till the earth, how best to plant and reap the crops. Still others gave advice on raising cattle or sheep. There was a blacksmith to show them how to form and repair farm implements, and how to set up their own forge.

The Cheyenne men turned a deaf ear to all this. The United States could send instructors until the great mountains turned to sand, and it would do the government little good. Warriors were meant to hunt and fight, not grow crops. The idea of ranching appealed only slightly more than farming, though they could see the sense in replacing the diminished wildlife with cattle. However, they would tend to their own cattle in their own way, and if they decided to raise sheep they would do so in their own time.

In the wake of these advisors came preachers, and teachers, and missionary women. This sudden onslaught of white intruders onto the reservation was confusing, upsetting, and extremely irritating. There was little to be done about it, however, since soldiers had been assigned to guide them to the camp and guard them against harm. The government had ordered it, and the Indians had to endure this interruption in their lives until the whites became uninterested once more.

''Their concern will not last,'' Panther predicted. ''Soon they will tire of trying to teach what we do not want to learn. Then they will go and leave us to our own ways once more.''

''Why do they bother at all?'' Summer asked. ''Why now, after ignoring us for so long and failing to uphold the terms of the treaty all these years?''

"It has to do with their plans for this Dawes Act," Windrider explained. "Once the reservation is broken into individual plots and farms, they wish us to remain peaceful and productive. I heard one man speaking with the agent. They were saying that officials of the Oklahoma Territory are preparing for the time when they will petition for admittance to the United States as a state. It is to their benefit to display us as farmers and peaceful landowners."

"I see," Summer said, her own voice laced with disdain. "So they send teachers to educate us, preachers to convert us, and missionaries to show us the error of our ways."

Winter Bear nodded. "They think to divide our land and our people, to replace our own customs with their own, and reform us into their own image."

Tanya laughed scornfully. "They think to erase the Indian from the earth, as if he had never been here to begin with. It is their way of easing their guilty consciences I suppose, if they have them." She flung her arm out in a dramatic gesture, tears of bitterness swimming in her eyes. "Behold! The savage has been tamed!" she exclaimed. "He has been remolded, converted and properly trained! He is now a common, placid, ordinary citizen. Behold what wonders the white man hath wrought!"

Her emotional outburst echoed what lived in each of their hearts: all the smoldering hatred, all the untempered disdain and resentment that lay just below the surface of seemingly resigned attitudes.

Summer had her own personal encounter to deal with a few days later. Sitting outside her lodge with Singing Waters and Snow Blossom, the three young women were talking and working together in the hot sun. While Shadow Walker and Long Feather hung in their cradleboards in the shade of the overhang, the women were softening pieces of tanned deerhide to make into new moccasins.

The day was hot and still, with barely a breeze from the river. The air hung heavily, laden with moisture that stifled and sapped the energy from every living thing. Far off, beyond the horizon, a storm was brewing. Though the clouds could not yet be seen, every Cheyenne could read the signs well. Before the coming night was done, Nature would display her awesome power in a summer thunderstorm. It would be a welcome relief after weeks without rain. They could only hope the storm would not be over-violent, deluging the parched land with such a hard, driving downpour that flooding occurred. What they needed was a good steady rain, the kind that lasted all night, refreshing the land and restoring lifegiving moisture.

The unrelenting heat was almost unbearable. Sweat ran in rivulets between Summer's breasts and down her soaked back. With a gesture of impatience, she blew at the damp strands of hair that clung to her face, despite the fact that she had carefully plaited her hair that morning to keep its length off of her neck.

"I wish I had some sugar candy made," Summer commented offhandedly. "I would gladly trade some of it, if one of the children would stand in front of me and fan me with a blanket—anything to create a breeze!"

"When we are finished here, let us take the babies and go down to the river and swim," Singing Waters suggested. Just the thought of the water, even as tepid as it was now, was deliciously tempting.

"Are you not afraid the fish demons will attack

you?'' Snow Blossom teased her friend. While most of their tribe learned to swim, there were still those, especially the older members, who believed that the evil spirits of wicked women transformed into fish when they died. They would attack the unaware and gobble up small children. Many Indians would not swim except when absolutely necessary, and would not eat fish unless they were starving, for fear that the evil demon would enter their bodies and possess them.

"It is not the fish demons I would beware of," Singing Waters said, "so much as being seen by one of the white men who wander about the camp so freely. Have you noticed how they leer at us so lustfully, even when our men are near to see their looks? It is a wonder Two Arrows has not sliced a throat or more already!"

"Windrider has warned me to be wary of them. While they are here, I do not leave the village seeking firewood by myself, as I often did before. It is safer and wiser to walk together, two or three of us at least." Summer sighed irritably. "This annoys me that their lack of respect hinders our usual movements, but it would be foolish not to fear what we see on their faces; just as it would be foolish to be forced to kill one of them in defense of our honor. It is best to avoid trouble of that sort, if possible; just as one circles in a wide arc to avoid a rattlesnake, rather than walk in front of it and risk being bitten."

As they sat talking, a group of white women approached them. One of them Summer recognized as a teacher. Another was the wife of one of the soldiers. The other two were from the Christian Missionary Society. To Summer the last two seemed like drab black crows in their dark dresses, their hair pulled back into severe, unattractive buns. Their voices drifted ahead of them to Summer and her friends.

"I can't believe people would live this way!" The old missionary lady wrinkled her nose in disgust. "You would think these people had never heard of soap and water, or even a broom! The filth of this place makes my skin crawl!"

Though she did not raise her head from her work, the woman's words had caught Summer's attention. Nostrils flared in anger at the white woman's critical remarks, she listened carefully as the teacher replied, "That is why we are trying so hard to educate them, Mildred, so the younger ones will not follow in the same ignorant footsteps of their elders. Once they truly understand the need for cleanliness, I'm sure they will seek to better their living conditions considerably."

Summer snorted softly, her lip curled up scornfully. The small sound drew her friends' attention. Reluctantly, she translated the women's comments. Then she added, "Do they think a piece of soap will dispel the dust of this dried earth, or the mud that turns the land into quagmires in the spring? Will it give life and color to this barren land the whites have so benevolently allotted us? Will it grow crops from poor soil and make trees and grass grow more abundantly? Will it replace the buffalo and game that once roamed here so freely—that sustained our families so richly before the white man's touch destroyed it all?"

The soldier's wife was speaking now. "Frank says that if these people would just learn to farm, and stop trying to live as they have in the past, they would be able to feed and clothe themselves properly. They are not prone to change, or to hard work, for that matter; otherwise they would build decent cabins in which to live, instead of these crude shelters they have now."

"And what would we use for lumber?" Summer mumbled beneath her breath. "Or would the government supply that as efficiently as it did the blankets and food that have never been delivered as promised?"

"Like as not, we are wasting our time and money trying to educate these savages. I don't know about you, but it gives me the shivers every time one of those naked warriors glares at me with those hard dark eyes. It's like looking into the face of the Devil himself!" This from Mildred, who had a face that would stop a ten day clock.

"As if she needed to worry about being ravaged!" Summer thought, rolling her eyes in disgust. "She looks as if she were rode hard and put away wet! Any brave in his right mind would rather slit his own throat than lay with her!" This she told her friends after again translating the missionary's words.

Though they pretended ignorance and went on with their work, the three Cheyenne women listened avidly. They knew that the white women would never speak so candidly if they suspected their conversation was being understood and related.

Suddenly the younger missionary spoke up. "Oh, look!" she exclaimed. "Babies! Oh, aren't they darling?" She stepped forward eagerly to get a better look at the two infants.

"All animals are cute when they are young," Mildred said curtly. "It is when they are grown that they become dangerous." She pulled the girl away. "Don't touch them. They are probably alive with lice and vermin."

Summer's temper fairly sizzled, and it was all she could do to sit quietly and pretend to ignore the woman's blatant hatefulness.

"They are not animals, Millie," the younger girl defended. "They are human beings, the same as you and I. They are merely less fortunate."

"Think what you like," Mildred replied. "Preacher James is right when he says that without God, they are all hellbound demons, big or little. Given the chance, any one of them would slit your throat in a minute, and not blink twice. Besides, they live like rats and breed like rabbits. They are ravaging beasts, with no remorse. After the atrocities they have inflicted on white settlers, they deserve no better than they have now. I say let them rot in their own filth, and good riddance if it kills them!"

Summer had had more than enough. She'd had a belly full of this crude, rude woman. She could remain silent no longer. Her eyes flashed golden daggers as she drew herself up to face the four women. Aware that their friend was more furious than they had ever seen her, Singing Waters and Snow Blossom rose to stand beside her, ready to defend Summer if need be.

Proud and regal, her face a mask of unleashed fury, Summer Storm glared at the woman called Mildred. "You!" she hissed. "You self-righteous bitch! How dare you wear the mantle of Christianity when your dark heart is filled with more venom than the most poisonous of snakes!"

At her words, spoken in clear and precise English, four sets of eyes grew wide in amazement, and four jaws hung open. "Why, you're white!" the teacher exclaimed in astonishment.

"I am Cheyenne," Summer corrected haughtily, drawing herself up to her full height, her head proudly erect.

"But your eyes!"

Overcoming her own surprise somewhat, the soldier's wife shook her head. "No, Vera," she said quietly. "It may not mean she's white. Many of the soldiers have bedded Indian women."

"But she speaks such perfect English! How can she not be white?" Vera argued, her eyes searching Summer's features.

"Your friend is mistaken," Summer sneered. "My father is a Cheyenne chief, not a lowly cavalry soldier."

The younger missionary gasped. "Then your mother had to be white. Oh, how dreadful! How awful for her!"

"Save your pity for someone who wants it, white woman. My mother will proudly claim that she, too, is Cheyenne. Here she comes now. Ask her for yourself, if you doubt my words."

Four heads turned toward the woman walking serenely toward them. A collective gasp echoed between them as they immediately saw her gleaming wheat-colored hair, and the same set of golden eyes she had bequeathed to her daughter.

Tanya stopped next to Summer. "What is happening here, daughter?" she asked in Cheyenne.

Briefly, Summer explained about the women's derisive comments and her own righteous anger. "I could not help it, Mother. I could take not one more word from that she-dog's vile mouth."

Tanya nodded, her own anger rising at some of the things Summer had repeated. "You are right to defend your family and your friends."

Turning to the white women, Tanya said calmly, yet forcefully, "My daughter has told me the things which you have said. You could not be more wrong in your thinking. Rather than you coming to convert and instruct the savages, perhaps we should be teaching you. At least we know when to speak and when to hold our tongues. It may also serve you well to remember that, though our lot may not now be a pleasant one, this was not always so. Once we were a rich people, rich in land and freedom. At one time, every bit of this nation you call America belonged to the tribes, to my people. Bit by bit you have pushed us from it, until we are left only with what you see about you—the most meager of lands, lands so poor the white man disdains to claim it.

"Yet we ask not for your pity, or even your help," Tanya continued, pride lancing every word. "You come, you see, you conquer," she misquoted, "yet you destroy more than you gain. It is you who deserve the pity, for you do not know how to care for that which you now claim. There will come a day when you regret your carelessness and lack of respect for the land. I can only hope that I do not live to see it; not for your sakes, but for the land which has been scarred and bled and will die beneath your neglecting hands."

"You may be right," the teacher conceded, "but how can you speak as if you are one of these people? You are obviously as white as any of us."

Tanya shook her head. "No. I am Cheyenne. My children and grandchildren shall be Cheyenne. My heart and soul are Cheyenne. This is so and shall always be."

"Hogwash!" Mildred the missionary exclaimed. "You are nothing more than a filthy savage's squaw—a hell-bound, low-life harlot!"

Tanya whirled to face the foul-mouthed woman, her eyes flashing golden fire. Summer was already confronting the missionary, her knife drawn and held threateningly before her. "One more vile word from that viper's tongue of yours, and I will slice it from your mouth," she growled, her eyes narrowed into glowing slits. "I have done so before, and I would not hesitate to do so again—with much more pleasure."

"And I will force it down your hateful throat until you choke on it," Tanya added vengefully, "along with your pious Christian religion that you defile by your every word and action."

White-faced and trembling, the four women backed slowly away. Mildred's fear-glazed eyes never left the knife in Summer's hand. At last they turned and scurried hurriedly on their way.

"That's right, Mildred!" Summer called tauntingly after them. "Run and hide under the very rock from which you slithered, and never dare to show your face here again."

"Savages!" they heard one of the women say. Tanya and Summer looked at one another and burst out laughing. "Yes, Savages!" Tanya agreed on a chuckle. "We Savage women are tough to deal with!"

"Grandmother Rachel certainly knew what she was doing when she chose our surname!" Summer agreed. "Nobody runs roughshod over us and walks away unscathed!"

In that moment Tanya and Summer shared a feeling of intense pride and family loyalty. More than that, they shared a mutual respect for one another, and a deep sense of honor and love for the Cheyenne heritage that bound them both.

15

Summer sat at the entrance of the tepee and watched the storm break around her. Ahead of the rain, the wind came, fierce and strong, heralding the arrival of the storm itself. Lightning adorned the sky with jagged blue-white streaks, and thunder roared like a wounded bear, shaking the earth with its tremendous growl. Then the rains came, pounding down upon the earth like a drummer gone berserk.

Ever since she could recall, Summer had loved storms. Perhaps it was because she had been born in the midst of one, because they were her namesake, but she had always been drawn to them, ever fascinated by the awesome display.

As Summer Storm sat entranced, Windrider watched her. There was something different about her tonight. Perhaps it was only the storm and its effect on her, but she seemed so—so serenely strengthened. It was an odd description, he knew, but the only one to come to mind. It was as if some calm power had come into her, giving her more assurance and yet endowing her with added peace and tranquility at the same time. Whatever it was, it sat well on her, making her more alluring and beautiful than he had ever seen her as she stared out into the night.

When at length she turned to him, her face was aglow with life, her golden eyes gleaming with a new awareness. "Today, for the first time, I truly acknowledged myself for who I am," she said softly. "I finally know myself as a whole being, not a confused girl torn in two different directions."

"And what have you discovered?" he asked gently, somehow very aware that this was a momentous revelation for her.

"Once, long ago, I told you I was not Cheyenne, and neither was I white. I recall telling you that I was nothing; nobody. I was wrong, Windrider. I was so very wrong! I am Cheyenne. Even with the blood of my white ancestors flowing through my body, I am Cheyenne. Today, in my righteous anger, I finally fully realized that, and all that it means to me."

She met his piercing look confidently. "It felt so right and good to proclaim my heritage with pride, to let my heart feel the full measure of my love for my father's people—for *my* people. I don't believe I really appreciated my Cheyenne blood before now. Suddenly I want to demand the honor and respect due to our people, to hold myself tall with pride and dignity before the world and proclaim unashamedly that I am Cheyenne. More than that, I am Summer Storm." Her solemn gaze trapped his as she came into his arms. "I was born in a storm such as this. It witnessed my first breath. It is fitting that it storm again tonight, for this night I am reborn to my people and my heritage, more strong and sure than ever before. I am Summer Storm, and never again will I doubt or deny that, to myself or anyone else."

It was uncanny that just when Summer Storm had finally resolved this inner conflict, that Jeremy should arrive in camp the very next day. He rode into the village at a gallop, his horse lathered and near dead from the wicked pace Jeremy had set. This, and the solemn look on his face, foretold that this was not a casual visit. Nor was it to be a pleasant one.

Panther took one look at Jeremy, as did Tanya, and knew something was terribly wrong at home. He stepped forward to greet the younger man. "Jeremy, you have come bearing bad news. What is wrong?"

Jeremy, who had no time or patience for the amenities just now, came straight to the point. "It's Dawn. Roger Watkins tried to rape her."

"Oh, my God! My baby!" Tanya was completely unprepared for the shock of Jeremy's news. Her usual composure deserted her altogether. "Is she badly hurt? Where is she? Will she be all right?"

White-faced and shaken, she looked to her husband for the strength and comfort she needed so desperately. Panther held her tightly to him, his big hand gently stroking her golden head. "Come, Jeremy. We will go to my lodge, and there you can tell us everything as quickly and completely as possible."

The entire family gathered in Panther's tepee to hear Jeremy speak. The men wore grim faces; their lips tight and angry, their jaws taut against clenched teeth. The women were still stunned. Their eyes were large and frightened, their lips and hands trembling as they listened. Summer was as shocked as her mother, and in this state she gave no thought to the fact that it was Jeremy who now related this unwelcome news. Her concern was all for her little sister.

"It probably would never have happened if Roger had not been drinking so heavily," Jeremy was saying.

"He has been resentful since the day Summer Storm said she was going to marry Windrider," Panther said.

"Yes, but he has never done anything more than complain and malign Summer to his friends," Jeremy pointed out. "He has never taken revenge of any active sort until now."

"Only because his kind is usually too cowardly to do more than whine," Mark jeered, his eyes narrowed to mere slits. "It is the drink that gave him the false courage he needed to seek revenge on Dawn, who never harmed him in any way. He would never have challenged anyone as strong as himself, but chose someone weak and defenseless! He is the lowest of bastards!"

"How is she?" Tanya asked fearfully. "How is my baby? Who is looking after her?"

"She is fine; frightened and shaken, and a bit bruised, but otherwise, all right," Jeremy quickly assured her. "It may take her awhile to forget, and to trust again, but she is not seriously injured. Rachel has insisted that she stay with her until you get home."

"How badly bruised?" Tanya was not to be that easily put off.

Jeremy hesitated a moment, but Panther's sharp look told him to speak freely and truthfully. "Her arm was wrenched fairly badly, from Watkins pinning it behind her as he held her down. She has bruises on her arms and legs—and on her throat."

"Go on." Coal from the pits of hell could not have been blacker than Panther's eyes as he thought of his youngest daughter struggling helplessly beneath that animal.

"She received a nasty bump on the back of her head, and a lump on her jaw. Watkins evidently hit her when she tried to fight him."

Summer swallowed the lump in her throat and blinked back hot tears. "Evidently?" she repeated. "Didn't Dawn tell anyone if he hit her?"

A bleak look of regret shone in his emerald eyes as Jeremy answered, "Dawn hasn't spoken a word since the attack."

"Oh, no! No!" Tanya exclaimed, imagining the stark terror Dawn must have felt.

"It's all my fault!" Summer blurted. "If I hadn't made such a fool of Roger in front of everyone, he would never have taken his spite out on Dawn."

"No, daughter," Panther corrected. "Do not blame yourself for the actions of that swine. He made the fool of himself."

Panther turned to Jeremy again. "What about Watkins? Does Tom Middleton have him in jail?"

Jeremy shook his head. "No, Adam. No one has seen hide nor hair of Watkins since. Tom can't arrest him if he can't find him. Several of the younger men from the Watkins' ranch are also gone. I suspect they have gone off with Roger to help protect him, or to provide him with an alibi and witnesses, or both. When Hunter heard Dawn's screams, he ran to help her as fast as he could, but Watkins heard him calling for her, and he ran. Hunter got a good enough look to recognize him, but he couldn't catch him. Besides, Dawn needed him, and he figured they could always deal with Watkins later, since he knew who was responsible. First he had to see to Dawn."

Nodding agreement, Panther told Tanya, "Pack only those provisions we will need to travel light and fast."

"We are going home to our daughter," Tanya concluded.

"No, not yet. First we are going to track down her cowardly attacker and his no-good friends. We must alert no one to our arrival, except for Hunter.''

"Not even Dawn or your mother?'' Tanya asked confusedly. "Panther, our daughter needs us.''

"Mother will take care of her as if she were her own. It is imperative that Mother not know we are near, for she would tell Tom.''

Mark frowned. "Why shouldn't Tom know? He's the sheriff. It is his job to see Watkins arrested and properly punished.''

"No,'' Panther insisted, his pride hardening his noble features, "it is our responsibility to see Watkins pay for his attack on our beloved Dawn Sky. Under white law, he would be dealt with too lightly, since he did not succeed in his intentions. I intend to extract my own brand of revenge, and I promise you that Roger Watkins will never again attempt to dishonor any woman. Before he dies, he will regret his actions heartily.'' Panther's voice rang with vengeance, and he could already taste the sweet revenge he planned.

Jeremy's eyes widened in disbelief as he, and everyone present, realized what Panther meant to do. "You can't, Adam!'' he exclaimed. "You can't play judge and jury like this, as well as executioner!''

"I can and I will,'' Panther vowed with an evil smile that sent shivers down Jeremy's spine. "I assure you that he will live only long enough to wish he had never dared to touch my daughter. He will know who takes revenge against him, but no one else will ever be able to prove it. You see, we will not have arrived in the area yet. Watkins and his men will have been attacked by unknown assailants. No one will be left alive to carry tales.''

"I should like to accompany you on your mission,'' Windrider said.

Panther had been expecting this. "Come, then. Let us prepare our weapons and our horses. Mark, see to a fresh mount for Jeremy. His is too exhausted for the pace at which we must travel.''

As the men rose to leave, Summer detained her husband with a gentle touch upon his arm. ''Husband,'' she said softly, her steady gaze seeking his. ''May I ride with you? After Watkins has been found and dealt with, I would like to see my sister. And I want to be there to witness this spineless snake's death, for my guilt still lies heavy on my heart.''

''If your father has no objections, you have my permission to come with us. Prepare our son for his journey, for your grandparents will be pleased to see him.'' Windrider's hand came up to stroke her dark braid in a gesture of comfort, for he knew Summer Storm was deeply hurt at this news of her sister's attack.

''Dawn Sky has always adored babies,'' Tanya added. ''Perhaps seeing Shadow Walker will aid in her recovery.''

Jeremy was speechless. He hadn't been aware that Summer had borne a child. Though it was extremely bad manners, especially among the Cheyenne, to ogle another man's wife, Jeremy could not help himself. His eyes searched for some sign of motherhood, yet her figure was just as trim and lovely as he remembered.

Jeremy had observed with envy the intimate exchange between Summer and Windrider. Now it was Windrider's turn to watch Jeremy's eyes upon his wife. Windrider's nostrils flared slightly with displeasure, and his firm lips flattened in irritation. For just a moment he considered rescinding his permission for Summer Storm to travel with them.

His temper cooled somewhat when he noticed that his beautiful wife was already helping her mother pack for the journey, paying no undue attention to

Jeremy. Still, he knew that her mind was preoccupied with thoughts of Dawn Sky just now. She was not purposely ignoring her former love; she had merely suffered too great a shock over her sister's attack to truly notice anything or anyone else just yet.

Windrider concealed a fretful sigh. The ride ahead would be a long one, with plenty of time for Summer Storm and Jeremy to speak together. Windrider vowed to be ever alert. Though Summer Storm now claimed to love him, she had once loved Jeremy also. If any old sparks were in danger of being rekindled, Windrider would be quick to douse them before they could flame to life. He would not lose his wife's heart now that he had tasted fully of her love, and he would kill Jeremy before he would let him lure Summer Storm away from him. She belonged to him alone, and only death would release her from the unbreakable bonds that tied her to him.

Even as fast as they traveled, pushing their mounts to their limits, it was five hard days of riding to reach Pueblo. That first night, when they finally made camp, Summer was too busy helping her mother and tending to Shadow Walker to do more than acknowledge Jeremy's presence.

It registered faintly on her weary mind that seeing Jeremy had not brought old yearnings flooding back. Nor did it hurt to have him near, as she had once thought it would. While she still cared for him in many ways, that wild desire she had once felt had fled, leaving behind a warm feeling of friendship and a sincere happiness at knowing him. When she had finally given Windrider her heart, she had done so totally, with no regrets, no lingering sadness for what might have been.

For this she was thankful, though she could sense

Windrider's unease as she settled herself next to his tense body when they bedded down for the night. She suspected the reason was Jeremy's unwelcome intrusion into their lives. Tentatively Summer reached out and touched her husband's arm. "Sleep easy, my love," she whispered softly, in her own way trying to reassure him without wounding his pride.

His hand closed over hers, squeezing it tightly for just a moment. His dark eyes bore into hers, seeking truth and trust in their golden depths. A tender smile curved his firm, masculine lips. "You, also, Wife of My Heart."

If Summer was not bothered by Jeremy's nearness, Jeremy was not as fortunate. When he had first set out for the Cheyenne camp, knowing he would see Summer once again, knowing she was now married to Windrider, he had expected to feel regret and heartache, but nothing like this! He had never thought to feel such pain! The agonies of the Damned could not be worse! Each loving look, each soft word Summer sent Windrider's way, was like a sharp knife twisting into his heart. Just being close to her and knowing that she belonged forever to another man was agony. The thought of Summer sharing Windrider's bed each night for the rest of her life, the tender love the two of them undoubtedly shared, made Jeremy want to scream aloud in pain.

Dear God, how could he have been such a fool to let her go? Jeremy castigated himself for not making her his when he'd had the chance. Now it was far too late. The minute Summer had said she would marry Windrider, it had been too late for Jeremy—too late for both of them. Her promise had bound her to Windrider as firmly as the actual marriage vows which had followed weeks later. Now they had a child to tie them even more closely. Even as Jeremy was glad that Summer was not suffering regrets, that she seemed to be so happy and content in her marriage, envy gnawed at him. Just the sight of her glowing face and smiling golden eyes was a severe blow to his bleeding heart.

Yet he could not let her see his suffering. Instinctively he felt that if he hid his feelings, he could at least maintain their friendship, and he desperately needed at least that small part of her to cling to. As much as it hurt him to be near her now, it hurt much more to be away from her. He needed to know that she was well and happy. He needed to see her smile and hear her voice. This was to him like food to a starving man. Though he did not want her to guess the depth of his pain and pity him, he knew he would treasure her friendship. This he would grab greedily and consider himself blessed. Anything, any small part of her, was better than nothing at all.

So Jeremy smiled and tried not to let his own pain shadow her happiness. Knowing he had no one but himself to blame, he swallowed his jealousy, extending his friendship to Summer's husband. It was not an easy task, but it was the fair and honest thing to do, and Jeremy had always been a fair person. He'd always liked Windrider, from the time the Cheyenne brave had been but a boy. Jeremy had gone out of his way to be kind and understanding when Windrider had lived with the Savage family and gone to school in Pueblo. He had admired the boy's spunk then, and beneath his envy, he had to admit that he admired the man Windrider had now become.

If Windrider had put that glow of love into Summer's cheeks, that sparkle of joy in her golden eyes, Jeremy told himself to be glad for her. Evidently, the Cheyenne was a good husband, and for that Jeremy was sincerely thankful. Where Jeremy had stupidly thrown away his best chance at true love, Windrider had been wiser. The man obviously adored his wife and child. Jeremy knew the young brave would provide for and protect them with his very life. The possessive look Jeremy had seen on Windrider's face had told him this much. It also warned Jeremy to step lightly if he wanted to earn a place of friendship in their lives.

Jeremy sighed heavily. "Well, old man," he told himself, "when you make a mistake, you make it big. Now you are going to have to live with it the best way you know how. If you can't have her, at least be grateful that she has found happiness with someone else—someone as fine and deserving as Windrider. Don't be a dog in the manger about this. At least you are not both suffering for your own blind mistake." With this lecture to himself, Jeremy set his mind toward accepting the fact that Summer and Windrider had found love together. His only hope was that the two of them would accept his offer of friendship and let him share their lives in this small way at least.

It was during a rest break on the second afternoon, that Jeremy sought her out. "I was surprised to learn that you have a child already, Summer. Congratulations. He is a fine, handsome son, much like his father."

Summer gave him a slight smile in return for his compliment to her precious son. "Thank you, Jeremy. I am very proud of Shadow Walker. As most mothers undoubtedly do, I consider him a wondrous miracle. It is still hard to believe that I had part in creating such a perfect little being, even though I carried him within my body for so many months."

"As I recall, you always favored birthings to any other part of veterinary medicine."

She nodded.

"Are you as happy as you appear?" he asked.

"Yes." Her clear amber eyes gave truth to her reply.

"You love Windrider very much, don't you?"

Though she could read the love and regret in Jeremy's expressive green eyes and had no wish to hurt him further, Summer answered honestly. "I adore him with all my heart. My one wish for you, my friend, is that you too might find the love and contentment I have discovered."

Jeremy mustered a weak smile. "I am glad for you, Summer. I am happy to see that you have adjusted so well to your new life, and yet I am troubled by some of the changes I sense in you."

"Oh? What changes are these?"

"You seem harder somehow, more cynical and cold-hearted."

"You speak of my reactions to Dawn Sky's attack," she surmised.

"Yes. The Summer I once knew would never have been so vindictive, or sought such deliberate and cruel revenge."

"Are you so sure, my friend? When I lived with my parents on the ranch, I was sheltered from many of life's cruel realities. Even there, once I had been exposed to them, I would probably have reacted similarly. If you will recall, I have always been rather willful and stubborn." Again she smiled, this time a bit wryly. "It is not hardness you see in me now, but strength—an inner strength I had never uncovered before, simply because there was no need. In the past year, I have grown and matured in many ways."

Jeremy nodded. "I thought it was motherhood that had brought that new serenity to your face. Perhaps I was mistaken."

"I'm sure that is part of it, Jeremy, but much of it comes from resolving my own confusion about my mixed heritage. I had to come to accept my Cheyenne blood without shame or regret. Windrider has helped me to do this. His love and pride have made me whole and given me my own sense of honor and pride in my Cheyenne ancestry. It is an invaluable lesson he has led me through, and my reward is the priceless gift of self-respect."

"He is good for you then."

"More than good. He has become the very center around which my life revolves."

Even as poignant pain pierced Jeremy's heart, a breathless sigh of relief coursed through Windrider at Summer Storm's words. His silent approach had gone unnoticed. He had stood listening for many minutes, hearing most of their conversation. Now he quickly retreated as quietly as he had come. His heart swelled to bursting at his wife's freely offered confession. It sang with a fierce love and pride for her. If he lived to be a thousand, Summer Storm could never give him a greater gift than she had just unwittingly bestowed upon him by professing her love so openly and willingly, never guessing that he would hear her words.

They reached the ranch undetected in the middle of the night, rousing Hunter from a sound sleep. His guilt at failing to protect his sister was eased by the thought of helping to track down Watkins and repay him for his treacherous assault on Dawn Sky. Before the dawn had begun to tinge the eastern sky with its pale pink fingers of light, he had collected his things and joined them in their pursuit. They were well away from the ranch when the first cock crowed in the first barnyard, announcing the start of the new day.

Though the trail was cold, it had been fairly undisturbed, and they had little trouble following it once Panther had located its faint beginnings. It led west, into the mountains, and though a white man may not have been able to trace its path, these Cheyenne easily read the signs that pointed the direction.

Not until late the next morning did they come across the small cabin hidden away on the mountainside. While the others hid in the surrounding trees, Panther and Windrider stealthily approached the cabin, peering through the windows to see if Watkins and the others were all inside. Luck was with them, for they had counted six horses tethered at the rear of the cabin and Watkins and five other men were all in the cabin. Four were playing cards around a small table in the center of the single room. Another was asleep in a rear bunk, and the last was wolfing down an open can of beans as if it were his last meal—which it would be, if Panther had his way. All were blissfully unaware of their approaching doom.

Panther motioned for the others to move in close to guard all exits in case any of their intended victims should somehow escape Panther's first surprise appearance. Then he, Mark, Hunter, and Windrider crept around to the door, and with a burst of speed and strength, kicked the door wide on its creaking hinges.

The men inside were caught completely unprepared. None, most especially Roger Watkins, stood a prayer of escaping the wrath gleaming in Panther's hot black eyes. Two tried, however. As one dived headlong out the window, breaking glass and splintering braces, another was right behind.

While her menfolk dealt with the remaining four in the cabin, Summer, on lookout outside, suddenly found herself face-to-face with two very burly and very desperate men. Both were armed with handguns, though neither had yet had the opportunity to draw it from his holster. The two men seemed just as stunned to see her as she was to suddenly confront them, and for several seconds all three stood staring at one another in mutual surprise.

Summer recovered her wits first, drawing back on her bowstring, a single deadly arrow pointed toward the men. Therein lay her problem, causing Summer to curse her luck. One man she could have handled easily, but two? Even as she proudly faced them down, she knew that, together, they could overpower her. This fact was quick to occur to the men, too.

"Go ahead, woman," the first drawled, a sly smile curling his lip. "You might get one of us, but not both." His hand crept toward the butt of his gun as he spoke. Summer saw the other man doing the same.

Her blood ran cold with fear, a chill finger of dread shivering down her spine, yet she spoke bravely. "Don't do it, fellows."

Once more, surprise flashed across their faces as the Indian woman before them spoke faultless English. For just a moment they hesitated, but it gave Summer the time she needed. Launching her body forward, she barreled into both of them, knocking them apart from one another before either could draw his pistol. One went sprawling into the dirt, but the other kept his footing.

Her bow useless at this point, Summer flung it from her, drawing her knife from its sheath at her waist. As she lunged at the man standing less than three feet from her, the cowboy on the ground fired his gun. The bullet whistled past her ear, making her wince involuntarily, but not deterring her from her chosen target.

Her opponent stood a foot and a half taller than Summer and was more than twice her weight, but as her slim body slammed into his, her training took over. One small, moccasined foot caught behind his and pulled him off balance, tumbling them both to the ground. He toppled like a giant oak, and Summer swore she felt the earth quake beneath them as she fell atop him. Her dominant position was not held for long, however, as her forward motion and his superior strength caused them to roll. Suddenly he was over her, his angry face glaring down at her as his huge hands manacled her wrists. Within seconds, the hand holding the knife became numb, and Summer knew he would soon disarm her.

The second cowboy fired another shot, this one passing scant inches from her nose. The man astride her jerked upward and hollered, ''Damn it, Joe! What ya tryin' to do, shoot me? Ya dumb son of a . . .''

The knee Summer sent crashing upward between his legs cut his words short. While he bellowed in pain, Summer pushed him off of her. Her arm came about, and before she was quite aware of what she was doing, her knife had plunged deep into his chest. His huge body jerked once at the deadly intrusion, his eyes staring into hers in mute shock, and then he was still.

Summer tore her gaze from him in time to see the man called Joe leveling his gun at her. A shot rang out. Even as she waited to feel the bullet slam into her body, anticipating pain and death, she saw Joe pitch backward, the gun dropping from his lifeless hand. A quivering sigh tore through her, boundless relief weakening her quaking limbs as she turned to see Jeremy lowering his smoking pistol.

Their eyes met and held in a turbulent gaze. ''You

saved my life," Summer breathed shakily, her lips quivering so badly she could barely speak. She swallowed hard. "You said you weren't going to become involved in this filthy raid of revenge."

Jeremy's green eyes glittered with unspoken emotion. "I could hardly stand by and let him kill you, could I, Summer?" His look turned bitter as he stared first at her, then at the man he had been forced to kill in her defense. "Damn, but I didn't want any part of this!" he swore angrily. Jamming his gun back into his holster, he turned and stalked away, brushing past Tanya without a word as she rushed toward Summer.

"What happened?"

Summer merely shook her head in confusion. "I'll explain later, Mother, when I am sure myself," she answered softly.

While Summer was contending with her opponents outside, her brothers, father, and husband quickly dealt with the remaining four men in the cabin. The poor fool in the bunk never knew what hit him, as Mark's arrow pierced his heart before he had fully awakened. Windrider's tomahawk ended the life of another. The third lay sprawled on the cabin floor, Hunter's knife in his throat and the spoon still clutched tightly in his fingers. Within seconds, only Roger Watkins was left alive to face these angry Cheyenne avengers.

Even beneath the fearsome warpaint, Roger recognized Adam. Gulping at the lump of fear that clogged his throat, Watkins backed warily away from the man he knew had come to kill him. "I didn't really hurt her, S–Savage," he stammered. "I just scared her some. I was drunk!"

Panther sneered, his feral smile sending chills chasing down Watkins' backbone. "Am I supposed to accept that as an excuse, Watkins? You were drunk, so I am supposed to understand why you tried to brutally rape my daughter? You and I both know that Hunter's timely arrival is the only thing that spared her.''

Slowly, one taunting step at a time, Panther stalked his prey. "How does it feel to be so scared you can barely breathe for the fear, Watkins? Can you taste it yet? Can you smell your own cowardly sweat pouring out of your shriveling body? There is no escape, Watkins, as there would have been no escape for Dawn if Hunter had not heard her frightened screams. You will scream, too. This I promise you, but there will be no one to run to your rescue.''

In a surprisingly quick move, Roger went for his gun. Panther's knife buried itself into the man's wrist before the gun cleared leather. Watkins screamed, his hand dangling uselessly at his side.

"Leave us," Panther commanded, ordering the three younger men from the cabin. "Watkins is mine alone to deal with.''

Summer was standing with her mother when Hunter, Mark, and Windrider joined them. Jeremy had not yet returned. When Summer would have questioned him, Windrider shook his head. All of them stood silently outside, awaiting Panther.

A few seconds later, an earsplitting shriek of pain and terror rent the air. Minutes later, Panther emerged from the cabin, a grim look of satisfaction on his face. Wordlessly he led his family to where Jeremy now waited with their horses.

No one spoke until they were several miles from the cabin. Finally Panther broke the silence. Gesturing to Windrider, Hunter, and Mark, he said, "I want you three to go back and cover our tracks completely. Jeremy and I will take the women back to our camp, where we will all meet later. When we are certain

Watkins has been found, we will ride into Pueblo, and no one will know we have been here. We will make them think that we have just arrived from Oklahoma Territory to see our ailing daughter. Even if they suspect, no one will ever be able to prove otherwise, or that we had anything to do with Watkins' death.''

This was exactly the issue being debated immediately upon their arrival at Tom and Rachel's house a few days later.

"We both know it was you who killed Roger Watkins,'' Tom Middleton argued heatedly. "You know, Adam, and I know it.''

"And we both know you can't prove a thing,'' Adam pointed out.

"Who the hell else would have reason to extract such revenge?'' the sheriff shouted. He enumerated the sequence of events on his fingers. "First Dawn gets attacked, then Jeremy races off to fetch you, then Watkins and his men meet with some mysterious persons who just happen to be skilled with bows and arrows, knives, and tomahawks. Finally, you arrive just days afterward, all concerned for Dawn and cool as a cucumber when you find out Watkins was killed.''

"Don't look a gift horse in the mouth, Tom. Whoever did this just saved you, the judge, and a jury a lot of time and fuss,'' Tanya added. "And if justice was served in the process, who is to complain? I'm satisfied.''

"Well I'm not! That's not justice! It's murder, plain and simple!''

Tanya's eyes flashed in anger. "And my daughter was attacked, beaten, and terrorized to the point that she will not speak of it! That animal attacked my baby, and if not for Hunter he would have raped her! He deserved everything he got and more!'' Impassioned

287

tears filled her eyes.

"I'm sorry, Tanya," Tom sighed. "I know how this hurts you, and believe me, I was doing everything I could to try and find Watkins. He wouldn't have gotten away with it. But now his father is after me to have you arrested, Adam. He's sure you are behind what was done to Roger."

"Why is everyone so certain it was me? My God, Tom! It could have been anyone who knew and loved Dawn. It could have been you, for that matter, or Tanya's father, or Uncle George. Maybe it was a friend, or a beau."

"They wouldn't have used those weapons," Tom insisted. "They would have used guns." His sharp gaze narrowed on Adam. "And they wouldn't have done to him what you did. Only a father bent on revenge would do that, Adam," he added cryptically, casting what seemed to be an embarrassed look at the listening women.

"Now, Tom, you can't be sure of that," Rachel put in softly but firmly. "Maybe they just wanted it to look like Indians were responsible."

"I know it as well as I know my own name," he disagreed, "but I can't prove it. I don't have a single, solid ounce of proof, and it's for darned sure Watkins can't tell me."

His weary, accusing look included all of them. Tom shook his head in disgust. "You were all in on this, weren't you? I could stand on my head and stack marbles from now until Hell froze over, and none of you would admit to knowing anything. Not that it really surprises me that much, except for you, Jeremy. I never thought I'd see you get mixed up in something like this."

Jeremy merely shrugged. "Sorry, Tom. I can't tell you a thing about it."

"That figures. Well, I can at least understand why you all did it. Dawn is like my own flesh and blood granddaughter, and I love her, too. I can't say I approve of your methods, however. Taking the law into your own hands was wrong. That is my job, not yours, and I'll thank you to leave it to me from now on. If any of you ever oversteps the bounds again, you'd blamed well better be positive I can't prove it, or I swear I'll arrest you on the spot. Being relatives by marriage won't stop me, and no excuse will be good enough."

"Now, Tom, how often have I caused you any problem in the last twelve years?" Adam asked. "I've been a model citizen, upright and as straight as an arrow."

Tom rolled his eyes heavenward. "Just stay out of trouble, Adam, and keep the rest of your hotheaded family in line. That's not too much for an old man to ask, is it?"

"Well, I'll try, Tom," Adam promised with a sly grin, "but Mother's the worst of us all, and she rarely listens to me anymore. I guess she's your problem now."

16

Summer's visit with her family was short, but satisfying. Upon seeing her mother, Dawn Sky broke out of her stupor and began to cry. The flood of tears was just the emotional release she needed to begin to heal. Though she shied away from any mention of Roger Watkins, and started visibly whenever a male member of the family approached her too suddenly, she was much improved. Her physical injuries were fast healing, and hopefully, in time, her emotional bruises would disappear too. With love and care, Dawn would soon forget the terror that had held her in its evil grasp, or if not forget entirely, at least the memory of that dark fear would be dimmed.

Summer's grandparents instantly fell in love with Shadow Walker, as did Great Aunt Elizabeth and Uncle George. They were nearly as taken with Windrider, for it was obvious to all that he loved his young wife and child to distraction, and that she returned his affections.

Within the family, Summer ran into no problems. The Kerrs, who had long been family friends, readily accepted her back into their circle, Cheyenne husband and all. It was with the townspeople that she found a few raised eyebrows and outright snubs. That caused Summer little concern. It was when two of her former best friends refused to talk to her that she truly felt hurt. It helped that two others of her closest friends still accepted her.

"Don't pay any attention to Wanda. She always was a bit of a snob," Colleen comforted. "And Dorothy Ann thinks everyone is below her now that she is married to Harry Groves. Heavens, you would think he was the bank president instead of a mere teller."

Summer smiled ruefully. "What about Miss Peabody, our old grammar school teacher? She stood right in the mercantile and called me a heathen! And I used to be one of her favorite students!"

Marla Denning laughed. "I'd say you've lost favor with her now, Summer. But, then, who in their right mind ever wanted to be in good standing with that meanie? I've never liked her since she stood me in the corner in third grade for wetting my pants after Freddie York tickled my ribs."

Summer was learning a valuable lesson in friendship on this visit. Her fair-weather friends could not be counted on when the going was less than smooth, but her really true friends would stand by her, now and always, as she would for them. In a way, it was good to discover now who her friends really were.

While Summer was busy renewing friendships, Windrider stayed fairly close to the ranch, calling as little attention to himself as possible. That Summer Storm had reverted so readily to ribbons and pretty dresses and shoes concerned him somewhat, but since she had been raised this way for years he could understand her actions. He told himself it did not affect her feelings for him, and tried to convince himself that she would not balk at returning to the reservation when the time came. He hoped he was right.

Since their first talk with Sheriff Middleton, Jeremy had made himself fairly scarce, but it was hard for him to stay away from the ranch when Summer was so close at hand. Mid-morning of the third day found him riding into the Savage ranchyard.

"Is Summer here?" he called to Tanya through the back screen-door.

"No, I think she went off to visit with Marla and Colleen again. Then she was going to stop by my Aunt Elizabeth's for a bit."

Jeremy's face clouded in disappointment. "She'll be gone all day, then."

"It appears likely. I'm sorry you missed her, Jeremy."

He nodded. "Tell her I stopped by."

He walked back to where he had tethered his horse to find Windrider waiting for him. "Why do you seek my wife?" the Cheyenne warrior asked bluntly.

Jeremy grimaced inwardly at the unrelenting look in Windrider's stony black eyes. He had known this confrontation would come sooner or later. "I thought she might want to accompany me on a veterinary call nearby. Cal Jones' mare is about to birth twin foals, which is an uncommon occurrence to witness," he answered.

"Summer Storm is no longer free to go about with you, Field. She belongs to me."

"I can see it is time we talked, though my time is short at the moment," Jeremy said with a sigh. "Ride with me, Windrider. There are things we need to make clear between us."

"Matters having to do with Summer Storm and your feelings for her," Windrider surmised.

"Yes, and matters of honor and friendship."

A few minutes later, they were riding across the field. "I love Summer very dearly," Jeremy confessed, breaking the short silence between them.

Windrider inclined his head. "I am aware of that, Field. It is very obvious to me, but she is mine and I will never let her go; not even if she wished to, which she does not."

"I know she loves you very much." Jeremy chose his words with care. "You have made her very happy, for which I am glad. You and your son are her whole life now. There is no room for me in her heart, except as a friend."

"I am glad to hear that you accept this," Windrider stated flatly.

Jeremy pulled his horse to a halt and met Windrider's piercing gaze with his own steady look. "Once, long ago, you and I were also friends, Windrider," he said. "I thought you knew me well enough to know that I would never do anything to bring dishonor upon my friends or myself. Summer made her choice, and her choice was you. Though I might regret it, I will abide by it. Never would I attempt to woo her away from you, for I still consider you a friend. My respect for you is too great for me to deal falsely with you."

"How can we remain friends when you desire my wife?" Windrider said. "For two men to desire the same woman is always trouble."

As he shook his head, Jeremy's smile was wryly amused. "I can be content to remain friends with both of you, Windrider. Besides, I couldn't steal her away from you if I tried, as you well know. Summer nearly worships you. I ask only that you allow me to share your lives from time to time, to at least have her friendship to enjoy, and yours. I can bear to lose her love, for she is very happy with you, and I wish only the best for her. But to lose her friendship, too, would be a wound that would never heal. She has been a part of my life since she was a small child, and I greatly value the years we have spent together.''

A half-smile pulled at Windrider's mouth also. ''I may be a fool, Field, but I believe you. Your words ring with truth, and I have always felt you were an honorable man, even though you are white. You may continue to be a friend to me and my wife. You are welcome in our camp at any time, but if you ever betray the trust I now place in you, what Watkins suffered will be as nothing to what I will do to you.''

''Have no fear of that, my friend,'' Jeremy assured him. ''I have great respect for you, as well as my fair share of self-pride. I will guard our friendship well, and treasure it all my days.''

It was thus that a strange and lasting alliance was formed between the most unlikely of friends.

When it came time to leave, Summer was saddened at the thought of not seeing her friends and family again for many months, but she was not devastated by it. She was going home with her husband and son, to her other friends and family, to the life she had built for herself there.

''We are going to miss you, Summer,'' Colleen said. ''It was like old times having you home again.''

''Besides, it gave me a wonderful excuse to come out to the ranch and be around Hunter,'' Marla confessed a little guiltily. ''I think he finally really noticed me. He actually told me I looked lovely in my new dress.''

"Hunter said that?'' Summer exclaimed in mock amazement. "Lands, the man must be smitten! He never notices unimportant things like dresses and bonnets. If it is not something to do with the ranch or his precious cattle, he's uncommonly blind and deaf.''

Marla smiled shyly, her blue eyes twinkling happily. "Not any longer. I asked him to Sunday supper with my parents, and he said he'll come.''

"Ah, me thinks I hear a heart a flutterin','' Colleen teased with a dramatic sigh, "and it's not me own!''

Marla shot her friend an exasperated look. "You can stop the Irish theatrics any time, Colleen. You are just as silly over John. If he hadn't started courting you when he did, I feared you would throw yourself in front of his horse to gain his attention.''

Summer laughed. "I'm going to miss all this banter. I wish you could come and visit me sometime.''

"With any luck at all, maybe I can come with your family next year,'' Marla said wistfully. "That is, if Hunter will cooperate with my plans for the future.''

"You have all fall and winter to convince him that he can't live without you,'' Summer told her friend. "Just pretend an interest in cattle and bake his favorite blackberry pie twice a week, and my dear brother will fall at your feet in stunned adoration. You'll be a bride before he realizes what hit him.''

Mark had decided to return to camp with Windrider and Summer. Before they left, he had a serious conversation with his father. "Did you have an opportunity to approach Winter Bear about a marriage agreement between Sweet Lark and me, Father?''

Adam nodded. "Winter Bear is agreeable.''

"Yes, but what about Sweet Lark? Perhaps she

would prefer other suitors, rather than to wait for me to finish my schooling."

"She seems favorable to marriage with you, as she seems content to wait," Adam told his son.

"Winter Bear has spoken with her, then?"

"Yes. Sweet Lark has agreed to your proposal, but I would present her with a courting gift as soon as possible, if I were you," Adam advised. "It will seal the contract and give notice to others that Sweet Lark is formally promised to you."

Mark was deliriously happy on the way to the village. His wide grin stayed perpetually on his face, causing Windrider and Summer to tease him unmercifully, but he did not seem to mind. He was too delighted to let anything intrude on his joy.

"Have you ever seen anyone that daft over a woman?" Summer commented aside to Windrider.

"Only myself over you, my sweet Summer Storm," he confessed lovingly.

Mark's blissful state was shattered immediately upon return to camp. All was havoc. A mile from the village they could hear wailing, and upon entering the village, everything was in a state of disorganization and confusion.

"What has gone on here?" they wondered.

Their curiosity was soon satisfied. "The missionary women call it 'chicken pox'," Winter Bear explained, coming out to greet them.

"Oh! Then it is nothing to be too concerned about," Summer said with immense relief. "For a moment I feared it was some dreadful disease."

"To us it is," the chief answered solemnly. "While to the whites it is a common childhood malady, to us it seems to be much more serious. Already, six of our people have died, and many more lie ill. Even now, Sweet Lark is fighting for her life in our lodge.''

Mark was starting to understand. This was one of those contagious diseases, much like measles, to which the Indians seemed to have little or no immunity. Never having been exposed to the disease before the white man brought it West, their bodies had not built up any resistance to this illness; whereas the white world had been fighting it for years, and what might once have been a fatal disease to them, too, was now not much more than a nuisance.

Windrider was already dismounting when Winter Bear stopped him. ''No, my son. You and your family have not been in contact with this illness. You must go away from here until it has passed.''

''He is right, Windrider,'' Mark agreed. ''Take Summer Storm and Shadow Walker upstream a few miles, and set up camp there until it is safe to return. I will stay here. Perhaps my meager medical knowledge will be helpful.''

''But, Mark,'' Summer said. ''I have already had the chicken pox when I was six. I can not get them again, can I?''

''No, but you might be able to carry the disease to your husband and child. I am not sure about this.'' He had already guessed her intentions.

Summer's solemn gaze traveled between the three men. ''I want to stay and help, since I would be in no danger. I agree that Windrider and Shadow Walker should not be exposed, but I want to stay.''

''You are still nursing Shadow Walker,'' Windrider quietly reminded her.

Summer's mind was set. ''He will do well for a few days on sweetened water and stewed vegetables that are well mashed.'' Her stubborn gaze linked with his. ''Can you manage to fend for yourself and our son without me for that long, Windrider?''

It was a subtle challenge—one he accepted, but reluctantly. ''We will not be far. Send word when you wish for my return.'' His dark eyes lingered on her face for a long moment before he took his son and rode away.

The next couple of weeks were one long endless battle for everyone. Summer worked until she nearly dropped from exhaustion. Mark did twice what she did, appearing to be everywhere at once, scarcely even sleeping, barely eating, and never faltering. Summer didn't know where he found the strength.

All but a few of the whites had deserted the village at the onset of the epidemic. Two missionaries, the teacher, and a minister were the only ones to stay and help.

Summer had never seen anyone as sick with chicken pox as these people. Several of her friends back in Pueblo had had them, herself included, but nothing like this. Winter Bear had not exaggerated. Sweet Lark was deathly ill when they arrived. Her fever raged and even in her delirium she complained that her head ached unbearably. All they could do was sponge her burning body and force liquids into her and wait for the spots to appear. When they did, she was covered with blotches from head to toe. Then came clear blisters, and suddenly Sweet Lark's fever was of lesser concern as the young girl now had trouble breathing. This continued for four days, until Mark was sure there was not one more clear area on her body for the blisters to cover.

''She is through the worst of it now, I think,'' he said, rubbing wearily at his red-rimmed eyes. ''Next the blisters will yellow and form crusts. Our main problem then will be to prevent her from scratching, for they will itch terribly. If she scratches the scabs before they are ready to come off, they could seep and form more pox, or become infected. Also, it can produce scars that will stay forever.''

As sick as she had been, Sweet Lark recovered fully, with only three small pock marks to serve as reminders, and those in places that did not show. Others were not so fortunate. Before it was over, fifteen villagers died from the disease, while seven more succumbed to an infection following their bout with the chicken pox. Many could not keep from scratching, and were obviously scarred. Some mothers, in order to prevent the scratching, tied their children's arms to their sides, or padded their little hands with leather or fur.

When Shy Deer came down with the fever, Mark was doubly concerned. He was not sure how this would affect her or the child she carried within. As a medical student, he was aware that it was dangerous enough for a woman her age to be pregnant, let alone to contract a serious illness. Fortunately, she had an extremely light case, with only a dozen blisters in all. She barely felt ill. Mark was grateful for this small favor in the midst of such havoc, and for the fact that some Cheyenne such as Winter Bear did not get the sickness at all.

At the end of one week, Windrider came to the edge of the village for news of his people. Over the space of thirty paces separating them, he and Summer Storm stared at one another hungrily. Self-consciously, she brushed at her wrinkled clothes and straggling hair. She knew she looked haggard. Her only consolation was that everyone here looked awful just now. Even Windrider, who had not been ill, looked weary with worry.

''You must not come nearer, my love,'' she called to him. ''It is not safe yet.''

"How is my sister?" he asked. "And my parents?"

"Sweet Lark has passed the feverish stage. It appears she will recover, but now your mother seems to be catching it. Four more of our people have died, but many are getting well. Others are just now beginning to sicken."

"What of Two Arrows and Singing Waters?"

"They are nearly well now, and so is their son. Snow Blossom is very bad, but Gray Rock has not become sick yet, nor your father."

"You look tired," he said. "Are you ill?"

"No, just weary. So is Mark; he works like a demon to save lives here. You look tired, too."

"I have been worried about all of you."

"Is Shadow Walker doing well?"

Windrider held the baby up for her to see. "He is fine, but he misses his mother, as do I."

"I miss you too, dearest husband, but you must stay away and keep yourself and our son safe from this disaster."

"How much longer do you think it will last?"

Summer sighed heavily. "Mark says at least a fortnight, maybe more."

Finally, after what seemed an eternity but was actually little more than a month in all, the crisis was over. When she was sure her last patient would live, Summer went back to her tepee and fell into an exhausted sleep. She slept for two entire days, and when she at last opened her eyes, it was her joy to find Windrider and Shadow Walker back with her again.

In celebration of the end of the epidemic, to thank the spirits for sparing most of their lives, Chief Winter Bear decreed that a feast be held. During the festivities, Mark and Summer Storm were honored for their dedicated work; as was Root Woman, who had labored tirelessly among her people once she had recovered from her own bout with the disease.

Then, much to Summer's surprise, a special ceremony took place during this celebration. Summer Storm was called to stand before Chief Winter Bear, who bestowed upon her the prized eagle feather for her hair, that esteemed symbol of a Cheyenne warrior.

Summer was not sure what was really happening, afraid she had misunderstood yet another Cheyenne ritual, but Winter Bear's words of praise cleared her confusion. "You, Summer Storm, by your participation in a raid of revenge led by your father, have counted coup on your white enemy. In doing so, you have completed your training and earned your new status as a Cheyenne warrior."

Nearly as surprised as his sister, Mark, too, had gained the same exalted rank. Though already a warrior, Windrider was awarded another feather for his warbonnet. Hunter, too, was now considered a warrior by his deeds, though he was not present to collect his praise this night. It was a proud night for Summer Storm and her family, though she regretted that the attack on Dawn Sky had been the means for her to achieve her new ranking.

Life returned quickly to near normal after that. Winter was fast approaching, and there was still much to be done before moving to their winter site. The selected cattle were slaughtered, and the meat smoked and dried and packed away for the long months ahead. A hunting party went off in search of added game, while the women collected nuts, ground their corn, dried fall berries and organized a honey-gathering expedition. Winter garments were repaired, replaced, or mended as needed. The epidemic had set them behind in their work, and all must be readied before the first snows caught them unprepared.

The white men had brought more than one disease to the Cheyenne camp that summer, it seemed. They had also brought liquor, popularly called firewater because of the burning sensation upon swallowing the potent brew. More and more, it became common to see a brave or warrior stumbling about on his way through the village. Normally reserved men suddenly became rowdy; honorable warriors turned loud and lewd; friends and brothers became violent toward one another; peaceful families were now shouting and fighting; loving husbands were suddenly beating their wives and children with little or no provocation—all because of this debilitating drink introduced to them by the white man. It was disgraceful and humiliating to the entire tribe. It was also a new and growing problem for the tribe, and one without a ready solution.

Another disturbing problem had to do with the women. It seemed their white visitors had availed themselves of the willing services of the tribe's harlots, visiting that particular lodge with amazing regularity. Now several of those women found themselves expecting the offspring of the white men. When this news became known, everyone was angry. Something had to be done!

A council meeting was held, where it was learned that several of the soldiers had also dared to approach a number of Cheyenne maidens and young wives, assuming in their arrogance and ignorance that all Indian women were of loose morals and eager to be bedded by a virile white man. When they had dared to refuse, the men became angry. Not wishing to sully the family honor, most of these women kept silent about these incidents, but it had soon become common practice to go about the camp in groups of two or more, for safety's sake.

"We said exactly the same thing," Singing Waters recalled.

"Yes, and several times I saw one or another of the white men coming from the 'bad' women's lodge," Snow Blossom added. "They made no secret of their visits there. I naturally thought everyone knew of it, and of course, it is not something to be discussed openly."

In the course of the ensuing investigation, it was discovered that two of the maidens and one of the wives were also pregnant by white men. The girls finally admitted that they had succumbed to the soldiers' demands under threat of bodily harm. They had been frightened when the men had become violently angry and abusive. Thereafter, they had never gone anywhere alone again, and had hidden their shame from their families. One of the girls said that the soldier who had forced her to lay with him had warned her not to tell, or he would shoot her father. The other had been too ashamed to face her family, and afraid of what her father might do; not only to her, but of the trouble it might bring to the tribe if her father was to confront the soldier with his deeds.

The young wife claimed she was raped by one of the missionary men. There were many of the tribe who believed her, having known what a sweet and truthful person she had always been. She and her husband had been very happy together, and they had a young son of their own.

The result of this incident was tragic, and Summer's heart ached for the family, for it was obvious that her husband loved her dearly and was severely hurt by all this. Love her or not, the young brave could not abide having his wife bear a white man's child. In the end, he rejected her, throwing her out of his lodge and out of his life. According to tribal custom, if no one else would take her in, she would either have to enter the harlots' lodge, or be ordered out of the village altogether, whichever the tribal leaders decided.

This was a difficult and trying decision for the tribal leaders, and one they feared they would have to decide many times more in the future. The white men contaminated everything they came in contact with and there was no avoiding their effect upon tribal life altogether. With each passing year, the white influence became more evident, and problems arose more and more frequently.

The Cheyenne leaders were at a loss as to what to do to stop it. Bound to the reservation, with all their rights and freedoms severely restricted, there was little they could do but try to police their own people. Though the reservation land might belong to the tribe by treaty, it was well known that the Indians had no real authority over it whatsoever, and certainly not enough to openly accuse or punish a white man, no matter how vile his crime.

In the end, all the pregnant harlots and the young wife were banished from the tribe. This virtually meant death for most of them, for no other tribe would take them in or give them aid. On their own, with no food or shelter, and no means of obtaining either, they would soon die. They could stay within the bounds of the reservation, but that was of little comfort. With winter coming soon, they would all starve or freeze within weeks.

If they left the reservation lands, a similar fate awaited. Only if they were extremely lucky and found some white person to take them in, would any of them survive for very long. Even then, chances were good that they would be beaten and mistreated, for white people always considered any Indian far below them. A dog would receive better treatment than most Indians at the hands of the whites.

The two young maidens who had been disgraced were not banished with the others. They were exiled only as far as the harlots' lodge, where they would spend the rest of their lives in scorned, secluded shame, since no Cheyenne man would now claim them. To their families, they would be as dead, their names never again spoken. Their innocent babies, when born, would be adopted by another Cheyenne family and be raised within the tribe as any other child, with the full rights and privileges of any Cheyenne son or daughter.

On the day that judgement was passed upon the women, they were publicly escorted to the edge of the village and turned out. Except for those in the harlots' lodge, every other member of the tribe gathered together to jointly repudiate these unworthy women. It was one of the worst customs Summer had ever witnessed, and one she would have preferred not to participate in, but it was required of her as well as everyone else.

Not one tribal member looked fully upon the faces of any of the exiled women, for they were no longer considered people. In the Cheyenne manner, they simply no longer existed. Summer caught a fleeting glimpse of the tear-streaked face of the banished wife, and her heart wrenched at the knowledge that this young woman was forced to leave her small son behind, as well as everyone else and everything she had always known and loved. It seemed an unbearably high price to pay for a white man's brutal lust.

17

Wrapped tightly in Windrider's embrace, her slender body touching his, Summer asked, "Would you ever cast me out, as Slippery Beaver did his wife?"

Windrider looked down into her solemn amber eyes, "If you had been unfaithful, I would have no choice but to do so, Summer Storm. It would be the only way I could maintain my honor among our people, though I would rather rip my heart from my own breast than lose you. Why do you ask this question?"

"I wanted to weep for her today, Windrider. It was not her fault. She was cruelly raped, and now she is punished yet again."

He nodded. "I know, but there is nothing anyone could have done. She was Slippery Beaver's wife and it was his decision. This could not have been easy for him, either."

"What if I were to be raped? Would you do the same? Would you force me to leave my son and be exiled from you?''

Windrider brushed a strand of her silky black hair from her cheek, stunned to find it wet with her silent tears. ''I love you more than my life, Summer Storm, more than is good for me. If some other man would forcefully take what is mine alone, I would be consumed with hatred, but not toward you, I think. I could not hurt you more than you had already been harmed.''

She kissed his open palm, caressing it with her lips. ''What would you do with me?''

''If there were to be a child, I would have to send you away until it was born, for I could not bear to see you grow round with another man's seed. When the child was born, you could return to me, but I could not raise it as my own, no matter how innocent the babe would be. Another family would have to take it, and I would make you swear never to acknowledge it as yours. Does that seem too cruel to you?''

''No, Windrider. It seems very fair. If there were no child, what would you do then?''

His hands caressed her perfect, naked form. ''I would love you, Summer Storm, for I cannot imagine loving you less than I do now.''

Summer sighed, loving how his hands felt as they slid over her smooth skin. ''Would you not think me tainted?''

''Never,'' he promised, teasing his tongue along the sensitive cord of her shoulder. ''To me you will always be perfect.''

His tongue traced the delicate shell of her ear, and she shivered in delight. ''Will you still love me if I become fat and lose all my teeth?'' she giggled, pushing at his broad chest to make him stop tickling her ear.

"Even then," he murmured.

"Even if I get horrid warts on my face, and big wide buffalo hips?" she teased, nibbling seductively at his lower lip.

He tugged his lip from between her sharp teeth. "I shall love you even if you grow a horn from the center of your head," he chuckled.

Summer laughed merrily. "I shall probably need one to hold up my halo."

"What is this 'halo' you speak of?" he muttered distractedly, his lips tracing her stubborn jawline even as his fingers toyed with an erect rosy nipple.

Past a gasp of growing desire, Summer said breathlessly, "It is a glowing ring of light over the head of an angel. The Christians believe in benevolent spirits called angels, who protect mere mortals from harm. They are absolutely perfect spirit-beings."

"Mmm, I like the idea of having my own angel, for you are surely as perfectly formed as any could be." His fingers skimmed along her skin, making her arch into him on a wave of longing.

A throaty moan of raw desire escaped her parted lips. Her hands caressed him, urging his body ever closer to hers. Her lips followed the line of his collarbone, making tiny bites and soothing them with kisses. "Come into me, Windrider. Make love with me."

"Do angels make love?" he asked, already lowering himself to her hot, waiting body.

"This one does." Then speech was impossible as she received him with a glad cry. With soft sighs and passionate loving, they ascended on gossamer wings to glorious heights. There they found heaven's ecstasy in a celestial realm all their own.

A few days later, the tribe moved to their winter grounds, again in the wooded hills, but in a different area than the previous year. No sooner had they settled there, than the Washington delegates came to again discuss the Allotment Act. When the tribal leaders again refused to sign, the head delegate informed them that leaders of the bill were coming from Washington to meet with them in St. Louis, Missouri. President Cleveland himself had hand-selected these important men to meet with them on this issue. The Cheyenne tribe was to do the same, sending their own representatives to the talks. They would travel the first two hundred miles on horseback. Then, near Tulsa Town, they would board a train for the remainder of the five hundred fifty mile journey to St. Louis.

It was typical of the government representatives to disregard the fact that winter would soon send deep snows throughout the territory. Getting to St. Louis should be no problem if they hurried, but coming back again was another problem. By the time the meetings were concluded, the Indians could be trapped in St. Louis until spring, unable to get home through drifted snow and freezing temperatures.

They had three days in which to prepare for a journey of indeterminable length. Summer had been to St. Louis once before with her parents, and she knew it was a thriving, bustling city. She was also aware that it housed some very elite society. If these dignitaries were staying there, she was sure they would not be hobnobbing with the riffraff, and she and Windrider would surely be called upon to meet some very aristocratic citizens. In preparation she packed their best clothing, for Summer was determined that neither she nor Windrider be a laughing-stock.

Ten days of hard riding brought them to the railway station where they would catch the train to St. Louis. Summer was glad then that she and Windrider had not ridden their own horses, for the horses provided were now stabled until their return, and Mist was too dear to her to leave stabled in a strange town.

The train was dirty, noisy, and crowded. The passenger car smelled like coal dust and sweat. The rank odor from the cubicle that hid the chamber pot nearly made Summer gag as she passed by. She and Windrider shared a look of disgust as they seated themselves opposite the two men delegated to accompany them.

They made a strange sight, these two well-dressed gentlemen and the two Indians seated together. Many a head turned in curiosity. They had tried to get Windrider to dress in a black broadcloth suit, but he had refused. It had never dawned on them that the second Cheyenne representative would be a woman. Not only did they have no appropriate clothing to offer her, which she too would have refused, but they were at a loss as to how to deal with her. Their attempts at courtesy were awkward at best. Their relief that both of their Cheyenne guests were fluent in English was laughable.

''Now don't you be frightened at all the noise when the train starts, ma'am,'' one man, the one called Swanson said, leaning forward to speak to Summer.

Summer merely gave him a weak smile and settled Shadow Walker's cradleboard more firmly on her lap. It would serve no purpose to correct the man's mistaken impression, so she saved her breath.

At noon, the other man, Mr. Wilke, produced

cheese sandwiches from a hamper he'd had packed in town before boarding the train. That, a cup of room-temperature tea, and an apple constituted lunch; after which Summer breastfed Shadow Walker, her bodice modestly concealed with a small blanket over her shoulder.

The hours dragged by in the crowded, smelly traincar. The cigar smoke hung over their heads like a gray cloud and stung their eyes terribly. Summer was thankful that Shadow Walker slept so much of the time. The stuffy car and the smoke made her sleepy, and she rested awhile, her head pillowed on Windrider's hard shoulder. Barely a word was spoken among them all day.

It was very early the next morning when the train finally pulled into the station in St. Louis. Swanson hired a carriage to take them to their hotel. Summer Storm could not recall being this weary since the chicken pox epidemic, so she wasn't in any mood to put up with the belligerent desk clerk who looked down his puny nose at them when they arrived.

"We have two rooms reserved under the name of Swanson," the delegate told him.

The desk clerk shook his head. "We don't cater to no Indians here."

"Look here, fellow. You took our money in advance, now give us the keys."

A smirk creased the clerk's sullen mouth. "They'll have to sign the register first. Rules is rules."

Windrider stepped forward, a menacing look on his face. When the hateful little man behind the desk stepped hastily backward in fear, Windrider merely snatched the pen from the desk and swiftly signed his name. Then he handed the pen to Summer Storm, who promptly did the same.

Windrider held out his hand. "The keys," he said.

The clerk hesitated, then he grabbed the key from its peg and tossed it on the counter. "The price don't include meals, and baths in the room are extra. 'Course I don't expect you're too familiar with those anyway."

With deliberate ease, Windrider reached across and took hold of a huge handful of the man's shirt, nearly lifting him from the floor. "Little man with the big mouth, I don't like you. You would be wise not to anger me further, or I might become violent."

He released the clerk with a sharp shove that sent him stumbling. Without waiting for further comment, he took the key and led Summer up the stairs to their room. They fell wearily into bed, both of them wondering if their poor reception here was any indication of what awaited them on the rest of their mission.

The situation did improve, but not by much. St. Louis had seen its share of Indians for many years, but when it had been explained that Windrider was a chief's son and Summer Storm a chief's daughter, interest perked immediately. This was a new oddity for the citizenry to view. Windrider wasn't certain he cared for this attitude any better. It made him feel like a trained bear on display and he could sense the bigotry behind the carefully constructed smiles of the people they met in the following days. Summer wasn't fooled either. She had met her share of prejudiced snobs before, and these people were cut from the same bolt of cloth. The faces were different, but the attitudes the same.

Almost from the start, plans went awry. Though they met the government officials, and some of the representatives of other tribes who also opposed signing the new treaty, many of the Indian delegates had not yet arrived, and the meetings were delayed. Then, just as it seemed business might get underway, the Thanksgiving holiday took precedence.

Since one of the white men in charge of the talks had relatives in the city, all of the tribal representatives were invited to a holiday feast at the home of Hiram and Mary Williams. They arrived to find at least forty white guests already there, elaborately attired and awaiting them with ill-concealed curiosity.

Mary Williams met them at the door of her elegant home. "Oh, do come in!" she gushed. "I was just telling a few of our other guests how wonderful it is to have you celebrating Thanksgiving with us this year. Why, it will be like that very first Thanksgiving all over again, Indians and whites feasting together!"

Summer barely bit back a groan at the woman's naive excitement, and when she slid a quick glance in Windrider's direction, she could see that he was torn between disdain and outright laughter.

One of the original delegates sent to the tribes served as interpreter for the Indians, since most of them did not understand English. Looking about, Summer was dismayed to see that several of the leaders of other tribes had been convinced to dress in white men's clothing. They looked ridiculous and uncomfortable in their ruffled shirts and formal evening-wear, and their long dark braids and decorated headbands. Those who had chosen to wear their usual attire might look out of place in this elegant setting, but they had also preserved that special dignity and pride that Summer so admired.

Equally at home in either situation, Summer had still opted to dress in deerskin for this occasion, as she and Windrider were representing their Cheyenne tribe. Windrider looked particularly handsome in his best buckskin shirt and leggings. Elaborately fringed and decorated with beadwork, it was as fine as anything the white men wore. The previous winter, Summer had sewn him a thick fur coat from the hide of a bear he had killed, and she saw several admiring glances sent his way as he removed it and handed it to a waiting servant.

Summer, too, was receiving her share of appreciative looks. The faces of some of the white women were openly envious as Windrider helped her out of her full-length fox fur cape. No fancy silk or satin gown could have complimented her more than her creamy doeskin wedding dress, which she had chosen to wear this evening. Only on her wedding day had Summer looked more beautiful. She stood proudly before these strangers now, her unbound hair flowing like wavy black silk over her shoulders, her golden eyes gleaming from beneath her intricate headband. The shining silver discs jangled merrily as she shook her hair back from her face and transferred Shadow Walker to her other arm.

As Summer eased the covering from over her son's face, several of the women came forward eagerly to see the baby, and the tension of the moment was broken. Windrider watched in amusement as his wife was led to a nearby divan and instantly surrounded by chattering ladies. As he joined a group of men, he smiled to himself. Men might differ greatly, but women the world over were basically the same. Show them a baby, a pretty dress, or a new recipe and their interest was instantly aroused.

"Oh, dear! I wish that interpreter would come over here!" Mary Williams lamented. "There are so many things I would like to ask you!"

Summer chuckled. "Then ask, Mrs. Williams. I understand you perfectly." She thoroughly enjoyed the startled faces of the women around her.

"Oh, my goodness!" Mary exclaimed. "I'm so sorry! I had no idea you spoke English. Most Indians don't, do they?" The petite woman's brow wrinkled in confusion.

"Not usually," Summer agreed calmly.

Introductions were made, though Summer was certain she would never recall all their names correctly.

"Where did you learn to speak such perfect English, dear?" an elderly lady questioned.

"My parents taught me when I was young," Summer replied simply. Not wishing to elaborate on her mixed heritage, she left it at that.

A young woman by the name of Jean asked, "That tall Indian who helped you with your coat—are you his squaw?"

Even though she knew the question was perfectly innocent and not intended to harm, Summer's hackles rose. Forcing her irritation aside, she explained. "Windrider is my husband. I am his wife, not his squaw. That is a term badly misinterpreted by white men. It generally refers to a woman living with a man without benefit of marriage."

Several faces burned red in embarrassment, and Jean hastened to apologize. "I meant no offense, Mrs. Rider."

Slightly taken aback, it took a moment for Summer to realize the woman's thinking. Jean had naturally assumed that since Summer was married, she would adopt her husband's surname, as in white society. Therefore, she had addressed Summer as Mrs. Rider. As the evening wore on, others made the same mistake, or called her Mrs. Windrider. Many simply blustered about, not knowing how to address her, and it amused Summer greatly. In the end, she simply asked them to call her Summer Storm to eliminate confusion.

In a private moment over dinner, she shared the joke with Windrider, who laughed delightedly. "Summer Storm Rider?" he suggested amusedly. "No, you are the Storm—I am the Storm Rider." The roguish gleam in his eyes told her he would demonstrate this fact once they were alone in their room.

Dinner itself was a bit of a fiasco, but everyone managed to muddle through. The warriors were used to eating separately from the women, but they bowed to white custom for this occasion, though some were not pleased at doing so. Dining at a table, with chairs and linen and china, was a new and strange experience for most of the Indians present. While the table knife and spoon were recognizable utensils, the fork was a mystery to them.

To ensure that they would not be ridiculed or greatly embarrassed, Summer Storm quickly and quietly explained in Cheyenne the white customs and table manners which were considered proper etiquette. Those who understood her words interpreted to their fellow Indians by means of sign language. Though a few took offense at instruction from a woman, most understood her good intentions and were grateful to be spared being made to appear foolish before these white people. Many a fork or napkin slipped from clumsy fingers, but they managed with fair success that made Summer ache with pride for them.

The food was delicious, and much of it was not uncommon to the Indian palate. There was smoked turkey, grouse, scalloped corn, and sweet candied yams. There were mounds of chestnut dressing and fluffy mashed potatoes, and fresh creamery butter and flaky biscuits. These foods seemed to please the warriors, though few of them cared for the baked ham, deviled eggs, or tart cranberries that accompanied the meal. Dessert consisted of plum pudding and mincemeat and pumpkin pie with frothy toppings of whipped cream.

The item that met with the most favor, however, was the freshly-cranked ice cream. Having never experienced this cold, creamy confection, or anything like it, the Indians exclaimed over it with delight. Completely fascinated, their stern faces melted into broad smiles. Like wide-eyed children, they savored the feel and taste of it on their tongues and lips. Several abandoned their spoons in curious delight, to poke at the strange mixture with their fingers. Still others licked it studiously from their spoons, enthralled with the way it melted from the heat of their mouths. Many a noble mouth and chin dripped sticky streams before all was said and done. The meal ended with much laughter and shared joy; something no one had really expected from this unusual gathering.

Thanksgiving now over, the meetings started in earnest, though with little success. With serious intent, the government officials argued, persuaded, and pleaded their case; but the tribal leaders, as a whole, stood firm in their refusals. As the days and weeks dragged on, neither side was gaining concessions. It seemed they were at a stalemate, with little hope of breaking it, yet they continued to meet and talk.

Windrider was fast becoming frustrated. Despite

his impassioned speeches, he could not convince these white leaders that dissolving the reservations into individually owned farms of specific acreage would be detrimental to his people. He tried to make them see that in doing so the government would be taking still more of the Indians' precious land—how harmful it would be for their hunting—but these men were not impressed. Though they sympathized somewhat, they kept arguing that if the warriors would only learn to farm, they could survive very well on small homesteads. White settlers did it all the time and turned a tidy profit. They simply could not understand the Indians' aversion to farming, no matter how the Indians tried to explain it to them. The cultural barriers of two entirely different ways of life stood between them, and neither side could fully appreciate or enlighten the other.

Time wore on and tempers grew short. Patience was at a premium as Christmas approached. Many tribal leaders wanted to stop this useless negotiating and return home to their reservations, but the U. S. officials asked them to stay until after the start of the new year. They would take a short break for the upcoming holidays, and reconvene the first week of 1889.

Summer had attended a few of the meetings at first, but as time dragged on and no significant progress was made, Windrider suggested that her days would be better spent coaxing opinions and intentions from the white wives. Men often discussed important issues with their ladies, and much valuable information had been related in the relaxed atmosphere of the bedroom. It became Summer's mission to unobtrusively obtain these bits of news and pass them on to Windrider.

She spent much of her time with Mary Williams, whose husband was deep in Thomas Brown's confidence, and with Jean Dover, whose husband was another of the officials. The two women had readily taken Summer under their wings, partly out of a morbid curiosity about the Indian lifestyles, and partly to become the envy of the other ladies. They claimed it was quite an honor to entertain a genuine Cheyenne princess, and soon had everyone else convinced and jealous into the bargain.

The teas and luncheons to which they dragged Summer were tedious at best, and often very trying on her temper. The stupidity and outright nosiness of these white women was amazing and extremely irritating. Summer came to detest these meetings, where she was pelted with the most outrageous, rude questions. Never would she have dreamed of asking another woman some of the things she was asked!

"If you and this man are really married, where is your wedding ring?" one dim-witted woman asked almost accusingly.

Summer pinned her with a piercing look from her amber eyes. "Not many of the white customs are also ours," she said, clenching her teeth and trying to stem her rising irritation. "These are my wedding bands." With a flourish, she displayed the wide gleaming wristbands. The intricately engraved copper was quite impressive.

"Is it true that two or more families often occupy one of your tepees?" another lady asked.

Summer nodded. The woman was only partially satisfied, for with a sly look, she commented, "Then however do you preserve any modesty at all, dear girl? Isn't it also true that Indians wear no clothing to bed?"

Summer looked the woman square in the eye with

all the royal hauteur she could command. "Have I yet asked you what color your husband's nightshirt is, or if he bothers to wear one?"

The woman puffed up like a banty hen and stalked off in an offended huff. Summer could not have cared less. She was sick and tired of their endless, idiotic questions. They asked everything from how many children the average family had, to whether they ate skunks and snakes for dinner. They were morbidly curious about tortures they had heard of, to which Summer merely laughed and said that she had never witnessed anyone burned at the stake or skinned alive; those were only gross exaggerations. Not for all the gold on earth would she have told them of actual tortures her mother had recounted to her, or of her own participation in one particular occurrence.

The women were surprised and obviously doubtful when Summer admitted that Cheyenne brides were virgins and that fidelity was not only expected but demanded. These white women believed, as did the men, that Indian women were promiscuous by nature and that it was commonplace within the tribe. One woman had even heard from somewhere that Indians didn't bother with marriages or keeping to one mate, but mated with anyone and everyone in the tribe, and that no one really knew whose child was whose. Summer was sickened and flabbergasted at this blatant fabrication of outright lies. Someone certainly had a wild imagination and a malicious tongue!

If not for the tidbits of information she gleaned now and then, Summer would have declined further invitations. Truthfully, she did not mind Mary and Jean, for they were basically kindhearted women. They truly tried to be helpful and they did not make such personal inquiries or snide remarks as some of the others did.

Perhaps even harder to take was the women's overt interest in Windrider. They ogled him at every opportunity, issuing undisguised invitations. Even the married women eyed him openly, flirting with him behind their husbands' backs.

To his credit, Windrider ignored them, but his cool disdain only piqued their interest further. The afternoon Summer accidentally overheard a conversation between two of the most wanton of them, she'd finally had enough. She had once again attended a luncheon with Mary, and she was just entering the ladies' powder room when the mention of Windrider's name brought her up short.

"Yes," the one woman was saying, "he is one of the most handsome men I've ever seen. Land sakes, but I do adore his muscles! I've never seen such arms on a man before. I can't help but wonder what it would be like to be held in those arms, caressed by those long, strong fingers!"

"Oooh! Betsy, please do be quiet! I swear I'm going to die just imagining what he is like in bed! He just looks at me with those jet-black eyes, and I positively melt! He's such a magnificent savage."

The first woman laughed. "And you are bound and determined to discover if he is just as savage and wild between the sheets. Sadie, you are a prostitute at heart, but I can't say I blame you where he is concerned. He's surely one fine stallion to look at, and every woman he's met is panting after him."

Summer had heard quite enough. With a strength born of rage, she flung the door wide, nearly bouncing it through the wall. Eyes blazing with golden fury, she stared at the two startled women before her. An angry hiss escaped her clenched teeth. "You are the lowest, most despicable harlots God ever put breath into! You are unfit to even speak my husband's name!"

"Now, honey, don't get into a snit!" the first woman said. "No one's going to take your man from his faithful little squaw and new papoose. We were just letting our imaginations run wild a bit. There's no harm in that."

Summer was not to be placated. "There will be plenty of harm done, and I will be doing it, if I ever catch you within ten feet of my husband again. Even dare to let your eyes wander in his direction, and you will know my wrath. This I promise you!"

The one called Sadie spoke up. "Dear girl, it was only talk. You are getting all upset over nothing, and jealousy is such an ugly thing to see."

"It will be beautiful compared with what you will see reflected in your own mirror if you dare to approach my husband with your brazen smiles and fluttering lashes once more," Summer sneered. "No man will ever look upon you with yearning again, unless it is with the desire to retch at the very sight of you."

Both women had paled at her words, yet still tried to hide the fear they were beginning to feel. "You wouldn't dare harm either of us. That is an empty threat, and you know it."

The cold, confident smile that barely curved Summer's generous lips sent chills racing down both their spines. Her piercing gaze never wavered from theirs. "Would you stake your life—or rather, your beauty—on that?" she asked mockingly. So fast that neither of them saw her hand move until it was too late, Summer drew the small knife from its hidden sheath in her belt and sent it whizzing through the air.

It passed between their heads, which were just inches apart, and lodged in the wall behind them. Over their startled gasps, Summer said, "Look behind you, *ladies*. It is no accident that you shall each find strands of your hair clinging to my blade."

Tentatively, with wary glances at Summer, they peered at the knife still quivering in the wall. Sure enough, strands of both blonde and red hair hung from the wall, pinned there by the sharp blade.

"Be wise and heed my warning well, for I will not repeat it," Summer advised. "And you might spread the word to all your wanton friends. I am through with watching women throw themselves at my husband like she-dogs in heat." With that she calmly retrieved her knife and left.

Early that evening Windrider returned to their hotel room to find Summer in tears. Alarm raced through him, for she never cried. "What is it, my dove? What has caused these tears that stain your lovely face?"

He waited anxiously as she swallowed a last sob. "Oh, Windrider, I want to go home! These people are so hateful, and the women flaunt themselves so brazenly, lusting after you so openly, as if I had no eyes to see what they do before my very face! Today I had to threaten two of them away from you, for you would never believe how boldly they spoke of their desire for you! Please! Let us pack our belongings and go home."

Her tearful, pleading gaze made his heart turn over in his chest. "Soon, Golden Eyes. I have given my word that we will stay until the new year when the talks resume, and I must honor my promise. We will leave as soon after that as we can manage. I will have no one putting tears in your lovely golden eyes again. No useless treaty with the United States government is worth that to me.''

18

As much as Summer dreaded staying in St. Louis any longer, Mary Williams promised her a lovely Christmas, and it looked as if she seriously meant to deliver just that. The tale of the confrontation between Summer and the two white women had made the rounds, much embellished by the time it met Mary's ears. Mary and Jean were both furious. They had tried so hard to nurture good relations between Summer and the other women. Now to have all their efforts destroyed by these two brazen, vile-tongued vipers was the last straw! Mary called a conference of all the women in her particular social circle and gave a tongue-lashing of her own. When they left the Williams home that day, not one was left in doubt of Mary's feelings. She would not abide having her Cheyenne friend harmed further, either by vicious gossip, nosy questions, or unwelcome flirtations. Anyone who did so would no longer be admitted to her home, and Mary was a very influential person in St. Louis society. It would not pay to cross her.

Once this was established, there were no more incidents. Those women who tended to be nasty kept their comments to themselves, and those who wanted to be friends went out of their way to be nice to Summer. With Christmas fast approaching, there was much to be done. There were cookies and candy to be made, decorations to hang, and a tree to be found and decorated. There were gifts to be bought and wrapped.

Summer had no money of her own with which to buy gifts, and she was not about to accept charity. Neither would she ask Windrider, for even if he had some, which she doubted, she could not buy his gift with money he had given her.

In the end, it was Jean who inadvertently offered a solution. "I would dearly love to have a deerskin dress such as yours to take home to Washington and display to my friends," she said.

"If I had the skins, I could make one for you, but I imagine deerhide is difficult to find in St. Louis," Summer offered graciously.

"Not as hard as you would think," Mary told them. "A lot of trappers still come through here to trade. I know just the place to look."

She took them to a small dingy store down along the waterfront in a rather seedy section of town. Here they found exactly what they were looking for. As Summer browsed through the stacks of hides, searching out the best doeskin, just the smell and feel of the soft hides made her terribly homesick. She came away with the material she needed, and a deep yearning for the sight of old friends and family.

By diligent labor, she finished the dress for Jean, and one for Mary, with time to spare. Mary had decided she, too, wanted an authentic doeskin dress. She would wear it to her Christmas party, in honor of her new friend. Though not as fancy as Summer's wedding dress, they were still quite lovely. It helped that the doeskin had already been properly scraped and softened, and smoked to prevent shrinkage. All Summer had to do was cut and sew the dresses to fit. Then she decorated them with fancy beadwork and long, heavy fringe.

With the money Mary and Jean had paid her, Summer went Christmas shopping. It gave her a great deal of pleasure to buy small gifts for several of the women who had been friends to her. She bought sachets and handkerchiefs for them, though for Mary and Jean she had made elaborate headbands to match their dresses.

With special care, Summer purchased small toys for Shadow Walker. At six months, he was now sitting up and grabbing at anything that his chubby little fingers could curl around. He was a very alert and active little fellow for his age, and he was even now attempting to crawl about on his own. No longer quite so content in his confining cradleboard, he had to be watched constantly when given his freedom from it. Summer never left him alone on a bed or divan, for the rascal would soon roll to the edge, and she feared he would fall and seriously hurt himself. His bright amber gaze was captured by anything bright or colorful, and everything he touched found its way into his mouth. Summer had already fashioned a soft leather chewing ring for him, for she could see two tiny white teeth about to poke through the surface of his lower gum.

With the leftover scraps of doeskin, she had already sewn him new leggings, shirts and tiny moccasins, for he had fast outgrown the ones she had brought with them for the trip. Now she sought out gaily painted wooden toys and rattles to entertain her bright, handsome boy. This was Shadow Walker's first Christmas, and she wanted to commemorate the occasion, since they might never celebrate it again once they were back on the reservation.

It took much shopping before Summer found the gifts she wanted for Windrider. Once she saw them, she knew they were perfect for him. It took every cent she had to buy the superbly crafted hunting knife with the razor-edged steel blade and the elegantly carved bone handle, and the elaborately hand-tooled leather belt and sheath for it. She could hardly wait to see his face when she presented them to him.

Windrider had plans of his own for this holiday spent among the white people. For Hiram Williams, Bill Dover, and Thomas Brown, he fashioned fancy drawstring tobacco pouches, while for a few others he made the braided string ties they seemed so fond of. Then, needing money for additional gifts, he set about winning it by teaching several of the white men some of the more favored Cheyenne games of chance. With his winnings in hand, he went in search of a special Christmas gift for his beloved wife.

As before, the holiday dinner was held at the Williams' house. Afterward, a small party was scheduled. Traditional Christmas carols were played on the piano, to the delight of their Indian guests, who joined in the singing with guttural chants that somehow matched the melodies. Eggnog and freshly baked doughnuts were passed around, and then the Christmas candles on the massive Christmas tree were lit. The Indians stood and stared in awed silence at this spectacular sight. Even the small gifts of tobacco did not impress them more than the sight of the gaily decorated pine, its graceful boughs outlined by brilliant light.

Windrider had received tobacco and a beautifully carved pipe from his white friends. For Summer there were scented soaps, packets of pins, and colorful hair ribbons. Many of the women had also bought small toys or cookies for Shadow Walker. Summer was touched to tears, but this time they were tears of gladness.

Summer waited until they had returned to their hotel room to give Windrider his gifts. The stunned look on his face as he reverently touched the magnificent knife and traced the intricate designs of the belt and sheath were reward enough for her diligent search.

In turn, he presented her with two small gaily-wrapped packages. Eagerly she tore the wrapping from the first to find a bottle of her favorite perfume. "How did you know?" she asked in wondrous delight.

He smiled at her obvious pleasure. "It is no great mystery. When we were visiting at your parents' ranch, I noticed a near-empty bottle on your dresser. I remembered the name and thought you might enjoy another bottle. Now open the other package."

Once the paper was removed, Summer lifted the

lid of the small box. Never, in her wildest imaginings, had she expected such a spectacular gift! With trembling fingers she reached inside to remove a small, tear-shaped topaz pendant and matching drop earrings, all suspended on fine gold chains. Words failed her as tears of joy made her eyes glitter as brightly as the gems in her hand. "Oh, Windrider!" she choked. "They are absolutely beautiful!"

"When I saw how they matched the color of your eyes, I had to have them for you," he told her. "Put them on so I can see how they look on you."

She hurried to do as he requested, her hands shaking so in her excitement that she could scarcely manage the tiny clasps.

For good measure, she dabbed a bit of the perfume behind her ears and at the base of her throat. Then she turned and faced her husband, impatiently awaiting his opinion.

"The jewels are lovely," he said, noting how the pendant lay nestled in the pulsing hollow of her throat, "but your eyes still outshine them. You, my enchanting wife, are more beautiful than any jewel the earth offers, and many times more precious."

Without another word, he approached her. One by one he removed each item of clothing from her body, his smoldering dark eyes never leaving hers. Then, leaving only the gleaming jewels and her wristbands to adorn her naked form, he picked her up in his strong arms and carried her to the waiting bed.

With his hands and his lips, he adored her body. Each toe, each ankle, each arch knew his special touch. He traced a warm, wet, tingling path of fire up her quivering body, and when he at last reached her brow, he started down once more. She tingled, she burned. She caught fire and glowed more brilliantly than any sunlit gem beneath his sensual touch. She shimmered for him alone, arching into him as he worshipped at the altar of her glorious womanhood. So sweetly did she respond to his every caress, calling out her desire in soft, muted cries. She was a dancing flame held brightly in his hands; luring him, enticing him ever closer to her consuming heat.

Then he was a part of that dazzling blaze, twisting and twirling higher and higher, like sparks caught in a whirlwind. White-hot passion exploded through them, searing them with breathless bursts of radiance that went on and on into eternity until nothing was left but gently smoldering embers glowing softly in the night.

They left St. Louis in mid-January, after further talks had failed to produce a solution to the impasse. Everyone was tired, disappointed and disgruntled. The whites still insisted on employing the Dawes Allotment Act, and the tribes still staunchly refused to acknowledge it. Tempers had grown short toward the end, both sides flaring up in bouts of angry words. As they boarded the westbound train for home, Windrider suspected that the government would do as it wanted anyway, and that all the time and effort spent here would be not only fruitless, but ultimately useless. It had all been an exasperating exercise in futility.

The delays had now thrust them into the worst of winter. The train took them to Tulsa, where they suddenly found themselves stranded. When they attempted to retrieve the horses that were to have been waiting for them there, the stable owner disclaimed any knowledge of the mounts. Yes, he remembered them, but no, the horses were no longer here. A couple of soldiers had collected them nearly a month before.

Their situation was critical. Left in the middle of nowhere, with no food and no horses, and only a few dollars between them, they had no way to get home. Certainly, they could not walk over two hundred miles through the dead of winter. Neither could they stay here, for their meager funds would barely buy a decent meal.

Windrider considered stealing mounts for them, but he would also need to steal food and supplies as well, and already the people in this small town were eyeing them with suspicion. They wouldn't get five miles before being caught and hung. There were also several men who had been openly leering at Summer Storm, and the sooner they left this place, the better.

They had few options, and they had to find a solution quickly. There was Shadow Walker to consider, and they needed shelter immediately. They could either stay here for the remainder of the winter and try to find some means of supporting themselves, or they could find a way out of this hostile little town.

It was growing dark when Summer suddenly hit upon any idea. "Let us return to the railway station, Windrider. There is something I wish to check on." She explained on the way.

Once there, she boldly approached the ticket agent. "Is the line still open to Pueblo?" she asked.

The man barely glanced at her. "Yeah. The train

leaves at ten in the morning," he grumbled.

His dismissive attitude annoyed her.

"Is there a telegraph office and a bank in this spit-and-miss town?" she snapped irritably.

The man glowered at her. He jerked his thumb in the direction of the main street. "Just follow yer nose, Pocahontas. You can't miss it."

The telegraph operator was almost as amiable as the ticket agent. "I would like to send a telegraph to Pueblo, Colorado, to a Mr. Adam Savage," she told him.

"Savage?" the fellow snickered, his gaze flickering over all three of them. "You are kidding, aren't you?"

"Mister, I'm tired, hungry, and my feet are freezing. I am in no mood for jokes. I just want to send the wire."

His look sharpened, taking in her golden eyes. "Say, are you white?" he asked.

"No, I'm Chinese."

"No need to get snappy," he grumbled. "Just show me your money and I'll send the message."

The message sent, they waited in the small office for the reply.

"This could take a while," the operator warned.

"We'll wait," Windrider replied tersely. They had nowhere else to go, and as cramped and uncomfortable as this tiny cubicle was, it was warm and dry.

"Listen, I usually close up at six and go home. There probably won't be an answer till morning anyway. I really hate to turn you out, but you'll have to leave then."

Windrider nodded. "We'll wait here until you

close.''

A few minutes later, the town sheriff walked in, shaking fresh snow from his coat as he entered. His glance narrowed as he noticed the Indians. Windrider was standing erect as usual, but Summer was slumped against the wall, hugging Shadow Walker to her. Her eyes were closed, and every line of her face showed fatigue.

''Trouble here, Amos?'' the sheriff asked.

''Not really,'' came the reply. ''These folks just sent a wire and were hoping for the reply before six. I told 'em it probably won't be till morning, though.''

At the voices, Summer wearily opened her eyes to find the sheriff's hard gaze upon them. ''Where are you two from?'' he asked brusquely.

In her present mood, Summer was tempted to tell him they were from New York, or somewhere equally ridiculous, but she stood quietly and let Windrider answer.

''Oklahoma Territory.''

''Indian reservation?''

''Cheyenne.''

''You're a ways from home, aren't you?''

There was no need to reply to such an obvious observation.

''Who'd they send the wire to, Amos?'' he asked the telegraph operator.

''Some fellow in Pueblo by the name of Savage. Can you beat that?'' Amos chuckled.

The sheriff frowned at them. ''Okay, what's the story here? What kind of mischief are you up to?''

Summer blew up. ''Oh, for sweet pity's sake! Not a blasted thing has gone right since we left St. Louis!

We end up stranded in this one horse town, and now it's against the law to send a telegraph to my own father!'' Her eyes shot golden flames at the stunned sheriff. ''Go ahead! Arrest me! Arrest us all! At least we'll have a place to lay our heads tonight!

''Just make sure that message gets through!'' she said aside to the grinning Amos. ''Charlie Plagger gets forgetful in his old age.''

''You're white!'' the sheriff said in surprise.

''Nope. She's Chinese,'' Amos put in with a chuckle.

''Damn it, Amos, pipe down!''

To Summer, he said, ''Okay, lady. Let's hear it.''

Summer glared at him belligerently, obstinately refusing to open her mouth. Windrider was also suddenly struck mute, and the sheriff certainly wouldn't get any information out of Shadow Walker.

After a few tense moments, the sheriff barked, ''Amos! Send another wire to Pueblo and find out if this Savage fellow actually exists. I want a reply straight from Sheriff Tom Middleton personally, and I want it immediately!''

''But I was just about to go home and have some supper,'' Amos complained.

''Don't tell me your problems. I have enough of my own. You just stay right here until that reply comes in, and I don't care if it takes all night. Do you hear?'' he bellowed.

''Half the town probably heard you,'' Amos mumbled irritably.

''Alright you two,'' the sheriff said to Summer and Windrider. ''We're gonna take a nice little walk down the street to my office, and don't try anything funny.''

"There's not a humorous bone left in my body,'' Summer retorted with a glare.

The sheriff marched them the few doors down to his office. There he promptly locked them in one of the two cells in the one-room building. Seating himself behind his desk he stared at them through the bars. "Let me know when you're ready to talk.''

"Don't we at least get a last meal?''

Irritation flared in the sheriff's face. "Lady, just shut that smart mouth of yours, and I'll think about feeding you.''

Half an hour later, they were dining on mouth-watering chicken and dumplings from the cafe across the street. The coffee was strong and steaming, helping to revive their waning energies, and the apple pie was heavenly.

"At least I got us a meal and a place to sleep,'' Summer told Windrider sheepishly, embarrassed that she had not let him handle the situation.

"And arrested,'' he added dryly. "The only reason I am not angry with you is that I know that Tom Middleton and your father will verify that you are related to them and we will soon be free.''

She nodded. "And as soon as Father can wire the ticket money, we will be on our way to Pueblo. I hope you don't mind, but that was the only solution I could think of.''

Windrider shrugged. "Anything is better than being stuck here all winter. At least we will be with your family until the weather clears, and not among strangers.''

It was close to midnight when the sheriff came

storming back into his office, madder than a hornet. "What's the idea of not telling me you are Sheriff Middleton's granddaughter?" he shouted. "And for crying out loud, what are you doing dressed like an Indian?"

"I *am* an Indian!" Summer shot back.

The sheriff groaned. "I don't even want to hear this." He sighed heavily. "I have a message from Tom and one from your father. Tom says for you to try to stay out of any more trouble until you get home; your father has wired money for you. You can stay here for what is left of the night. In the morning, I'll escort you to the bank so you won't cause a fuss there, and I will personally see you aboard the ten o'clock train to Pueblo. Then, if there is still a God in Heaven, I'll never set eyes on either of you again."

"Back again already?" Hunter teased when they had at long last arrived at the ranch. "It seems like you just left."

"Don't joke about it, brother dear. After all we have been through, it really is not very funny."

"It is good to see you, Summer," Tanya said, coming up to kiss her daughter's cheek. "And you, Windrider."

Shy as always, Dawn Sky had hung back. Now, seeing Shadow Walker, she stepped forward. "Let me take him, Summer," she offered. "You and Windrider get something to eat. You must be starved after your long trip."

As Dawn Sky disappeared down the hall, Summer asked, "How is Dawn, Mother?"

"Much better. By the time spring arrives, she

should be completely recovered. Being fairly well snowed in serves her purpose well just now, but she cannot remain reclusive forever.''

"Has she said anything about the Church?'' Summer asked tentatively, not sure if her parents knew of Dawn's wishes yet.

Tanya pressed her lips together in momentary agitation. "Yes. I told her we would speak of it later. She is still too young to make such a decision.''

"She is fifteen, Mother. You were engaged to Jeffrey Young at that age.''

"Yes, and what a terrible decision that was! I hate to think what my life would be if I had married that maniac.''

Though she enjoyed her visit with her family, Summer was anxious to get back to her own life. When the first week of February brought a freak thaw, she and Windrider decided to chance crossing the plains to Oklahoma. There would be risks, but if good fortune were with them, they could be home in half a moon's time.

With horses and supplies from Adam, they set out. For seven days, they followed the thaw, or it followed them. Whichever, the mild weather continued to aid them in their travel. Over the next few days, the temperature dropped gradually, and clouds formed over the mountains behind them. Then just two days' ride from their destination, the storm caught up with them.

It started with a freezing rain and a howling wind out of the northwest, which soon had them chilled to the bone. As soon as the storm had threatened, Summer had removed Shadow Walker from the cradleboard hanging from the pommel of her saddle and strapped him securely to her middle, snug inside her fur cape. At first he had squirmed about, not liking the dark confines, but soon he settled against her warm body and slept. It was a bit stuffy, Summer was sure, but he would be much more comfortable. As it was, the part of her stomach against which he now lay seemed to be the only warm spot on her body. The rest was pure goose-flesh.

Soon the rain changed to snow, driven so hard by the wind that they could barely see an arm's length ahead of them. The temperature had plummeted suddenly with the onset of the storm. "We must find shelter soon," Windrider called to her, "but first we must cross the river while we still have daylight." This was the last river that lay between them and the Cheyenne camp.

Having hunted this area before, Windrider was fairly familiar with it. He chose a stretch of river which was a bit wider than some, but which he knew to be the most shallow, with less dangerous currents and eddies.

As he had shown her on other river crossings, Summer pulled her legs up and half-crossed them, creating a safe cradle for her son and at the same time preventing her clothing from getting soaked in the icy water. Then she let her horse have its head as Windrider led the way into the freezing river. She held her breath and prayed, for this was the part of the journey she hated most. If her horse should stumble, both she and Shadow Walker could be drowned, or at least catch pneumonia from the dunking. Chances were good that they would freeze before they could get dry.

Three quarters of the way across, Summer suddenly felt her horse's hooves slipping from beneath him. As the horse struggled for balance, so did she, flinging herself forward and grabbing at his neck instinctively. She let out a strangled cry for Windrider, even as Shadow Walker gave a startled shriek at being crumpled between his mother and the horse. Her horse thrashed about, trying to gain a foothold on the slippery river-bottom and Summer rocked precariously on his back, one foot still up and the other struggling to find the stirrup. Then Windrider was there, calmly leading her horse to firmer ground and on up the shallow bank on the other side.

Summer breathed a shaky sigh of relief and quickly checked on her son. Shadow Walker gave her a sour look that told her exactly how displeased he was with her. His lower lip protruded in a pout, and his little chin thrust out stubbornly, but he did not cry. She soothed him as best she could and bundled him back inside her coat.

Now that they were across the river, they could seek shelter among the trees. Windrider quickly selected a little stand of small pines that would best suit his purpose. It was the best the terrain had to offer and he would make do. Working quickly, with Summer's help, he bent the boughs and lashed them together to form a small hut. They unsaddled their horses and sheltered them nearby. Then he, Summer Storm, and the baby squeezed inside out of the wind and snow. There was barely room inside for a tiny fire, and as soon as he had warmed up a bit, Windrider went in search of whatever dry wood he could find.

SUMMER STORM

The storm lasted all night and halfway through the morning. Cramped as they were, they stayed warm and dry, none the worse for their adventure. By noon they were on their way again and by nightfall of the following day, rode into the Cheyenne camp, home at last.

19

It was good to be home, to their own lodge and their own lives once more. The next few days were spent in happy reunion with friends and family. While they relayed their own news, there was so much here to catch up on.

Snow Blossom was expecting her first child in midsummer. Already she carried a round little tummy. Compared with Shy Deer, who was near the end of her term, Snow Blossom's stomach appeared small, but she was delighted to share her glad news with Summer.

As ungainly and uncomfortable as she was, Shy Deer had not lost that calm, sweet demeanor that endeared her to everyone. She patiently went about her day, waiting for the time when her child would be born.

All was well with Singing Waters and Two Arrows and their infant son. Sweet Lark asked anxiously for news of Mark. All Summer could say was that he sounded fine from his letters home, that he was busy and that he'd asked about Sweet Lark. Mark would return again in summer.

It was in the following moon, the Bud Moon, that Shy Deer gave birth to her second son. Though it was a long hard labor, both mother and baby came through fine. He was a beautiful child, with a mop of black hair and chubby little arms and legs. When his proud father heard his son's first sharp cry, he named him Crying Eagle, for the piercing cry of the majestic bird.

Later that night the drums beat out the news for all to hear. Chief Winter Bear had another son. It was a time for great celebration.

While Shy Deer rested and the rest of the camp prepared to celebrate, Summer Storm returned to her own lodge. Sweet Lark had been tending to Shadow Walker while Summer Storm aided Shy Deer in the birthing.

The moment she ducked beneath the entrance flap, Summer felt queer shivers race over her skin. Sweet Lark lay before the fire, as if asleep, but something told Summer this was not so. Summer's eyes raced about the tepee, her alarm rising as she failed to see her son.

Swiftly she bent over Sweet Lark. As she gently rolled the girl to her back, Sweet Lark moaned, her hand coming up slowly to touch her head. With a deft touch, Summer found the bloody bump on the side of Sweet Lark's head. "Sweet Lark!" she called softly. "Sweet Lark, what happened? Where is Shadow Walker?"

Slowly the girl opened her eyes, moaning with the pain. "Is he not here?" she mumbled.

"No. What has happened? Who did this to you?"

Sweet Lark cradled her head in her hands. "I do

not know. The last thing I recall was sitting here preparing the meal. Then I felt this terrible pain. Someone must have hit me from behind, but I heard no one.''

"Sweet Lark, will you be all right by yourself? I fear someone has taken Shadow Walker, and I must find him. I must get Windrider."

"Yes. Yes, go on. I will be fine."

Sweet Lark looked far from fine, but Summer had to leave her and search for Shadow Walker. "I will send someone to watch over you," she promised as she fled from the tepee. Even in her haste, she stopped to examine the tracks outside the tepee, but to no avail. The latest snow had melted within the village, and the more traveled paths were mucky streams and puddles of oozing mud. There were plenty of footprints, all going different directions and melting together.

Summer ran to the council lodge, where she knew she would find Windrider. Hurriedly, fighting back tears, she told him of Shadow Walker's disappearance from their tepee. "Someone has taken him, Windrider!" she cried fearfully. "Why would someone steal our child?"

Windrider was alarmed by her words, yet he sought to calm her—and himself. "Perhaps there is some explanation. Perhaps someone discovered Sweet Lark's injuries and went to get help, taking Shadow Walker along."

"No!" Summer shook her head. "No, someone struck your sister on the head. That person stole my child. Oh, Windrider, what shall we do? We must find our son!"

"Where was War Bonnet?" Windrider wondered. "He usually guards Shadow Walker when Pouncer is off prowling for his meal.''

"I do not know. I have been with your mother for hours. Perhaps War Bonnet is hunting. Since Sweet Lark was with our son, perhaps he felt it was safe to fly off for a while."

A quick council was held, and the entire village searched immediately. Shadow Walker was nowhere to be found, yet not another person was missing from the camp.

"Could it have been someone from another village, perhaps some enemy counting coup on us?" Two Arrows suggested.

Windrider shrugged. "It is possible, but I doubt this. We must search outside the camp. It will be dark soon, and hard to read sign."

The search party divided into groups, each going in a different direction to search for a trail or some sign of the child.

Summer was frantic with worry as she stumbled along after Windrider. Strangled sobs bubbled into her throat, and panic threatened to overwhelm her. As the sun lowered across the sky, it was becoming colder. The coming night promised to be clear and freezing, and her baby could be out here somewhere, exposed to the weather and the night-stalking creatures.

"Why doesn't he cry?" she babbled, straining her ears for the slightest sound. "Oh, why doesn't he cry so we can find him?"

Windrider cast a sympathetic glance at his wife. He, too, was worried sick over Shadow Walker's safety, but he was trying to keep a clear head. Obviously Summer was beyond that, or she would not have asked such a question. As all Cheyenne children were taught from birth, Shadow Walker had been schooled not to cry. In former days, a crying child could alert enemies to the tribe's location. The tradition of teaching the child to be quiet was still being passed down even now that they resided peacefully on the reservation.

They had searched for nearly two long, desperate hours, and Summer was nearly witless, when suddenly War Bonnet came screeching across the tree tops above them. His piercing cry sounded again and again as he circled over their heads. Swooping low, he landed briefly on Summer's shoulder, then flew off almost immediately. He circled again, swooped down nearby, and rose to the sky.

Summer gazed at Windrider, a tiny ray of hope on her tear-stained face. "Could he be trying to alert us? Could War Bonnet have found our son?"

Windrider could barely stand to hope it, but he was wondering the same thing. "The eagle's keen eyesight is well-known. We are fast losing the light. It is our only chance now."

Though it seemed crazy, stranger things had happened. They followed War Bonnet, keeping him in sight as they wound their way through the trees. At last they came upon a small creek. They followed it for a short way. Then they saw him. Lying on the cold ground, just paces from the water, was Shadow Walker. A large cougar lay nearly on top of him, and for just a moment Summer's heart hammered in her throat until she recognized Pouncer. The big cat was warming and guarding her son, for when Shadow Walker suddenly rolled over in the direction of the creek, Pouncer gently nosed him away again.

Two Arrows stopped short, frowning. "Your cat stole your son?" he wondered.

"No," Summer concluded. "Whoever did this has undressed my son, for he was clothed when he was taken. Pouncer could not have done this." Gently she picked him up and held Shadow Walker to her breast. He was cold—so cold that his little toes and fingers were stiff and red, and his lips and face were bluish-gray. "I would sell my soul to know who did this."

Windrider's eyes were narrowed in anger, his nostrils flared in his drawn face. "We will discover who has done this deed. You have my word." He removed his shirt and wrapped it securely about his son. "Come. We must return to camp, and warm our son before he becomes ill. Pouncer's attempts to warm him have probably saved his life, but now we must get him home and warm him thoroughly."

Windrider signaled the other searchers that the babe had been found, and they started back. It was a long walk back to the village in the dark, but Summer had her son safely in her arms and scarcely noticed anything else. She held him tightly to her, giving thanks that they had found him relatively unharmed.

Once inside their tepee, Summer bundled Shadow Walker in thick furs and laid him as near the fire as possible. She heated stones in a pot of water over the fire, wrapped them, and stuck them inside the covering to further warm her baby's chilled body. Gradually the color returned to his tiny face, and his lips stopped quivering.

While she was busy doing this, Windrider questioned his sister. She remembered hearing or seeing nothing. Other than the nasty bump, which was not severe, Sweet Lark was not harmed.

Then Windrider walked slowly about the tepee, his eyes roving carefully over every item, noting the smallest of details in their familiar settings. Suddenly he stopped, his eyes narrowing as he frowned. Slowly he stooped to pick something from the thick fur of a buffalo robe nearest Shadow Walker's cradleboard. it was an amulet of unique design—the special charm always worn about Morning Moon's neck. In all the village there was none exactly like this, worn only by Morning Moon.

Summer looked up to find Windrider studying the object in his hand. "What is it, Windrider? What have you found?"

His face was set in stern anger, his black eyes blazing. "It is Morning Moon's special charm," he said evenly. With determined steps he headed from the tepee, grabbing several long leather thongs on his way. "Look after our son well, Summer Storm; I will tend to Morning Moon." He was gone before she could ask him just what he intended to do.

Before too long he was back again, but Summer had other problems on her mind. Shadow Walker's breath had begun to rattle in his tiny chest and he was beginning to feel feverish. A quick consultation with Root Woman produced pine and cedar shavings, which she simmered in a pot of boiling water. Then, using a blanket to hold the vapor close, she created a steamy tent about the infant. All night long she worked worriedly over her small son while Windrider looked on and Pouncer paced the tepee with lashing tail.

Toward dawn his fever broke and his breathing was nearly normal. With a sigh of relief, Summer sought her own sleeping mat. Just before she succumbed to blessed, beckoning sleep, she thought to ask, "How did you deal with Morning Moon?"

"The white man's religious book, the one called the Bible, says 'an eye for an eye, a tooth for a tooth'," he said mysteriously. "I have done just that."

Sleep claimed her before she could question him further. Whatever it meant, she would find out in the morning.

Shadow Walker had a stuffy headcold and a scratchy throat for several days, but these were the only aftereffects of his long hours of exposure on that cold March afternoon. Summer was profoundly thankful, for if he had been lost overnight, he would probably have died. The temperature that night had dipped below freezing, with a brisk west wind that had made it feel much colder. The skies had clouded quickly the next morning and before midday, the snow had been ankle-deep.

When Summer asked Windrider again about Morning Moon's punishment, not a muscle flicked in his bronze face as he answered calmly. "If you go to the place where she left Shadow Walker, you will find her."

Summer frowned thoughtfully. "Is she dead?"

Windrider shrugged nonchalantly. "Possibly—or perhaps not quite yet, but soon."

His evasive answer roused her curiosity. "What have you done with her?"

"Exactly what she intended for our son. She is helplessly exposed to the forces of nature, unable to return to the warmth and comfort of her lodge. Like Shadow Walker, she is unclothed; unlike him, she is now dangling from a limb overhanging the river, her feet immersed in the icy water. It is the very fate she wished for our son, with one exception. She has been beaten until the blood runs in streaks down her body, for I wish her to know great pain before her body becomes numb with the cold, and if the forest creatures are attracted by the smell of her blood and her fear, so be it.''

"It is fitting that she suffer the very fate she herself devised," Summer admitted. "I am glad that she will no longer be able to inflict her twisted vindictiveness upon us.''

For nearly one full moon, their lives went smoothly. Windrider worked with his horses, and Summer tended to her home. The smell of spring came on the wind, and each day Sun walked across the land a little longer and with more warmth, heating the earth for its spring birth. Soon it would be time to move to their summer camp again. Soon Summer's family would return for their annual visit.

It came as a surprise when Jeremy and Hunter arrived in mid-April. As before, Jeremy's news was not good. With them they had brought a printed notice, put out by the U. S. government.

"Look at this!" Hunter exclaimed, ready to explode with anger. "This is how trustworthy the white officials are toward the tribes!" He waved the paper before Windrider's nose.

Taking the paper, Windrider read it with growing dismay and fury. All those long hours of negotiation in St. Louis had gone for nought. All that time and all those words wasted! In his hands he held an announcement declaring certain Indian lands in the Oklahoma Territory open for white settlement. There was to be the first of several "land runs" on April twenty-second, just days from now.

"What does this mean, Windrider?" Summer asked as she, too, read the notice.

A muscle jumped near his temple, and his face was grim as he answered flatly. "It means that our fine 'friends' in Washington have once again betrayed their

'Indian brothers.' It means that over all our objections and refusals, the Dawes Allotment Act has been officially enacted, and what lands the whites have already decided are surplus have been declared open for white settlers. Lands directly in the middle of Indian Territory are now to be granted to whites, invading our holdings and splitting the tribes even further.'' His dark eyes gleamed with deep resentment.

"And this 'land run'? What exactly is it?''

Jeremy explained. "It is the same as the 'land rushes' or 'land grabs' held in other territories. The authorities set a certain time for the land to be declared available. All those who wish to participate gather, and when the gun goes off to mark the start of the race, they rush off to stake claim to the particular plot they wish to own. Usually they have to agree to make some improvement upon the land in order to keep it; build a home, raise a crop, and so on.''

"Sort of squatter's rights,'' Hunter grumbled.

"Only it is our land they intend to squat upon, with the government's smiling approval,'' Summer added. "Is there nothing we can do to stop this?''

"Probably not,'' Jeremy said discouragingly. "It has already been decided, and there is no stopping it. In a week's time there will be white settlers scrambling for land right in the heart of Indian territory.''

"And in one week's time, they will regret their greediness heartily,'' Windrider snarled. "The time for talk and peaceful acceptance is done.''

"What do you intend to do?'' Hunter asked.

Windrider drew himself up proudly. "For too many years I have seen these white worms eat away at our land and our pride and stood helplessly watching. No more! This time I shall stand and fight like a warrior."

Hunter nodded agreement. Like many young braves and warriors, he had long wanted to strike out against the white tyranny that ruled the tribes, even here on their own pitiful reservation lands. Their fathers and grandfathers had fought bravely against the white invasion, even though they had lost the war in the end. The young men of Hunter's generation had never had that opportunity—until now. Now, win or lose, they too would make their anger felt with singing bows and flying arrows.

"I will join you on your quest, my brother," Hunter said, his golden eyes aglow, "as will many of our tribe and other tribes who resent this intrusion."

"This will not solve anything," Jeremy put in with a concerned frown. "It will only stir up trouble and bring government troops down upon your necks. You are going to get yourselves killed by your hotheaded actions if you attack these settlers."

"Then we shall die as proud Cheyenne warriors, not weak-willed old women!" Windrider declared vehemently. "I have no wish to die a toothless old man upon my sleeping mat. To be killed in battle with one's enemy brings no dishonor. On the contrary, it brings great honor and glory to a warrior's name and to his family. When I die, may it be with my weapons in my hand and my war cry echoing upon the land."

"What of your wife and son?" Jeremy asked. "What are they to do while you are out raiding?"

Summer spoke up almost before Jeremy had finished speaking. "We shall be at his side, of course."

As Windrider bestowed upon her a look of intense pride, Jeremy exclaimed, "Summer, you can't! My God, girl! The cavalry is going to be all over this band of renegades like a swarm of riled hornets! You will be risking your life every minute you are with them."

"Should I sit back like a coward, Jeremy?" she suggested, disgust written clearly on her beautiful face. "I am a Cheyenne warrior, as my mother was. It is not merely an honorary title, but one I earned. At the first opportunity to truly prove myself, you think I should not defend what I believe, that I should not fight for what is right?"

"You'll be placing your son in danger," Jeremy argued.

"He has already seen danger in his short life, and he will do so many times before he becomes a man," Windrider stated firmly. "That is the way of things in this life."

"We must do what we feel is right, Jeremy," Summer said.

Windrider nodded. "There comes a time when a man must defend his beliefs with pride, not from his knees but on his feet, straight and tall before his enemy. Now is that time."

"He is right. For too many years our warriors have lived without pride, restricted and ridiculed. It is time we behaved as warriors and struck back. Too many treaties have been broken, and we are tired of being treated like dogs!" Hunter defended his brother-in-law.

Jeremy agreed to some extent. "I know you are angered by this, and I agree that it is unjust that the government should do this. When you went to St. Louis, it was in good faith, to try to negotiate in a peaceful manner."

"And now the whites have once again knifed us in the back. They show us one face over peace talks and another when we turn our backs."

"But is this the best way to deal with the problem?" Jeremy insisted.

"Have you a better suggestion?" Windrider asked simply.

"No. No, I don't," he admitted helplessly. "I just hate to see you put yourselves in such danger, to pit yourselves against such overwhelming odds."

"We may win nothing more than our pride, but is that not a worthy prize, for what man can live without it?"

Later that evening Hunter approached his sister, a sheepish look on his face. "I have not even thought to tell you the news from home," he said apologetically.

"I understand, Hunter. The notice of the land run was more important at the moment. How is everyone? How is Dawn Sky?"

"Everyone is fine. Dawn has agreed to postpone becoming a nun for the time being. Mark is due home soon. Marla sends greetings."

This last comment brought Summer's head up from the sewing in her lap. "Are you still courting her, as you were when we last visited?"

Summer had never seen her oldest brother blush before, and she stared in fascination as color rose to his face. "I—uh—Marla and I were married last month. I guess I forgot to mention that, too!" he confessed in utter embarrassment.

As the shock of his blunt announcement passed, Summer burst out laughing. As Hunter watched in confusion, she laughed until her sides ached and tears of mirth rolled down her cheeks. Finally she choked out, "Was it the pies or the cattle that won you over, dear brother?"

"What are you talking about? You are making no

sense whatsoever.''

Past a lingering chuckle, she said, ''Not to you, perhaps, but Marla would understand perfectly. Congratulations, Hunter, you have a wonderful woman for a wife, even if it did take you a while to notice the fact.''

''I know.'' Hunter shook his head in wonderment. ''Who would have guessed that pretty little Marla Denning was so interested in ranching? She was raised in town all her life.''

Fresh peals of laughter bubbled from Summer's throat as she rocked with glee. Hunter frowned at her in frustration. ''Now what is so funny?'' he snapped.

''Nothing,'' Summer squealed. ''Nothing at all.''

Many of the younger warriors agreed to follow Windrider on raids against the white settlers. They were tired of living under white domination, sick of being humbled and humiliated. More than willing to risk their lives for their honor and the glory of battle, they elected Windrider as their leader.

In a special ceremony that brought tears of pride to Summer's eyes, Windrider was elevated to the status of chief by vote of the tribal council. Not since Panther, had the tribe needed a war chief. Chief Winter Bear was a tribal negotiator, a decision maker, a decider of tribal disputes—he was a ruling chief in times of peace. Chief A-Panther-Stalks had been the tribe's war chief, the one who led them in battle, the one who planned raids and attacks with the warriors. Now Windrider would take his place. It was fitting that Panther's son-in-law, and Winter Bear's son, would now try to match Panther's legendary cunning and countless coup.

Though they respected Windrider's need to

avenge this latest humiliation, some of the older warriors declined to join the raiding party. "We have had our time of glory, our day of battle," one said. "Go and do what you must. Bring honor to yourselves and your Cheyenne tribe. Let the whites feel the sting of your angry arrows. We will watch and be proud, but it is time for the younger warriors to earn their honors and count their coup."

Summer thought perhaps there was more behind these generous words than was being voiced, but she held her tongue. She suspected that some of the older warriors felt the raids would be futile, that the cavalry would soon end the fledgling battle and the white settlers would gain the land regardless. Perhaps they were right, but she would follow her husband into battle—she would follow him to the ends of the earth if need be.

Another very special and very rare ceremony was held before they left, one that neither Summer nor any other woman could attend. It was the sacred ceremony for the purification and renewal of the sacred medicine arrows. For four days the warriors secluded themselves in the ceremonial lodge. There the four sacred stone-headed medicine arrows, revered for their mysterious powers of protection in battle, were carefully rewrapped with fresh sinew and the old feathers replaced with new. Prayers and chants went up for the safe return of these young warriors who were about to do battle with their enemies. *May the benevolent spirits guide and protect them in their mission.*

In the soft pink light of dawn, the day after the land run, the warriors and their families rode from the village. It would be many days before they returned, for they would camp elsewhere, not wishing to bring the angry soldiers down upon those who remained peacefully behind in the village.

Summer bid a fond farewell to Chief Winter Bear and Shy Deer. She kissed Sweet Lark on the cheek and held baby Crying Eagle for a final time. Then she mounted her gray mare, checked to be sure Shadow Walker's cradleboard was secure about her pommel, and joined her friends in the procession.

The women and children were centered in the group, surrounded by warriors to protect their flanks. Horses with disassembled tepees and household goods strapped to them were led by the women. They would find a secluded area and set up camp. From there they would conduct their raids, then move on to a new location.

Later Summer would ride at her husband's side, but for now she rode with Singing Waters and Snow Blossom, who was now big with child but determined to follow her husband. Their pack horses in tow, the women rode after their husbands, each wondering to herself what the days and months ahead would bring. With a soft sigh, Summer trained her gaze ahead, a smile lighting her golden eyes as she spotted her husband at the head of the group, the new Chief Windrider proudly leading his band of renegade warriors to do battle for Cheyenne honor.

20

So began yet another phase of Summer Storm's ever-changing life. Within days they had made their first raids, swooping down upon the newly arrived settlers in the midst of Indian territory. Though warned that something of this sort might happen, the land-hungry farmers were ill-prepared. They ran from their covered wagons, their hastily erected tents and crude shelters, seeking cover anywhere they could find, but there was nowhere to go, no place to hide. Many burned alive, as the warriors set fire to their flimsy homes and canvas wagons.

This small band had little use for captives, so rarely was one taken. Their raids were swift and sure, and quickly over. They struck unexpectedly, burned, killed, raided, and left as swiftly as they'd come. Those settlers who survived these lightning attacks, and lived to tell about it, told of painted devils riding down upon them with all the fury of Hell, their wild war whoops nearly as terrifying as their flaming arrows. Many a fresh scalp found its way to a Cheyenne belt, and many a horse was claimed as prize for a day's successful raid.

Word soon spread throughout the territory of these renewed raids, and of this bold new chief who led them. Tales of these swift and varied attacks were retold by whites and Indians alike. The cavalry was soon called into action after years of relative peace, but try as they might they could not locate the renegade warriors. They always seemed to strike where least expected and then vanish. Troops were sent to various villages, but no one seemed to know from whence this avenging band had originated—that or they simply were not telling what they knew.

Rumor had it that Cheyenne Chief Winter Bear's son was behind the raids, but when a cavalry troop was sent to investigate, the chief indignantly produced his newborn son, to the vast humiliation of the bewildered troops. "I truly doubt my son is capable of such deeds as yet," Winter Bear jeered. "It would be a wondrous thing to behold if it were possible. My pride would know no bounds."

"Then you have no idea who this Chief Windrider is?" the lieutenant persisted uneasily.

"I have heard of him, as you have, but there is no such person in our camp," Winter Bear answered evasively.

Meanwhile, the raids continued, never in more concentrated areas, but on small, secluded farms. Like an irritating mosquito, they would strike and be gone, leaving in their wake a string of burning farms and dead or terrorized settlers.

Each report told of larger parties of warriors and more widespread destruction. Knowing how these tales could be exaggerated, the cavalry tended to discount much of what they heard.

Windrider's band was, indeed, growing in size. Hearing of their daring routs, young warriors from other tribes joined the select group. Wisely, Windrider carefully selected his new recruits, making it understood from the start that he would brook no challenge to his authority. If others wanted to join, they would have to accept his leadership.

With each new raid, Windrider's fame grew and so did Summer's. As the sole female warrior among them, she drew a lot of attention. Recalling tales of another female warrior with golden eyes, many thought they were one and the same. Others said not, for this one had hair as black as sin, where the other had light hair. Besides, the other warrioress had fought twenty years before, and this woman was young, by all reports.

Then stories began to circulate that both women had been seen riding with the renegade band, and the soldiers shook their heads in confusion. It was bad enough trying to catch these elusive warriors without having the tales of their bold attacks embellished. After each raid they seemed to vanish into thin air like smoke, leaving no trail to follow and no indication of where they might next appear. To top it all, word now had it that the famed Chief A-Panther-Stalks had joined the band, having been recently seen riding at the head of the warriors alongside Chief Windrider. This was all too confusing and ridiculous to be believed. Chief Panther had not been seen in a dozen years at least. Surely he was long since dead, killed and buried in some unknown place.

This rumor was also based on fact, unbeknownst to the baffled cavalry. Tanya and Adam had both joined Windrider's band for the summer, as had

Hunter. Even Mark rode with them from time to time. Dawn had stayed behind in the Cheyenne village, living with Winter Bear and his family, but Hunter's new wife, Marla, had daringly come along to be near Hunter.

Though she knew next to nothing about the Cheyenne way of life, she stubbornly set out to learn. "If you could do it, Summer, so can I," she told her friend. "I won't be left behind when Hunter visits his Cheyenne relatives."

"Yes, but I spent my first seven years growing up among the Cheyenne," Summer reminded her. "I've known the language and many of the customs since I was a small child. Besides, this is not the typical Cheyenne village these days. Here we are in constant danger, ever on the move and on the lookout for the cavalry."

Marla made a wry face. "I'll survive." Summer had to admire her friend and new sister-in-law's spunk. She sincerely hoped Hunter realized what a rare treasure he had for a wife.

Shadow Walker was now one summer old and already charging about on his chubby legs. Once he'd found that his feet were for something other than to play with, there was no stopping him. He was like a small whirlwind, trying to go in several directions at once. His naturally inquisitive nature often got him into trouble with his mother.

"He is a rascal!" Summer told Tanya, who only laughed and recounted some of the escapades Summer and her brothers had gotten into. "If not for Pouncer and War Bonnet, the little stinker would have long since seriously hurt himself. Just yesterday War Bonnet caught him by the hair and saved him from toppling headlong into the fire. Shadow Walker had decided he wanted the rabbit I was roasting. He now has a sore scalp, but at least he was not burned.''

Having been told the story of Morning Moon's treachery, Marla asked, ''I've wondered why neither animal carried Shadow Walker home that day. Why did they merely find and guard him until you reached him?''

Summer shrugged. ''I suppose it was because Morning Moon had removed his clothing. Perhaps they had nothing to clamp hold of without hurting him. I really have no idea. I am just thankful they found him and guided us to him. He would never have survived the night.''

''You were very fortunate to find him in time,'' Tanya said, shuddering at what might have been.

''I know,'' Summer admitted, pulling her small son away from his father's quiver of arrows. ''Now, if he can just survive his babyhood.''

Shadow Walker grinned up at his mother, proudly displaying his shiny white teeth. ''Ma–ma!'' he exclaimed, poking his finger at her eye.

''Imp!'' she retorted with a smile, melting like warm butter as she gathered him onto her lap. ''We should have named you Trouble.''

Singing Waters' son was not far behind Shadow Walker in growth or antics. The two boys spent many hours playing together. Then, in late July, Snow Blossom added another infant to the small tribe. She gave birth to a tiny, delicate daughter. Bright Star was the most adorable, perfect baby girl Summer had ever beheld.

''She is absolutely precious!'' Summer exclaimed in awe. ''She is going to be as sweet and beautiful as her mother one day.''

"Shall we arrange to have our children marry when they are grown?'' Snow Blossom teased.

"Oh no! As wonderful as my own marriage is to Windrider, I will never do that to my own children,'' Summer vowed. ''They will choose their own mates.''

As much as she had changed since coming to the Cheyenne camp and marrying Windrider, Summer was not without qualms about the continued raids. Their lives were fraught with danger at every turn. Though she had confidence in Windrider's leadership as war chief, and her own abilities as a warrior, Summer still worried over their safety.

Then too, there were times during one of their raids when her conscience smote her mightily. Battles were not all glory and excitement. They were also blood and guts and the agonized cries of the wounded. Innocent women and children were often victims in warfare, and it was no different now. It tore at Summer's heart to see this happening, though it was an unavoidable part of battle, one she had no power to change.

To their credit, the Cheyenne had always revered children, and even in these intense raids, if they could spare an infant's life, they often would. Sometimes a child was taken with them rather than left alone to die of starvation or fright. Often it was given to a childless couple to raise as their own. This was done only with small children, however; the ones young enough to forget their white parents and the horrors they had witnessed. Too often though, when the whites realized that the battle was lost, they would slay their children and women themselves rather than have them face untold tortures at the hands of the red savages, little realizing that their babies would not have been harmed, but adopted into the tribe and raised as Indian children.

Scalps, and the taking of such, was another thing Summer found abhorrent. This was one dislike she shared with her mother, for Tanya had always detested this particular custom herself. When they could, both women avoided this and left such dubious rewards to the men.

All through that summer and late into the fall, the band raided the small farms and settlements, successfully avoiding the soldiers. It was during a late summer raid that Summer literally stumbled across Angela.

The warriors had raided a group of three small cabins built alongside a riverbank. Behind the cabins, fields had been cleared, and crops planted. Most of the harvesting had been completed by the time Windrider's band of warriors attacked early that fateful morning. All was peaceful as they rode upon the tranquil farm scene. Even the barnyard rooster had yet to crow his awakening cry to the dawn, and the milk cow still dozed in the lean-to shed attached to the far cabin. The unsuspecting families still slept snug in their beds, unaware of the fate that was so soon to befall them.

There was no warning. One minute all was quiet. The next, whooping savages had burst into all three of the cabins, tomahawks and knives gleaming in the pearl-gray dawn. For a few brief moments, pandemonium broke loose, and then it was over. Four men, two teenage boys, and one young woman lay dead. Another older woman was led alive from the first cabin, the sole survivor.

This particular morning, by luck of the draw, Summer had been allotted the duty of seeing to their horses as the others had crept quietly up to the cabins. Once the signal had been given, she joined her fellow warriors in searching the cabins and outbuildings for food and other useful items before the buildings were burned.

Upon entering the third cabin, she saw the farmer dead in his bed, half in and half out of it, as if he had tried to leap up at the first sign of trouble. Obviously he had not been quick enough. Nor had his neighbors. His young wife must already have been up, however, for her body was lying near a rocker in front of the far fireplace, a poker still in her hand. Whether she had been stoking the fire or trying to defend herself with it, Summer could only guess.

For several seconds Summer stared down in pity at the lifeless form of the pretty young woman so near her own age. Then, with a resigned sigh, she stepped forward to explore the rest of the small cabin. The toe of her moccasin became entangled in the soft threads of a pile of knitting yarn spilling from a basket on the floor, nearly tripping her. With a soft curse at her unusual clumsiness, Summer bent to disentangle herself. It was then she saw the tiny foot poking out from beneath the colorful yarn still filling the basket.

Quickly she brushed aside the layers of yarn, and beneath it she found the hidden babe. With an exclamation of dismay, Summer saw that the tiny child, only weeks old, had somehow wrapped itself tightly in some of the lengthy strands—so tightly that its little face was nearly blue from the strands drawn about its throat.

"No wonder you did not cry out!" she exclaimed, her fingers working frantically to free the strangling infant. Finally, after what seemed an eternity, she succeeded, but by now she could not detect any movement of the tiny chest.

"Oh, little one, do not die now!" She grabbed the infant from its tangled nest and tossed it over her bent knees. Thumping it gently on its fragile back, she half-sobbed, "Breathe! Please breathe!"

From behind her, she heard Windrider ask as he approached, "Who are you talking to, Summer Storm?" Then, over her shoulder, he saw.

"Give the child to me," he directed, reaching for the baby.

Summer thrust it into his outstretched hands. "Oh, Windrider!" she cried, her face frantic. "The child was strangling, and now I cannot make it breathe again!"

As she watched anxiously, Windrider looped his long fingers about the impossibly small ankles and proceeded to dangle the babe headlong from them. For just one horrifying instant she feared he meant to dash the tiny head against the nearby fireplace. Then she saw him slap his big hand sharply against the babe's bottom, and once again on its little back. A thready gasp filled the baby's chest. Flipping the child face-down and cradling it in one large palm, Windrider placed his other hand on its back. Gently he compressed his hands, and with it the little chest between them.

All at once, the infant began to cry weakly. Then it promptly vomited the contents of its stomach onto the floor and Windrider's moccasins. With a wry grin, he handed the wailing child back into Summer Storm's waiting arms. Eyeing his milky moccasins with mock regret, he said, "I should have realized that would happen."

Summer laughed delightedly, the baby cradled securely against her shoulder. Her tender gaze lingered gratefully on her husband's face, then swung to the child in her arms. "Just look at her, Windrider," she breathed in awe. Now that the child was calming, its face was becoming its natural color, and Summer was entranced with the delicate pink and white face so near hers. A small upturned nose was set between two pudgy pink cheeks, and below that a perfect rosebud mouth quivered slightly. A dusting of impossibly long brown lashes framed large round eyes of the deepest sea-blue she had ever seen. The tiny head was capped with a downy covering of hair so light blonde it was nearly white. "She is beautiful!"

There was no doubt in Windrider's mind as he watched Summer Storm caress the child with her expressive golden eyes that she coveted this baby for her own. He resigned himself to that fact then and there. "Do we have a new daughter now, wife?" he asked, already knowing her answer.

"Yes, please." Then, in case she was somehow mistaken in her guess, she quickly checked inside the baby's loose diaper. Black eyes laughed into gold as she nodded eagerly. "Yes, a daughter. And is she not a precious bundle? She reminds me of the angel Aunt Elizabeth has atop her Christmas tree each year, so pink and white and delicate. A darling little angel."

Angela, as she came to be known, was the only survivor of the raid that day, for the older woman's heart had promptly given out. She had died outside her cabin even before Summer Storm and Windrider had emerged from the far cabin with the infant. There was no one to say what the child's name had been before, for no Bible was found with the family's names recorded therein; and there was no one to claim her from Summer's arms or from the heart that had already begun to love her.

SUMMER STORM

Summer's life was full, if not calm, with an inner peace that came from loving and being loved. If possible, she grew even more beautiful in her new maturity. Jeremy, when he arrived in early autumn, was stunned anew by the depth of his feelings for her. As usual, however, his urgent news superseded all else.

"Several forts are combining their efforts in a full-out reconnaissance of the area," he related grimly. "I have managed to learn that they intend to come in from all four sides, gradually tightening their circle about you until they have you trapped. Though they have not been able to predict your pattern, or where you might strike next, they have fairly well narrowed down the general area of your raids, and they have guessed accurately this time," he warned. "They are determined to catch you before the first snows. They have already begun their campaign.

"Also, from your father I have learned that they are constantly harassing those villages they suspect your warriors come from," he told Windrider. "They are watching for you. Knowing what you look like from the descriptions of several survivors, they are also on the lookout for your wife, the one they now call Golden Eyes." Jeremy gave a troubled sigh. "Thankfully, they do not know her real name, but the moment they see her they will know her—and you. It is not safe to return to your father's village this winter."

"It is good of you to warn us yet again, Jeremy," Windrider said thoughtfully. "With winter coming soon, perhaps we should disband until spring. Several of my warriors have families and wish to return to them. Others of us can split into smaller groups, some to go north and some south. We can meet again when the snows begin to melt.''

Panther, who would soon be returning to his ranch, agreed. He had a further suggestion. ''Once we have escaped the boundaries of the cavalry's search, our smaller groups should make a few surprise attacks in our varied directions. This will confound the soldiers further, for they will not know which way to go, or where to search.''

''You and Summer Storm could spend the winter with us,'' Tanya suggested hopefully. ''The soldiers would never think to look for you there.''

Windrider graciously declined the offer. ''No, my second mother, though I thank you for the offer. My soul would suffocate within the confines of your ranch, lovely as it is.''

Tanya could not take offense, for she understood his feelings and respected them. ''Then take care and we shall see you in the spring.''

Jeremy was immediately taken with the baby Angela, though he was also somewhat outraged. ''Summer, why don't you let your mother take the baby back with her to Colorado? She would be much better off there.''

Bristling with resentment, Summer asked haughtily, ''Are you saying that I cannot care for this child properly, Jeremy? She is well-fed and loved. She is clothed.''

''It's not that, Summer. God knows you are a wonderful mother.'' An ache tugged at his heart to know she would never hold his child tenderly to her breast as she did Shadow Walker and Angela.

''What then?'' she demanded, her golden eyes flashing dangerously.

"Your life is in such upheaval now," he attempted to explain. "You are constantly on the move. Danger lurks at every turn."

"Countless generations of Cheyenne have grown and thrived on just such a life," she countered stubbornly.

"Perhaps, but Angela is not Cheyenne. What would happen if the cavalry should find you and discover you have stolen a white child from its family?"

Summer's shoulders stiffened in anger. "I did not steal her. Her mother was dead, and so were all of the other whites. Angela would have died, had we left her. Windrider and I saved her from strangling in that basket of yarn in which her mother had hidden her."

"She is white," Jeremy insisted. "She should be raised by her own people—white people like herself. If I had a wife, I would take her myself."

"If you had ten wives, I still would not give her up to you!" Summer retorted sharply.

The stricken look on Jeremy's face brought her tirade to an immediate halt. Of all people, she had no wish to ever hurt Jeremy as she knew she had just done. "Oh, Jeremy! I am so sorry!"

He looked down at her, all the heartache he felt showing openly in his sorrowful green eyes. "Don't you know by now that I would die before I see any harm come to you or those you love?" he asked softly. "I cherish everything about you, and that includes your children, even the adopted ones. I respect and admire the man you have chosen to spend your life with. There is no spite in my heart for you, Summer, only love."

Her fingers came up to gently cover his lips. "Say no more, Jeremy," she entreated softly. "Do not let words such as this come between us and the friendship we now share.''

His deep sigh was heartfelt. ''You are right, Summer. It was not fair of me. I beg your pardon.''

''And I yours, for I would trust you with my life. I did not mean to wound you so deeply with my thoughtless words, but Angela is now my child. She is very dear to my heart and I will not give her up to anyone, not even my own mother—not while I still draw breath.''

''I understand, but I would ask one thing of you.'' At her inquiring look, he said, ''If you are ever in trouble, if ever you need help, promise me that you will turn to me. I will always be there, Summer, ready to help in any way I can.''

''You have my word, Jeremy.'' Then she smiled up at him impishly. ''In turn, you must promise to stop bringing alarming news with you each time you come to our camp. It is beginning to appear that you are a jinx.''

The small camp broke up shortly thereafter. Panther, Tanya, Hunter, Marla, Jeremy, and Mark returned to the ranch in Pueblo. Several families chose a southern direction for their escape. Others rejoined their respective tribes. Windrider took the small remaining group north toward the Black Hills for the winter, assured that the cavalry would not risk the winter's snowbound terrain to follow them there. They would be safe until the spring thaws.

As planned, each retreating group made several raids off of their chosen routes. These sudden diverse attacks in several different directions served to confuse the cavalry leaders. They had no idea what was going on, or which of the attacks were instigated by

Windrider's infamous band of warriors, and this time no survivors were left alive to tell them. Foiled in their best attempts to corner him, they were forced to retire to their respective forts for the winter, disgruntled but determined to catch him come spring.

It was after their last raid that Windrider returned with a captive. Summer had stayed in camp during this final raid, preparing needed provisions with the other wives. With so much to do, she sometimes had to forego her warrior activities in order to maintain her household properly.

Going out to greet her husband, she was unpleasantly surprised to see the young captive he had brought back with him. Summer's brows drew together in a dark frown. It was a young girl seated behind Windrider, her arms tied firmly about his waist. She looked to be about fifteen or sixteen, with large dark eyes and long auburn hair. What was her husband thinking of to bring this young girl back to their camp?

Windrider rode directly up to their lodge, where Summer awaited him. He could see the confusion in her beautiful features. With a flick of his fingers, he deftly untied the thongs binding his captive to him. He shoved the frightened girl to the ground at Summer's feet. "Greetings, Wife of My Heart. I have brought you a slave to help with your many chores about our tepee."

Summer debated the wisdom of telling him she needed no help, but she held her tongue for now. This was something to be discussed in private, solely between the two of them. "Greetings, husband," she said as calmly as she could manage, schooling her features into more untroubled lines. "I have awaited your return with eagerness, and my heart is glad to find you well. Your meal is ready whenever you wish.''

Though her words were properly welcoming, there was a distinctly cool edge to her voice that she could not disguise from his sharp hearing. He knew she was displeased, and he was shrewd enough to know that it had to do with the new captive he had dragged home. Surely his lovely wife was not jealous of this scrawny white girl? This was a new thought for him to ponder.

"If you will see to your new slave, I shall tend to the needs of my horse," he told her. "We shall talk later."

"As you bid," Summer said with a terse nod. Taking the girl by the arm, she led her into the lodge. There she sat her a safe distance from the entrance, away from the weapons hanging there. Seating herself opposite, she studied the girl with critical eyes. Though frightened, the girl also watched Summer, her dark gaze a mixture of fear and curiosity.

"Do . . . do you speak English?" the girl finally stammered. When Summer failed to respond and merely stared at her with those intimidating golden eyes, the girl fell silent again. After several minutes, she pointed to herself. "My name is Dora. What . . . what are you going to do with me?" Her voice broke on a frantic sob. "Are you going to kill me? Are you? Why won't you tell me?" She was nearly shrieking now.

Though Summer could understand the girl's fears, she saw no need to reveal the fact that she could understand her words. With sharp gestures and Cheyenne words, she commanded the girl to be silent. Once more the two young women sat and stared at one another in strained silence.

This is how Windrider found them when he entered the tepee. Ignoring the girl, he addressed his wife. "What bothers you, Summer Storm? I had hoped the girl would please you."

"Does she please *you*, Windrider?" Summer countered irritably.

His wry smile rankled even more. "No, Summer Storm, she does not. My purpose for bringing her to you is to help you with all your work."

"She will be more hindrance than help, husband. It will take time and effort to train her properly, and she will have to be watched constantly, lest she escape."

Windrider shrugged indifferently. "Then sell or trade her to someone else, if you do not care for her. I thought only to ease your burdens when I captured her, not add to them."

Summer eyed him cautiously. "You truly do not find her attractive, Windrider?" she asked. "If she stays, you will not wish to bed with her?"

Windrider laughed outright, his teeth gleaming white in his handsome bronze face. "What need have I of her skinny body when I have you to warm my mat, My Heart? You are nearly more than I can manage, with your insatiable demands. You may put your great imagination to rest, before your wondrous golden eyes turn green with jealousy. I do not desire your slave. She is yours alone, to do with as you wish."

A satisfied smile lit Summer's face. "Then thank you for the gift, Windrider. I shall keep her for now, but if she proves to be more trouble than she is worth, I shall be soon rid of her."

21

That winter of 1889–1890 proved more harsh than anyone suspected. With it came all the perils and struggles to survive the winds, snow, and freezing temperatures. The meat the warriors provided by diligent hunting proved their only salvation. Even with that, by the first of February, The Moon When the Babies Cry for Food, their meager supplies were nearly depleted. The month was sure to prove worthy of its name. In desperation, the men braved the deep snows and wild winds to hunt farther and farther from the camp in search of food for their hungry clan.

It was during one of these longer hunts that peril struck. A sudden, fierce storm roared down on the hunters. Far from camp, the immediate need for shelter was imperative. With wind-driven snow, visibility was soon reduced to mere paces ahead. Everything was a blur of white. The temperature plummeted to a bone-numbing cold. Within minutes none of them could feel their fingers or toes.

Good fortune alone seemed to lead them to the

cave in the side of the mountain, for they stumbled on it quite by accident just when it seemed they were doomed to freeze to death. The mouth of the cave was wide enough to shelter even the horses from the worst of the weather. Inside, it was the width of the average lodge for perhaps ten paces. Then it narrowed into a smaller passageway, the ceiling of which seemed to slope steadily downward. This was just a guess of course, for none of the warriors was inclined to investigate the dark tunnel. Their sole concern now was getting warm and keeping safe until the storm was over. At least the elk and the mule deer they had killed would not spoil before they could get it back to their waiting families.

To the leeside of the ledge into which the cave was carved, Two Arrows found enough dead limbs and brush to start a small fire. The damp wood sent up a cloud of smoke, but the worst of it drifted down the dark tunnelway, which acted as a draft hole. Gray Rock tended to the horses, while Windrider and Brown Hornet cut strips of venison from the deer for their meal. Soon they would all be fed and warm again.

Windrider was kneeling on the floor of the cave, the deer carcass before him. His back was to the rear of the cave. With fingers still stiff from the cold, he wielded his hunting knife on the near-frozen meat.

"This meat will taste wonderful even half-cooked this night," he said to Brown Hornet.

The other warrior nodded. "Even raw it would fill our empty stomachs, but with the fire we shall eat very . . ."

Whatever else he said was drowned out by a tremendous roar so near behind Windrider that the cave floor beneath his knees trembled. That, and the look of absolute horror on Brown Hornet's face, was all the warning Windrider had. Whirling about, he faced the most massive grizzly bear he had ever seen, or even heard of. The gigantic animal was a good nine feet in length and was bearing down on him with the speed of an arrow and all the fury that only a recently awakened grizzly would possess.

Windrider barely heard the shouts of his fellow warriors as the great beast let out another wall-crumbling roar and lurched at him with all its thousand pounds of fur and fury, sharp white teeth bared in a feral snarl and ten razored claws bared for business. In the split instant it took him to react, Windrider clutched his knife and rolled to the side, but the bear was already upon him. With a giant paw as big as Windrider's head, it took one mighty swipe and sent Windrider barreling against the cave wall with a resounding crash. Stunned, Windrider barely had time to raise his knife as the beast descended upon him again. He heard his shoulder snap like dry kindling beneath the weight of the grizzly's immense paw, and through a red haze of pain, he heard his own agonized cry. His final thought as those two blazing eyes met his, those huge white teeth bared and lowering upon him, was that he would never see Summer Storm again, for he was looking death in the face.

Summer Storm had just finished skinning the lone rabbit she had been fortunate enough to trap for their supper. Dora was sullenly adding wood to the fire beneath the cooking pot, and the two babies were sleeping on nearby mats, huddled beneath thick fur robes. Pouncer was guarding them as they slept, and keeping a wary golden eye on Dora, whom the cougar had disliked on sight. War Bonnet was not particularly fond of the girl, either. This afternoon he was off hunting after the two day storm that had kept him grounded for longer than he liked. Pouncer was awaiting his turn to prowl for his dinner, and now he lay lashing his long tail to and fro impatiently.

Suddenly the huge cat's ears pricked up, his head rising and turning toward the tepee entrance in a listening stance. Alerted by the cat's actions, Summer Storm also listened, knowing Pouncer's hearing was much more acute than her own. Then she heard it; the sound of horses' hooves plodding slowly over the snow covered ground. When her ear at last picked out the guttural sounds of the Cheyenne tongue, she knew the warriors had returned from the hunt. With a happy smile, she rose to greet her returning husband. Pouncer was on his way before she had her fur cloak from its peg.

As she stepped from the tepee, the sight that met her eyes was not a joyous one. Two Arrows and Gray Rock were bearing her husband's limp body toward her, Pouncer loping fretfully at their heels. Summer's heart lurched into her throat, then plummeted to her feet, taking with it every drop of blood from her face. Her head swam alarmingly, and a loud buzzing sounded in her ears. Only with tremendous effort did Summer prevent herself from fainting. Raising fearful eyes from Windrider's fur-bundled body to Two Arrows' grim face, she whispered through stricken lips, "Does he live?"

The breath froze in her chest, and only when the warrior answered, "He lives," did she dare to breathe again. Hastily she raised the lodge flap, following the warriors inside.

They lay Windrider on a mat near the fire, gently unwrapping the robes from his battered body. Summer Storm could not prevent the sharp cry that escaped her anguished lips as she viewed her husband's badly mauled and bloody form. Falling to her knees beside his still length, tears raced down her face unheeded. With trembling fingers, she reached out to touch his torn cheek. "What happened?" she asked faintly.

"He was attacked by a grizzly bear, and has been badly mauled." Vaguely her stunned mind registered the fact that the other two men also had torn clothing and nasty looking wounds on their arms and shoulders.

Almost afraid to investigate further, Summer asked fearfully. "How bad is it, Two Arrows? Will he live?"

Two Arrows shook his head. "It is very bad, as you will see. I fear he may yet die. Since the attack, he has neither moved nor wakened. His mind and body are in the deep sleep that leads to death."

On a trembling breath, Summer sobbed. "Thank you for returning him to me, Two Arrows. If my love alone could heal him, he would surely live. Now I must tend to him with my meager knowledge of healing and do my best to save his life. Go and have your wife tend to your own wounds."

"I will send Singing Waters to help you with our chief," he promised solemnly.

Gray Rock added, "Snow Blossom will soon be here also."

Summer Storm nodded, her attention already on her wounded husband. Gently she peeled the blood-soaked buckskin from his torso, wincing as dried shreds of skin and clothing came with it. "Stoke the fire and bring the water to a boil," she commanded the watching Dora.

"What?" The girl stared at her dumbly, her huge dark eyes flickering to Windrider's torn body.

No longer caring if the girl learned she could

speak English, Summer instantly repeated the demand in precise English. "Hurry, you foolish girl! Do not stand there staring. Do as I tell you, quickly!"

Dora snapped out of her surprise and scurried to bring in more firewood to add to the flames. Later she would ponder the fact that her strict mistress with the flashing golden eyes spoke perfect English. For now she must do as she was told, for Summer Storm brooked no disobedience. She had no doubt the chief's wife would beat her senseless if she dallied now, while Windrider's life hung in the balance.

With warm clear water and gentle hands, Summer Storm removed her husband's tattered, bloody garments. Ever so tenderly she washed the blood from his body, revealing the full and startling extent of his many wounds. Not once did Windrider stir from his deep sleep. Not a muscle twitched nor a moan escaped while she ministered over him. His skin was hot and dry with fever, drying the water almost as soon as it touched his body.

An agonized moan escaped her own stiff lips as she gauged the extent of his injuries. His left side had borne the brunt of the attack, for several ribs on that side were cracked and broken. Summer could only hope there was not severe internal injury as well. Windrider's left hip had been dislocated and there were five deep gashes in his thigh that ran nearly from hip to knee. His left shoulder was broken, a chunk of meat torn away from the fleshy part of his arm just above the elbow. A ragged row of claw marks ran from his shoulder to the middle of his broad chest. Least serious of all, but still heartrending, were the three bloody gashes from near the outer corner of his left eye down across the upper ridge of his high cheekbone. They stood out like brightly painted streaks on his pain-paled face, though Summer judged only one to be deep enough to leave a lasting scar on his handsome features.

Summer had her work cut out for her and she knew she must work quickly to save her beloved's life. Pushing her shock and grief aside, she drew on that inner strength she knew must sustain her through this terrible trial. Later, when Windrider was safe and sound, she would give in to the tears and trembling that threatened to overwhelm her. Now she could not afford such a luxury—and neither could Windrider. His life depended now on her cool competence and quick actions.

To Summer's immense relief, Singing Waters and Snow Blossom were soon there to help her. Together they labored over their chief's broken, torn body. While they held him according to her directions, Summer called upon all her veterinary and medical knowledge to set his broken bones and relocate his dislocated hip. They bound his ribs against further damage and cleansed the open cuts. A cleansing healing salve was applied to reduce the chances of infection, and the gashes were drawn together and bound with clean cloth. The deeper gashes were carefully sewn with the finest of stitches, and covered with salved bandages.

All the while, Windrider slept, never flinching, never flicking so much as an eyelash. In one way, Summer was glad that he had not awakened to the pain their healing hands were inflicting upon his tattered body, gentle though they tried to be. Yet his deep sleep bothered her, for it was not a natural healing sleep, but one of intense shock that sent the mind into hiding from its pain. Such shock alone often killed a person, Summer knew.

Now the waiting began, and this was perhaps the most difficult time for her. Time and again she bathed his fevered body, repeatedly checking his wounds for signs of fresh bleeding or the beginnings of infection. On those wounds that seeped, she changed the dressings, replacing soiled bandages with fresh ones. With her friends' help she forced water and nourishing broth into him, gently massaging his throat to cause him to swallow the strength-giving liquids his unconscious body needed so badly in order to heal itself.

For three long, nightmarish days Summer never left his side. Singing Waters and Snow Blossom quietly took her children into their own lodges, frequently checking on Summer and Windrider, and thoughtfully providing meals she barely touched in her worry over her husband. Under the other women's directions, Dora performed the necessary chores in Summer's lodge, replenishing the wood, bringing fresh water, keeping the fire burning. Life went on around her as Summer anxiously watched over her husband, her mind and heart solely concentrated upon him, to the exclusion of everything and everyone else about her. In all that time she worked and prayed over him; barely dozing, rarely eating, hardly daring to tear her gaze from him, torn with the irrational fear that he would die if she ceased her faithful vigil at his side.

On the evening of the third day, Windrider stirred. Summer's weary mind barely registered this new development until he moaned fitfully in his sleep. Instantly she was alert, her hand flying to his brow. Though still warm to her touch, it was noticeably cooler than before. All through the night she watched over him; bathing him, talking softly and reassuringly to him, touching him with her gentle hands and reaching out to him with her heart and soul.

With the dawn, he awoke. The terror of not knowing where he was, and of remembered pain, shone briefly in his dark, fevered eyes. Then she spoke, and his eyes found the solace of hers, and the fright fled. His lips and tongue attempted to move, but words refused to form. In their stead, a deep moan of agony emerged, tearing at Summer's heart.

"Do not try to speak, my love. Do not attempt to move. I am here, and you are safe. Sleep, my brave warrior. Sleep and heal. I will watch over you, and my love will protect you." She moistened his dry lips with her own in a tender kiss. "Sleep and know that I love you."

Within a few moments his even breathing told her he had drifted off again, but this time it was a healing sleep. Curling up at his side, alert to his every movement, Summer slept beside him. Two days later, his fitful fever finally broke, drenching him in sweat, and she rejoiced, weeping tears of joy and relief.

Windrider's injuries were extensive and his recovery took a long time. For a while Summer continued to tend to him, as their lives gradually returned to near normal. Once he could sit up and feed himself, however, she felt it safe to leave him in someone else's care for part of the time.

"I am going out hunting," she announced abruptly one day. "Singing Waters has said she will look after the children, and Snow Blossom will check on you. Dora can cook your meal and fetch anything you might need until I return."

Windrider's face clouded over. "The men have been providing for us. They gladly share what they have with their chief's family. There is no need for you to hunt with them."

Summer merely smiled. "Husband, I think I have spoiled you very badly these past days. Now you expect my constant attention." From habit, she checked the cutting edge of her hunting knife before returning it to its sheath at her belt.

"The warriors will provide meat for our lodge," Windrider repeated sternly.

"I, too, am a warrior," she reminded him. Then she added, "The snows are very deep and the game takes shelter from the freezing wind. Game is hard to find these days, Windrider. The warriors return with precious little meat to feed our people. I will do my share in helping to provide for our hungry band."

Unable to move about as he wished, Windrider was already straining at the limitations his injuries forced upon him. He cast her a sulky look that reminded Summer very much of Shadow Walker when he could not have his own way. "I do not like you riding with the men when I cannot accompany you," he told her.

"You may put your jealous mind at rest, dearest heart," she laughed. "It is not my intention to hunt with the other warriors."

"You cannot go alone. It is too dangerous. As your husband and chief, I forbid it."

Summer shrugged into her heavy fur coat. "Then by taking Pouncer and War Bonnet along, I will not be disobeying you." She came to him and gave him a loving kiss on his firm lips, her fingers tracing the healing scratches along his face. "Why I did not think to use their fine hunting abilities for our own needs sooner, I do not know." Before he could object further, she stepped from the tepee and was on her way.

Summer's two unusual hunting companions worked with her very well in helping to provide game for her little family. War Bonnet could easily spot their prey from high above, and Pouncer would help her track and trap the beasts. Often he would aid in the kill. After giving her strange partners their fair share, she would take the rest of the meat home, where Dora would help to prepare it. For the most part, the arrangement worked very well, for the two animals also served as Summer's protection on her hunting ventures.

Dora was another matter. For all her help, the girl was sullen and uncooperative unless constantly prodded. Still, she helped to cook the food Summer now provided and to keep the tepee in livable condition. She also watched the children and catered to Windrider's needs while he was unable to move about. Just how well and how amiably the girl did this last chore, Summer was unaware until she entered her lodge unexpectedly one afternoon to find Dora bent close over Windrider.

Summer Storm stood silently for several long seconds surveying the intimate scene before her, too shocked to move. Clad only in his breechcloth, Windrider lay on his mat, his scarred but still magnificent body open to Dora's avid gaze. The girl was bent over him, a tender smile curving her lips, her unbound hair falling lightly over him as she changed the dressing of his shoulder wound. The lacings of her dress were half undone, giving Windrider a perfect view of Dora's pert breasts.

As Summer watched, Dora removed the old bandage, her hands lightly caressing Windrider's shoulder. "I could kiss it and make it feel better," she said softly, her eyes coming to meet his unreadable dark stare. "Would you like that, Windrider?" she murmured. Her free hand slipped down to lay upon his bare thigh.

Before Summer could react, Windrider's strong hands clamped tightly about Dora's wrists, making her squeal in pain. "You overstep your duties, slave," he said coldly, his black eyes now blazing with scorn and anger.

"Indeed!" Summer now stepped forward, making her presence known.

With a shove from Windrider, Dora tumbled at Summer's feet. Those famed golden eyes flashed daggers at the hapless girl, who waited warily for Summer's reaction.

For long moments, Summer said nothing, merely staring at Dora with contempt. When at last she spoke, her words were in English, making certain that the girl understood. "It seems you more willingly serve a master than a mistress," Summer sneered. "That being the case, you should please Slippery Beaver very well. Since putting his wife away from him, he has had no woman to see to his needs. For his many fine deeds, he deserves a reward, and you will do nicely, I believe. Come, slave! We go to meet your new master!" Grabbing a handful of Dora's hair, Summer yanked the girl to her feet.

"No!" Dora screeched. "You can't do this!"

Summer laughed spitefully. "I can do anything I please with you, girl. If I so desired, I could kill you, and no one would say a word in your defense. As my slave, you have no say in these matters."

Eyes round with fright, Dora exclaimed, "I am Windrider's slave, not yours. He is the one who captured me and brought me here."

"And he gave you to me that first day," Summer corrected, her eyes gleaming with hatred. "Now I, in turn, will make a gift of you to Slippery Beaver. I would tread carefully around my new master if I were you, Dora. He has a quick temper and much less patience than I have shown you. It would be disastrous for you to make any rash assumptions with him, as you have done here."

With vast relief, Summer gave Dora into Slippery Beaver's keeping. "Use her well and in good health," she said in parting, a cunning smile curving her lips. If Dora was the only one dissatisfied with the bargain, all the better for the manipulative little twit. Summer was well rid of her.

A few days later, Jeremy rode unexpectedly into their camp, leading three well-packed mules behind him. "What disastrous news do you bring to us this time?" Summer joked by way of greeting as she watched him dismount.

Jeremy grinned at her, his emerald eyes sparkling in his wind-chapped face. "None, thank God! I come bearing gifts." He gestured toward the laden mules. Following her inside the tepee, he continued to explain, "Your parents thought your supplies would be running short by now, so they decided to send provisions. Devoted friend that I am, I volunteered to deliver them." With a rueful smile, he added, "Never mind that I nearly froze my stupid arse in the process. This is a damned uncomfortable time of the year for travel, I'll tell you."

From his mat, Windrider grinned at his friend's colorful speech. "Welcome, Jeremy. Come warm yourself at the fire and tell me of your journey."

Jeremy's gaze swung to Windrider, and widened in surprise at the bandaged warrior. "What the devil happened to you?" he exclaimed.

"You and Windrider exchange tales," Summer suggested. "I will tend to your animals, and if you brought coffee among your treasures, I will brew us all a cup when I return."

Though Jeremy listened with awe and amazement to Windrider's tale of his encounter with the huge bear, he said very little about his recent trials. He hadn't been joking when he'd said that he had nearly frozen trying to deliver their supplies. He'd started out just after the holidays, knowing it would be hard going in the deep snows and storms. Still, it had been months since he'd seen Summer, and with winter at its worst in years, he had to make sure she was faring well. He had gladly volunteered to deliver food to their camp.

The trail had been rough, but Jeremy had made good time, all things considered. He'd reached the Black Hill country the first week of February, when suddenly a fierce winter storm swept down out of nowhere. After hearing Windrider's tale, Jeremy was sure he'd been caught in the same storm, just as unaware and unprepared as the warriors had been.

In all his years, Jeremy had never seen anything like that storm, and he hoped never to do so again. Once was one time too often for him with storms of that nature. A freezing north wind had driven the snow so fiercely that Jeremy could not see the mule he led just behind him. In fact, he could not see his own horse's nose! When, minutes later, his face and hands were already numb with cold, Jeremy knew he must find shelter—and fast! Blinded by the white, driving snow, numb with cold, and deaf to all but the shriek of the howling wind, it was not he, but his horse, who found the sheltering glade.

Nothing more than a pile of brambles shaded by overhanging pines, it looked like heaven to Jeremy at that minute! Shoving his horse and the balking mules through the stiff branches enclosing the small space, Jeremy followed them out of the worst of the wind. After he'd unloaded the mules and taken the saddle from his horse, he spread out his bedroll smack in the center of the four animals, draping them with saddle blankets, tarps, anything he could find to hold their combined body heat within. Then he'd settled down to wait and pray and think of Summer, all the while wondering if he would live to see her dear face again.

Shivering so hard that his teeth clattered in his head, Jeremy had grimly watched as the blizzard continued to display its ferocity. Even surrounded by a wall of warm bodies, he felt chilled to the marrow of his bones. Only thoughts of Summer seemed to warm his soul.

In his mind, he recalled every moment he could remember having spent with her, especially those sweet times since she'd been grown. It was funny how clearly he could envision her in his mind, her golden eyes flashing out an amber challenge. He could see the stubborn tilt of her head, the way her long dark lashes shadowed her eyes in a stunningly provocative manner. And he could see her midnight black hair, not in braids as she had worn it the last couple of years, but flowing loose and wavy down her back, shiny as a raven's wing and oh, so silky, like ebony satin.

Jeremy's tortured mind conjured up the soft, full shape of Summer's mouth. That tempting mouth—oh, God! He could almost taste its sweetness, as he had once known it, could almost feel those velvet-soft lips against his! Jeremy bit back a groan at the memory of her firm young breast cradled in his palm, the naturally seductive sway of her hips, the glow of her face and the feel of her skin.

The colder Jeremy had become, the more he had thought of her and how very much he loved her. He let his most secret longings wash over him, joy and regret combined; for each emotion, each memory, was a priceless treasure he had hoarded like a miser for years. All his unvoiced feelings flooded his heart, and in the privacy of his own mind, he told her of his love;

and only in his deepest hidden dreams did she love him, too.

Jeremy had awakened with a start. For a moment, completely surrounded by blinding white, he thought he had surely frozen to death and gone to heaven. Then one of the mules shifted and brayed, and the illusion passed. Besides, he was too cold to be dead! With a short laugh, Jeremy looked about. Though it was still absolutely freezing, the wind had died down. All about him the pristine snow lay pure and clean, decorating the landscape in a mantle of beauty. The air was crisp and clean, though it nearly seared the lungs, it was so cold, and Jeremy drew a deep breath. It was good to be alive!

The snow may have been heavenly to look at, but it was sheer hell to travel through, as Jeremy could soon attest. He lost count of the number of hours he plodded along on foot, dragging the floundering animals behind him through waist-high snow and drifts taller than he was astride the horse. There were many, many times he truly doubted he would make it to the Cheyenne camp, or anywhere at all in this snowbound wilderness. In his most morbid, self-pitying moments, he wondered if Summer would grieve over his death. Only thoughts of her kept him going, prevented him from giving up entirely.

Then, one day, when Jeremy was certain he could go no further, he looked up to find himself within hours of his destination. Relief assaulted him so strongly that he sat astride his horse and wept, long heartfelt sobs shaking his broad shoulders. He would see his secret love once more after all, and dear Lord, but he was grateful to be alive!

Jeremy stayed through Windrider's long recuperation. Summer was glad of his help. No longer did she feel she had to hunt, for Jeremy now rode with the warriors in search of fresh meat for their lodge. When she was busy with chores about the village, he often helped Windrider watch the children. With Jeremy to keep her husband occupied, Summer could now visit with her friends, a leisure denied her for some time.

With Jeremy's help, Windrider was soon on his feet again. While he complimented Summer on her fine treatment of Windrider's wounds, Jeremy's own superior knowledge now came in very handy. Used to treating animals that often had to regain the strength and mobility of injured limbs and muscles, he worked long and hard with Windrider once the warrior's bones were sufficiently healed. He devised exercises to loosen stiff joints and strengthen the bones without inflicting further damage.

Under his advice and guidance, Windrider made great strides. Soon he was walking with barely a limp. With the stitches removed, he soon regained use of his left arm, which Summer had feared might be hopelessly impaired. As much as it pained him, Windrider faithfully exercised his arm and shoulder. Though it remained somewhat stiff, and ached terribly after a day's use, he could soon use it nearly as well as before. It would probably never be perfect, or as strong as it once was, but Windrider was grateful to be able to function normally, with two arms again. His numerous scars began to fade somewhat as they healed, and he was left with only one noticeable scar, high on his cheekbone, to mar his handsome face.

"It gives your face character," Summer told him, "and makes you look fierce and formidable as a warrior."

"I would not want to look too fierce," he said, pulling her down with him upon his mat, "for then I might frighten my lovely young wife and she would not care to join with me on my mat."

As his lips found hers, she murmured, "I will always wish to join with you, Windrider." With eager hands, she returned his heated caresses, and for several minutes she forgot all else.

With a start, she recalled that Jeremy now shared their lodge. Pulling slightly away, her breath shortened with desire, she panted, "What of Jeremy, Windrider? I would not have him walk in on our lovemaking."

"Jeremy is staying in Two Arrows' lodge this night. I told him I needed to be alone with my shy wife."

A wild blush rushed to her cheeks and she buried her hot face in his shoulder. "He will guess what we are doing," she groaned in embarrassment.

Windrider's chest vibrated with laughter beneath her. "He would be stupid not to know."

He pulled her more fully atop him. "Tonight, since I am yet recovering my strength, you may expend most of the effort." His dark eyes twinkled with merriment as her blush deepened with his words.

"Are you sure you are well enough?" she asked hesitantly. "I would not want to cause you pain."

"Golden Eyes, I shall surely die of my pain if you do not make love with me this night," he assured her. "Please me, my love," he murmured, raising her up to tease at her breast with warm lips. "Pleasure me as I shall do to you."

With all the love in her heart, Summer treated Windrider to a night of splendor neither of them soon forgot. With her playful tongue, she teased him, her moist lips gliding smoothly over every inch of his bronze body. Generous kisses sprinkled across his skin, her warm breath wafting over his wounds as if she would heal him with her love alone. Her hands caressed him, exciting him with the light touch of her fingertips as they traced the contours of his masculine form.

With gentle hands, he unbound her braids, and the silken strands floated down about them like a midnight veil, shutting out all else but the passion they now shared. The long, wavy tresses tickled his thighs and his stomach as her mouth worked its seduction upon him. A groan of intense pleasure rumbled in his throat, like the satisfied purr of some great cat. With a sound close to a growl, he again pulled her over him, entwining her long legs with his. His hands about her hips, he held her poised over him. "Come ride the wild stallion you have roused," he entreated, his dark eyes blazing into hers. "See if you can tame him with your sweet warmth."

One swift plunge, and they were united. A cry of joy escaped her lips and tremors instantly shook her, as if some great earthquake had its center within her. When the spasms ceased, she began to move upon him, his hands guiding her hips in a gentle rhythm. Then the wondrous desire began to build again, more and more, increasing the pace and intensity of their fierce loving. Clinging to him, his name an endless chant upon her lips, her head tossed back in glorious rapture, she rode the untamed passion he brought to her.

Together they raced headlong through colored clouds of ecstasy that burst about them in magical splendor, only to enclose them once more in a shimmering glow of shared elation.

Jeremy was noticeably remote the next day, and for several days thereafter. Throughout an evening, he would often sit inside the confines of their tepee staring moodily into the fire and saying little. Though never rude, he contributed little to the conversation now, and the easy camaraderie the three of them once had shared now seemed forced, on Jeremy's part, at least.

One evening, as Summer was sharing a bit of friendly gossip with the two men, Jeremy suddenly leapt to his feet and stalked out of the tepee without a word. Summer's dumbfounded gaze flew to Windrider's. "What is wrong with him these days?" she wondered aloud.

Windrider shook his head. He had his suspicions about what was bothering their friend, but if he was right, it was something Jeremy had to resolve within himself. Of all people, Windrider could not help him. It was a matter of pride, honor, friendship, and love all warring within one heart, and though Windrider could sympathize somewhat, he knew Jeremy well enough to be sure that honor and friendship would win the battle yet once again.

Summer stood and stared at the tepee entrance. "I think I will go after him and try to get him to tell me what has been bothering him. He has been behaving so strangely lately."

Windrider gazed up at his wife, seeing the concern on her face. For a second, he thought to tell her not to go after Jeremy, but then he thought better of it. Perhaps it was a good idea that Summer talk with Jeremy. It might serve to clear the air and Jeremy's befuddled mind. "Take your coat," he advised. "The night air is bitter cold."

Summer found Jeremy at the edge of the clearing, leaning against the trunk of a tree. He was smoking a cigar and staring morosely up through the leafless branches. At her approach, he glanced at her grimly and grunted, "What do you want, Summer? I came out here to be alone."

Summer frowned back at him. "I wanted to talk with you, Jeremy, to see if I could help with whatever is bothering you. These past few days you have been as prickly as a porcupine! Why?"

It was as if Jeremy had been walking around with a stick of dynamite in his hand, and Summer had just lit the fuse! Even in the dark, she could see the angry glitter of his green eyes as he whirled on her. "For God's sake, woman, are you that dense?" he ground out through clenched teeth. "Don't you know how it tears my guts out each time you smile so tenderly at your husband, or watch him with your heart in your eyes? Can't you see what it does to me to see him touch you, to see the love you share?"

Summer stared at him aghast. "Jeremy, you are our friend! You should not say these things to me."

"Maybe it's past time I said what I feel, Summer. Oh, don't look at me with those huge, hurt eyes, as if I am some monster! Windrider has known all along what you have preferred not to see. I'm not about to betray him, or you, or myself. I admire Windrider. I respect him and your marriage. Besides, I do have some honor and pride left, tattered though it may be!"

"Jeremy, I do not want to hear this."

"That's just too bad, princess!" He stood glaring down at her. "You marched out here wanting to know what the problem was, and now you are going to listen, like it or not! Lord knows it's little enough for the hell you've put me through, sashaying your sweet bottom about day after day doing your wifely chores right under my nose! I've noticed the seductive looks passing between you and Windrider when you think I'm not looking. I've seen the telltale glow on your face, or that shy, half-embarrassed look you get when I've inadvertently walked in on an embrace, though I've done my damndest to make myself scarce lately!

Then, adding salt to the wound, I have sat there night after night and watched you unbraid your hair and brush it, and it has been all I could do not to reach out and run my fingers through those inky tresses. I can barely sleep knowing you are resting curled up in your lover's arms, when all I can dream about is holding you and loving you."

"Stop it!" she demanded angrily. "Say no more! You have no right to say these things, no right to— to . . ."

"To want you?" he supplied. "I'm a man, Summer, not a stone or a saint! I have the same hot blood running through my veins as you do; as Windrider does. And you are an extremely beautiful woman, not to mention the fact that I have always been in love with you!"

Summer's chin rose sharply. "It might be best if you went back to Pueblo, Jeremy," she said stiffly, "before you say more and damage our friendship irreparably."

Jeremy gave a weary sigh and closed his eyes briefly. "Oh, Summer, Summer. How do I make you understand? I've always felt this way, yet I have still been your friend all this time. I have just never said anything to you before, though Windrider knows; and I'm sure if you think about it, you will see that you have also known deep down. If you hadn't pushed me tonight, I would have remained silent, and you would not be angry now. I probably shouldn't have said anything tonight, but nothing has really changed by voicing my feelings. We can all still be friends for many years to come. I am not belittling the love you and Windrider have, nor trying to destroy it. It is just that sometimes I wish that I had been wiser, sometimes my regrets weigh heavily on me, and sometimes I get a little green with envy." This last was said with a wistful smile. "I am human, Summer. Merely human."

Summer nodded, her heart aching for him and all that he had admitted this night. She hated to see him hurting this way, and she dearly wanted to keep him for her friend. She believed him when he said he admired and respected Windrider. She had seen the bond between the two men, and she did not want to see it broken merely because she had been too hasty to poke her nose into Jeremy's private feelings. "I will try to forget what was said here tonight, Jeremy, for all our sakes," she said finally. "I will try not to let it affect our friendship, if you will hold your silence on the subject in future."

Jeremy let out the breath he had unconsciously been holding. "I will keep my feelings to myself, as I have done in the past."

"Then let us return. Windrider will be waiting."

"You go ahead," he told her. "I will be along later. Tomorrow I will move my things to Two Arrows' lodge for the remainder of my stay. Under the circumstances, I feel that would be best."

Summer did not disagree.

Jeremy stayed until Windrider was fully recovered. For a few days following his heartfelt confession, the relationship between the three friends was strained. Gradually it returned to normal, though Jeremy did not again share their lodge. By the time Jeremy left for Pueblo, it was as if the strange conversation had never taken place. They had all silently agreed to put the episode firmly behind them.

22

When spring had come to stay, spreading a blanket of green across the land, Windrider led his band south once more, onto the prairies. With the space of winter between now and their last raids, Windrider felt it safe to return to their village for a short time. His warriors agreed with this, for they were all homesick to see their families again. Their fellow warriors would find them there when and if they decided to resume their raids against the intruding whites.

Summer was elated to see Shy Deer and Sweet Lark once more. She hardly recognized Crying Eagle, who was now fourteen moons old and toddling about on chubby legs. While she exclaimed over him, Shy Deer did the same over Shadow Walker, who would soon see his second birthday.

This would be the last summer that Mark would court Sweet Lark. With one final year of schooling ahead of him, by this time next year, he could claim her as his bride. Nearly sixteen now, she had blossomed into a lovely young woman.

With no new raids in the territory, the soldiers seemed to have forgotten about Windrider's band, at least temporarily. This was fine with Summer, for she was enjoying their time here, and the peace that came with it. If they never went back on the warpath, she would be very happy, but if Windrider decided to resume the raids, she would follow alongside him wherever he led. Meanwhile, she settled into this more tranquil existence with a glad heart, content to raise her two small children and plant her spring crops with the other women of the tribe.

It was twenty years to the day since Summer Storm had been born. This day, too, was proving very stormy, nor did it show any signs of clearing for long. Just as one cloudburst passed, another followed in its wake. Strong winds blew up from the southwest, bringing rains that pelted the earth. Just yesterday the breezes had been warm, joining the sun in heating the earth. Now the rains were cold by comparison, causing Summer to shiver as she lashed the tepee entrance more firmly shut.

"Nature seems not able to decide what to do this year," she commented to Windrider, who was braiding a new halter for one of his horses. "First, it is so hot you can barely breathe, now we need a fire to ward off the chill."

Windrider nodded. "It is strange. Even the beasts seem restless today, as if they sense something unusual."

Summer had noticed Pouncer's restless pacing, but she had assumed he was merely anxious to be off to his mountain rendezvous with his mate. At Windrider's words, she now realized that War Bonnet had also been particularly flighty all day.

A particularly strong gust of wind rattled the tepee, sending rain pelting against the sides. Then the sound changed, the pounding becoming louder and harder against the taut skins until it sounded as if they were inside a giant drum. Curious, Summer lifted the edge of the entrance flap to look out. Her eyes grew wide with amazement as she exclaimed, "Windrider! Come look at this! I have never seen hail this time of year, and never such large pieces! Some of them are bigger than your thumb!"

Rising, Windrider joined her at the entrance, a worried frown creasing his brow. Grabbing a deerskin covering, he said, "I must see to the horses. They are probably crazed with fear at the stinging they are receiving from these big balls of ice."

Seconds after he had left, the hail stopped as abruptly as it had come, and within a few minutes the rain had also ceased. Suddenly the air was unbelievably still, as if the sky held its breath in waiting. Summer had never seen such a strange day, and she shook her head in confusion as once again she tied the entrance flap open.

It was then she noticed the odd yellowish cast to the sky. It gave the earth an eerie look that somehow made Summer uneasy. As she watched, the wind began to blow once more, and she sighed in exasperation, wondering how many times she would be required to open and close the entrance flap. It seemed she had done nothing else all day.

She was just reaching for the lashings yet again when Windrider came dashing up to the lodge. "Get the children and follow me!" he yelled. "Hurry!" Even as he spoke, he grabbed Shadow Walker from the floor, tucking him securely under his arm. "Summer

Storm, hurry!'' he shouted again, pulling at her as she lifted Angela to her chest.

Summer had never seen her usually calm husband so frantic. Stumbling along beside him, buffeted by strong winds that threatened to knock her from her feet, she shouted breathlessly. ''What is it? What is going on?''

Still running, Windrider gestured toward the southwest, where a dark whirling cloud descended from sky to earth in the shape of a twirling funnel. Even as she watched with startled eyes, the cloud drew nearer, sending bits of dirt swirling into her face, stinging her skin and eyes. She drew Angela closer to her in an effort to shield the child with her body.

They were running toward the river as fast as they could manage against the fierce buffeting of the wind. Summer staggered and nearly fell, but Windrider reached out and pulled her after him. When they reached the sloping edge of the riverbank, Windrider nearly threw her and the children over the muddy incline. Following them down, he pushed them hard against the bank, nearly crushing Summer and the children beneath his weight as he lay over them. His harsh breathing sounded loudly in her ear. ''Lie still and hold tightly to the babies,'' he panted.

Angela was whimpering beneath her, and Shadow Walker clung as tightly to her side as a second skin. She could feel his small body trembling to match her own, though he made no sound to voice the fright he was surely feeling.

All about them the wind howled and tugged at them like a mighty, grasping hand. A tremendous roaring filled the air, a deafening sound that shook the earth with its ferocity. The very breath seemed to be sucked from her body, and even with Windrider's large bulk covering her, she could feel the pull of the wind as if it were trying to tear the skin from her bones. She could only guess how much worse it felt to Windrider, who was sheltering his small family with his own body. His fingers bit into her arm as if seeking something firm to hold on to.

Mere feet away, a large tree was torn from its mooring, roots and all, and flung to the ground with a resounding thud. Summer shrieked with terror as its outer branches covered them, creating a bizarre green world about them. Windrider's arms tightened about her in a fierce hug. "It is alright, Summer Storm," he shouted near her ear. Just the sound of his voice was comforting in the midst of this nightmarish turmoil.

Then it was over. For the space of a few seconds, all was calm again. Then the rain began to pound down upon their leafy bower. With a tremulous sigh of relief, Windrider loosened his hold on her and the children. "It is past," he huffed breathlessly.

Sitting up and pushing her straggling hair from her eyes, and a pesky branch from her face, she asked shakily, "What was it?"

"The twisting wind," he answered, peering out of the branches to see if it was indeed safe to leave their meager shelter. "The white man calls it a cyclone, or a tornado. By any name, it is a killer."

Clearing a path from the branches, he pulled Summer and the two babies free. "Come. We must see how much damage was done to the camp and if all our people have survived."

As they climbed back up the riverbank, Summer saw others doing the same, other persons who had also sought this lower ground as shelter against the raging storm. Muddy as they were, it was a wonder they could recognize one another, but she identified several of their friends. With much relief she spotted Chief Winter Bear and his family, all safe.

Summer had never viewed such vast destruction as she saw when she gazed in stunned disbelief at what remained of the Cheyenne village. Nearly every tepee had been blown over, some literally shattered into bits. Debris was scattered for nearly a mile, mixed with what was left of their belongings. Everything lay in ruin, open to the drenching rain that now poured steadily from the sky.

"What are we to do now, Windrider?" she asked helplessly, looking about her in despair.

"We will sift through the rubble for what we can salvage, find what we can of our belongings, construct new lodges and be grateful that we are alive. It will be a great deal of work, but our people have started with less and survived before."

Ashamed of her weakness, Summer straightened her slumped shoulders and waded determinedly into the twisted mess before her. Windrider was right. Regrets were of no use now. Only hard work and determination would set things right again.

From the splintered wreckage of what were once lodge poles, roughly half were usable. The rest were reduced to kindling. Many of the skins were so torn and twisted that they were ruined for use again on the tepees. The women salvaged what they could. Luckily, the large council lodge had not been damaged beyond repair. Within hours it housed several families. Other friends and families constructed one new lodge from the usable parts of two or three that had been toppled by the storm. In this way, everyone at least had shelter by nightfall. In the coming days, the women would replace the lodge poles with new ones from slender poplars along the riverbanks. The skins to use for coverings would not be so easily replaced, however.

The tribe counted itself extremely fortunate. Only three of its people had been killed in the storm; a baby, one old woman, and a young boy. Several others had bumps and bruises and broken bones. One warrior had been hit hard in the head and would be several days recovering, but there were few serious injuries, which was miraculous considering the tremendous damage to the camp itself.

Bits and pieces of their lives were strewn over miles of open land. They collected what they could and immediately set to making replacement tools and weapons. If she had had the time, Summer could have wept. In this she was not alone, for their lives were all in shambles, and it would be many months before it would be close to normal again.

Several horses had been killed in the storm, and most of the rest had fled in fright. While they now had fresh horsemeat to live on, the most important thing was to retrieve their ponies so the men could hunt again.

Early the next morning, Windrider set out with the other warriors to round up the horses. "I shall try to find Mist for you," he promised, kissing her before he left.

"And I will find more of our belongings in this turmoil," she said, gesturing about them. With new lodge poles, she was fairly certain she could salvage enough skins to reconstruct their lodge. For the next few days, they would be staying in her parents' tepee, which had been rolled and tied in waiting until their arrival. In its tightly lashed, disassembled form, it had sustained hardly any damage at all. Even the fur robes her mother had wrapped inside it were still there. If worse came to worse, she was sure they would let her use anything she needed for as long as she wished. Indeed, for a while, everyone would be sharing utensils and tools with fellow members of the tribe, to the benefit of all. It was the Cheyenne way.

One week after the tornado, Summer's family arrived. Though most of the debris had been cleared, it was still obvious that some sort of disaster had occurred. Learning what had happened, they immediately set to work to aid their tribe.

While he and Tanya helped around the village, Panther sent Hunter and Mark back to Pueblo. "Bring all the heavy canvas you can manage to locate," he told them. "It will do very well to replace the lodge coverings; perhaps not as well as skins, but it will work. Also have your grandparents and Uncle George send all the blankets they can spare from the mercantile. There is no way my people can replace all the thick robes they will need for next winter. We will need knives and hatchets and metal for arrowheads."

Tanya sent a list of her own with them. Included were such items as iron cooking kettles, spoons and bowls, large yarn needles, hoes and fish hooks, and anything else she could think of that the women would need in preparing food and new clothing. "It is a shame we have no place in which to buy the hides we need for clothing," she bemoaned. "It will be nearly impossible to properly clothe everyone on what little the men will bring home before winter."

"There was a store in St. Louis that Mary Williams took me to once to buy doeskin to make a dress for her," Summer told her mother. "It was where the trappers and traders sold their goods. You would not believe the stacks of hides the man had for sale." Summer sighed dejectedly. "Of course, even if it were not so awfully far away, we have no money with which to buy the skins, though the prices seemed fair."

Tanya's eyes lit up at this bit of news. "I will speak with your father. When Hunter and Mark return from Pueblo, perhaps he can send them there. Surely we can afford to buy some of what we need so desperately."

Summer was astounded at the extent of her parents' generosity, for though they were very successful ranchers, she knew they were not extremely wealthy, either. In addition to everything else, her father had instructed Hunter to purchase food supplies for the tribe, and had ordered cattle to be driven to the reservation, out of his own herds. Also, several of his best cow ponies were to be brought to help replace those lost in the cyclone.

"Mother, can you and Father afford to do all this?" Summer questioned.

Tanya gave her a level, serious look. "These are our people, Summer. There is nothing within our power we would not do for them. As a chief, your father is still very much aware of his responsibilities to the tribe, even though we no longer live among them as we might wish."

As Tanya had suggested, Hunter left for St. Louis almost as soon as he had arrived back at the village. Jeremy had also come, helping to drive the wagons and herd the livestock, and now he also went to St. Louis, while Mark stayed in camp with the other warriors.

"Never has there been such a fine friend to us," Windrider said of Jeremy. "We are fortunate to know this man whose heart is so good. Surely in his heart he is Cheyenne."

With so much to do to recover from the calamity that had struck such a devastating blow to the tribe, Windrider's plans to regroup for more raids were set aside. There was barely enough time for hunting this summer, let alone for attacks on the white settlers. It seemed a peaceful if hectic summer was in store for the Cheyenne warriors. Much time and energy was spent rounding up their ponies and restoring the village. Autumn winds were blowing across the land before normalcy returned. By then it was too late to bother planning raids for this year.

Hunter and Jeremy returned with many more skins than the delighted women had expected. "How did you manage to purchase so many?" Tanya asked in surprise, knowing Panther had not sent that much money with them.

Jeremy stood grinning as Hunter explained. "We looked in on Summer's friend, Mary Williams, while we were in St. Louis. When she learned of the disaster and our reasons for being in town, she called all her friends together. They all donated to what they called 'Summer and Windrider's Tornado Fund'. By the time they were satisfied, we had money enough to buy all the skins we needed, plus some furs for lining winter garments."

By the time Hunter was done speaking, Summer's eyes swam with warm tears. It seemed she and Windrider had made many friends in St. Louis, regardless of the U.S. government and their damnable Allotment Act.

It was in autumn when word spread of a new religion among the tribes. With great excitement, they learned of a visit from the Christ to the Indian tribes. The Wondrous Messiah had come down to earth to

414

speak to the tribes, to spread his words of peace and comfort among The People. The Paiutes called him Wovoka; others said he was the Great White Spirit, though he did not resemble a white man. Rather, he looked like an Indian, and he spoke in their tongues that all might understand his words. Others knew him as the Great Spirit.

The Messiah brought a message of hope and peace to the tribes. He taught them songs and the Ghost Dance, which he wanted all The People to learn. He told of a time when he would again come to them, if they believed his words and faithfully learned the dance he required of them. When he came again, he would restore their lands to them. Game would return to the plains, and great herds of buffalo and wild horses would be theirs once more. The land would be fresh and new and green again, with no white man upon it.

The Great Spirit would bring back all the dead Indians, making them live again. The old would once again be young. The blind would see, the lame walk, the mute speak, and the deaf hear once more. Life and the land would be sweet and good again, with only the tribes upon it; but they must believe, and they must dance the Ghost Dance while they awaited his return to earth.

Like prairie fire, word spread from tribe to tribe. Soon, on nearly every reservation, men and women alike were dancing this Ghost Dance in hopes of reviving dead ancestors and loved ones. This and the promise of having their land renewed to them had everyone eager to learn of the Messiah's words and his special dance.

There was to be a special ceremonial dance, where one of the men who had actually seen the Great

Spirit and heard him speak at Walker Lake would talk to the Cheyenne and Arapahoe. He would tell them all that he had learned from the Great Spirit and teach them the Ghost Dance. The gathering would be held in the hills between the two reservations, a place advantageous to both nations. Also, it would perhaps keep the soldiers from noticing, as the cavalry was becoming very upset over all this dancing and celebration. It was making the whites very nervous, though they had been told that the celebrations were of a peaceful religious nature, with no plans of war or raids in mind at all.

"We shall go to this Ghost Dance," Winter Bear said. "We shall go and learn the songs and the dance, so that we might also be included when the Great Spirit comes to give our land and our great ancestors back to us."

So it was decided. Summer wished her family had stayed long enough to learn of this, but they had left for the ranch some weeks before. It was all the more surprising then, to have Jeremy arrive back in their camp the very day they were to leave for the meeting. Nearly packed and ready to ride on the four day journey, Windrider went to greet him.

"What brings you back to us so soon, my friend?" he asked.

"On the way back to Pueblo, we heard tales of the Great Spirit visiting the tribes and of a Ghost Dance. The military is sending troops to halt the celebrations wherever they find them, for the whites fear a major uniting of the tribes and a great uprising. Have you heard of this yet? Panther sent me back to see if your tribe was thinking of holding one of these dances and to warn you to beware of the soldiers."

Windrider nodded. "Our thanks once again for

your warning, but we are aware of all you have said. My father and the council have decided we will go and learn more—learn the Ghost Dance for ourselves.''

"Is that where you are heading now?'' Jeremy asked, noticing the tepee being disassembled. ''I thought perhaps you were merely relocating to your winter grounds.''

"First we go to the ceremonial meeting with the other tribes,'' Windrider said. ''You are welcome to come and see for yourself what is said.''

"Perhaps I'd better,'' Jeremy agreed. ''Then I could tell Panther all I learn firsthand. Are you sure the others won't object? I thought this gathering was for Indians only.''

"If you are with us, they will say nothing.''

Upon reaching the meeting grounds, the women erected the tepees while the men wandered about greeting old friends from other tribes. They had arrived the evening before the actual ceremony of the Ghost Dance was to take place. It was early November, still in the Moon When the Leaves Fall Off, and the air was crisp and cool, the nights getting cold, though they had seen no snow as yet.

After she had put their children to bed, Summer sat by the fire and waited for Windrider to return. He would be late, for he and the other warriors would sit for hours and talk. Old war tales would be told, great coups recounted, news exchanged. Still she would wait up for him, for she felt very restless this night. She tried to tell herself it was all the excitement of gathering together with the other tribes for the Ghost Dance, but it was more than that. There was an eerie feeling dancing through her, almost a warning. She was depressed and jittery all at the same time, and it was very upsetting, for she had never felt this way before.

When Windrider at last entered their tepee, he found Summer staring into the flames, a dreamy, lost look about her. It took several seconds for her to notice him, and when she did, she smiled, but it was a sad sort of smile.

"What is wrong, my Golden Eyes," he asked, seating himself beside her and pulling her into his strong embrace. "Why does this sadness sit upon your face?"

"I do not know, Windrider," she said with a helpless little shrug. "It is nothing I can touch, or see, or explain. I have never felt quite this way before."

"Could you be with child again?" he suggested gently.

Summer shook her head. "No, I am sure that I am not, but I wish this gloomy feeling would leave me."

"Come lay with me on the mats, and I will soon chase these dark shadows from your mind. I will fill your heart with gladness and your mind with joy."

Summer laughed lightly. "And what magic will you use, oh, handsome sorcerer?"

His onyx eyes smiled into hers. "The magic of my touch upon your lovely body, and all the secrets of love in my heart."

Summer rose to her feet. Standing silently before him, her golden eyes glowing with love and desire, she removed her dress. It fell to her feet, leaving her body open to his adoration. Her skin glowed like polished copper in the light from the fire. With nimble fingers she untied her braids, combing her fingers through the loosened strands so that it fell in long ebony waves to her waist. Her body shimmered through the dark curtain of her hair in tantalizing glimpses as she bent toward him, holding out her hand to him.

"Come show me your sorcery then, my love," she invited.

Taking the hand she offered, he rose. "It is you who casts the spell, sweet Summer Storm."

With eager hands, she removed his shirt and unlaced his leggings. Her fingers found the ties that held his breechcloth about his slender hips, and with one quick motion it fell to the floor. Windrider stepped out of his moccasins as Summer swiftly unbound his braids.

Then they were kneeling face to face upon the mat, their eyes openly adoring one another. "Tell me what you see, when you look upon my scarred body with such sweetness glowing from your face," he entreated softly.

"I see my special love; my beloved. My eyes see not the scars, but the power and beauty of your body." Her hands caressed him as she told him all she longed for him to know. "Here your shoulders are so wide, so full of power, and here your arms show such strength." Lifting his hand, she placed her lips upon each finger. "These are the hands that provide so well for our small family, the fingers that fashion your weapons, yet touch me with such tenderness." She laid her cheek within his palm, holding it there tenderly, then placed a kiss within its center.

Her hands rose to lovingly cradle his handsome face, her fingertips measuring his wide brow. "Here I see the intelligence of a great man, a leader among his people. And here," she traced his proud straight nose and his high cheekbones, "I find nobility and pride. Your jaw reveals your stubborn streak and I adore your firm lips, especially when they hold a smile for me.

"Most of all," she said, her gaze trapping his, "I love your eyes. There are times when they snap with anger or laugh with such humor, and times when they glow with desire. In your eyes I see the world as I wish it could be, and all the love I shall ever need shimmering in their dark depths. Oh, my darling, I wish I could find the words to properly express just how deeply I love you."

"There are no words," he confessed softly, "or I would have used them to say all that you mean to me. You are the brightest star that lights my life. You are my greatest happiness, my only love, my cherished treasure."

Their lips met and clung in a kiss of such unbearable sweetness that it brought tears to Summer's eyes. His arms enfolded her in that protective embrace that made her feel so absolutely cherished. Together they slid to the mat. With his body he told her what words alone could never begin to say. His hands spoke eloquently of her perfection as they tenderly traversed the curves and hollows of her feminine form. His lips told her of his abiding love, and of his yearning as they adored her face and figure, lingering here and there as if to sip the sweet nectar that was uniquely hers. As his kisses deepened and his heated body pressed more urgently into hers, she knew of his unending desire, the limitless passion she alone inspired in him.

It was a passion that matched her own. As her heart and body responded to his, she surrendered to the desire that engulfed her; and when he came into her, she melted about him like warm honey, drawing him further, until she was sure he had invaded her very soul. It was like dying and being reborn, more perfect and wonderfully than ever, for her body sang with boundless joy and tingled with wondrous delight. Together they journeyed through undiscovered realms of beauty, splendid places touched only by the two of them and the love they shared.

When at last they lay quietly in one another's arms, sleep was a long time claiming them. Their passions sated, they simply lay together, touching with loving caresses not meant to arouse but to soothe, to convey their love. It was a time of wondrous sharing that both were reluctant to relinquish too quickly, a rare moment too precious to sacrifice for slumber's sake.

Long after Windrider's deep, even breathing told her that he slept, Summer gazed lovingly at his face, almost as if she were committing each beloved feature to memory. Her restless fingers seemed compelled to lightly stroke his bronze skin, so warm and firm beneath her touch. Time and again her lips were drawn to him, gently kissing his shoulder, his brow. Curving her long body into his, she laid her head on his chest. Beneath her ear his heart thumped reassuringly, lulling her to sleep with its steady rhythm, and she slipped into slumber with the scent of him surrounding her.

23

Summer's feelings of unease grew steadily the next day, though she could not say why. As she seated herself next to her friends, her children tucked securely by her side, she told herself she was being silly. With the talks and ceremonies about to begin, her mind was probably dwelling overmuch on ghosts. As eager as she had been to see this famed Ghost Dance, she was now glad that the many people gathered about had forced her further back toward the fringes of the crowd. Windrider sat not far from her, though his status as a chief could have earned him a better view had he desired it. Jeremy, Gray Rock, and several others of their warriors were seated around him.

By the time the honored guest finished telling them of the Great Spirit's words and instructions, all sat in awe at the tale. By now it was dark, and the fires had been lit. The speaker had taught them songs to sing with the dance, and now it was time to learn the Ghost Dance itself. As the drums beat out a steady rhythm, the steps were demonstrated with deliberate care, for this was the special dance designated by the Great Spirit himself, and must be done exactly. The teacher chose several people to learn the intricate movements with him while the others watched and chanted the accompanying song.

In turn, they would all learn the Ghost Dance.

Above the singing and dancing, Summer heard a sharp report that could only be from the firing of a rifle. Her head swung about sharply, just as a second shot sounded. Her eyes widened in stunned disbelief to see a troop of uniformed cavalrymen bearing down upon the crowd at full gallop. Suddenly all was chaos as everyone scrambled for cover.

Instinctively, Summer crouched low as she ran toward her tepee, Shadow Walker clutched tightly under her arm and Angela to her chest. Close behind her, she heard a woman scream in pain and prayed it was no one she knew. Ducking to one side, she swerved barely in time to avoid the pounding hooves of a cavalry horse. It passed so close she could have reached out her hand and touched the striped pantleg of the soldier.

Then, miraculously, Windrider was there with their horses. Grabbing Shadow Walker from her, he literally threw her onto Mist's back, Angela still in her arms. All she got was a quick glance of the mayhem about them. Many Indians lay wounded or dying already, while others such as themselves had reached their horses or weapons. Shots ripped through the night air and arrows were flying in every direction as she kicked her horse into a gallop, racing off into the cover of darkness.

In the dim light, she saw the gleam of Jeremy's blond hair as his horse raced alongside hers. Windrider was behind her, as well as several other mounted warriors and women. A group of soldiers was in hot pursuit.

More shots rang out. Suddenly Summer's horse stumbled, almost throwing her and the baby to the ground. Though Mist quickly recovered, precious seconds had been forfeited. Summer had lost ground, falling behind the others. A quick glance behind her told her the soldiers were fast gaining on her. Then Windrider was at her side, thrusting Shadow Walker into her lap, where he clung to her waist like a big-eyed frightened monkey. Windrider's hand came down smartly on Mist's rump, sending the fleet mare racing after the others.

In her efforts to keep tight hold on both of the children and remain seated herself on the wild ride, it was several moments before Summer was aware that Windrider was not immediately behind her. He had fallen back to confront his enemies in defense of his small family. He was gallantly giving her added time to escape, at great risk to his own safety.

An awful dread filled her, and Summer wanted to cry out to him, to tell him not to chance his life to save hers. If not for the two babies relying on her for their own well-being, she would have spun about to join him, but she dared not. As he wanted, she urged her horse ever faster, soon catching up with those ahead of her. Shots sounded behind her and she winced, but rode on. Before too long, Windrider reappeared at her side, pushing his horse up between hers and Jeremy's, and Summer breathed a sigh of vast relief.

On and on they rode through the dark night, skirting hills and dashing around trees in their head-long flight. At last, in the density of the trees, they lost their pursuers. Still they rode on, putting the distance of several hills and miles between them and the soldiers before they finally felt it safe to stop and rest their horses for a few minutes.

Summer slid shakily from her horse, her knees still weak with fright. She set Shadow Walker on his own wobbly feet, and was looking about for a place to lay Angela. As she turned, she watched in horror as Windrider toppled from his horse onto the ground. Racing to his side, she threw herself down next to him. By the dim light of the moon filtering through the treetops, she saw the dark stain that had spread itself over his chest.

Panic struck her full force as she realized it was blood. "Windrider!" Her cry was but a whisper, yet it echoed in her head like a death knell.

He turned his head to find her gaze upon him, and his hand reached out to touch hers. "Summer Storm," he murmured, "let me see my son one last time before I die."

Tears gushed down her cheeks as she grasped his hand tightly. "Oh, Windrider," she sobbed. "We will make camp here and I will tend your wounds, just as I did after the bear attacked you. Soon you will be well again. Please do not speak of death, for I could not bear to lose you."

Jeremy knelt at Windrider's other side, Shadow Walker in his arms. The look of pity on his face told her more than she wished to know as he said, "Shadow Walker is here, Windrider."

The warrior chief gazed upon his son, pride and sorrow showing through the pain. "Raise him well, Summer Storm, for I shall not be there to guide his steps toward manhood."

"No! Oh, Windrider, no! Please do not die and leave me, for I would only wish to die with you." She was sobbing uncontrollably now, her tears falling to mix with the blood on his chest.

"Your promise," he insisted weakly.

"Yes, yes! Anything! Just do not die, for you possess my heart and soul, and how can I go on living without them—without you?"

His pain-glazed eyes sought Jeremy. "I give my wife and my children into your care, Jeremy. You must watch over them for me, protect them as I would."

Past the lump in his throat Jeremy vowed, "You have my word."

"Take Summer Storm back to her own people, where she can find peace again. I do not wish to think of her living out the rest of her life on the reservation, where there is so little freedom."

He was gasping for every breath now, his speech halting and labored as he addressed his wife, his eyes lingering on her tear-streaked face. "Go now, Summer Storm, before the soldiers come near. Know that I love you still, now and always, even as my feet begin the long walk into the next world. Do not grieve too deeply, for we shall meet again, when I will once more claim you for my bride."

Her own shimmering eyes caressed his face, her hand coming up to tenderly touch his cheek. "I love you," she whispered past a shuddering sob. "I will always love you to the very deepest reaches of my heart." Bowing her head, she kissed him sweetly on his lips one last time. "Goodbye, my love."

Rising, she fled on stumbling feet toward her horse, tears blinding her as she struggled to mount the mare, Angela clutched tightly in her arms. Someone helped her onto the horse's back and only when she looked down into his sorrowful face, did she recognize Two Arrows.

"Stay with him, Two Arrows," she implored. "Place his weapons in his hands, for that is how he wishes to die."

Two Arrows nodded gravely. "We will take his body back to our village, where he will be buried with all the honors of a chief and warrior," he pledged. "We will tell Chief Winter Bear of Windrider's wishes for you so they will not worry."

"We must go now, Summer," Jeremy broke in softly. "The soldiers will be searching for us." He sat beside her, Shadow Walker before him on his horse.

Drawing her knife from her belt, Summer quickly whacked off both her long black braids. Handing them to Two Arrows, she said, "Place these upon his body, as symbols of my great grief, that he might have something of me to carry with him on his travels into the next world, though he carries my love with him wherever he journeys."

Summer and Jeremy had ridden several minutes when a blood-chilling war cry rent the night. A great sob caught in Summer's throat as she recognized Windrider's war whoop. It was the last time she would ever hear his voice. He had died a warrior's death, as was his wish, his weapons in his hand and his war cry echoing over the land. She bent her head and wept.

All through the night they rode, stopping only briefly to rest their horses. Neither spoke, both steeped in grief over Windrider's death. Summer rode like a silent ghost upon her horse, guiding him purely by instinct as she followed Jeremy's lead. Near dawn, they topped a rise, looking down upon a peaceful valley below.

It was then Summer broke from her stupor, her

red-rimmed, swollen eyes widening in disbelief. She could scarcely fathom the sight before her eyes. Down in the valley, all alone in his supreme magnificence, stood a pure white buffalo.

Her breath caught sharply, drawing Jeremy's attention to the sight at which she stared in awe. "I've heard of such an animal, but I've never seen one," he breathed softly.

Reverence filled her voice, as she looked upon the sacred white buffalo, who seemed to be calmly returning her gaze. "It is the Sacred White Buffalo, and he is rarely seen by anyone. It is said he is the power of the Great Spirit reborn in animal form, sent to guide and comfort his people in times of trouble. His flesh is never eaten, nor is his skin tanned by any woman of the tribe. Only a shaman can touch this animal, and his hide is usually presented as an offering to the Great Spirit, for it is said to possess great powers."

As she watched, the great beast seemed to nod his head at her. Then it turned and ambled off, disappearing into the mist that layered the valley floor.

"What do you think it means?" Jeremy wondered half to himself.

Summer merely shook her head, not willing to voice her thoughts. To her it was a sign that her beloved Windrider had found favor with the Great Spirit. It was meant to comfort her with the knowledge that her husband would find freedom and happiness in the next world—that he would live contentedly until she joined him there upon her own death. Fresh tears stung her eyes, but her broken heart now held some small measure of peace as she followed Jeremy down off the hill.

As they rode into the snow-covered ranchyard, Tanya was at the door to greet them, curious as to who her unexpected visitors might be. The shock on her face immediately changed to heartfelt dismay as she viewed her daughter's sorrowful face and shorn braids. She dashed off the porch, calling out loudly. "Adam! Adam, come quickly!"

Adam came flying from the barn in response to his wife's urgent call. He stopped short upon seeing Jeremy and Summer, then hurried to their side.

Tanya held both her daughter and Angela in a fiercely protective embrace, tears shining in her eyes. "Windrider is dead," she chokingly told her anxious husband, echoing Summer's single heartbroken explanation.

Adam took his daughter into his arms, hugging her tightly to him, as if to absorb her immense pain. "Daughter," he said softly. "My dear, sweet Summer."

Cradled against his broad chest, her tears rained onto his coat. "Oh, Daddy!" she whispered brokenly, her body quaking against his. It had been many long years since she had called him that instead of Father, since she was a small girl. Adam blinked back tears of his own. "It hurts so badly! I wish I could die too!" she cried.

"But you cannot, Summer," he crooned, his big hand caressing her short hair. "You must find the strength to go on, and to raise your children, who need you very badly now." He led her gently into the house, the others following with the children.

As Tanya comforted her weeping daughter and made sure that the children were seen to properly, Adam heard the story from Jeremy. "It was all so unnecessary, so uncalled for," Jeremy said toward the end of the lengthy explanation. "There was no reason

430

for the military to come charging down on that peaceful gathering. Without warning, they were shooting everything in sight. The attack was vicious, and absolutely horrifying! I still can't believe they would massacre these people as they did."

"They have done so many times in the past," Adam reminded him solemnly.

"But they were holding a religious ceremony!" Jeremy exclaimed in confused irritation. "It was only a dance, for God's sake!"

"Precisely, and isn't it ironic that they should attack the tribes for worshipping the same Christ they have tried so hard to teach them about all these years."

"Why? Why couldn't they understand? How could they fail to see what was going on?" Jeremy was beside himself with anger and sorrow for the needless loss of lives.

"They will never understand our ways," Adam told him. "They do not care to, and they simply will not. There might be peace in the years ahead, but there will never be true understanding between the whites and the tribes, not as long as the government insists that the Indians change to suit its purposes and gives no thought to their needs."

"It surprises me that Windrider should want you to bring Summer home to us," Tanya said, casting a concerned glance at Summer, who now sat staring at nothing.

Jeremy gave Tanya a baffled look. "You are her family. Where else would she go?"

"He might have wanted her to stay with the Cheyenne, where his parents could help her raise his son."

This raised another question. "What of Winter

Bear and his family?'' Adam asked. "Did the rest of Windrider's family escape safely?''

"I think so. As we rode out, I saw the chief and several warriors riding in another direction. His wife and son were with him, and Sweet Lark as well. Two Arrows was in our small band, and he was to take Windrider's body back and break the news to Winter Bear.''

"I should have been at Windrider's burial, to mourn and place my braids upon his body myself,'' Summer murmured from her chair. "I should have been the one to wash his body and dress him in his best ceremonial garments. Shadow Walker should have been there.'' She turned tormented golden eyes toward her mother. "How do I explain Windrider's absence to his small son? How will I keep his memory alive to a mind that will soon forget even the look of his father's face?''

"You will find a way,'' Tanya told her. "As your own mind clears of its grief, you will find the answers to many of the questions that plague you now.'' In her wisdom, Tanya knew that only time would heal her daughter's bleeding heart, and ease the pain of Windrider's death.

In the days that passed, Summer was lost in her deep sorrow. Her grief knew no bounds, and there was no consoling her. She would mourn for him until time alone dulled her anguish. She wandered about like a lost child, her own children giving her the most comfort. Still, each time she looked into Shadow Walker's small dear face, a miniature reflection of Windrider's features, a shaft of intense pain would pierce her wounded heart.

Through the long days and nights, her soul

grieved for her lost love. Tears were never far from her doleful eyes. Hardly a night went by that she did not cry herself to sleep, hugging her pillow to her in Windrider's stead. Even in her weary sleep, she wept, her heart crying out in despair for its missing half.

Summer began to join her father in his morning prayer chants, Shadow Walker cuddled in her lap, that he might learn this ritual from Adam. Often she sat there long after Adam had taken Shadow Walker in for breakfast, watching the sun rise in the east, where her beloved was buried miles away from her. Only the freezing cold would eventually drive her back into the house.

Summer had no concern for her looks these days. The only man she wanted to be beautiful for was gone from her forever. She slept poorly and her appetite was nil, and she grew terribly thin and pale. Her short hair, though curly now, was dull and lifeless. "Summer, you have got to stop this," Tanya admonished one day. "Have you no pride in yourself? What would Windrider think if he could see you now?"

With a careless shrug, Summer replied, "He would know that I miss him, and yearn to be with him."

"He would also think you a fool for treating your body with so little respect," Tanya said sharply. "Have you looked in a mirror lately? You are as thin as a rail! A good wind would blow you away."

"Mother, food holds no appeal for me these days."

"Regardless, you must eat or you will become ill and not be able to care for your children as Windrider wants."

Her mother's stern reminder served its purpose. With shame Summer recalled Windrider's wish, and knew she could not fail to uphold that vow to him. From then on, she forced herself to eat, though the food was tasteless to her much of the time. Her young body soon responded to the better treatment and Summer's deliberate attempts to attend to her appearance. Her face soon lost that gaunt look and her clothes ceased to hang on her thin frame. Her short black hair, which curled delightfully to frame her lovely face, shone with highlights. Her dresses began to fit properly once more, showing her perfect figure to its best advantage, and slowly but surely the purple shadows beneath her eyes began to fade.

It seemed a bit strange to dress in cotton skirts and blouses once more, or warm wool. As much as she had always adored satins and lace, and ribbons and bows, she found herself missing her doeskin dresses. In her present mood she could not truly appreciate the lovely colors and fabrics that now filled her wardrobe. Though she wore them without comment, she did not fuss or exclaim over them as in the days of her youth. To her now dulled senses, they were merely coverings for her body.

In an effort to cure Summer's sleepless nights, Tanya suggested long walks, and when the weather permitted, they rode about the ranch. Gradually Summer began to help about the house, but more and more she was drawn to the stables, her love of horses awakening once more. Soon her skin began to glow with renewed vitality, and with the added exercise she began to sleep less fitfully.

Thanksgiving came too soon after her arrival for Summer to be in an appropriate mood for the holiday. After all, what had she to be thankful for these days? Her husband was dead, her children fatherless. Even in the midst of her loving family, loneliness sat like a dark cloud over her. Halfway through the meal, she excused herself and went to her room to brood in solitary sorrow.

Everyone did their best to comfort and cheer her. Marla and Hunter were living at the ranch, and though her friend was miserable in her last weeks of pregnancy, she often took time to talk with Summer. Dawn had blossomed into a dark-eyed golden beauty in the last year, but she was just as sweet and dear as ever. At seventeen, she had poor Steven Kerr falling over himself for her attention, and even in her grief Summer took delight in her sister's splendid recovery from Roger Watkins' attack. She no longer spoke of entering the convent. Now she talked about Steven and his plans for their future.

A year and a half older than Dawn, Steven wanted to be a lawyer like his father. When he went off to the university next fall, he wanted Dawn to go with him as his wife. Coming from a wealthy family, he could well afford to support her and himself as he attended his classes, and he swore he was too much in love with her to leave her behind. Thus far Dawn had not given him a definite answer to his proposal, but she was strongly considering accepting him.

"I do love him, Summer," Dawn admitted.

"Then what is the problem?" Summer asked, drawing herself out of her doldrums to listen to her little sister.

"I'm not sure I want to move away and live in a strange town. You know how awfully shy I am."

"You'll make friends, Dawn. Every one who meets you loves you."

"Except . . ." Dawn could not bring herself to mention Roger's name, but Summer knew from the way Dawn's eyes clouded whom she meant.

"Why dwell on that now?" Summer advised. "You have known Steven all your life. He adores you. He would do anything for you, and he would never hurt you in any way. You've been friends forever. Don't you trust him to take care of you?"

"Of course, I do," Dawn frowned. "It is just that I'm not sure I could ever be the kind of wife he needs. Men seem to set such great store on the physical side of marriage, and frankly I don't think I'll care for it much."

Summer shook her head, knowing her sister would have to conquer the fears Watkins had instilled in her. "Roger was a poor example of what love should be, Dawn. It is not pain and fear, but wondrous beyond belief." She sighed sadly, for not only did she grieve for Windrider, her young body would not forget the long nights of passion spent in his arms. It yearned for his arms about her, his lips plying hers with sweet kisses, his hard body seeking the softness of hers. "Lovemaking can be one of the most beautiful experiences a woman will ever know, and when a child is born of that love, you will know a fulfillment beyond measure."

"I hope you are right, but you were never as frightened as I was by a man."

"Go talk with Melissa," Summer suggested softly. "Steven's mother was badly treated by her Cheyenne captor, yet she overcame her fears and married Justin. Perhaps better than anyone else, she can set your mind at ease and erase your doubts. She does not seem to dislike Justin's advances."

Dawn giggled. "You should have seen them when he caught her under the mistletoe last Christmas! You are right. I will speak with Melissa."

SUMMER STORM

Mistletoe soon hung again in the wide archway leading into the ranch house *sala*, the big front parlor. Christmas was upon them before Summer was prepared to deal with it. Memories of the Christmas she had celebrated with Windrider in St. Louis haunted her. Though she knew she should shop for gifts for her family and friends, Summer had little heart for it. In the end, she shut herself up in her mother's sewing room and made gifts from material her mother had stored there. In this way, she never had to leave the ranch. She didn't have to face the pity or contempt of the townspeople she might otherwise meet, and she would not have to talk to anyone. Though she knew its was cowardly to hide away from prying eyes, she could not help herself. She wanted only to mourn in solitude and nurse her broken heart in the peaceful surroundings of the ranch.

Jeremy stopped by often in the days following their return to Pueblo. Summer sometimes marveled that he managed to traverse the snowbound roads when no one else seemed willing to risk it. He made no secret of the fact that he came to see her, to check on her and the children, who absolutely adored him.

Shadow Walker had clung to him like a bear cub to a tree all the way back to Pueblo. The little tyke had become very attached to this tall blond man with the bright green eyes. Angela merely worshipped him. At a year and a half, she was very particular about who held her and who didn't, and Jeremy was a favored perch. She would crawl into his lap, bat her huge blue eyes at him, pop her thumb into her pudgy-cheeked mouth, and dare him to attempt to dislodge her. Her tiny rosebud lips would pucker into a pout if he failed to pay her proper attention. Often he would hold her until she slept, her little blond head nestled close to his. It was plain to see that he loved both children dearly.

At first Jeremy was sympathetic toward her grief. He, also, mourned the loss of his friend. But as time went on and she continued to mope about, he voiced his objections.

"You really should get into town a bit, Summer. You haven't set foot off this ranch since you've been back."

"I haven't wanted to, Jeremy."

"Has it occurred to you that you are hiding out here much the same way Dawn did after Watkins attacked her?"

Summer bristled, but Jeremy did not care. This was the only emotion other than grief she had displayed since Windrider had died. Anything, even anger, was better than the bland lifelessness she wore these days.

"Are you calling me a coward, Jeremy?" she said heatedly.

"Yes." he answered bluntly. "I realize you mourn Windrider, Summer, but your friends and family are very concerned about you. The least you could do is visit them once in a while. As it is, if they want to see you, they have to come all the way out here. Your grandparents and George and Elizabeth are not all that young any more, Summer. It is much easier for you to make the trip into town. Besides, what are you so afraid of? A little gossip never killed anyone."

"It's more than that. I have my son to think of. You know how Windrider was treated when he was a boy attending school here."

"Yes, and I also know that Hunter and Mark could have suffered the same prejudice, but your parents would not stand for it.''

"What exactly are you saying, Jeremy?"

He met her look squarely, his emerald eyes flashing a challenge. "When your mother first came to Pueblo with her two small sons, everyone knew she had been captured by the Cheyenne. They also knew that Hunter and Mark were half Cheyenne. Tanya did not have an easy time of it at first, but she faced this town head-on, daring anyone to ridicule her or her sons in her hearing. She proudly proclaimed her love for her Cheyenne husband, and she bowed to no one, man or woman, who tried to sully his name or hers. She would have spit in the eye of anyone who dared, and she protected her sons like a tigress with new kittens. She walked straight and tall in this town and no one criticized her openly.''

"Obviously, you feel I should do the same," Summer commented haughtily.

"Can you do less—for yourself and your own children?" he countered smoothly.

It was a challenge, plain and simple, but one she could not deny. With much trepidation, she began venturing into town on short excursions, as the weather allowed. At first it was just for brief visits with the grandparents. Then she added Colleen and a couple of other friends to her list of calls. Next she began dropping into the mercantile to shop, or merely to browse. Finally she worked up enough courage to brave church services with her family, knowing the entire town was watching her and her children curiously. It took her till spring to begin going to tea with her friends, or to spend an afternoon of shopping with them.

Through much of her tentative venturing, Jeremy was there, urging her on with quiet encouragement or outright dares, whatever it took to get her to socialize. It did not happen overnight. Summer was still wrapped too tightly in her grief to give up her reclusive mourning so quickly, but bit by bit he pulled her out of her solitary shell.

Christmas was a trial in itself. The gaily decorated house contrasted sharply with Summer's forlorn mood. In addition to everything else, Jeremy had come with Great Aunt Elizabeth and Uncle George for the holidays, and he was pestering her no end about her morose attitude and unsmiling face.

"What do you expect, Jeremy? I am still mourning my husband, not yet dead two months. Should I burst into song and dance on the rooftop?" she snapped irritably.

"Well, it would be a sight to see," he grinned. Then, more solemnly, "Couldn't you at least try to smile once in a while, for the children's sakes?"

Rachel had finally convinced nearly everyone in the family to attend Christmas Eve services at church. Summer had declined, as had Marla who was not feeling well enough for the ride into town. Hunter decided to stay at home with his wife, and Jeremy had also volunteered to help Summer look after the children.

Everyone else had left, and Summer and Jeremy had just finished putting Shadow Walker and Angela to bed. All four adults were enjoying a quiet moment together in the *sala*, and for once Jeremy was not annoying her. All at once Marla stiffened noticeably in her seat, her hands clenched into tight fists at her sides.

Summer frowned in concern. "Marla, dear, are you in pain?" she ventured.

Marla started to deny it, then nodded affirmatively. "Yes!" she hissed through clenched teeth.

Hunter eyed his wife with a mixture of fear and awe. "Oh, my God!" he exclaimed.

"No, oh, your *baby*," Summer corrected with a rare chuckle. It amazed her that such big strong men should suddenly quake at the thought of their own children being born.

"Relax, Hunter," Jeremy said. "Believe me, these things take a while. You'll have plenty of time to panic later."

Marla smiled apologetically. "That's what I thought. That is why I haven't said anything before now."

Hunter's brows rose in alarm. "How long have you been having these pains?"

"Since just before lunch," she admitted sheepishly.

Hunter stifled a groan at her answer, and Marla suppressed one of her own as another sharp pain ripped through her enormous stomach.

Summer rose to her feet. "Well, Jeremy, do you feel like helping to deliver a Christmas baby, or are Marla and I on our own this time?"

Jeremy grinned up at her. "Just like old times, eh, Summer?"

"What should I do?" Hunter asked anxiously.

"Can you knit booties?" Summer teased.

"Of course not!"

"Then just sit here and wait, or pace the floor. Pour yourself a whiskey and relax."

"Shouldn't I boil water or something?"

Summer laughed, the first real laugh Jeremy had heard from her since the cavalry attack. "Only if you want to do the laundry. Mother has everything already prepared and ready for just this event."

"Don't worry, darling," Marla comforted as Summer and Jeremy helped her from her chair. "I don't think you'll have to wait much longer."

Marla was correct in her estimation. Working as a team, Jeremy and Summer helped her deliver a son barely two hours later.

Jeremy handed the squalling newborn to Summer once he had cut the navel cord and tied it off. Quickly she cleaned the slippery infant and laid him gently in his mother's arms. "Your son, dear sister," she said, her voice a bit husky with the sentimental tears she was holding back.

Just as Jeremy was about to leave to give Hunter the good news, Marla stiffened with yet another pain. "Wait a minute, good doctor," Summer called to him. "Marla is still in labor."

"It is just her body expelling the afterbirth," he explained from the doorway. "You've seen enough of birthings to know that."

"No, Jeremy, this is definitely labor," Summer insisted as Marla let out a long groan.

A few minutes later Jeremy held a tiny, squirming baby girl in his big hands. "I'll be switched!" he said in awe. "I would never have guessed you carried twins, Marla."

Marla laughed weakly. "I'm rather surprised myself. Are you sure we're done now?"

Summer placed her baby daughter in Marla's other arm. "We are if you are," she laughed. "Let's get you ready to greet the new father."

"I'll go prepare him for the shock," Jeremy offered gallantly, grinning from ear to ear.

An hour later, Summer's family returned, gaily singing Christmas carols as they entered the house. To their vast surprise, they were invited to meet the newest Savage children.

Hunter magnanimously offered to let his sister and Jeremy have the honor of naming the twins, which greatly surprised Summer since her brother was notoriously Cheyenne in his thinking most of the time. After consulting together and with Marla, for her approval, they named the babies Christopher and Caroline, for the Christmas carols their grandparents were singing so soon after their birth.

24

Gradually Summer was beginning to heal, though she sometimes felt so very guilty when she forgot her solemn demeanor and laughed at one of the children's antics or a particularly funny comment someone made. Jeremy was a frequent visitor to the ranch. He would sit and talk with her for hours, drawing her out from under her mantle of grief. She enjoyed his quick wit and his sparkling emerald eyes that often teased her out of her gloom. He played with the children, told her of his latest veterinary calls, and did not try to cover the fact that he came primarily to see her, though she did nothing to encourage him.

Though she had never considered herself particularly talented in painting or drawing, she soon found herself caught up in it quite by chance. One day, as she watched Shadow Walker playing contentedly with his new Christmas toys, she was again struck by how much he resembled Windrider, except of course for his golden eyes. A great yearning grew in her that

Shadow Walker should remember his father, and what he looked like.

Taking pencil and paper, she set about to try and recapture Windrider's image. Her first attempts were clumsy and rough, but with each try she improved, until at last she had a portrait that satisfied her. In it she had captured all the pride and nobility of his character, but also his warmth. His dark eyes sparkled in his handsome face, showing humor and intelligence; his chin hinted of his strong stubborn streak. It was a portrait born of love.

After the first, Summer was compelled to draw more. She drew him mounted upon his stallion, racing across the open prairie, his long braids flying out behind him. She pictured him breaking a wild horse, and one where he sat chanting his morning prayer before the rising sun. In an effort to show Shadow Walker all the various facets of his proud, handsome father, she portrayed him as he held his son in his arms, as he hunted, as he gazed solemnly into the starlit night. She showed him in all his many moods; laughing, serious, haughty, angry.

As she labored over these gifts for her son, Summer was receiving a blessing herself, though she barely realized it then. It came gradually, but with each picture, each loving memory, she was releasing a bit of her grief. Though she often thought of him and wept, now she could also think of him and smile. A new warmth was creeping into her heart, replacing that cold, bereft feeling that had lodged there for so long. The terrible loneliness was easing, letting her laugh again, giving her the freedom to enjoy the feel of the sun upon her face and the wind in her hair once more. She was beginning to live again.

Along with her drawings, an older interest was

also blossoming anew—her love of horses. The more she was around them, the more she wanted to learn. That old dream of someday owning a horse ranch and breeding thoroughbreds had never truly died. It had only been deeply buried during her short marriage to Windrider. Now, though they were her father's horses, Summer could indulge her whims. With Jeremy's advice and guidance she set about to learn all she could about these marvelous animals.

Jeremy was elated that Summer would want his advice. It gave him one more reason to be around her, though he really needed no excuse. Still, it brought him one step closer to winning her heart. As each week passed, he could see her gradually recovering from her deep sorrow, and his hopes rose a bit more. As spring approached, an idea planted itself in his mind, and the more he thought about it, the more right it seemed. With eager anticipation of the rich rewards, he set his scheme into action, though he told no one else of his plans. He dearly hoped the element of surprise would tip the scales in his favor if he needed added help in his campaign to win Summer's love.

With all his grand dreams and hopes, it came as a shock to Jeremy to learn that Summer intended to return with her family to the Cheyenne village when they went for their annual visit that summer. They would leave as soon as Mark returned from school. In fact, Adam and Tanya were soon going East to attend Mark's graduation from medical college. In a few weeks he would be both a full-fledged doctor and a new husband, for he was to marry Sweet Lark at long last.

It seemed the year for weddings in the Savage family. Once Mark and Sweet Lark were properly wed, they would return again to Pueblo for Dawn's marriage to Steven. She had at last put the poor man out of his misery and accepted his proposal. They would be married and have a short honeymoon before Steven had to start college in the fall. Now if Jeremy could only rekindle Summer's love for him, all would be perfect. She had loved him once. Surely she could find room in her heart for him again.

When Jeremy heard of her intentions to return to the Cheyenne camp, he decided it was time for a serious talk. Without preamble, he said straight out, "Summer, I love you and I want to marry you."

Summer's head jerked up in surprise at his blunt announcement, coming suddenly out of thin air. She had just shown him her latest drawing of Windrider, and she had been expecting a comment on the art. Gathering her wits, she said quietly, "Jeremy, it is too soon to speak of such things."

"It has been six months," he pointed out.

"I am still grieving. Though I have grown accustomed to the awful loneliness it is my constant companion, as is my deep sorrow."

Jeremy had known all this. With determination he said, "I won't rush you, Summer. I merely wanted you to know my intentions. Just keep in mind that I can't wait forever. I'm not getting any younger, you know."

Summer had to laugh at this. "You are not an old man yet, Jeremy. You are only thirty-four. Surely you won't be ready for a cane and a rocking chair for at least a year or two," she teased.

Jeremy shrugged. "It is time I married and had a family. You know how I've felt about you all these years. I stood by and watched you marry Windrider, and I tried to bury my love for you behind a face of friendship, knowing how much you loved him. I thought I had lost you forever. Now I have been given a second chance, and I do not intend to give you up a second time.''

Her golden eyes clouded, and he knew she was remembering her life with Windrider. If he thought he could shake her memories from her, Jeremy might have done so then.

''Jeremy, I am not ready to remarry. I may never be ready,'' she said softly.

Jeremy's short laugh held no humor. ''You can't make widowhood a life's commitment, Summer. It's just not for you. You are much too passionate a woman for that.''

''Perhaps once, but passions fade,'' she told him, her face taking on that stubborn look.

That small chin jutting out at him and the defiant look creeping into her eyes was too much of a challenge for him to pass up. ''Yours haven't. I'm willing to bet you have plenty of passion just simmering under the surface. Shall we put it to the test, princess?'' He took a step toward her, his emerald eyes gleaming dangerously. ''Shall we see how quickly all those dormant desires can be awakened?''

Summer's eyes widened in alarm, and she backed slowly away as he continued to stalk her. ''No! Jeremy, I am warning you. Don't you dare touch me!''

''Oh, but I've touched you before, and you loved it. Don't you remember, Summer, how you begged me not to stop? Have you forgotten how you declared your undying love for me? I haven't. Lord knows, I haven't.''

His hand flashed out to catch her wrist and pull her tightly to him. Then, without further warning, his lips captured hers. Her angry shriek was buried within his mouth as his lips forced hers to open beneath his. She twisted in his embrace, trying to break free, but his strong arms held her fast. A frantic sob rose to her throat as she fought him, emerging as a whimper.

The sound seemed to trigger a protective tenderness in him. Even as he continued to trap her lips with his, the kiss gentled. Where demand had bruised, now sweetness soothed, and it was Summer's undoing. She could fight his aggressiveness, but the slow seduction of his lips and tongue caressing hers was her defeat.

Desire snaked through her like a slowly twisting fire. Oh God, but it had been so long! So long since she had been held like this; so long since firm lips had covered hers with such warmth and sweet persuasion. With a tremulous sigh, she surrendered. Her lips softened and moved beneath his; tasting, testing, reveling in the feel of him. Her body melted into his, no longer straining to be free, but seeking contact with his hard length. Arms that had pushed against his chest now crept willingly about his neck, her fingertips delving into the thick gold hair at his nape.

It was only when his broad hand at the base of her spine pressed her against his insistent arousal that Summer jerked to her senses. With renewed effort she twisted her lips from his and pushed herself free. "How dare you!" she screamed, her hand whipping up to slap him smartly across the face.

"How dare I do what, princess? How dare I love you? How dare I want you? How dare I make you want me?"

Angry tears made her eyes glisten like rain-washed gold. "You have no right!"

"I have every right. My love for you gives me the right to need you. Windrider has given me the right to look after you and the children. He gave you into my care.''

"And you are abusing his trust!" she accused.

Jeremy shook his head at her, his eyes holding hers in a solemn gaze. "No, Summer. You deceive yourself if you think Windrider did not know of my love for you. He knew exactly what he was doing when he asked me to take you. Why else do you think he did so, rather than have you and Shadow Walker go back to the Cheyenne camp?"

"You act as if he literally gave me to you that night, as a person would bequeath a possession upon his death."

"He did, Summer. Haven't you realized that yet? The only reason I've held off is out of respect for your grief and Windrider's memory. He was my friend, as well as your husband. I am not betraying his trust by wanting to claim you as my own. Rather, I am fulfilling it. Windrider would want you to be happy again, and he believed you could find that happiness with me, perhaps because we once loved one another. Once, he took you from me, and upon his death he gave you back again."

"You are out of your ever-blooming mind, Jeremy Field!" She was sobbing angrily now. "I am not a vase or a horse, to be passed on from one owner to another!"

"I know that, love." Jeremy sighed. How had things gotten so out of hand, when all he had wanted was to declare his love for her? "I can wait until you are ready to love again, but when you are, I'll be first in line to claim you. Just don't shut me out of your life, for I've never loved another woman the way I have loved you. These past four years, loving you and knowing you belonged to someone else, have been a living Hell. I apologize if I've upset you, but I am not sorry I kissed you. I've waited a long time to be able to hold you and kiss you like that. I treasured every moment of it, and if you are truthful with yourself, you enjoyed it, too.''

About to deny it, Summer found she could not lie to him. She had enjoyed his kiss, much to her dismay and confusion. Refusing to affirm or deny his claim, she swung on her heel and stomped angrily away from him, though whether she was more angry with herself or him, she could not say.

''Why are all men such arrogant jackasses?'' Summer muttered furiously as she walked through the kitchen.

''I beg your pardon?'' Tanya gave her daughter an amused glance as she stirred the vegetables in the cooking pot.

''I said, why are all men such . . .''

''I heard what you said,'' Tanya broke in. ''What I'd like to know is, why? Who are you angry with now?''

''Jeremy.''

''Why?'' Tanya repeated.

''Because he loves me!'' Summer exclaimed irrationally.

Tanya shook her head in confusion.

''Jeremy is a jackass because he loves you?'' she asked. ''That's rather uncomplimentary to yourself, don't you think? You are really not making much sense.''

''I don't want him to love me.''

''Whyever not?''

Summer swallowed a sob, her eyes brimming

with tears. "Because I'm afraid I'll love him back. Because I loved him once, before Windrider, and it would be all too easy to fall in love with him again."

"Would that be so awful, Summer?" Tanya asked softly, beginning now to understand.

"I loved Windrider! Oh, Mother, I loved him so much!"

"Are you afraid you'll lose Jeremy, too, if you let yourself love him; or do you feel you would be betraying Windrider?"

"Both, I think."

Tanya nodded in understanding. "Windrider is gone, Summer," she said gently. "He was a fine man. He loved you every bit as much as you loved him. This is how I know that he would not begrudge your finding a new life and a new love to fill your years. He liked Jeremy, and he respected him. If you should discover love in your heart for Jeremy, I somehow think Windrider would approve and wish you well."

Summer sighed. "I have much to think on, Mother. Suddenly everything is very confusing."

"Jeremy is a good man," Tanya added. "I have known him since he was twelve years old. He is honest and dependable, and he would be a loving husband and father. He also loves your children, which is admirable. Many men could not accept another man's children as his own, let alone a child that is mostly Cheyenne."

"He's also very bossy."

"And very handsome," Tanya argued.

"That doesn't give him the right to think he owns me."

"He also loves you very much."

Jeremy came to see Summer off before she left to go to the reservation.

"I hope this visit does not stir up too many painful memories for you, Summer," he said. "You've been through so much already."

Summer's eyes searched his. "I thought you would be going with us to see Mark and Sweet Lark married. A Cheyenne wedding between chiefs' sons and daughters is quite a celebration." Her own ceremony came to mind, bringing a poignant sadness with it.

"No," Jeremy answered. "This is something you must do on your own. Besides, I am very busy on a special project of my own just now, and I cannot spare the time away from it."

"What project is this?" she asked, unaware that he had been working on something special. He had not mentioned anything to her.

"You'll see it when it is finished," he promised. "Just hurry back home again." He was afraid she might get so caught up in her memories that she would want to stay with the Cheyenne. "Try to miss me a little, while you are gone."

"I'll give your regards to Winter Bear and Shy Deer."

"Do that—and do something else for me."

"What is that?" she asked.

His hands came up to gently cradle her face, his eyes tracing her features lovingly. "When you are surrounded by memories, when you are sifting through the bits and pieces of your marriage to Windrider, spare a thought for me, and remember that

I love you. And remember this, too."

With infinite tenderness, he kissed her, all the love and longing he held for her pouring forth from his lips to hers. Caught by surprise, Summer was unprepared for the hot wave of yearning that washed through her.

When he finally released her and stepped back, her face was red with embarrassment.

"You really shouldn't do that, Jeremy," she whispered shakily.

His keen gaze noted her breathlessness and the way her breasts had perked, telling him of her desire. With a grin, he said, "I think I should do it more often, princess." Pulling her back into his arms for a quick hard kiss, he said, "Think about this while you are gone, Summer. Think of how well you fit into my arms, how my lips feel on yours, how much you desire me, how quickly you flame to life at my slightest touch."

He bounded off the porch. Over his shoulder he called, "Dream of me, princess!"

Summer was surprised to arrive in the Cheyenne camp and find her lodge erected and waiting for her, as if she had never left. It gave her a strange feeling, and her heart lurched crazily in her chest. For one breathless moment she expected to see Windrider come striding out of their tepee and greet her. Tears stung her eyes as hopelessness struck her anew.

Windrider may not have been there, but everyone else was. Shy Deer came forward to embrace Summer and to take Shadow Walker into her arms. Sweet Lark stood gazing shyly at Mark, who could not take his eyes from his fiancée. Panther immediately greeted Winter Bear, telling him of their sorrow over the death of his son.

Singing Waters and Snow Blossom came forward. For a moment Summer and the other two women stood staring at one another forlornly. Then, regardless of who was watching, they fell into one anothers' arms and wept.

"Oh, Summer Storm! How can I tell you of our sorrow for you?" Singing Waters wailed.

"We have missed you and worried over you," Snow Blossom hiccuped.

"And I you."

It was soon learned that several members of their tribe had been killed during that fateful raid, as well as many from the other tribes gathered that night for the Ghost Dance. Summer was relieved to find that none of her close friends or other relations had been killed, though Gray Rock had received a bullet wound to his thigh. He had long since recovered.

Summer sobbed quietly, tears running silently down her cheeks as Shy Deer haltingly related the details of Windrider's burial. For many minutes the two women held one another, Summer crying out her grief over the death of her beloved husband, and Shy Deer mourning her handsome young son; together they shared their deep loss.

Later that evening, alone with her children in her own tepee, Summer sat staring sleeplessly at the remnants of over three years of her life. There, near the entrance, were the leather halters Windrider had fashioned with his own hands. Nearby was the beautiful cradleboard he had labored over so lovingly before Shadow Walker's birth. On a peg hung his bearskin coat, on another his buckskin shirt and leggings.

One peg near the door was glaringly empty. It was here Windrider had always hung his weapons; his bow and quiver, his tomahawk. These, his feather-bedecked lance, and the bone-handled knife Summer had given him that one Christmas were gone. Dressed in his best garments, all his coup feathers and headband, he had been laid to rest with his weapons at his side, that he might have them with him to hunt again in the abundant lands to which he had traveled.

With a trembling sigh, Summer arose. She went to where his fringed shirt hung, one she had sewn for him. Was it only her imagination, or did the shirt still retain the smell of him, that special scent that was his alone? Hugging it tightly to her, Summer cried, and when at last she slept, her hands still clutched the garment, needing some small part of him near to her.

Then the dreams began—strange, fragmented dreams over which she had no control. First she was riding Mist. They were flying over the ground, with Windrider and his horse keeping pace next to her. His dark eyes glowed with happiness, and she shared his joy. They were racing across the land and laughing as the wind tugged at their clothes and hair. When next she turned to him, it was not Windrider who rode beside her, but Jeremy. He gave her that special crooked grin of his, the green of his eyes brighter than new spring leaves. Summer saw herself return his smile, and on they rode together.

The dream changed, and across a misty meadow she saw Windrider standing so proud and handsome.

She called to him and he smiled, but as she went to join him, his image faded. Peering through the mist, her eyes strained to see him again. Then, when she finally caught a fleeting glimpse of him, he was walking slowly away from her. Though she called to him once more, he kept on walking, until he was swallowed by the swirls of mist and she could not find him again.

Then she was lying on the mossy ground beneath a large shade tree. Windrider lay beside her, tickling her bare breasts with the tip of his long black braid and laughing at the way she squirmed and giggled. He bent his head to hers and stole a long, loving kiss. When at last her lashes fluttered open, it was Jeremy's face she saw above hers, Jeremy's dancing green eyes smiling down into hers. His lips came down to cover hers, and she surrendered her mouth to his with a soft sigh, already feeling that hot sweet yearning begin to flow through her.

Summer awoke with a start, wondering what had awakened her. Glancing quickly about, she saw nothing unusual. The children were sleeping peacefully on their mats, and the entrance flap was still tied shut from within. Fragments of her dreams still haunted her, causing her heart to beat unusually loudly. It was her dreams, she supposed, that had caused her to awaken so suddenly.

Then her eyes caught the flash of metal near her sleeping mat. A startled gasp escaped her lips as she beheld her own copper wristbands lying end to end near the head of her mat. Never before had they been off of her wrists; not since Windrider had placed them there upon their wedding. A long eagle feather ran through the center of the bands, resting where her wrists should have been.

With a cry of dismay, Summer reached out to retrieve them. How had they come to be off of her wrists? The bands fit very snugly, and could never have come off by themselves. Neither did she believe she had removed them herself in her sleep, for where had the eagle feather come from?

Then she recognized it, and a shiver ran up her spine like icy fingers. This was one of Windrider's coup feathers. She was sure of it, from the way it was notched. Each of a warrior's coups were recorded in this special manner, and by the notching a person could decipher whom the feather belonged to, and for what deed he had been awarded the token. This was Windrider's, from one of their raids. Summer's father had awarded him this very feather, and it had gone with him to his burial.

Though she knew she would see nothing more, her eyes searched the shadowed interior of the tepee. Her shaking fingers caressed the feather. "Windrider?" she called softly. There was no answer, but Summer knew he had been here. He had come and removed her wedding bands from her wrists, leaving the eagle feather behind as a sign. It was a private message to her, telling her in the only way he could that she was now free to go to Jeremy, with his blessing. Summer sat in the silent tepee staring pensively at the feather and the copper bands. Finally, when dawn sent streaks of pink to light the eastern sky, she got up and found the small leather bag in which she kept her jewelry. Inside the bag were her wedding earrings, her silver hair discs, and the armbands and amulet that pronounced her a chief's daughter. At the bottom of the bag was the small box with the topaz pendant and earrings Windrider had given her. With lingering reluctance and great reverence, she placed her copper wristbands inside the bag and closed it. With a trembling sigh of sorrowful resignation, she turned and walked from the tepee. Windrider had placed the bands upon her wrists, and he had removed them. Summer knew she would never wear them again—at least not in this world.

After that morning, a new peace came upon Summer, a calm that entered her heart and lent her comfort. Her eyes no longer swam with tears as she thought of Windrider. Rather, a warm contentment filled her, a gladness that she had known and loved such a wonderful man. Only one other time did a brief sorrow tear at her heart. As Sweet Lark stood beside Mark, wearing her doeskin wedding dress, and Mark looked with such pride and love upon his bride, memories of her own wedding crowded her mind.

It saddened her that Pouncer and War Bonnet were no longer in the village. Neither animal had been seen since Windrider's death. Summer would have liked to have seen them one last time.

Summer spent her days in pleasant companionship with friends and family, for once she had gone, it might be a very long time before she met with them again. Her nights were filled with thoughts and dreams of Jeremy. Never again did dreams of Windrider plague her.

More and more, her thoughts turned to Jeremy, and by the time she dismantled her tepee for the final time, she knew that she did, indeed, love him. He had crept into her heart and filled the void left by

Windrider's death. When they left the Cheyenne camp to return to Pueblo, Summer's heart ran ahead of her. With joy and anticipation she turned her horse toward home—and Jeremy.

25

It was the first of August before they finally reached home again. In three weeks time, Dawn would marry Steven Kerr, and there were still many preparations to be made. Sweet Lark had come back to the ranch with Mark, where they would live until Mark had set up an office in town. When he had a decent practice established, they would find a house in town to buy, or perhaps build. If they tired of the long ride into Pueblo before then, Aunt Elizabeth had offered them room in her big old house. They were welcome to move in, bag and baggage, any time they wished.

Summer anxiously awaited Jeremy's appearance, for she had decided she would tell him at the first opportunity that she would marry him. Until she saw him, however, she kept her plans to herself, for she had no wish to detract attention from Dawn's wedding. She wanted her sister to have the most wonderful wedding possible, with all the joy and anticipation she deserved.

For this same reason, Mark also decided that a quiet family service be held at the ranch to unite him and Sweet Lark according to white law. Though Mark considered himself already well and truly wed to his bride, Adam had convinced him that the second ceremony would be wise. That way no legal problems could crop up later, and no one could criticize either Mark or his new wife.

When two weeks had passed and no one had seen or heard from Jeremy, Summer was a mass of nerves. Where was that man? How dare he pester the daylights out of her before she left, then fail to show himself upon her return? Especially when she was so anxious now to relay her good news.

By the time Dawn's wedding day had arrived, and still no Jeremy, Summer was frantic. Was he hurt, lying injured somewhere? Worse yet, had he met with an accident in some out-of-the-way place and been killed, while no one knew of it? Had he changed his mind about wanting to marry her?

Summer was beside herself with worry, and it annoyed her that no one else seemed the least bit concerned. When she had asked Aunt Elizabeth if she knew of Jeremy's whereabouts, her great aunt had calmly replied, "He's a big boy, Summer. He'll show up in his own good time."

Uncle George and Grandad Martin were just as bad. "All he said before he rode out was that he might be a while. He had some things to take care of that would keep him busy, and we were not to worry."

"What things?"

"We don't know. He didn't say, and we didn't ask. A man has a right to his privacy."

"Men!" Summer stalked off in a huff.

SUMMER STORM

Summer was matron of honor at her sister's wedding. Kept busy for most of the morning, and caught up in the turmoil once they'd reached the church, she did not catch sight of Jeremy until she walked up the aisle ahead of her sister. With the ceremony underway, she could not speak with him then, of course. She was forced to wait until after the wedding.

As she stood in the front of the church, Summer stole a glance at him from the corner of her eyes. The aggravating man looked disgustingly healthy to her, and annoyingly attractive in his fine suit and tie. Where on earth had he been—and doing what?

Jeremy caught the frown that marred Summer's lovely face as she looked his way. He smiled mockingly, knowing she was angry with him for his long disappearance. He considered that a very encouraging sign, and his smile broadened.

Summer had no more time to think of Jeremy just now. Dawn was being led down the aisle on their father's arm. Elegantly attired in snow white satin and lace, she looked absolutely radiant. Steven's eyes lit up at the sight of her, and a collective gasp of appreciation rippled through the gathering of guests. Summer had never seen her sister look so beautiful, and with all her heart she wished her and her groom all the happiness in the world.

As the sacred vows were being exchanged, Summer's gaze again met Jeremy's. She had no idea what promise and love shone in her golden eyes, or how it made Jeremy's heart flip over in his chest. She knew only that his emerald gaze had trapped hers and refused to release it. She saw only the adoration glowing from his face to hers, and hope swelled in her heart again.

The reception was being held at Aunt Elizabeth's, and Summer again had no opportunity to speak with Jeremy, as the wedding party was hurried into waiting buggies for the short ride from the church. She could only hope Jeremy planned to attend the celebration.

A short time later, she found herself face to face with him at last.

"Have you been avoiding me, Jeremy?" she blurted out, not bothering with a normal greeting.

"In a manner of speaking," he agreed with a quick nod.

Summer's full lower lip protruded in an annoyed pout, a trait left over from her precocious childhood. "Why?" she asked, unable to mask the hurt in her voice.

Jeremy held back the grin that threatened to erupt. "I've been busy."

"So I've heard!" Summer snapped. "Doing what, may I ask?"

Jeremy smiled blandly. "No, you may not ask. You and everyone else will find out in due course."

Properly put in her place, Summer bristled. "I've been wanting to speak with you, Jeremy," she said stiffly.

"About what?" he asked a bit warily.

"About us."

"What about us?"

"Jeremy, you are making this extremely difficult! Do you, or do you not, still wish to marry me?" It took all the courage Summer could muster to ask that last question.

"That depends."

Summer didn't know whether to scream or cry. "On what?" she asked in a small voice.

"On your feelings for me, of course," he answered.

Summer heaved a sigh of relief and smiled. "I love you, Jeremy. I suppose I should have told you that first."

Jeremy still was not satisfied. "As a friend or a lover?"

Summer blinked in confusion. "Both," she answered softly. "I wouldn't agree to marry you otherwise."

"And are you agreeing, Summer? You haven't really said as yet."

Summer ventured another smile at the stubborn man before her. "Yes, I most definitely am accepting your kind proposal, Dr. Field."

A wide smile finally lit his face, and he pulled her into his arms, not caring who might be watching. "It certainly took you long enough!" he grumbled good-naturedly. Then he kissed her, and the earth fell away from beneath her feet.

The rest of the day was a blissful blur for Summer. The only thing she clearly recalled was the surprise on everyone but Jeremy's face when she caught the bridal bouquet. Summer was deliriously happy!

When he escorted her home, she was surprised to learn that Jeremy wanted a traditional church wedding with all the trimmings.

"For heaven's sake, why? Jeremy, neither you nor I have ever attended church very regularly."

"I'll most likely marry only once in my life, Summer, and I want to do it right. I want you to have a wedding you will always cherish in years to come; gown, flowers, music—everything just as it should be, as every girl imagines her wedding ought to be."

"That will take some time to arrange, you realize," she told him.

"Then you'd better start planning it right away, princess. I'll give you a month. By that time I should be fairly well finished with my own work."

"That secret project of yours?" she guessed.

"Yes, and don't bother to ask me about it, because I'm not about to tell you. It's a special surprise."

Changing the subject slightly, she said, "Jeremy, I can't marry you in a white gown."

"That's all right. I hadn't really planned on wearing one anyway," he answered with a perfectly straight face, though his emerald eyes danced merrily.

Summer burst into laughter. When she finally stopped giggling, she said, "I meant me, and you know it. I've already been married and have two children. It would not be appropriate to wear white, as Dawn did today."

"Wear any color you want, darling, except black. You'll look ravishing in anything."

"I still don't see why you should be so adamant about a big church wedding," she said. "I'd certainly be satisfied with a small, intimate ceremony. Most men would give their eye-teeth to avoid all that fuss."

"Ah, but I'm older and wiser than most grooms," he teased. "You see, I want plenty of witnesses when you promise to love, honor and obey me—especially the 'obey' part."

Four weeks later, Summer again walked down the church aisle, only this time she was the bride on her proud father's arm. Not the typical mother-of-the-bride, Tanya sat smiling broadly, Shadow Walker and Angela on either side of her. With faces scrubbed to a rosy glow, the two children watched as their beautiful mother met their new father at the altar. Jeremy had already started proceedings to adopt the two of them.

After a short, private honeymoon for their parents, they would be a happy family of four.

Summer had chosen a pale yellow gown that complimented her skin and made her eyes glow like golden candlelight. In her midnight hair, which was now long enough to be worn in a loosely upswept style, she had a garland of late summer daisies. To Jeremy she was the most perfectly beautiful woman he had ever seen, and he could hardly believe that the day had finally come when he could claim her for his own.

Summer could scarcely take her eyes from the tall, handsome man whose name she would soon take for her own. With all her heart she loved him, and she would gladly spend the rest of her life proving to him just how much he meant to her.

The dignified traditional ceremony was touchingly beautiful, and Summer savored every bit of it, knowing it would be one of her most cherished memories. Only when she caught the devilish twinkle in Jeremy's eyes as she solemnly vowed to obey him, did she come close to losing her composure. A smile just for him curved her lips as they shared this private joke on their special day of joy. The tender kiss he gave her at the close of the ceremony was a tantalizing promise of more to come.

Summer could sense Jeremy's growing impatience as they endured the reception afterward. It seemed forever before they could slip away from their guests. Jeremy had not told her where they were to spend their honeymoon. "Trust me," he'd said. "You'll love it." Obviously, her parents had been privy to this highly guarded secret, for her bags had been packed and sent ahead.

With Jeremy as her guide, they rode north and west for several miles. Then, in a secluded location she judged to be roughly in the same area as her father's ranch, though further west then she'd ever explored, they stopped.

"Pass your horse's reins to me, and close your eyes," Jeremy instructed mysteriously. "Don't peek, or you'll spoil the surprise."

Feeling supremely silly, Summer nevertheless did as she was told. Even with her eyes tightly shut, she could tell that they were climbing a slight incline.

When they halted again, Jeremy said, "Now, open your eyes, Summer, and look at your new home."

The sight that met her eyes made her gasp in delight. Below them lay a small hidden valley as lovely as any she had ever seen, and nestled within it was a newly-built little ranch house, a fresh coat of white paint glowing like a beacon. Behind the house stood a barn, and there were fenced pastures and corrals widening out from the buildings. Everything was so peaceful and serene, a pleasure to the eye.

"It's so lovely!" she breathed, still stunned by the picturesque scene below.

"Then you like it?" he asked anxiously.

"Oh, yes! Did you say we are to live here?"

"Yes. I bought the land shortly after you came back to live with your parents."

Summer noticed how carefully Jeremy refrained from mentioning Windrider's death. "It's alright, Jeremy," she said softly. "You can say Windrider's name without fear of stirring up hurtful memories or yearnings. My wounds have healed. Though I'll always love and remember him, it is you who claim my heart now, wholly and wonderfully. This, too, I promise you on our wedding day."

Jeremy reached out to touch her cheek with

loving fingers. "Thank you, sweet princess. You could give me no greater wedding gift than that."

As they rode down to their new home, Jeremy explained. "This was the project that kept me so busy all these months. I wanted to complete it before today, and I barely managed it. There are still a few things left undone, but they require a woman's touch and I thought you would prefer to finish those yourself."

"Such as?"

"Just the usual touches, like curtains and bedding and such. I also left the floors bare so you could choose the rugs, and there is only the most essential of furnishings, so it may seem a bit empty to you now. I thought we could choose the rest of the pieces together."

Summer frowned thoughtfully, suddenly realizing that something else was missing from the scene. "Why all the pasture, when I see no cattle?" she questioned. "Will the livestock come later, too?"

"I'll explain all that soon enough." They had reached the house now, and Jeremy was there to help her dismount. When he did not release her right away, but continued to carry her in his arms as he approached the steps, Summer asked, "What are you doing now?"

"Why, Summer Field! Have you no romance in your soul?" he laughed. "I am carrying you over the threshold of your new home, as every good groom should." He proceeded to do just that.

After a long, sensuous kiss that set her blood bubbling, he set her on her feet inside the door. Standing back proudly, he awaited her reaction as she viewed their new home. For now there were just five rooms, but they were all beautifully finished and freshly painted. There was a parlor, a dining room, a kitchen, and two bedrooms all on one floor.

"Later, as our family grows, we can always add on more rooms," Jeremy told her, a roguish glint in his green eyes.

"Planning on a large family, are you?" she teased.

"Only if all our children are as sweet and lovely as you."

"I'll try," she said with a slow smile, "but I can't make any promises. They may all be as handsome and stubborn as you."

"Now I have another surprise," he announced suddenly.

Summer's eyebrows rose. "I wondered when you'd get around to that."

Jeremy laughed. "That comes later. First I have something else to show you." Taking her by the hand, he led her out the back door and across the ranch yard to the barn. Inside, he directed her attention to five stalls. "Take a look."

Curious now, Summer looked into the first stall. There, to her amazement, stood a beautiful thoroughbred mare. Before she had time to properly exclaim over it, Jeremy pointed to the other stalls. The next three also held mares, of the same beautiful conformation as the first. The last stall, located further apart from the rest, housed the most magnificent thoroughbred stallion Summer had ever encountered.

Turning to him with tears of wonder in her eyes, Summer whispered dazedly. "Oh, Jeremy! They are marvelous! Are they ours?"

He nodded, enjoying the awed expression on her face. "As I recall, you've repeatedly expressed the wish to own a ranch and breed thoroughbreds. This is my wedding gift to you, for making me the happiest man in the world."

Summer was still stunned. "This has been a dream of mine for longer than I can remember, and now you have made it come true. Thank you, my love. From the bottom of my heart, I thank you."

He drew her into his arms, gazing longingly into her glistening eyes. "Together we'll make all our dreams come true, my princess."

Just before his lips claimed hers, she murmured. "Why do you always call me 'princess'?"

"You'll always be my lovely Cheyenne princess to me. I've thought of you that way since I first laid eyes on you, and it's too old a habit to break now."

The kiss they shared threatened to set the barn afire. "Let's go into the house," Jeremy suggested eagerly after several minutes. "I'd really hate to consummate our marriage on a scratchy pile of straw, when there is a nice comfortable bed awaiting us inside, and if we don't get there soon, I'm sure to take you where you stand."

While she prepared herself for him, Jeremy unsaddled and stabled the horses they had ridden from town. After a quick wash in the kitchen, he joined her.

If he lived to be a thousand, Jeremy could not imagine a more beautiful or alluring sight than Summer as she awaited him. Propped against the pillows on the big bed, she sat in a filmy blue negligee. Her ebony tresses were undone and flowed in soft waves across her bared shoulders. A soft smile played on her lips and in her golden eyes—an inviting smile as old as Eve and meant for him alone.

Shedding his own clothes, he joined her on the bed. "You are so lovely you take my breath away," he told her softly.

"I love you, Jeremy. I don't think you quite know

how totally I love you.''

Her lips caught his in a seeking kiss, and she curled herself into his strong arms. His hands caressed her through the silken material of her gown as his lips took command of hers. Their seeking tongues performed a mating dance of their own, as a prelude to passion yet to come, as a wildfire spread itself insistently through their inflamed senses. His lips left hers to chart a course across her face, as if memorizing every lovely feature by touch alone. ''Sweet heaven, but you are beautiful,'' he murmured, his warm breath sending shivers through her as his teeth gently nipped a slow pattern across her shoulder and downward.

With trembling fingers, he brushed the slender straps of her gown aside, and the bodice fell to her waist, revealing her perfect breasts to his hungry gaze. Unable to stop himself, he sought one beckoning dusky rose peak, gently rolling the nipple between his lips.

A shaft of white-hot desire shot through her, leaving a throbbing ache in its wake. With a moan of intense longing she arched into him, her thigh brushing his aroused manhood and leaving her in no doubt of his own desire for her. Eagerly she presented her other breast for his loving attention, her fingers delving into his golden hair to press him ever nearer to his goal.

Long, strong fingers traced a path of molten lava along the burning lines of her body; down across her stomach and the curve of her hip, then up the silken flesh of her thighs. She opened her legs to his silent command, and received the wondrous reward he sought to give her, as his fingers found that most sensitive bud of desire. ''Yes, oh yes, my love,'' she sighed as blissful ripples washed over her.

He found her warm and welcoming as a summer's day, and he could bear to wait no longer. Bracing himself above her, he made them one. Summer shuddered as ecstasy captured her in its grip. Then he was moving within her, becoming a vital part of her. Faster and faster they spun in a mad whirlpool of passion, with only each other to cling to. With a wild cry, she felt herself being sucked down into its center, where spinning lights sent shafts of color about her, even as her body shattered into joyous splinters of rapture. Jeremy's cry echoed her own as he joined her in that twirling, twisting paradise of passion's most glorious pleasures. Sweetly shared words of love and purest promises lulled them gently to sleep.

Sometime later, Summer awoke to find Jeremy standing by the open window near their bed. Rising, she went to him, wrapping her arms about him as he enclosed her in his warm embrace.

"If I had known how wonderful love would be with you, I don't know how I could ever have waited so long to claim you," he confessed quietly.

She snuggled even nearer, her head resting on his broad shoulder. "I'm going to adore making babies with you, Jeremy, and I'm going to love you for a long, long time."

They stood silently looking out at the starlit night, the moon shimmering over the peaceful landscape. Quite suddenly there came the screeching cry of an eagle, and as Summer watched, it soared gracefully across the face of the moon. A serenity filled her heart at the magnificent sight. On a silent sigh, a secret smile upon her lips, she whispered inwardly, "Goodbye, Windrider."

Turning to her husband, Summer took his hand in hers. "Come my darling. Come back to bed with me, and let me show you what I have in mind for us for the next hundred years or so." Her smile held a world of promise as Jeremy picked her up and laid her gently upon the bed.

BE SWEPT AWAY
ON A TIDE OF PASSION
BY LEISURE'S THRILLING
HISTORICAL ROMANCES!

Make the Most of Your Leisure Time
with
LEISURE BOOKS

Please send me the following titles:

Quantity	Book Number	Price
_____	_____	_____
_____	_____	_____
_____	_____	_____
_____	_____	_____
_____	_____	_____

If out of stock on any of the above titles, please send me the alternate title(s) listed below:

_____	_____	_____
_____	_____	_____
_____	_____	_____
_____	_____	_____

Postage & Handling _____

Total Enclosed $_____

☐ Please send me a free catalog.

NAME _____
(please print)

ADDRESS _____

CITY _____ STATE _____ ZIP _____

Please include $1.00 shipping and handling for the first book ordered and 25¢ for each book thereafter in the same order. All orders are shipped within approximately 4 weeks via postal service book rate. PAYMENT MUST ACCOMPANY ALL ORDERS.*

*Canadian orders must be paid in US dollars payable through a New York banking facility.

Mail coupon to: **Dorchester Publishing Co., Inc.**
6 East 39 Street, Suite 900
New York, NY 10016
Att: ORDER DEPT.

Love's
Leading Lady

CATHERINE HART

Bestselling author of SILKEN SAVAGE

SUMMER STORM — *She was as soft and warm as a sweet summer rain — as tempestuous and unpredictable as a thunderstorm over the desert.*

WINDRIDER — *He was destined to lead his people as a warrior chief and to tame the woman named Summer Storm. Though she had given her heart to another, he vowed their tumultuous joining would be climaxed in a whirlwind of ecstasy.*

02465

0 29398 00395 0

ISBN 0-8439-2465-9 NB2I

Printed in U.S.A.